"Krueger aims higher and hits harder with a stand-alone novel
that shares much with his other work. . . .
narrator and reader alike." —*Kirkus R*

"Elegiac, evocative. . . . A resonant tale of f
—*Publishers Wee*

"A wonderful coming-of-age novel." —*Providence Journal*

"A thoughtful literary mystery that is wholly compelling . . .
[and] anything but ordinary." —*BookPage*

"Not often does a story feel at once fresh and familiar.
But *Ordinary Grace* is both, and it is affecting." —*The Denver Post*

"The tone is much like *To Kill a Mockingbird*, with its combination
of dread and nostalgia." —*The Detroit News*

"A quiet novel that unfurls its sad story slowly, but eloquently,
leaving its mark on your heart." —*The Missourian*

"There's such a quiet beauty in Krueger's prose and such depth to his
characters that I was completely captivated." —*Minneapolis Star-Tribune*

"Luminous." —*St. Paul Pioneer Press*

"Juxtaposes loss with mercy in fresh and unexpected ways." —*Click*

"Everything about this book . . . is beautiful." —*The Globe and Mail*

Praise for

ORDINARY GRACE

"Besides being a terrific story that examines a powerful range of human experiences and emotions, it was the authentic voice of the teenage narrator, Frank Drum, that kept me reading late into the night. Though the tone is quiet, Krueger artfully layered the story with suspenseful examinations of family life, death, fury, spiritual fiber, and redemption."

—Beth Hoffman, *New York Times* bestselling author of
Saving CeeCee Honeycutt

"Krueger's stylish writing describes the town and its collection of people so well, one can taste, smell, feel what's on the page. Krueger's haunting story delivers with universal themes of guilt, innocence, love for family, tested friendships, and the pain of being thirteen."

—*Omaha World-Herald*

"A superb literary novel."

—*New York Journal of Books*

"I realized within pages this would be one of the best books I've read in recent years. The gathering threat and its consummation are satisfying and meaningful. This is an intelligent and compelling story told with great heart. . . . A perfect book club read, truly a book to love and read more than once."

—*Historical Novel Review*

"Extraordinary. . . . A moving story, replete with authentic characters who grow in wisdom and grace and learn to accept what they cannot change."

—*Shelf Awareness*

"Deeply human. . . . Reads like an autobiography, not a novel, which is a compliment to Krueger. The voice is pure; the characters are real."

—*Killer Nashville*

"A beautiful and engaging story . . . revealing in even the smallest ways how grace enters into brokenness and loss and grief and provides hope."

—*Englewood Review of Books*

"Astonishingly deeply moving. . . . A book that you can't put down and don't want to end. . . . It deserves as wide an audience as it can get."

—*Men Reading Books*

"Krueger has created characters that sharpen our instincts."

—*The Bowed Bookshelf*

"This delicate, sturdy, suspenseful, sensitive, and amazing story will stay with you long after you've finished the last page. . . . I've read it twice and am already looking forward to revisiting it a third time. If there are any better books written this year, or for several years to come, I'd be very surprised."

—*Aunt Agatha's*

"Inevitable comparisons will be made to *Stand By Me,* and that's not far off the mark. Beautifully written and, at times, heartbreaking, *Ordinary Grace* is a must-read."

—*Crime Fiction Lover*

ORDINARY
GRACE

ORDINARY GRACE

A NOVEL

WILLIAM KENT KRUEGER

ATRIA PAPERBACK

NEW YORK   LONDON   TORONTO   SYDNEY   NEW DELHI

ATRIA
PAPERBACK

An Imprint of Simon & Schuster, Inc.
1230 Avenue of the Americas
New York, NY 10020

Copyright © 2013 by William Kent Krueger

First Atria Paperback edition March 2014

ATRIA PAPERBACK and colophon are trademarks of Simon & Schuster, Inc.

For information about special discounts for bulk purchases,
please contact Simon & Schuster Special Sales at
1-866-506-1949 or business@simonandschuster.com.

The Simon & Schuster Speakers Bureau can bring authors to your live event. For more information or to book an event contact the Simon & Schuster Speakers Bureau at 1-866-248-3049 or visit our website at www.simonspeakers.com.

Designed by Jill Putorti

Manufactured in the United States of America

33 35 37 39 40 38 36 34

The Library of Congress has cataloged the hardcover edition as follows:

Krueger, William Kent.
Ordinary grace : a novel / by William Kent Krueger.—1st Atria Books
hardcover ed.
p. cm.
1. Families—Minnesota—Fiction. 2. Murder—Minnesota—Fiction.
3. Grief—Fiction. I. Title.
PS3561.R766O73 2013
813'.54—dc23   2012034884

ISBN 978-1-4516-4582-8
ISBN 978-1-4516-4585-9 (pbk)
ISBN 978-1-4516-4586-6 (ebook)

For Diane, my extraordinary grace

Acknowledgments

For their kindness and generosity in sharing with me their experiences as ministers in small Minnesota communities in an earlier time, I'd like to thank Reverend Robert Rollin and Reverend Greg Renstrom, two men who selflessly answered the calling.

The heart has reasons that reason does not understand.

—BLAISE PASCAL

Prologue

All the dying that summer began with the death of a child, a boy with golden hair and thick glasses, killed on the railroad tracks outside New Bremen, Minnesota, sliced into pieces by a thousand tons of steel speeding across the prairie toward South Dakota. His name was Bobby Cole. He was a sweet-looking kid and by that I mean he had eyes that seemed full of dreaming and he wore a half smile as if he was just about to understand something you'd spent an hour trying to explain. I should have known him better, been a better friend. He lived not far from my house and we were the same age. But he was two years behind me in school and might have been held back even more except for the kindness of certain teachers. He was a small kid, a simple child, no match at all for the diesel-fed drive of a Union Pacific locomotive.

It was a summer in which death, in visitation, assumed many forms. Accident. Nature. Suicide. Murder. You might think I remember that summer as tragic and I do but not completely so. My father used to quote the Greek playwright Aeschylus. "He who learns must suffer. And even in our sleep pain, which cannot forget, falls drop by drop upon the heart, until, in our own despair, against our will, comes wisdom through the awful grace of God."

In the end maybe that's what the summer was about. I was no older than Bobby and didn't understand such things then. I've come four decades since but I'm not sure that even now I fully understand. I still spend a lot of time thinking about the events of that summer. About the terrible price of wisdom. The awful grace of God.

1

Moonlight pooled on the bedroom floor. Outside the chirr of crickets and other night bugs gave life to the dark. It was not yet July but already hot as blazes. That may have been why I was awake. In 1961 no one but the rich in New Bremen had air-conditioning. During the day most folks battled the heat by closing their curtains against the sun and at night fans drew in the promise of cooler air. In our house there were only two fans and neither was in the bedroom I shared with my brother.

As I tossed about on top of the sheet trying to get comfortable in the heat the telephone rang. My father often said that nothing good came of phone calls in the middle of the night. He answered them anyway. I figured it was simply another part of his job, another part of all the things my mother hated about what he did. The telephone sat on a small table in the hallway outside my room. I stared at the ceiling and listened to the brittle ring until the hall light came on.

"Yes?"

Across the room Jake shifted in his bed and I heard the frame squeak.

My father said, "Any damage?" Then he said, tired and polite, "I'll be there in a few minutes. Thank you, Cleve."

I was out of bed and trotting into the hallway before he hung up.

His hair was wild from sleep, his cheeks shadowed blue with stubble. His eyes were weary and sad. He wore a T-shirt and striped boxer shorts.

"Go back to sleep, Frank," he told me.

"I can't," I said. "It's too hot and I'm already awake. Who was it?"

"A police officer."

"Is somebody hurt?"

"No." He closed his eyes and put the tips of his fingers against his lids and rubbed. "It's Gus."

"He's drunk?"

He nodded and yawned.

"In jail?"

"Go back to bed."

"Can I go with you?"

"I told you, go back to bed."

"Please. I won't be in the way. And I can't sleep now anyway."

"Keep your voice down. You'll wake everybody."

"Please, Dad."

He had energy enough to rise and meet his duty but not the strength to blunt the assault of a thirteen-year-old looking for adventure in the middle of an oppressive summer night. He said, "Get dressed."

Jake was sitting on the edge of his bed. He already had his shorts on and was pulling up his socks.

I said, "Where do you think you're going?"

"With you and Dad." He knelt and in the dark under his bed dug for his sneakers.

"Like hell."

"You said hell," he said, still digging.

"You're not going, Howdy Doody."

He was younger than me by two years and two heads shorter. Because he had red hair and freckles and freakish ears that stood out like the handles on a sugar bowl people in New Bremen sometimes called him Howdy Doody. When I was pissed at him I called him Howdy Doody too.

"You're not the b-b-b-boss of me," he said.

Jake almost always stuttered in public but around me he only stuttered when he was mad or scared.

"No," I replied, "but I can p-p-p-pound the crap out of you any time I want."

He found his sneakers and began to put them on.

Night was the dark of the soul and being up in an hour when the rest of the world was dead with sleep gave me a sinful thrill. My father often ventured out like this on some lonely mission but I'd never been allowed to go. This was special and I didn't want to share it with Jake. I'd already wasted precious time however so I left off arguing and got myself dressed.

My brother was waiting in the hall when I came out. I intended to argue with him some more but my father slipped from his bedroom and shut the door behind him. He looked at Jake as if about to say something unpleasant. Instead he sighed and signaled us both to go before him down the stairs.

Outside the crickets were kicking up a frenzy. Fireflies hung in the still black air flickering on and off like the slow blink of dreamy eyes. As we walked to the garage our shadows glided before us, black boats on a silver sea of moonlight.

"Shotgun," Jake said.

"Ah, come on. You're not even supposed to be here."

"I called it."

Which was the rule. In New Bremen, a town platted and populated by Germans, rules were abided by. Even so I complained until my father broke in. "Jake called it," he said. "End of discussion, Frank."

We piled into the car, a 1955 Packard Clipper the color of canned peas that my mother had named Lizzie. She christened every automobile we ever owned. A Studebaker she called Zelda. A Pontiac Star Chief was Little Lulu after the comic book character. There were others but her favorite—the favorite of us all except my father—was that Packard. It was huge and powerful and elegant. It had been a gift from my grandfather and was a source of contention between my parents. Though he never came right out and said so I believe it hurt my father's pride to accept such an extravagant gift from a man he didn't particularly like and whose values he openly challenged. I understood even then that my grandfather considered my father a failure and not good enough for my mother. Dinner when these two sat at the same table was usually a storm about to break.

We pulled out and drove through the Flats which was what we called the part of New Bremen where we lived. It lay along the Minnesota River below the Heights where the wealthy families resided. There were a lot of people living above us who weren't rich but no one with money lived on the Flats. We drove past Bobby Cole's house. Like all the others we passed it was totally dark. I tried to wrap my thinking around the fact of his death which had occurred the day before. I'd never known a kid who died and it felt unnatural and sinister, as if Bobby Cole had been snatched by a monster.

"Is Gus in t-t-trouble?" Jake asked.

"Some but not serious," my father replied.

"He didn't bust up anything?"

"Not this time. He got into a fight with another fellow."

"He does that a lot."

"Only when he's drunk," I said from the backseat. Making excuses for Gus was usually a responsibility that fell to my father but he was noticeably silent.

"He's drunk a lot then," Jake said.

"Enough." My father held up a hand and we shut up.

We drove Tyler Street and turned onto Main. The town was dark and full of delicious possibility. I knew New Bremen as well as I knew my own face but at night things were different. The town wore another face. The city jail sat on the town square. It was the second oldest building in New Bremen after the First Evangelical Lutheran Church. Both were built of the same granite quarried just outside town. My father parked diagonally in front of the jail.

"You two stay here," he said.

"I have to go to the bathroom."

He shot me a killing look.

"Sorry. I can't hold it."

He gave in so easily I knew he must have been dead tired. "Come on, then. You too, Jake."

I'd never been inside the jail but it was a place that had always appealed greatly to my imagination. What I found was a small drab room lit by fluorescent tubes and not much different in most respects from my grandfather's real estate office. There were a couple of desks and a file cabinet and a bulletin board with posters. But there was also along the east wall a holding cell with bars and the cell held a prisoner.

"Thanks for coming, Mr. Drum," the officer said.

They shook hands. Dad introduced us. Officer Cleve Blake appeared to be younger than my father and wore gold wire-rim glasses and behind them were blue eyes that had an unsettling frankness. Even though it was the middle of a night humid as hell he looked clean and neat in his uniform.

"A little late for you boys to be out, isn't it?"

"Couldn't sleep," I said to the officer. "Too hot."

Jake said nothing which was his usual strategy when he was concerned that he might stutter in public.

I recognized the guy in the cell. Morris Engdahl. A bad sort. Black hair slicked in a ducktail and fond of black leather jackets. He was a year older than my sister who'd just graduated from high school. Engdahl didn't finish school. The story I'd heard was that he was kicked out for crapping in the locker of a girl who'd turned him down for a date. He drove the coolest set of wheels I'd ever seen. A black 1932 Ford Deuce Coupe with suicide doors and a shiny chrome grille and big whitewall tires and flames painted along its sides so that fire ran the length of the car.

"Well, if it ain't Frankfarter and Howdy D-D-D-Doody," he said. He had a shiner and when he talked his words came out slurred through a fat lip. From behind the bars he settled his mean eyes on Jake. "How's it g-g-going, retard?"

Jake had been called all sorts of things because of his stutter. I figured it had to get to him but usually all he did was clam up and stare.

"Jake's not retarded, Mr. Engdahl," my father said quietly. "He simply stutters."

I was surprised Dad knew Morris Engdahl. They didn't exactly run in the same circles.

"No sh-sh-sh-shit," Engdahl said.

"That's enough, Morris," Officer Blake said.

My father gave Engdahl no more notice and asked the officer what it was all about.

The officer shrugged. "Two drunks, a wrong word. Like putting a match to gasoline."

"I ain't no drunk." Engdahl sat hunched over on the edge of a long metal bench and stared at the floor as if contemplating the advisability of puking there.

"And he's not old enough to be drinking in a bar, Cleve," my father pointed out.

"I'll be talking to the folks at Rosie's about that," the officer replied.

Behind a door in the back wall a toilet flushed.

"Much damage?" my father asked.

"Mostly to Morris. They took it out to the parking lot."

The door in the back wall opened and a man walked out still working at the zipper on his pants.

"Doyle, I was just telling these folks how you came to bring in Engdahl and Gus."

The other man sat down and put his feet on the desk. He wasn't dressed in a uniform but from his look of comfort in that jailhouse I understood he was a policeman too. He said, "Yeah I was off duty at Rosie's. Watched 'em going at it in the bar, mouthing off to each other. When they took it outside, I figured it was time to break up the party."

My father spoke to Officer Blake: "All right if I take Gus home now?"

"Sure. He's in back." The policeman reached into the desk drawer for keys. "Crying shame about the Cole kid. I heard you spent most of yesterday with his folks."

"Yes," my father told him.

"I've got to say I'd much rather have my job than yours."

"You know that whole thing's got me wondering," Doyle, the off-duty officer, said. "I've seen that kid on those tracks hundreds of times. He loved trains, I guess. Can't figure how he came to get himself killed by one."

Officer Blake said, "What do you mean?"

"I talked to Jim Gant. He was the first deputy on the scene. Gant said it looked like the kid had just been sitting on the tracks. Didn't move at all when the train came. Real strange, you know? He wasn't deaf."

"Maybe he was retarded like Howdy Doody there," Engdahl said from his cell. "Didn't know enough to get his butt off that rail."

Doyle said, "One more word out of you and I'm coming in there and kick your ass."

Officer Blake found the keys he was searching for and shut the drawer. "Are they pursuing it?"

"Far as I know, nope. Officially an accident. No witnesses to say otherwise."

Officer Blake said, "You boys stay out here. And, Morris, you behave yourself."

My father asked, "Is it okay if my son uses your bathroom, Cleve?"

"Sure," the officer answered. He unlocked the metal door in the back wall and led my father through.

I didn't have to use the bathroom. It had simply been a ruse to get inside the jail. I was afraid Doyle might make a point of it, but he didn't seem at all interested.

Jake stood staring hard at Engdahl. Staring knives.

"What are you looking at, retard?"

"He's not retarded," I said.

"Yeah and your sister's not a harelip and your old man's not a friggin' pussy." He laid his head back against the wall and closed his eyes.

I asked Doyle, "What did you mean about Bobby?"

He was tall and lean and looked tough as jerky. He wore his hair in a crew cut and his head was shiny with sweat from the heat of the night. He had ears every bit as big as Jake's but he wasn't the kind of guy anybody in their right mind would dare call Howdy Doody. He said, "You know him?"

"Yes."

"Nice kid, right? But slow."

"Slow enough he couldn't get out of the way of that train," Engdahl said.

"Shut up, Engdahl." Doyle looked back at me. "You play on the tracks?"

"No," I lied.

He looked at Jake. "You?"

"No," I answered for Jake.

"Good thing. Because there are bums down there. Men not like the decent folks in New Bremen. You ever get approached by one of them men you come straight here and tell me. Ask for Officer Doyle."

"You think that's what happened to Bobby?" I was thunderstruck. It would never have occurred to me that his death wasn't an accident. But then I wasn't a trained policeman like Officer Doyle.

He began popping the knuckles of his fingers one by one. "I'm just saying you watch out for guys drifting along those tracks. Understand?"

"Yes, sir."

"Goblins'll get you if you don't watch out," Engdahl said. "They love tender meat like you and Retard."

Doyle stood up. He walked to the cell and motioned Morris Engdahl to come to the bars. Engdahl drew his whole self onto the bench and pressed to the wall.

"That's what I thought," Doyle said.

The metal door opened and Officer Blake came out. My father followed. He supported Gus who was stumbling. Gus seemed drunker than Engdahl but there wasn't a mark on him.

"You're really letting him go?" Engdahl said. "That's friggin' unfair."

"I called your father," the officer said. "He told me a night in jail would do you good. Take it up with him."

"Get the door, Frank," my father said and then looked at the officer. "Thank you, Cleve. I appreciate this."

"Keeps things around here simpler. But, Gus, you've got to watch yourself. The chief's at the end of his rope with you."

Gus grinned drunkenly. "He wantsa talk to me, tell him I'll be happy to discuss it over a beer."

I held the door and my father hauled Gus out. I looked back where Morris Engdahl sat on the hard bench. Now, forty years later, I realize that what I saw was a kid not all that much older than me. Thin and angry and blind and lost and shut up behind iron bars not for the first time or the last. I probably should have felt for him something other than I did which was hatred. I closed the door.

At the car Gus straightened up suddenly and turned to my father. "Thanks, Captain."

"Get in the car."

Gus said, "What about my motorcycle?"

"Where is it?"

"At Rosie's."

"You can get it tomorrow when you're sober. Get in the car."

Gus swayed a little. He looked up at the moon. His face was bloodless in the pale light. "Why does he do it, Captain?"

"Who?"

"God. Why does he take the sweet ones?"

"He takes us all in the end, Gus."

"But a kid?"

"Is that what the fight was about? Bobby Cole?"

"Engdahl called him a retard, Captain. Said he was better off dead. I couldn't let it pass." Gus shook his head in a bewildered way. "So how come, Captain?"

"I don't know, Gus."

"Isn't that your job? Knowing the why of all this crap?" Gus seemed disappointed. Then he said, "Dead. What's that mean?"

Jake spoke up. "It means he won't have to w-w-worry about everybody making f-f-f-fun of him."

Gus eyed Jake and blinked. "Maybe you're right. Maybe that's the reason. What do you think, Captain?"

"Maybe."

Gus nodded as if that had satisfied him. He bent toward the open car door to get into the backseat but instead stood there making awful retching sounds.

"Ah, Gus. All over the upholstery," my father said.

Gus straightened up and pulled his shirttail from his pants and wiped his mouth. "Sorry, Captain. Didn't see it coming."

"Get in front," my father said. He turned to me. "Frank, you and Jake are going to have to walk home. Do you have a problem with that?"

"No, sir. We'll be fine. But could we have the tire iron from the trunk? For protection?"

New Bremen wasn't at all the kind of town where you'd need a tire iron for protection but I nodded toward Jake, whose face had gone a little white at the prospect of walking home in all that dark, and my father understood. He popped the trunk and handed me the iron. "Don't dawdle," he said.

He climbed into the driver's side. "You have to puke again, Gus, puke out the window. Understand?"

"I read you loud and clear, Captain." He smiled gamely and lifted a hand to us as my father drove away.

Under the moon we stood on the empty square. The city jail was the only lit building we could see. On the opposite side of the green the courthouse clock bonged four times.

"It'll be light in an hour," I said.

"I don't want to walk home," Jake said. "I'm tired."

"Then stay here."

I started away. After a moment Jake came too.

We didn't go home. Not directly. At Sandstone Street I turned off Main.

Jake said, "Where are you going?"

"You'll see."

"I want to go home."

"Fine. Go home."

"I don't want to go home alone."

"Then come on. You'll like this, I swear."

"Like what?"

"You'll see."

A block off Main on the corner of Walnut was a bar with a sign over the door. Rosie's. A '53 Indian Chief with a sidecar was in the lot. Gus's motorcycle. Only one automobile was still parked there. A black Deuce Coupe with fire painted along its sides. I approached that beauty and spent a moment running my hand admiringly over the slope of the front wheel well where a silver snake of moonlight shot along the black enamel. Then I set myself and swung the tire iron and smashed the left headlight.

"What are you doing?" Jake cried.

I walked to the other headlight and once again the sound of shattering glass broke the stillness of the night.

"Here," I said and offered the tire iron to my brother. "The rear lights are all yours."

"No," he said.

"This guy called you a retard. You and Bobby Cole. And he called Ariel a harelip and Dad a pussy. You don't want to break something on his car?"

"No." He looked at me then at the tire iron then at the car. "Well, maybe."

I handed that magic wand of revenge to Jake. He walked to the back of Morris Engdahl's precious set of wheels. He glanced at me once for reassurance then swung. He missed and banged metal and the tire iron bounced out of his hands.

"Jeez," I said. "What a spaz."

"Let me try again."

I picked up the tire iron and handed it to him. This time he did the deed and danced back from the spray of red glass. "Can I do the other one?" he pleaded.

When he'd finished we stood back and admired our work until we heard the screen door of the house across the street squeak open and a guy shout, "Hey, what's going on over there?"

We tore down Sandstone back to Main and down Main toward Tyler. We didn't stop until we hit the Flats.

Jake bent over and held his ribs. "I got a stitch in my side," he gasped.

I was breathing hard too. I put my arm around my brother. "You were great back there. A regular Mickey Mantle."

"Think we'll get in trouble?"

"Who cares? Didn't that feel good?"

"Yeah," Jake said. "It felt real good."

The Packard was parked in the church lot across the street from our house. The light over the side door was on and I figured Dad was still inside putting Gus to bed. I set the tire iron on the Packard's hood and we walked to the door, which opened onto a set of stairs that led to the church basement where Gus had a room next to the boiler.

Gus wasn't related to us by blood but in a strange way he was family. He'd fought beside my father in the Second World War, an experience, my father contended, that made them closer than brothers. They stayed in touch and whenever Dad updated us on his old friend it was usually to report another in a long litany of missteps. Then one day just after we'd moved to New Bremen, Gus had shown up at our doorstep, a little drunk and out of work and with everything he owned stuffed in a pack in the sidecar of his motorcycle. My father had taken him in, given him a place to live, found him work, and Gus had been with us ever since. He was a source of great disagreement between my parents but only one of many. Jake and I liked him immensely. Maybe it was because he talked to us as if we weren't just kids. Or because he didn't have much and didn't seem to want more and didn't appear to be bothered by his questionable circumstances. Or because on occasion he drank to excess and got himself into trouble from which my father would predictably extricate him, which made him seem more like an errant older brother than an adult.

His room in the church basement wasn't much. A bed. A chest of drawers. A nightstand and lamp. A mirror. A squat three-shelf case full of books. He'd put a little red rug on the cement floor of his room that added a dash of color. There was a window at ground level but not much light came through. On the other side of the basement was a small bathroom which Dad and Gus had put in themselves. That's where we found them. While Gus knelt at the toilet stool and puked my father stood behind him and waited patiently. Jake and I lingered under the bare bulb in the middle of the basement. My father didn't seem to notice us.

"Still ralfing," I whispered to Jake.

"Ralfing?"

"You know. R-a-l-f," I said and drew out the word as if I was vomiting.

"That's it, Captain." With some difficulty Gus stood and my father handed him a wet cloth to wipe his face.

My father flushed the toilet and walked Gus to his room. He helped Gus out of his soiled shirt and pants. Gus lay down on his bed. He wore only his undershirt and shorts. It was cooler in the basement than outside and my father drew the top sheet over his friend.

"Thanks, Captain," Gus murmured as his eyes drifted closed.

"Go to sleep."

Then Gus said something I'd never heard him say before. He said, "Captain, you're still a son of a bitch. Always will be."

"I know, Gus."

"They're all dead because of you, Captain. Always will be."

"Just sleep."

Gus was snoring almost immediately. My father turned to where we stood in the middle of the basement. "Go on back to bed," he said. "I'm going to stay and pray for a while."

"The car's full of puke," I said. "Mom'll go berserk."

"I'll take care of it."

My father went up to the sanctuary. Jake and I went out the side door. I still wasn't ready to call it a night. I sat on the front steps of the church and Jake sat there too. He was tired and leaned against me.

"What did Gus mean?" he said. "Dad killed them all. What did he mean?"

I was wondering about that too. I said, "I don't know."

The birds had started to chatter in the trees. Above the hills that rimmed the valley of the Minnesota River I could see a thin line of vermilion in the sky that was the approach of dawn. And I saw something else. On the other side of the street a familiar figure separated itself from the cover of the lilac bushes that edged our yard. I watched my older sister sneak across the lawn and slip into our house through the back door. Oh the secrets of the night.

I sat on the steps of my father's church thinking how much I loved the dark. The taste of what it offered sweet on the tongue of my imagination. The delicious burn of trespass on my conscience. I was a sinner. I knew that without a doubt. But I was not alone. And the night was the accomplice of us all.

I said, "Jake?" But he didn't answer. He was asleep.

My father would pray for a long time. It was too late for him to go back to bed and too early to fix breakfast. He was a man with a son who stuttered and another probably on his way to becoming a juvenile delinquent and a daughter with a harelip who sneaked in at night from God knew where and a wife who resented his profession. Yet I knew it was not for himself or for any of us that he was praying. More likely it was for the parents of Bobby Cole. And for Gus. And probably for an asshole named Morris Engdahl. Praying on their behalf. Praying I suppose for the awful grace of God.

2

She wore a white terry-cloth robe and her feet were bare. On the table in front of her sat a cup of black coffee. Against the cup she'd propped a pamphlet. In her right hand she held a mechanical pencil. A stenographer's notebook was open on the red Formica tabletop. Beside it lay half a cigarette smoking in a ceramic ashtray on which the four presidents of Mount Rushmore were embossed in gold. Periodically she put her pencil down and took up the cigarette, inhaled thoughtfully, and slowly released a plume of smoke that hung over the kitchen table.

"Nervous as a loose shutter in a storm," she said. She mulled the words as she watched the smoke gradually dissolve. Satisfied she took up her pencil and wrote in the notebook.

This was during the period my mother was enamored of the work of Ayn Rand and had decided she too could be a world-famous author. She'd sent off to a writers' school in New York City for a test that would confirm she had the right stuff.

Jake ate his Sugar Pops and watched the diver he'd pulled from the cereal box slowly sink in a glass of water. Moments later it returned to the surface, lifted on an air bubble created by the baking soda he'd put in a tiny compartment on the diver's back. I ate a piece of toast covered with crunchy peanut butter and grape jelly. I hated the crunchy kind of peanut butter but because it was on sale my mother had dismissed my complaints.

My mother said, "The cat crept across the floor like . . ." She took up her cigarette and thought deeply.

"An assassin stalking prey," I said.

"Finish your breakfast, Frankie."

"Like a robber after some money," Jake said. His eyes never left the diver in his glass.

"Thank you, I don't need your help."

She thought a moment longer then wrote on the pad. I leaned over and saw that she'd written . . . *like love entering a heart.*

My father came in. He was dressed in his good black suit and white shirt and blue tie. "The service is at noon, Ruth."

"I'll be ready, Nathan." She didn't look up from her pamphlet.

"People will start gathering much earlier, Ruth."

"I've been to funerals before, Nathan."

"You boys, you see that you look sharp."

"They know what to do, Nathan."

My father stood a moment and stared at the back of my mother's head then walked to the door and went outside. As soon as he was gone my mother closed her notebook and laid the pamphlet on top. She stubbed out her cigarette and said, "Two minutes, then breakfast is over."

An hour later she came downstairs wearing a black dress. She had on a black hat with a black veil and black pumps. She smelled of bath powder. Jake and I were dressed for the service. We had the television on and were watching a rerun of *The Restless Gun.* My mother was beautiful. Even we her thoughtless sons knew that. Folks were always saying she could have been a movie star. Pretty as Rita Hayworth they said.

"I'm going to the church. You two be there in half an hour. And, Frankie, you see that you both stay clean."

We wore the only suits we had. I'd tied my tie and I'd tied Jake's. We'd washed our faces and wetted our hair and slicked it back. We looked presentable.

As soon as she was gone I said, "You stay here."

Jake said, "Where are you going?"

"Never mind. Just stay here."

I left through the back door. Behind our house was a small pasture. When we'd first moved in, a couple of horses had grazed there. The horses were gone now but the pasture was still filled with grass where wild daisies and purple clover grew. On the far side stood a house set off by itself, an old yellow structure surrounded by willows. A wood fence separated the backyard from the pasture. I crept through the wild grass. Like an assassin stalking prey. I sidled up to the fence which was a slapped-together affair full of gaps where the warped boards refused to meet. I put my eye to the space created by one of those refusals.

The house belonged to Avis and Edna Sweeney. Avis worked at the grain elevators at the edge of the Flats. He was a toothpick of a man with a huge Adam's apple. Edna was a blonde with a bosom like the prow of an aircraft carrier. The Sweeneys had a nice yard with lots of plants and flowers and Edna did the yard work. She did it dressed in tight shorts and a halter top that barely contained her breasts. I don't remember how I discovered the delight of Edna Sweeney but I was much addicted to the sight of her dressed that way and bent to her labor. I spent a lot of time that summer with my eyeball glued to a gap in the fence.

That morning Edna Sweeney was not in her yard but she'd done laundry. Among the whites hanging on her line were a couple of bras with enormous cups and some lacy underwear that I was pretty sure didn't belong to Avis. I didn't hear Jake coming up behind me. His hand on my shoulder made me jump.

"Jesus," I said.

"You said Jesus in the bad way."

"What are you doing here?"

"What are you doing here?"

"Nothing," I said. I grabbed him and tried to turn him back toward our house. "Let's go."

He shrugged off my hand and plastered his eye to the fence.

"Damn, Jake."

"You said damn. What are you looking at?"

"Nothing."

"You're looking at her underwear."

"Okay I'm looking at her underwear. You're looking at her underwear too."

He moved his head around a little and tried to position his eye for a better view.

"Come on." I took hold of his sleeve and gave a yank. He didn't budge but the seam along the suit coat shoulder split in a heartbreaking rend. "Oh, Christ."

Jake straightened up. "You said—"

"I know what I said. Lemme see." I turned him and took a long look at the damage I'd done. If I told the truth, the circumstances of the accident would be hard to explain. So the truth was not an option. But a lie would depend on Jake and that was a problem. Even if I was able to convince him to go along with some goofy story, he'd stutter and stammer so awful that our guilt would quickly be obvious.

Jake craned his neck so that he could see the tear. "We're going to get in t-t-trouble."

"No we're not. Come on."

I ran across the pasture through the grass and wild daisies and purple clover. Jake was right behind me. We raced through the back door and went upstairs to my parents' bedroom. I pulled my mother's sewing basket from the closet shelf and selected a spool of tan thread. I bit off a long section and speared the eye of a needle.

"Give me your coat," I said and got to work.

I was a Boy Scout. Not a good one. I liked the general idea of being trustworthy and loyal and thrifty and brave and clean and reverent but the effort it took to hang in there with all those weighty virtues was usually more than I cared to muster. I learned some pretty good stuff though. Like how to sew onto my uniform the patches that went along with being a scout. I wielded a mean needle. I did a quick baste so that unless you looked closely you wouldn't notice anything amiss.

"There," I said and handed the coat to Jake.

He looked at it skeptically and put it on and shoved his finger through one of the gaps between the loose stitching. "It's still b-b-broken."

"It'll be fine as long as you don't go poking it all the time." I put Mom's sewing basket back in the closet and checked the clock on the nightstand. I said, "We better hurry. The service is about to start."

My sister Ariel had turned eighteen in May and in June had graduated from New Bremen High School and was planning to attend Juilliard in the fall. When Jake and I entered the church she was at the organ playing something beautiful and sad that sounded as if it might have been by Handel. The pews were already pretty full. Mostly people we knew. Members of the congregation. Friends of the family. People from the neighborhood. A lot of folks who came regularly to my father's church weren't members. They weren't even Methodist. They came because it was the only church on the Flats. Jake and I took places in the last pew. My mother was up front where the choir usually sat. She wore a red satin robe over her black dress. She was listening to Ariel play and she was staring at the stained-glass window in the west wall with that same faraway look she'd had at the kitchen table when she was searching for inspiration. Part of it was the music itself but it was also the way Ariel played. To this day there are pieces I cannot hear without imagining my sister's fingers shaping the music every bit as magnificently as God shaped the wings of butterflies.

The casket was set in front of the chancel rail with a profusion of flowers flanking it on either side. The church smelled of lilies. Bobby's parents were in the front row. They were older people to whom Bobby had come late in life. I'd seen how they treated him with a great and gentle love. Now they sat together with their hands in their laps and stared dumbly beyond the casket toward the gold-plated cross on the altar.

My father was nowhere to be seen.

Jake leaned to me. "He's in there?"

I knew what he meant. "Yeah."

Until Bobby died I hadn't thought a lot about death but as I imagined him laid in that small casket I was struck with an awful sense of wonder. I didn't believe in heaven—the Pearly Gates version—so the question of what had become of Bobby Cole was mystifying and more than a little frightening.

Gus entered the church. It was clear from his unsteady gait that he'd been drinking. He was dressed in his Sunday best which was a dark secondhand suit. His tie was askew and there was a cowlick in his red hair that stuck out at the back of his head. He sat in the pew across the aisle from Jake and me and he didn't seem to notice us. He stared at Bobby's coffin and I could hear the bellows of his lungs sucking air.

My father finally appeared. He came from the door to his office, dressed in his black Wesley robe and wearing a white stole. He was a handsome man and impressive in his ministerial regalia. He paused as he passed the Coles and he spoke to them quietly and then he took his place in the chair behind his pulpit.

Ariel ended her piece. My mother stood up. Ariel laid her hands again on the organ keyboard and paused and prepared herself then began to play. And my mother closed her eyes and composed herself to sing.

When my mother sang I almost believed in heaven. It wasn't just that she had a beautiful voice but also that she had a way of delivering a piece that pierced your heart. Oh when she sang she could make a fence post cry. When she sang she could make people laugh or dance or fall in love or go to war. In the pause before she began, the only sound in the church was the breeze whispering through the open doorway. The Coles had chosen the hymn and it seemed an odd choice, one that had probably come from Mrs. Cole whose roots were in southern Missouri. She'd asked my mother to sing a spiritual, *Swing Low, Sweet Chariot.*

When my mother finally sang it was not just a hymn she offered, it was consummate comfort. She sang slowly and richly and delivered the heart of that great spiritual as if she was delivering heaven itself and her face was beautiful and full of peace. I shut my eyes and her voice reached out to wipe away my tears and enfold my heart and assure me absolutely that Bobby Cole was being carried home. It made me almost happy for him, a sweet boy who didn't have to worry anymore about understanding a world that would always be more incomprehensible to him than not. Who didn't have to endure anymore all the cruel mockeries. Who would never have to concern himself with what kind of man he would grow into and what would become of him when his aged parents could no longer protect and care for him. My mother's singing made me believe that God had taken Bobby Cole for the best of reasons.

And when she finished the sound of the breeze through the doorway was like the sigh of angels well pleased.

My father stood and read scripture from the pulpit but he didn't preach from up there. He came down the steps instead and passed through the opening in the chancel rail and stood finally beside the casket. In truth I didn't hear much of what he had to say. Partly it was because my heart was already full from my mother's singing and my head was already stuffed with too much wonderment about death. But it was also because I'd heard my father preach a thousand times. People said he was a good preacher though not as fiery as some of his congregation would have liked. He spoke earnestly, never passionately. He was a man of ideas and he never tried with overpowering rhetoric or dramatics to muscle people into believing.

It was quiet in the church when he finished and the breeze that swept through the open doors cooled us and the flowers beside the coffin rustled as if someone had passed by.

Then Gus stood up.

He stepped into the aisle and walked to Bobby's coffin. He put his hand on the polished wood. My father if he was surprised or concerned didn't show it. He said, "Gus, is there something you'd like to say?"

Gus stroked the coffin as he might have the soft fur of a dog. I saw that his body was shaking and I understood he was crying. Someone in the congregation gave a cough. It sounded phony, as if it had been done to break the moment. What it did was make Gus turn and face them.

He said, "Bobby used to help me take care of the cemetery sometimes. He liked the quiet. He liked the grass and the flowers. To me and you he wasn't much of a talker, but he used to whisper to the headstones like he was sharing a secret with the folks buried there. Bobby had a secret. You know what it was? It took nothing to make him happy. That was it. He held happiness in his hand easy as if he'd just, I don't know, plucked a blade of grass from the ground. And all he did his whole short life was offer that happiness to anybody who'd smile at him. That's all he wanted from me. From you. From anybody. A smile."

He looked back at the casket and anger pulled his face into sudden lines.

"But what did people offer him? They made fun of him. Christian folks and they said things to him hurtful as throwing stones. I hope to Christ you're right, Captain, that Bobby's sitting up there in God's hand, because down here he was just a sweet kid getting his ass kicked. I'll miss him. I'll miss him like I'd miss the robins if they never came back."

His face was a melt of tears. I was crying too. Hell, everybody was crying. My father held his composure and, when Gus had returned to his pew, said, "Would anyone else like to offer something in memory?"

I thought about getting up. I thought maybe I could tell them about Bobby at the back of the classroom in first grade. The teacher didn't work with him much. She gave him clay and Bobby spent his time at his desk carefully rolling out snakes which he arranged in rows, and every once in a while he would look up while the rest of us recited the alphabet and added two plus two, and his myopic eyes behind those thick, gold-rimmed lenses seemed contented. And I thought about telling them how I'd figured Bobby was hopeless but I was wrong and Gus was right. Bobby had a gift and the gift was his simplicity. The world for Bobby Cole was a place he accepted without needing to understand it. Me, I was growing up scrambling for meaning and I was full of confusion and fear.

I didn't stand up. I didn't say anything. Like everyone else I sat there dumb until my father offered a final prayer and Ariel began playing the final hymn and my mother stood up in her red satin robe and gave voice to the finality of it all.

And when she'd finished I heard the black hearse idling outside the open church door and everyone stood to follow Bobby to the hole Gus had already dug for him in the cemetery.

3

Something fishy about that boy's death," Doyle said.

It was Saturday afternoon, the day after Bobby Cole was buried. Jake and I had spent all morning working on my grandfather's yard. Mowing, clipping, raking. Chores we did every Saturday that summer. My grandfather had a big house on the Heights with a yard that was a beautiful green sea of thick grass. He was in real estate and claimed that the look of his own property said as much about him as any piece of advertising he put on a billboard. He paid us well but he oversaw our every move. By the time the job was done I never thought the money was enough.

Always when we were finished—hot and sweaty and covered in grass clippings—we hit Halderson's Drugstore where we could belly up to the soda counter for root beer served in a frosty mug.

At the back of the drugstore was an open passage to a storeroom. More often than not a curtain hung across the doorway but not that afternoon. I could see three men in the yellow light of a bare bulb that hung from the ceiling of the back room. They sat on crates. Two of them drank from brown bottles which I was pretty sure held beer. The one not drinking was Mr. Halderson. One of the other men was Gus. The third was the off-duty officer we'd met at the police station. Doyle. It was Doyle who was talking.

"I mean the kid was slow sure. But he wasn't deaf. He'd have heard that train coming."

"Maybe he fell asleep," Halderson said.

"On the railroad tracks? Be like lying down on a bed of nails like one of them sheiks."

"Fakirs," Gus said.

"What?"

"They're not sheiks. They're fakirs."

"Whatever."

Doyle drank long and noisily.

"All I'm saying is that there's more to that kid's death than anybody knows. I've picked up plenty of bums on those tracks. I mean guys no mother would claim. Got sickness in their heads you wouldn't believe."

"Surely they're not all like that," Halderson said.

"All it takes is the wrong one at the wrong place at the wrong time. That boy he was so simple he would have been easy pickings."

Gus said, "You really believe that?"

"The things I've seen during my years in uniform would make your stomachs turn," Doyle said. He tipped his bottle to his lips but caught sight of me and Jake at the counter, both of us clearly eavesdropping. He lowered his beer and waved us to him. "Come on over here, you two."

Jake looked at me. Joining these men was the last thing he wanted to do. I didn't mind the possibility of getting in on that backroom conversation. I slid off my stool. Jake followed but he followed slowly.

"You're the preacher's kids right?"

"Yes, sir."

"You ever play down on them railroad tracks?"

It was the same question he'd asked a few nights before in the police station. I didn't know if it was the two empty beer bottles sitting beside his crate that made him ask or if he'd forgotten that he'd asked or if he'd forgotten the answer I gave when he asked or if this was just what a cop did asking the same question over and over to see if he could confuse you. I wasn't confused.

"No," I lied. Just as I had before.

He had a wide jut of flat cliff for a forehead and in its shadow his eyes shifted to Jake. "You?"

Jake didn't answer.

"Well, boy?"

Jake's mouth twisted and he tried to reply.

"Come on, spit it out."

"He stutters," Gus said.

"I can see that." Doyle spoke sharp. "Tell me the truth, boy."

Doyle must have scared the piss out of Jake. In a way that was painful to bear my brother tried to comply. He contorted his face and looked at Doyle out of deep creases filled with the dark anger that came from his frustration. He finally gave up and fiercely shook his head.

"Yeah, right."

I hated the man for that. For putting Jake through torture and then dismissing the result.

Gus said, "Their father doesn't let them play on the tracks."

"You think they don't go there anyway?" Doyle shot me a look that seemed to contain a whisper of conspiracy, as if he knew me and didn't entirely condemn me for what he knew. As if in a way we were brothers.

I took a step back, hating the man more every minute. "Can we go?"

"Yes." Doyle dismissed us as he might have a couple of suspects he'd decided not to collar.

I put my arm around Jake who was staring angrily at the floor and I turned him. We left the men. Left Doyle laughing quietly and meanly at our backs.

Outside the day sweltered. The sun threw heat from above and the sidewalks gathered it and roasted the soles of our sneakers. The tar that filled the cracks on the pavement had turned to black goo and we were careful to watch our step. We passed Bon Ton's barbershop where the easy voices of men and the scent of hair oil drifted through the open door. We passed the bank which had been robbed by Pretty Boy Floyd and Ma Barker's boys in the thirties and which had long been the source of a good deal of my own daydreaming. We passed store after store deserted in the drowse of that hot day in late June. We kept to the shade of the awnings and didn't talk and Jake stared at the sidewalk and fumed.

We left the shops behind and walked Main Street toward Tyler. The houses on the hills were old and many of them Victorian and, though the heavy curtains were drawn against the heat, every once in a while we caught the sound of a baseball game broadcast from the cool dark inside. We turned down Tyler toward the Flats. I could feel Jake's anger hot as the concrete under our feet.

"Forget him," I said. "He's an asshole."

"Don't s-s-s-say that."

"But he is."

"That word I mean."

"Asshole?"

Jake shot me a killing look.

"You shouldn't let him get to you. He's nobody."

"Nobody's n-n-nobody," Jake said.

"Hell everybody's nobody. And I know I said hell."

Grain elevators rose beside the tracks on the Flats. Tall and white they were connected by catwalks and conveyor belts. There was a stark kind of beauty in the way they stood against the sky like sculptures made of bone. Next to them ran a siding where the hopper cars were rolled so they could be filled with grain but that afternoon the rails were empty and the elevators deserted. We strolled over the tracks at the crossing on Tyler. Jake kept walking toward home. I stopped and turned and began to follow my shadow stubby and black along the rails toward the east.

Jake said, "What are you doing?"

"What's it look like?"

"You're not supposed to play on the railroad tracks."

"Not playing. Just walking. You coming or you going to stand there and cry?"

"I'm not crying."

I walked a rail like a tightrope. Walked through waves of heat. Walked in the fragrance that rose up from the hot rock of the roadbed and the creosote of the crossties.

"And you're not coming either," I said.

"I'm coming."

"Then come on."

His shadow caught up with mine and he walked the other rail and together we walked out of the Flats and though we did not know it we were walking toward the second death that summer.

The valley of the Minnesota River was carved over ten thousand years ago by great floods released from the glacial Lake Agassiz which covered an area in Minnesota and North Dakota and central Canada larger than the state of California. The drain was called the River Warren and it cut deep and wide into the land through which it ran. What's left now is only a wisp of that great river. In summer the land along its banks is green with soy beans and cornstalks and fields of rye that roll in the wind with the liquidity of an ocean. There are stands of old deciduous trees whose branches cup the nests of Forster's terns and black terns and great blue herons and egrets and bald eagles and warblers and other birds so ordinary and profuse that they fill the air like dandelion fluff. The river runs nearly four hundred miles and it runs brown. It flows out of Lac qui Parle. The Lake That Speaks. At its end are the cities of Minneapolis and Saint Paul.

To this day for much of its length the river is shadowed by railroad. To a thirteen-year-old kid in 1961 that set of tracks seemed to reach to a horizon from beyond which came the sound of the world calling.

We walked to a place half a mile outside the Flats where a long trestle bridged the river. Wild rye and blackberry thickets and thistle grew to the edge of the railroad bed. Sometimes people fished from the trestle though it was a dangerous thing to do. This was where Bobby Cole had been killed.

I stopped and Jake said, "What do you want to do?"

"I don't know."

The truth was that I was looking for evidence of a thing I hadn't considered before. Bobby Cole was not a fisherman and so to my mind he'd come there looking to eat the blackberries that were ripe or to sit on the trestle and watch the river run below and look for the carp and catfish and gar that sometimes broke the surface. That's what I did there and Jake when he came with me. Or we'd toss a stick into the river and try to hit it with a harvest of rocks gathered from between the railroad ties. But Officer Doyle had speculated there was something more sinister in what happened to Bobby than just the tragedy of a boy too lost in his daydreams to hear the thunder of death approaching. That had me wondering.

Jake said, "Want to throw rocks?"

"No. Hush. Listen."

From down the riverbank near the trestle came a snapping like the break of a million tiny bones. A large animal was forcing its way through the brush. We sometimes found places along the river where deer had bedded and the flattened vegetation still carried the outlines of their bodies. We didn't move and our shadows roosted on the rails. From under a willow that overhung the bank and that was surrounded by bulrushes a man emerged plucking burrs from his clothing as he came. He seemed old to me because his hair was no longer black but the dull color of a long-circulated five-cent piece. He wore dirty khakis and a sleeveless undershirt and he swore at the burrs snagged in his clothing. He disappeared under the embankment where the rails crossed the river. I crept forward onto the trestle and knelt and peered down through the gap between the first two sets of crossties. Jake knelt beside me. Directly below us the man had seated himself on the dry clay of the riverbank and next to him was sprawled another man. The second man looked as if he was sleeping and the man who'd come from the bulrushes began going through the sleeping man's pockets. Jake tugged at my sleeve and pointed back down the tracks indicating that he thought we ought to leave. I shook my head and returned to watching the activity below.

Though it was a hot day, the sprawled man wore an overcoat. It was a dirty thing of pale green canvas much patched and mended. The first man dipped into one of the outside pockets and came up with a labeled bottle of amber liquid. He unscrewed the cap and sniffed the contents and tipped the bottle to his lips and drank.

Jake whispered in my ear, "Come on."

The man below who'd lifted his head to drink must have heard Jake because he tilted his head a bit more and eyed us where we gazed at him through the crossties above. He lowered the bottle. "Dead," he said. He nodded toward the man on the ground. "As a doornail. You boys want to, you come on down here and see."

It was not an order but an invitation and I stood to accept.

I look back now and I wonder at this. I have raised children of my own and the thought of a child of mine or a grandchild descending to be with a stranger that way makes me go rigid with worry. I didn't think of myself as a careless boy. What was inside me was a wonderment desperate to be satisfied. A dead man, that was a thing you didn't see every day.

Jake grabbed my arm and tried to drag me away but I shook him off.

"We should g-g-g-go," he said.

"You go then." I started down the slope of the railroad bed toward the riverbank.

"F-F-F-Frank," Jake said with fury.

"Go on home," I said.

But my brother would not desert me and as I stumbled down the bank Jake stumbled after me.

He was Indian the man who now held the bottle. This wasn't unusual because many Indians lived in the valley of the Minnesota River. The Dakota Sioux had populated that land long before white people came and the white people had by hook and by crook stolen it from them. The government had created small reservations farther west but Indian families scattered themselves along the whole length of the river.

He motioned us closer and indicated a place to sit on the other side of the body.

He said, "Ever seen a dead man?"

"Lots," I said.

"Oh?"

I could tell he didn't believe me. I said, "My father's a minister. He buries people all the time."

"Laid out in fine boxes with their faces painted," the Indian said. "This is how it is before they get them ready for the coffin."

"He looks like he's sleeping," I said.

"This here was a good death."

"Good?"

"I was in the war," the Indian said. "The First World War. The war to end all wars." He looked at the bottle and drank. "I saw men dead in ways no man should die."

I said, "How did he die?"

The Indian shrugged. "Just died. Was sitting there talking one minute. The next he was lying there like that. Fell over. Heart attack maybe. Maybe a stroke. Who knows? Dead's dead that's all she wrote." He drank some more.

"What's his name?"

"Name? I don't really know. Know what he called himself. Skipper. Like he was a sea captain or something. Hell, maybe he was. Who knows?"

"Was he your friend?"

"About as much friend as I got, I suppose."

"He doesn't look old enough to die."

The Indian laughed. "It's not like voting or a driver's license, boy."

He began again to go through the dead man's pockets. From inside the coat he pulled a photograph much handled and faded. He looked at it a long time then turned it over and squinted. "There's writing on the back," he said. "Lost my glasses a while back. Can you read it?"

"Sure," I said.

He held it out toward me across the dead man's body. I took it and looked at it and Jake who was next to me leaned over to look too. It was black and white and was of a woman with a baby in her arms. She wore a plain dress that appeared gray in the photo with a pattern of white daisies. She was pretty and was smiling and behind her was a barn. I turned the photograph over and read out loud the writing on the backside.

October 23, 1944. Johnny's first birthday. We miss you and hope you can be home for Christmas. Mary.

I handed the photograph back. The Indian's hand shook a little and I saw that his palms were dirty and his nails ragged. He said, "Probably called to service in the second war to end all wars. Hell, maybe he really was a sea captain." The Indian drank some more and leaned his head back against the embankment and looked up at the trestle and said, "Know what I like about railroad tracks? They're always there but they're always moving."

"Like a river," Jake said.

I was surprised that he spoke and that he spoke without a stutter which was a thing he seldom did around strangers. The Indian looked at my brother and nodded as if Jake had spoken some great wisdom. "Like a steel river," he said. "That's smart, son, real smart."

Jake looked down, embarrassed by the compliment. The Indian reached across the dead man and across me and put his hand with its dirty palm and ragged nails on Jake's leg. I was startled by the familiarity of the gesture and I looked at the stranger's hand on my brother's leg and the realization of the danger inherent in the situation descended on me like a flame and I leaped up dislodging the offending hand and grabbed my brother and yanked him to his feet and dragged him up the slope of the riverbank to the tracks.

Behind us the Indian called out, "Didn't mean anything, boys. Nothing at all."

But I was running then and pulling Jake with me and I was thinking about that Indian's hand and seeing it in my mind like a spider crawling Jake's leg. As fast as I could force us we returned to Halderson's Drugstore. The men were still in the back room drinking beer from brown bottles. When we stumbled in and stood before them breathless they ceased talking.

Gus frowned at me and said, "What is it, Frank?"

"We were down on the tracks," I said between gasps for air.

Doyle gave a grin stupid and satisfied. "His old man don't let them play on the tracks," he said.

Gus ignored him and said evenly, "What about the tracks, Frank?"

I spoke with an urgency that had been building all the way from the trestle and that had been fed by my rumination on the Indian's hand too familiar on Jake's leg and by my own guilt at the danger in which I'd placed my brother. I said, "A stranger was there. A man."

The faces of all three men changed and changed in the same frightening way. The stupid satisfaction left Doyle. Gus's dogged patience fled. Halderson abandoned his mild demeanor and his eyes became like chambered bullets. All three men stared at us and in their faces I could see my own fear reflected and magnified. Magnified to a degree I had not anticipated. Magnified perhaps by all the sick possibility that grown men knew that I did not. Magnified probably by the alcohol they'd consumed. Magnified certainly by the responsibility they felt as men to protect the children of their community.

"A man?" Doyle stood up and took hold of my arm and forced me to come close to him where the smell of beer poured from his mouth, a stream on which his words were carried. He said, "What kind of man? Did he threaten you boys?"

I didn't reply.

Doyle squeezed my arm so that it hurt. "Tell me, son. What kind of man?"

I looked to Gus hoping that he could see the pain on my face. But he seemed lost in the confusion of that moment which probably came not only from the confounding influence of the alcohol but also from the betrayal of the trust he'd put in me. He said, "Tell him, Frankie. Tell him about the man."

Still I did not speak.

Doyle shook me. Shook me like a rag doll. "Tell me," he said.

Halderson said, "Tell him, son."

"Tell him, Frank," Gus said.

Doyle shouted now. "Tell me goddamn it. What kind of man?"

I stared at them, dumbed by their viciousness, and I knew I would not speak.

It was Jake who saved me. He said, "A dead man."

4

On a minister's salary we ate cautiously but we ate well. That didn't mean the food was good; my mother was a notoriously bad cook. But she was a savvy shopper and made sure there was plenty to sustain us. Most Saturday nights my father made hamburgers and milk shakes and we ate these with potato chips. Salad was the lettuce and tomato and onion we put on our burgers though sometimes my mother would cut carrots and celery into sticks. We looked forward to dinner on Saturdays which we sometimes ate around a picnic table in our backyard.

That Saturday things were different and they were different because of the dead man and because Jake and I had reported him. My father had come to pick us up at the police station where we waited with Gus. We'd answered the questions of the county sheriff who was a man named Gregor and who'd been called into town from the small farm he operated on Willow Creek. He didn't look like a sheriff. He was dressed in overalls and his hair was stiff with hay dust. He treated us kindly though he was stern when it came to his admonition that the railroad tracks were no place for boys to play. He reminded us about the unfortunate Bobby Cole. He sounded truly sad when he spoke of Bobby's death and I had the sense that it meant something to him and I was inclined to like him.

Jake stuttered horribly when he was questioned and in the end I told the story for both of us. I didn't mention the Indian. I don't know why. The sheriff and the men in the police station hadn't been drinking and they seemed reasonable and I wasn't afraid that they'd do violence if they picked him up. But Jake in his utterance in the back room of the drugstore had omitted the Indian and in doing so had lied and the lie once spoken had taken shape as surely as if he'd chiseled it from a block of limestone. To undo it would be to put on my brother's shoulders the impossible responsibility of trying to explain why he'd dissembled in the first place. Since the moment when with astonishing clarity he'd spoken the lie, Jake hadn't been able to say a single word without stumbling through a long preamble of unintelligible utterances that were an embarrassment to him and to all who were present.

My father when he arrived was fully informed. He and Gus stood together while our questioning was completed then he ushered us outside into the Packard. Although Dad had cleaned the car thoroughly after Gus puked in the back, there was still a faint unpleasant odor and we drove home with the windows down. He pulled into the garage and we climbed from the car and he said, "Boys, I'd like to talk to you." He looked at Gus and Gus nodded and walked off. We stood in the open doorway of the garage. Across the street the church was bathed in the light of the late afternoon sun and its white sides had turned yellow as pollen. I stared at the steeple whose little cross seemed like a black brand against the sky and I was pretty sure of what was about to come. My father had never struck us but he could speak in a way that made you feel as if you'd offended God himself. That's what I figured was our due.

"The issue," he said, "is that I need to be able to trust you. I can't watch you every moment of every day nor can your mother. We need to know that you're responsible and won't do dangerous things."

"The tracks aren't dangerous," I said.

"Bobby Cole was killed on those tracks," he said.

"Bobby was different. How many other kids have been killed playing on the tracks? Heck, streets are more dangerous. Me and Jake could be killed a whole lot easier just crossing the street in town."

"I'm not going to argue, Frank."

"I'm just saying that anything can be dangerous if you're not careful. Me and Jake, we're careful. That dead guy today wasn't because we weren't careful."

"Okay, then this is the issue. I need to know that when I ask something of you you'll give it. If I ask you to stay away from those tracks, I need to know that you will. Do you understand?"

"Yes, sir."

"Trust is the issue, Frank." He looked at Jake. "Do you understand?" Jake said, "Yes s-s-s-sir."

"This is what's going to happen in order that you remember. For one week, you won't leave the yard without my permission or your mother's. Am I clear?"

All things considered I didn't think it was such a bad deal so I nodded to show that I understood and I accepted. Jake did the same.

I thought that was it but my father made no move to leave. He looked beyond us toward the dark at the back of the garage and was silent as if deep in thought. Then he turned and stared through the open door of the garage toward the church. He seemed to come to some decision.

He said, "The first man I ever saw dead outside a coffin was on a battlefield, and I have never spoken of it until now."

My father sat on the rear bumper of the Packard so that his eyes were level with ours.

"I was scared," he said, "and I was curious and although I knew it was a dangerous thing to do, I stopped and considered this dead soldier. He was German. Not much more than a boy. Only a few years older than you, Frank. And as I stood looking down at this dead young man, a soldier who'd seen a lot of battle stopped and he said to me, 'You'll get used to it, son.' Son, he called me, even though he was younger than I." My father shook his head and took a deep breath. "He was wrong, boys. I never got used to it."

My father leaned his arms on his thighs and folded his hands in the way he sometimes did when he sat alone in a pew and prayed.

"I had to go to war," he said. "Or felt that I had to. I thought I knew more or less what to expect. But death surprised me."

My father looked at each of us. His eyes were hard brown but they were also gentle and sad.

"You've seen something I would like to have kept from you. If you want to talk about it, I'll listen."

I glanced toward Jake who was staring at the dirt floor of the old garage. I held my tongue though in truth there was much I wanted to know.

My father waited patiently and gave no sign that he was disappointed in our silence. "All right," he said and stood. "Let's go inside. I'm sure your mother is wondering what's become of us."

My mother was in a tizzy. She gathered us to her bosom and made a fuss over us and swung between chastisement for our actions and delirium over our safety. My mother was a woman of deep emotion and also of drama and in the middle of the kitchen she poured out both on Jake and me. She stroked our hair as if we were pets and she dug her fingers into our shoulders and gave us each a stern little shake to set us straight and in the end she kissed the tops of our heads. My father had gone to the sink to run himself a glass of water and when my mother asked him about what had gone on at the police station he said, "Go on upstairs, boys. Your mother and I need to talk."

We trudged up to our bedroom and lay down on our beds in the heat that lingered from the day.

"Why didn't you tell them about the Indian?" I said.

Jake took his time answering. He had an old baseball that he'd grabbed off the bedroom floor and he tossed it and caught it as he lay. He said, "The Indian wasn't going to hurt us."

"How do you know that?"

"I just do. Why didn't you say anything?"

"I don't know. It didn't feel right."

"We shouldn't've been on the tracks."

"I don't think it was wrong."

"But Dad said—"

"I know what he said."

"You're going to get us in big trouble someday."

"You don't have to always follow me around like a sick dog."

He stopped tossing the ball. "You're my best friend, Frank."

I stared up at the ceiling and watched a fly with a shiny green body crawl across the plaster and I wondered what it was like to walk upside down in the world. I didn't acknowledge what Jake had said although it was something I'd always known. Except for me Jake didn't have friends and I wasn't sure the weight I should give the confession or the response I should offer.

"Hey, you two desperadoes."

My sister stood leaning against the doorframe with her arms crossed and a wry smile on her lips. Ariel was a pretty girl. She had my mother's auburn hair and pillowy blue eyes and my father's quiet and considered countenance. But what Morris Engdahl had said about her was true. She'd been born with a cleft lip and though it had been surgically corrected when she was a baby the scar was still visible. She claimed it didn't bother her and whenever somebody who didn't know asked her about it she gave a toss of her head and said, "It's the mark left by the finger of an angel who touched my face." She said it so sincerely that it usually ended the discussion of what some considered a deformity.

She came into the room and nudged Jake over and sat on his bed.

I said, "You just get home?"

Ariel waitressed in the restaurant at the country club south of the Heights.

"Yeah. Mom and Dad are having this big discussion about you two. A dead man? You really found a dead man? That must've scared you plenty."

"Naw," I said. "He looked like he was sleeping."

"How did you know he was dead?"

It was a question the sheriff had asked too and I told her what I'd told him. That we thought he might have been hurt and when he didn't answer our calls from the trestle we went down to check on him and it was easy then to see that he was dead.

"You said he looked like he was just sleeping," Ariel said. "Did you poke him to find out or what?"

I said, "Up close he looked dead. He wasn't breathing for one thing."

"You investigated this dead man pretty carefully," she said. She put her index finger to the scar on her lip which was something she did sometimes when she was deep in consideration and she looked at me a long thoughtful time. Then she turned to Jake.

"How about you, Jakie? Were you scared?"

He didn't answer her. Instead he said, "We weren't supposed to be there."

She laughed softly and said, "You'll be lots of places you're not supposed to be in your lives. Just don't get caught."

"I saw you sneaking in the other night," I said.

The moment of her playfulness vanished and she looked at me coldly.

"Don't worry. I didn't tell anybody."

"It doesn't matter," she said.

But I could tell that it did.

Ariel was my parents' golden child. She had a quick mind and the gift of easy charm and her fingers possessed magic on the keyboard and we knew, all of us who loved her, that she was destined for greatness. She was my mother's favorite and may have been my father's too though I was less certain of his sentiments. He was careful in how he spoke of his children, but my mother with passionate and dramatic abandon declared Ariel the joy of her heart. What she did not say but all of us knew was that Ariel was the hope for the consummation of my mother's own unfulfilled longings. It would have been easy to hate Ariel. But Jake and I adored her. She was our confidante. Our coconspirator. Our defender. She tracked our small successes better than our distracted parents and was lavish in her praise. In the simple way of the wild daisies that grew in the grass of the pasture behind our home she offered the beauty of herself without pretension.

"A dead man," she said and shook her head. "Do they know who he was?"

"He called himself Skipper," Jake said.

"How do you know?"

Jake shot me a look that was a silent plea for help but before I could respond Ariel said, "There's something you guys aren't telling me."

"There were two men," Jake said in a rush and it was easy to see that he was relieved to have the truth spill from him.

"Two?" Ariel looked from Jake to me. "Who was the other man?"

Thanks to Jake the truth was already there in front of us like a puddle of puke. I saw no reason to lie anymore especially to Ariel. I said, "An Indian. He was the dead man's friend." Then I told her everything that had happened.

She listened and the pillowy blue of her eyes rested sometimes on me and sometimes on Jake and in the end she said, "You guys could be in big trouble."

"S-s-s-see," Jake hissed at me.

"It's okay, Jakie," she said. She patted his leg. "Your secret's safe with me. But, guys, listen to Dad. He worries about you. We all do."

"Should we tell someone about the Indian?" Jake asked.

Ariel thought it over. "Was the Indian scary or dangerous?"

"He put his hand on Jake's leg," I said.

"He didn't scare me," Jake said. "I don't think he was going to hurt us or anything."

"Then I think it's okay to keep that part a secret." Ariel stood up. "But promise you won't goof around on the tracks anymore."

"Promise," Jake said.

Ariel waited for me to chime in and scowled until I gave her my word. She walked to the door where she turned back dramatically and gave a broad wave of her hand and said, "I'm off to the theater." She pronounced the word as *theatah*. "The drive-in theater," she said and finished by throwing an imaginary stole about her neck and exiting with a dramatic flourish.

My father didn't fix hamburgers and milk shakes that night. He was called to van der Waal's Funeral Home where the body of the dead man had been taken for disposition and where he discussed with van der Waal and the sheriff the burial of the stranger. He didn't get home until late. In the meantime, my mother heated Campbell's tomato soup and made grilled cheese sandwiches with Velveeta and we ate dinner and afterward watched *Have Gun—Will Travel*. The picture was snowy on the screen because of the poor reception in so isolated an area but Jake and I clamored to watch it every Saturday night anyway. Ariel left with some of her friends to go to the drive-in movies and my mother said, "Home by midnight." Ariel kissed her sweetly on the forehead and said, "Yes, Mother dear." We took our Saturday night baths and went to bed before my father returned and when he came home I was still awake and I heard my parents talking in the kitchen which was directly below our bedroom. Their voices came up through the grate in the floor and it was as if they were in the same room with me. They had no idea I was privy to every conversation that took place between them in the kitchen. They spent a few minutes talking about the burial service for the dead man which my father had agreed to perform. Then they moved on to Ariel.

My father said, "Is she out with Karl?"

"No," Mother replied. "Just a bunch of her girlfriends. I told her midnight because I knew you'd worry."

"When she's away at Juilliard and I have no say in the matter she can stay out as late as she wants but when she's with us and under our roof she's home by midnight," he said.

"You don't have to convince me, Nathan."

"She's been different lately," he said. "Have you noticed?"

"Different how?"

"I get the feeling something's on her mind and she's about to speak and then she doesn't."

"If something was bothering her she'd tell me, Nathan. She tells me everything."

"All right," my father said.

Mother asked, "When is the burial for that dead itinerant?"

Mother used the word *itinerant* because she said it was kinder than *hobo* or *bum*, and so we'd all begun to use that term when referring to the dead man.

"Monday."

"Would you like me to sing?"

"It will be just me and Gus and van der Waal at the burial. No need for music I think. A few appropriate words will do."

Their chairs scraped on the linoleum and they drifted away from the table and I could no longer hear them.

I thought about the dead man and I thought that I would like to be there when he was buried and I rolled over and closed my eyes thinking about Bobby Cole in his casket and about the dead man who would be in a casket too and I fell into a dark and unsettled slumber.

In the night I woke to the sound of a car door closing on the street in front of our house and Ariel laughing. In my parents' bedroom across the hall a dim light burned. The car drove away and a few moments later I heard the tiny cry of the hinges on the front screen door. The light in my parents' bedroom blinked off and their door closed with a quiet sigh. Ariel came up the stairs and then I was asleep.

Later I woke to thunder. I went to the window and saw that an electrical storm was sliding north of the valley and although the rain would miss us I could see quite well the silver bolts of lightning forged on the anvil of the great thunderhead. I slipped downstairs and out the front door and sat on the porch steps. A wind cooler than anything I'd felt in days breathed into my face and I watched the storm as I might have watched the approach and passing of a fierce and beautiful animal.

The distant thunder was like the sound of cannon fire and I thought about my father and what he'd told Jake and me about the war, which was a good deal more than he'd ever shared with us. There'd been many things I wanted to ask and I wasn't sure why I'd held back and though he'd done nothing to show it I knew my father was hurt by our silence which was the only return we gave for his difficult honesty. I'd wanted to ask about death and if it hurt to die and what awaited me and everyone else after our passing and don't give me that crap about the Pearly Gates, Dad. Death was a serious subject on my mind and I wanted to talk to someone about it. Standing with my father and brother in the dirt of the garage I'd been offered the moment but I'd let it pass.

As I sat on the steps I saw someone dash across the yard from the back of the house and head toward Tyler Street and up to the Heights.

We didn't have streetlights on the Flats but I didn't need a light to know who was sneaking away.

I stood up to return to my bedroom and looked one last time where the lightning stabbed the earth that rimmed and isolated our valley.

There'd been two deaths already that summer, and although I didn't have a clue, there were three more yet to come.

And the next would be the most painful to bear.

5

My father had three charges which meant that he was responsible for the spiritual needs of the congregations of three churches and every Sunday he presided over three services. As his family we were required to attend them all.

At eight a.m. the worship for the church in Cadbury commenced. Cadbury was a small town fifteen miles southeast of New Bremen. They had a strong congregation that included a number of Protestants of different denominations who had no church of their own near enough to attend easily and preferred the more informal service of the Methodists to the religious rigor of the Lutherans, who were as ubiquitous in Minnesota as ragweed. My mother directed the choir of which she was quite proud. Every week she drew from the men and women of the Cadbury church choir a sound that was rich and melodious and a joy to the ear. In this enterprise she had help. One of the men possessed a beautiful baritone that under my mother's tutelage he'd shaped into a fine instrument, and one of the women had a voice that was a strong alto complement to my mother's lovely soprano. The music pieces that my mother put together for the choir and that relied on the strength of those three voices were reason enough to come to church. Ariel was icing on the cake. Her skillful fingers coaxed from the pipes of that modest little organ music that was like nothing the congregation of the tiny country church had ever heard before. Jake and I trudged along to every service and mostly did our best not to fidget. Because it was the first, the service in Cadbury was not so difficult. By the third Sunday service our butts were sore and our patience sorely tested. So the Cadbury service tended to be our favorite.

My father was well liked in the rural churches. The sermons he preached, which were marked less by evangelical fervor than by a calm exhortation of God's unbounded grace, were well received by congregations composed primarily of sensible farm families who in most aspects of their public lives were as emotionally demonstrative as a mound of hay. He was also gifted in inspiring the church committees that were a part of every Methodist congregation. Most weekday evenings he was gone from the house attending some committee meeting in Cadbury or New Bremen or Fosburg, the site of his third charge. He was ceaseless in the execution of what he saw as his duty and if he was often absent as a father that was part of the price of his calling.

Cadbury lay in a hollow along Sioux Creek which was a tributary to the Minnesota River. As you crested the highway that dropped into town you were greeted by the sight of three church steeples rising above a thick green gathering of trees. Cadbury Methodist was the nearest of these steeples. From the front of the church you could look down the main street which was two blocks of businesses that in the boom of the post–World War Two years had prospered. The church was shaded by several tall elms and on summer mornings when we arrived the sanctuary was cool and quiet. My father unlocked the building and went to the office and Ariel went to the organ and my mother went to the choir room. Jake and I were responsible for putting out the offering plates for the ushers and if the sanctuary was stuffy we opened the windows. Then we sat in the back row and waited as the congregation gathered and the choir assembled.

That morning shortly before the service was to begin my mother came out from the choir room and stood near the altar and scanned the sanctuary with a concerned look on her face.

She came to me and said, "Have you seen Mrs. Klement?"

I told her no.

"Go outside and watch for her. If you see her coming, let me know right away."

I said, "Yes, ma'am."

I walked outside and Jake came with me and we stood looking both ways down the street. Mrs. Klement was the woman with the strong alto voice. She was my mother's age and had a son named Peter who was twelve years old. Because his mother sang in the choir Peter was orphaned during the service and he usually sat with Jake and me. His father never came to church and I'd gathered through conversations I'd overheard that he was not much inclined toward religion but was a man of unfortunate excesses who could have benefited from a bit of good solid Methodist discipline.

While we watched for Mrs. Klement a number of the congregation passed us on their way into the church and greeted us with pleasant familiarity. A man named Thaddeus Porter who was the town banker and a widower and who walked with a regal gait strode up to us and stopped and clasped his hands behind his back and looked down on us as a general might during inspection of his troops.

"I heard you boys found yourselves a dead body," he said.

"Yes, sir," I replied.

"Quite a remarkable discovery."

"Yes, sir, it was."

"You seem well recovered."

"The truth is, sir, it didn't bother me much."

"Ah," he said and nodded as if not being much bothered wasn't a bad thing. "Nerves of steel, eh? I'll see you boys inside." He turned from us and with measured strides mounted the steps.

Mrs. Klement never showed that Sunday morning nor did Peter. The anthem and the offertory hymn, my mother said afterward, suffered greatly due to her absence. After the service we stayed briefly for the social time in the church fellowship hall during which I was questioned a good deal about the dead man Jake and I had found. Each time I repeated the story I embellished it just a bit more and as a result suffered Jake's disapproving scowl. So much so that by the last telling I'd made him little more than a footnote in the tale.

When my father had finished with the final service that day, which was held at noon in the church in Fosburg a dozen miles north of New Bremen, he drove us all home. As always it felt as if I'd just spent a long time in hell and had finally been granted a divine pardon. I raced to my bedroom and changed my clothes and got ready to enjoy the rest of the day. When I went downstairs I found my mother in the kitchen pulling food from the refrigerator. She'd put together a tuna casserole and Jell-O salad the night before which I figured would be our dinner. My father entered the kitchen after me and it was clear he thought so too. He said, "Dinner?"

"Not for us," my mother replied. "It's for Amelia Klement. The ladies of the choir told me that she was quite ill and that was why she didn't come to church today." She pushed my father aside and walked to the counter with the pan of tuna casserole in hand. She said, "Amelia's life is a prison cell presided over by Travis Klement, who, if he isn't the worst husband in the world, is certainly in the running. She's told me more times than I can count that choir practice on Wednesday and church on Sunday are the two things she looks forward to most in a week. If she couldn't make it to church today, she must be very ill, and I intend to see that she doesn't have to worry about feeding her family. I'm going to finish this casserole, and then I'm going to deliver it, and you're coming with me."

"What about our dinner?" This slipped from my lips before I had a chance to think about the advisability of asking.

My mother gave me a scathing look. "You won't starve. I'll put something together."

The truth was that it was fine with me. I wasn't at all fond of tuna casserole. And I thought that if she and my father were driving out to Peter Klement's house I might go along and tell Peter about the dead man. I was really warming to the effect this story seemed to have on those who heard it.

Ariel came into the kitchen dressed for work at the country club. My mother asked, "Would you like a sandwich before you go?"

"No, I'll grab something when I get there." Ariel lingered and leaned against the counter and said, "What if I didn't go to Juilliard this fall?"

My father who'd plucked a banana from the bunch on the top of the refrigerator and was peeling it said, "We'd send you to work in the salt mines instead."

"I mean," Ariel said, "it would be cheaper if I went to Mankato State."

"You're on a scholarship," my father pointed out and stuffed a good third of the banana into his mouth.

"I know, but you and Mom will still have to pay a lot."

"Let us worry about that," my father said.

"I could continue to study with Emil Brandt. He's as good as anyone at Juilliard."

Emil Brandt had been Ariel's teacher since we'd come to New Bremen five years before. He was in fact much of the reason we'd come. My mother wanted Ariel to study with the best composer and pianist in Minnesota and that was Brandt. He happened also to be my mother's good friend since childhood.

I learned my mother's history with Brandt gradually over the whole course of my life. Some things I knew in 1961, others were revealed to me as I grew older. In those days I understood that when she was hardly more than a girl my mother had been briefly engaged to Brandt who was several years her senior. I'd also gathered that by the standards of the staid German population in New Bremen, Emil Brandt was a wild one, both a prodigiously talented musician and one of the high and mighty Brandts who knew he was destined for greater things. Shortly after he'd proposed to my mother Brandt had left her flat, gone off to New York City to seek his fortune without so much as a by your leave. By the summer of 1961, however, all of that was ancient history and my mother counted Emil Brandt as one of her dearest friends. Partly this was due to the healing property of time but I believe it was also because when he finally came home to New Bremen, Brandt was a very damaged man and my mother felt a great deal of compassion for him.

Mother stopped what she was doing and turned a stern eye on her daughter. "Is this about Karl? You don't want to leave your boyfriend?"

"That's not it at all, Mom."

"Then what is it? Because it's not about money. We settled that issue long ago. Your grandfather promised anything you need."

My father swallowed a mouthful of banana and said, "She doesn't need anything from him."

My mother ignored him and kept her eyes on Ariel.

Ariel tried again: "I don't know that I want to go so far away from my family."

"That's a feeble excuse, Ariel Louise, and you know it. What's going on?"

"I just . . . Never mind," she said and rushed to the door and left the house.

My father stood looking after her. "What do you suppose that was all about?"

"Karl," my mother said. "I never liked the idea of those two going steady. I knew he would end up a distraction."

"Everybody goes steady these days, Ruth."

"They're too serious, Nathan. They spend all their free time together."

"She went out with other friends last night," my father said.

I thought about Ariel sneaking off after she'd returned from the drive-in theater and I wondered if it was Karl she'd gone to meet.

My mother snatched up a pack of cigarettes from the windowsill over the sink and angrily tapped out a cigarette and struck a match and from behind a swirl of smoke said, "If Ariel's thinking that she might marry instead of going to college, I'll be happy to set that girl straight right now."

"Ruth," my father said, "we don't know anything of the sort. But it would be a good idea to sit down with her and find out what's going on. Discuss it calmly."

"I'll calmly tan her backside," my mother said.

My father smiled. "You've never hit the children, Ruth."

"She's not a child."

"All the more reason to talk to her like an adult. We'll do it tonight after she's home from work."

When they were ready to drive to the Klements' house I asked if I could go along to see Peter which meant that Jake would have to come too. My father saw no reason for leaving us behind especially in light of the constraint Jake and I were under not to go out of the yard without his permission. Jake didn't mind going. He brought along the most recent issues of *Aquaman* and *Green Lantern* to read in the car. We piled into the Packard and headed for Cadbury.

Mr. Klement operated a small engine repair business out of a shop that was a converted barn next to his house. His father had owned two hundred acres just outside town and on his death had passed it to his son who had neither the disposition nor the inclination to be a farmer. Travis Klement sold the arable acreage but kept the house and outbuildings and established his business there.

We arrived midafternoon and the heat lay oppressive on the land. We parked in the gravel drive in the shade of a big walnut tree. My mother took her casserole and my father took the bowl of Jell-O salad and they climbed the front steps and stood on the rickety porch and knocked at the screen door. Jake and I hung back. From the yard we could see the steeples of Cadbury just a quarter mile north. Between the Klements' house and town Sioux Creek crossed the road. Under the narrow bridge, on those occasions when we were able to slip away from some dull church function, we'd hung out with Peter and caught crawdads and had once observed a family of foxes scurrying into a thicket along the creek bank.

Peter came to the door and stood behind the screen and my father said, "Good afternoon, Peter. Is your mother home?"

"Just a minute," Peter said. He looked beyond my parents toward Jake and me in the yard and then he turned back and disappeared into the dark inside the house. A moment later his mother took his place. She was a woman plain of face but had long gold hair that she often wore in a braid and that hung like a silk rope down the middle of her back and that I always thought kept her from being in appearance completely unremarkable. She wore a simple sleeveless yellow dress which was something I'd heard my mother call a shift. She didn't open the door or look directly at my parents but kept her face behind the dark of the screen and tilted downward as if fascinated by the unpainted porch boards and when she spoke it was in a voice so quiet that I could not hear what she said. This was odd behavior toward a

minister and his family. People usually invited us in. I wandered onto
the porch and stood near enough that I could hear the adults talking.

"We so missed you this morning, Amelia," my mother was saying.
"The music isn't at all the same without you."

Mrs. Klement said, "I'm sorry, Ruth."

"We made do of course. But, Amelia, I hope you recover and can
be with us for practice on Wednesday."

"I'm sure I will," Mrs. Klement said.

"Well, anyway, we just wanted to bring over a little something for
supper so that you wouldn't have to worry about feeding your family
and you could rest and recover. Nathan?"

My father held out the bowl of Jell-O salad and my mother offered
the tuna casserole. Mrs. Klement seemed uncertain about taking them.
Finally she called for Peter and when he came she nudged the screen
open only far enough for the dishes to be passed through. Then she
stepped back quickly and let the screen door slap shut.

"I've been thinking," my mother said, "of a duet next Sunday. You
and me, Amelia. I think it would be quite a lovely piece."

I edged back and descended the steps and let the adults continue
talking. I walked around to the side of the old farmhouse. Most of the
grass in the yard was already dead and had gone brittle and I crunched
my way toward the open barn door with Jake close on my heels. We
stood in the doorway peering inside at disemboweled lawn mowers
and refrigerator condensers and motor parts that lay strewn about the
dirt floor and that made the barn seem to me like a gladiatorial arena
where the vanquished had been left dismembered. To the eyes of a
boy it was fascinating but the disarray also signaled something vaguely
unsettling to me.

I heard the crush of gravel at our backs and turned to find Peter
approaching. He wore a baseball cap pulled low as if to shield his face
from the brutal bake of the sun.

"Better come away from there," he said. "My dad might get mad."

I bent and peered into the shadow cast by the brim of his cap.
"Where'd you get that shiner?"

He touched his eye and spun away. "I gotta go," he said. "So do you."
Which was true. I saw my parents walking to the car and signaling

us to join them. Peter headed toward the back door of his house and went inside without another word and without looking back.

In the car on the way home we all were quiet. At the house my mother said, "Why don't you boys go out and play awhile? When you come back in I'll have Kool-Aid ready and some sandwiches."

We had a tire swing that hung on a rope from a branch of a big elm in the side yard and that's where we went. Jake loved that swing. He could swing in it for hours talking to himself the whole time. He climbed into the tire and said, "Spin me." I took hold of his shoulders and turned him and turned him until the rope was tightly twisted and then I let him go and stepped back and he spun like a top.

Through the kitchen window at my back came snatches of my parents' conversation.

"They lied, Nathan. Every one of the ladies in choir told me Amelia was sick. I should have known."

"And what did you expect her friends and neighbors to say? That her husband had hit her and she was embarrassed to show the bruises in public?"

"Not just her, Nathan. He hit Peter too."

Jake got out of the swing and began a wobbly walk, all dizzy from the spinning, and I lost track of the conversation in the kitchen for a moment. Jake fell down and I heard my mother's voice again with a tautness near anger.

"I don't expect them to tell me the truth, Nathan. I'm sure in their minds it's no one's business but the Klements'. But they should tell you."

"Because I'm their pastor?"

"Because you're her pastor, too. And if she can't turn to anyone else, she ought to be able to turn to you. People tell you their secrets, Nathan. I know they do. And not just because you're their pastor."

Jake finally got up and went back to the tire. I would have spun him again but he waved me off and began to swing normally.

I heard water run in the kitchen sink and a glass fill and then my father said, "He spent time in a North Korean POW camp. Did you know that, Ruth? He still has nightmares. He drinks because he thinks it helps him deal with the nightmares."

"You have nightmares. You don't drink."

"Every man handles in a different way the damage war did to him."

"Some men seem to have put their wars behind them easily enough. I've heard some men say being in the army was the best time of their lives."

"Then they must have fought in different wars than I did and Travis Klement."

From the swing Jake called to me, "Want to play catch?"

I said sure and started for the house to get the ball and our baseball gloves. My father came out the side door from the kitchen and walked toward the church. I quickly fell in step beside him and asked where he was going.

"To get Gus," he said.

"Why?"

I already suspected the answer. Gus was familiar with the drinking establishments in the valley of the Minnesota River and my father was not. If anyone would have an idea about where Mr. Klement was getting drunk it would be Gus.

"I need his help," he replied.

"Can I go?"

"No."

"Please."

"I said no." My father seldom spoke sharply but his voice made it clear that on this subject he would brook no argument. I stopped and he walked alone to the church.

Jake and I went inside the house where my mother had begun distractedly preparing lunch. Upstairs, my brother grabbed his ball glove from where it lay on the floor. I began digging through the closet in search of mine.

Jake sat on his bed and put the glove to his nose as if inhaling the good aroma of the old leather and said, "He never talks about the war."

I was surprised because I thought he'd been so involved with his tire swing that he couldn't have heard the kitchen conversation. Jake was always amazing me this way. I found my glove, an old Rawlings first baseman's mitt, and put it on and slapped the soft palm with my hard fist.

"Maybe he will someday," I said.

"Yeah, maybe someday," Jake said but not necessarily because he believed it. Sometimes he just liked agreeing with me.

6

Karl was the only child of Axel and Julia Brandt. Axel Brandt owned the brewery in New Bremen which had been built by his great-grandfather and was among the first businesses established when the town was originally settled. For more than a hundred years the enterprise had prospered. The brewery employed a significant workforce and was part of the economic lifeblood of New Bremen. In a way it was the town's crown jewel and the Brandts were about as near to royalty as you'd find in the Midwest. They lived of course on the Heights in a sprawling white-pillared mansion with a large marble patio in back that had a view of the town below and below that the Flats and beyond the Flats the broad crawl of the river.

Karl Brandt and Ariel had gone steady for almost a year and although my mother didn't like the idea, their relationship was more or less her doing. Every summer since we'd moved to New Bremen my mother had mounted a musical production that tapped the talent of the town's youth and that was presented in the band shell in Luther Park the first weekend in August. The citizens of New Bremen turned out in extraordinary numbers. For some time after the last bow of the final show had been taken the talk of the town was prideful, not only because the young people had displayed such extraordinary talent but also because they were evidence that New Bremen was fostering in its youth the kinds of values that would serve both the community and the country well. In the summer when they were seventeen, Ariel and Karl had been chosen by my mother as the leads in a musical called *The Boy Friend.* By the end of the production the pair of stars were inseparable. For a while my mother looked on the relationship as a natural extension of the time and energy the two teenagers had invested in the production and she predicted it would not last beyond the turning of the leaves in autumn. But another summer had come to the valley of the Minnesota River and Karl and Ariel's relationship seemed as consuming as ever. Its intensity alarmed not only my mother but also Julia Brandt who, whenever the two women happened to meet, was—my mother said in words that would have made the New York famous writers' school proud—"cold as an Arctic winter."

Despite her disapproval of the intensity of his relationship with her daughter, my mother liked Karl and often invited him for dinner. Ariel had never once dined with the Brandts, a fact not at all lost on my mother. Karl was polite and funny and an athlete who'd lettered in football and basketball and baseball. He'd been accepted to St. Olaf which was a college in Northfield, Minnesota, where he intended to play football and get a degree and then return to New Bremen to help his father run the brewery. When I looked up the hill from town and saw the walls of the mansion white among the greenery I thought Karl Brandt's future sounded pretty swell.

That Sunday evening Karl and Ariel were going boating. Karl's family owned a sailboat and a motor launch both docked at a marina on Lake Singleton. Ariel enjoyed boating. She said she loved the feel of the wind off the water and the clear blue circle of the sky overhead and the egrets and herons that walked stilt-like in the reedy shallows. She said she loved being freed from the stultifying solidness of dirt.

After supper she sat on the porch steps waiting for Karl. I came out and sat with her. Ariel always seemed happy to have my company. For that alone I would have loved her. My father hadn't yet returned from his search for Travis Klement and as we sat I watched Tyler Street for any sign of our Packard.

Ariel was dressed in white shorts and a top with horizontal red and white stripes and she wore white canvas slip-ons. Her hair was tied with a red ribbon.

"You look pretty," I said.

"Thanks, Frankie. With me a compliment'll get you anywhere." She lightly bumped my hip with her own.

"What's it like?" I asked.

"What?"

"Being in love. Is it all kind of gooey?"

She laughed. "At first it's lovely. Then it's scary. Then . . ." She looked toward the hills of town, toward the Heights. "It's complicated," she said.

"Will you marry him?"

"Karl?" She shook her head.

"Mom's afraid you will."

"Mom doesn't know everything."

"She says she worries because she loves you."

"She worries, Frankie, because she's afraid I'll end up like her."

I didn't know what that meant exactly though I knew as well as any of us that Mother was less than delighted with her life as a minister's wife. She'd said as much on a number of occasions. Her words usually went something like *When I married you, Nathan, I thought I was marrying a lawyer. I didn't sign on for this.* More often than not it was said after she'd had a drink which was not something a minister's wife was supposed to do but my mother did anyway. She had a fondness for martinis and sometimes would make a couple for herself in the evening and sip them alone in the living room while dinner bubbled over on the stove.

"She made Dad go look for Mr. Klement," I said. "Mr. Klement hit Mrs. Klement and Peter."

"I heard," Ariel said.

"I do a lot of stuff I figure I should get hit for but I never do. I just get yelled at. I deserve it. I'm not the greatest kid."

She turned to me and looked seriously into my face. "Frankie, never sell yourself short. You have remarkable strengths."

"I should be more responsible," I said.

"You have plenty of time to become responsible. And believe me it's not all it's cracked up to be." She spoke with a heaviness that weighed on me and I leaned against her and said, "I wish you weren't going away."

"Maybe I'm not, Frankie," she said. "Maybe I'm not."

Before I had a chance to press her further Karl drove up in his little sports car. For his eighteenth birthday his parents had given him a red Triumph TR3 and he drove it everywhere. He popped out of the car and bounded up the walk to where Ariel and I sat on the steps. He was tall and blond and smiling. He ruffled my hair and called me Sport and he said to Ariel, "You ready?"

"Home by midnight," my mother said through the screen door behind us. Then she said, "Hello, Karl."

"Hello, Mrs. Drum. Beautiful evening, don't you think? And I'll have her home before midnight, I promise."

"Enjoy yourselves," my mother said though not exactly with a full heart.

Ariel and Karl got into his car and sped up Tyler Street and out of sight. At my back I heard my mother sigh.

My father didn't return by suppertime and we ate without him. Mother had browned some hamburger and added to it a big can of Franco-American spaghetti and she kept this warm on the stove anticipating my father's return. Jake and I ate on television trays and watched *Walt Disney's Wonderful World of Color,* though for us it was in black and white, and on our old RCA console the world was a less-than-wonderful twenty-four-inches wide. The sun was down and the distant hills had taken on the blue look of twilight when there was a knock at the door and we found Danny O'Keefe standing on the porch scratching at a mosquito bite on his arm and telling us we should come outside and do something.

Despite the impression given by his name Danny O'Keefe was Indian. Specifically he was Dakota but in those days they were known as Sioux. He didn't like being called an Indian which was understandable given the image that had been acid-burned with ridicule and hatred into the minds of white Americans. In the valley of the Minnesota River—hell, maybe everywhere back then—it was dangerous to be an Indian. In 1862 the Sioux of the area had mounted a brief rebellion against the white settlers which all Minnesotans knew as the Great

Sioux Uprising. New Bremen had been besieged and many of the buildings burned. In the end, unconscionable death and suffering was visited upon the Sioux, who'd already endured years of mistreatment and deception at the hands of the whites. Even so, the uprising was usually given a spin in the classrooms that made the Sioux look criminally ungrateful. When we were younger and played Cowboys and Indians, Danny refused to take the part his genetics dictated.

Outside on our lawn there was a gathering of a bunch of the other kids from the Flats all of whom wanted to hear the story of how Jake and I had stumbled onto a dead man. I did the talking. By then I was reciting embellishments of the story that made it terribly exciting and full of moments of danger and suspense: We thought we heard voices. Arguing maybe. We were sure someone else had been there. Had foul play been involved in his death and were we in danger because we'd found the body? Jake eyed me with mild consternation but said nothing to contradict my version of the events and in the eyes of the others I saw a look of envy and respect that was intoxicating.

We played softball in the pasture behind our house until it was too dark to see and the others scattered back to their own homes and Jake and I went inside. My father still had not returned from his search for Travis Klement. My mother was standing at the kitchen sink smoking a cigarette and staring through the window toward Tyler Street. We asked for a treat before bed and she said we could have some ice cream which we ate while watching Ed Sullivan. We got ourselves ready for bed and kissed Mother good night and from the way she turned her cheek to us but not her eyes which held on Tyler Street it was clear that she was distracted. I didn't know what there was to be worried about because my father was often gone on a call to one of his congregation that ended up turning into a long visitation as he helped cope with some travail or he became part of a protracted vigil over illness or death.

Upstairs in our room Jake said, "You better stop telling that story."

"What story?"

"How you were such a hero finding the dead guy."

"I was sort of."

"I was there too."

"Everybody knows that."

"You make it sound like I wasn't."

"Then next time you tell the story."

That shut Jake up but I could sense him still seething on the far side of the room.

For Christmas we'd been given a clock radio with a timer that let you listen to it for an hour at which point it would shut itself off automatically. On Sunday nights Jake and I listened to *"Unshackled!"* which was a religious program broadcast from a place called the Old Lighthouse in Chicago. It consisted of dramatized stories of people whose lives spiraled into the darkest places imaginable where only the light of God was powerful enough to reach and save them. I didn't much care for the religious part of it but radio dramas were rare and I enjoyed being told a story that way. Jake usually fell asleep while the show was on and that night was no exception.

I listened until the radio clicked off and I began to drift into sleep and then I heard the return of the Packard and I woke up. Below me the screen door opened and I knew Mother had gone out onto the porch to greet my father. I went to the window and watched him walk from the garage with Gus at his side.

"Thanks, Gus," my father said.

"A good day's work, Captain. Let's hope it takes. Good night."

Gus left him and headed for the church. My father joined my mother on the porch and they came inside and went to the kitchen where I knew she would dish out the warmed-over spaghetti. I lay back down on my bed. Through the heat grate I heard the chairs scrape the linoleum as my parents settled at the table and the quiet that followed as my father ate.

"We finally found him in Mankato drinking in a bar," Dad said. "He was pretty drunk. We did our best to sober him up. Fed him something. We talked and I tried to convince him to pray with me, which he refused to do. In the end, though, he was better. He was ready to go home. He felt pretty bad about how he'd treated Amelia and Peter. He said things have been tough lately. He swore it would never happen again."

"And you believed him?"

I heard my father slide his fork across his plate as he gathered the last of his supper. "Ruth, I don't know that God can reach everyone. Or maybe it's just that I don't know how to deliver everyone to God. Travis isn't out of the woods. I worry about him and about his family. And I don't know what more I can do at the moment except pray for them."

I heard water run in the sink and the clatter of plate and fork as my mother laid them there and I heard silence and I imagined her turning back to my father still sitting at the table and the last thing I heard that night was her soft voice telling him, "Thank you, Nathan. Thank you for trying."

7

Monday was my father's official day off. After breakfast he usually took what he called a constitutional which was a walk from the Flats to the home of Emil Brandt. Because Brandt had a sister, Lise, whom Jake had long ago befriended, my brother often accompanied Dad. I didn't mind going with them on that particular Monday, as I was bound by my father's stricture to stay in the yard unless given permission to do otherwise. Accompanying him was like receiving a prison pass. Ariel went along but she was often at the home of Emil Brandt anyway, not only under his tutelage for her piano and organ keyboard work and her musical composition but also working with him to complete a memoir he'd been dictating for more than a year.

Although Emil and Lise Brandt were part of the royalty that was the Brandt family—they were the brother and sister of Axel Brandt and, therefore, uncle and aunt to Karl—they lived in a kind of exile in a beautifully renovated farmhouse on the western edge of New Bremen overlooking the river. They were Brandts in name and in fortune but they were different from the others. Emil was a piano virtuoso and a composer of significant reputation and in his youth he'd been a carouser of great celebrity. After he'd proposed to my mother and then left her, he'd gone to study music in New

York City and had become friends with Aaron Copland. Copland had just returned from Hollywood where he'd hit it big with a score for the film version of Steinbeck's *Of Mice and Men.* The composer had encouraged the struggling Emil to seek his fortune on the West Coast, and the young man had followed that advice. From the very beginning he did well, found easy work in the music side of the film business, and fell in with a good-time Hollywood crowd. He befriended Scott Fitzgerald in the author's final years of near obscurity, and the Andrews Sisters who were originally from Minnesota, and Judy Garland, née Frances Gumm, also of Minnesota. Until the war cut short his carousing with the stars he was a young musician with two roads before him: one that led to the glamour of continuing to compose for the big screen and the other that wound its way back to the land from which he came and the music that rose from black soil and strong wind and deep root. All this Ariel told me from what she'd learned typing the memoir he dictated.

Lise Brandt was another story. She'd been born ten years after Emil, born deaf and difficult. She was the child of whom the Brandts, if they spoke of her at all, spoke in somber tones. She hadn't attended school but had received what schooling could be given from special tutors who'd resided in the Brandt home. She was subject to tantrums and to fits of rage and only Emil seemed able to tolerate her outbursts and she for her part adored him. When Emil returned from the Second World War blind and disfigured and wanting only to feed in isolation on the meat of his bitterness, his family had purchased and completely renovated a farmhouse that was a stone's throw from the edge of town. For companionship they'd given him Lise who was in her midteens then and had no future that anyone could see. This union had served both damaged Brandts well. Lise took care of her brother and her brother offered Lise a place where, in all the isolated silent years ahead, she would have purpose and protection.

This too Ariel told me, but it would be a while before I understood the importance of these things.

When we approached the white picket fence Lise Brandt was already at work among the rows of her vegetable garden wearing soiled gloves and working the damp earth with the sharp edge of her hoe. Emil Brandt sat in a wicker chair on the porch and next to him was a white wicker table and another chair and on the table was set a chessboard with all the pieces arranged and ready for play.

"Will you have coffee, Nathan?" Brandt called out to us as we entered the gate.

He knew we were coming and the sound of the hinges had probably alerted him to our arrival but he loved to give the impression that although he was as blind as one of the fence posts he could somehow see us. He smiled as we advanced up the walk and he said, "Is that Ariel with you and those two hooligans you claim as your sons?" How he knew the exact makeup of my father's entourage was a mystery to me but my father spoke of him as the most intelligent man he knew and clearly Emil Brandt had his ways. Lise left off her hoeing and stood tall and plain and still as a scarecrow as she watched us intrude. Intrusion but for Jake who peeled away and ran to her where they communicated in signs and gestures and Jake followed her to the toolshed and came out with a garden rake and shadowed her as she began again the work in the garden.

My father mounted the steps and said, "I'd love some coffee, Emil."

The blind man said, "Would you mind getting it, Ariel? You know where everything is. And get whatever you'd like for yourself. I've left the tape recorder on my desk and there's plenty of paper for you at the typewriter."

"All right," Ariel said. She went inside in a way that seemed to me as familiar as entering her own house.

I sat on the porch steps. My father took the second wicker chair and said, "How is the memoir coming?"

"Words are different from musical notes, Nathan. It's a hell of an undertaking and I'm not sure I'm very good at it. That said, I'm having a fine time with the project."

The property of Emil and Lise Brandt was among the most beautiful in all of New Bremen. Along the fence Lise had planted butterfly bushes that bloomed red and yellow all summer long. Here and there about the lawn she'd created enclaves of flowers like islands that she'd edged with red brick and that exploded with blossoms of a dozen varieties in color and form. Her vegetable garden occupied a space as large as the foundation of our whole house and by the end of every summer the tomatoes and cabbage and carrots and sweet corn and squash and other vegetables grew huge and heavy on vine and stalk. Lise could not communicate well with the human world but she and plants seemed to understand each other perfectly.

Ariel brought my father coffee and said, "I'll just get started now."

"Fine," Brandt said and offered a smile that curled smoothly into the normal flesh of his right cheek but crinkled the thick scar tissue of his left.

Ariel went back inside and a few minutes later through the window of a room at the corner of the house came Brandt's voice on the tape recorder followed by the rapid tap of typewriter keys. As my father and Emil Brandt talked and began their weekly game of chess I listened to Ariel's fingers flying over the typewriter keyboard. My father had insisted that she take business courses and learn typing and shorthand because he thought that regardless of her dreams and intentions such training would stand a woman in good stead.

"E-four," Brandt said offering the opening move of the game.

My father advanced Brandt's pawn. He made all the moves for Brandt who could not see the board with his eyes but who had the marvelous ability to visualize the game as it progressed.

My father had grown up in the rough port city of Duluth, the son of a seaman who was often gone on long voyages, not a bad circumstance apparently because when the man was home he was prone to drinking and throwing an angry fist at his wife and son. I never met this grandfather of mine because along with twenty-nine other hands he'd been lost at sea when the coal carrier he was working on had gone down in a gale off the coast of Nova Scotia. My father was the first Drum to go to college. He planned to be an attorney, a litigator. My mother told us that when she met him he was whip smart and cocksure and she knew absolutely he would be the best lawyer in the Gopher State. She'd married him at the end of her junior year at the University of Minnesota, where she was majoring in music and drama. He was, her sorority sisters agreed, quite a catch. My father had just finished his final year of law school. This was 1942. He'd already enlisted and was preparing to go off to war. By the time he left to fight—beginning in North Africa, then through numerous campaigns all the way to the Battle of the Bulge—my mother was pregnant with Ariel. The war changed Nathan Drum, changed him dramatically, and completely altered his plans. He came home with no desire to fight battles in a courtroom. He went instead into the seminary and was ordained. By the time he took charge of the Third Avenue Methodist Church on the Flats, we'd lived in four other towns in Minnesota. A minister's family never stayed long in one place, a difficult aspect of the job we were all expected to accept without complaint. But because my mother had grown up in New Bremen and we came often to visit my grandparents we already knew the town well. Although my father and Emil Brandt were acquainted, it was the weekly chess that brought them close. The games had evolved gradually and were mostly an opportunity, it seemed to me, for my father and Brandt, two men of the same age and scarred by the same war, to relate in a manner that didn't require my mother's presence. Though Brandt had loved her and abandoned her, that didn't appear to be an issue. Or so I believed then.

"E-five," my father announced and moved his own pawn. "Ariel says it's fascinating. Your memoir, I mean."

"Ariel is a young woman and young women fascinate easily, Nathan. Your daughter is gifted in many ways but she has a lot to learn about the broader world. Nf-three."

My father lifted Brandt's knight and moved him to the proper square. "Ruth believes she's destined for greatness. What do you think, Emil? D-six."

"D-four. Ariel's a fine musician, there's no doubt about that. As talented as any I've heard her age. After Juilliard I suspect that she could audition and secure a position in any fine symphony orchestra. She's also a gifted composer. She still has a great deal to learn, but that will come with time and maturity. Hell, if she wanted, she could even be a fine teacher. What I'm saying, Nathan, is that she has enormous potential in so many areas. But greatness? Who can say? That's something, it seems to me, that depends more on God and circumstance than on our own efforts."

"Ruth has such hopes for her. Bg-four," my father said and moved his bishop.

"All parents hope greatness for their children, don't they? Or maybe not. I don't have children so what do I know? D takes E-five."

"B takes F-three. It may be a moot point. Ariel's talking about not going to Juilliard."

"What?" Brandt's sightless eyes seemed full of amazement.

"I'm sure she's just dragging her feet. Last-minute doubts."

"Ah," Brandt said and nodded his understanding. "Natural I suppose. I have to say, I'll miss her when she goes. I'm not sure I'll be able to trust my memories to someone else. Q takes F-three."

The work Ariel did for Brandt was part of the arrangement struck to compensate him for his time working with her to improve her playing and her music composition. My parents could in no way afford to pay properly for such a service. For a man of Brandt's stature it was paltry payment but his help was clearly offered as a favor because of his affection for my mother and his friendship with my father.

"What did Ruth say when Ariel dropped this bomb?"

"She went through the roof," my father said.

Brandt laughed. "Of course. And you?"

My father studied the board. "I only want her to be happy. D takes E-five."

"Bc-four. And what is happiness, Nathan? In my experience, it's only a moment's pause here and there on what is otherwise a long and difficult road. No one can be happy all the time. Better, I think, to wish for her wisdom, a virtue not so fickle."

"Nf-six," my father said hesitantly.

"Qb-three," Brandt immediately responded.

My father studied the board a minute, then said, "Qe-seven. Do you know Travis Klement, Emil?"

"No. Nc-three."

"He lives in Cadbury. His wife is a member of one of my congregations. He's a vet. Korea. Had a tough time over there. It's eating at him, I believe. He drinks. He's hard on his family. C-six."

"Sometimes, Nathan, I think that it wasn't so much the war as what we took into the war. Whatever cracks were already there the war forced apart, and what we might otherwise have kept inside came spilling out. You and your life philosophy, for example. You may have gone to war thinking you were going to be a hotshot lawyer afterward, but I believe that deep inside of you there was always the seed of a minister."

"And in you?"

"A blind man." Brandt smiled.

"I don't know how to reach Travis."

"I don't know that everyone you reach out to you can help, Nathan. A lot to expect of yourself, it seems to me. Bg-five."

My father sat back and stroked his cheek. "B-five," he said but not with great conviction.

"Dad," Jake shouted and came running from the garden. He had a rake in one hand and in the other he held a wriggling garter snake.

"Don't hurt it, Son," my father said.

"I won't. Neat huh, Frank."

"A snake? Big deal," I said. "When you find a rattler, let me know."

Jake's enthusiasm wasn't dulled by my response. He returned happily to the garden where Lise waited. They gestured to each other and Jake put the snake down and they both stood and watched it glide swiftly away among the stalks of sweet corn.

There seemed something preternatural about the relationship between the two of them and I have always believed it was because neither could communicate easily with the rest of the world. Though deaf, Lise had been trained to speak but was greatly reluctant to mouth the utterances that sounded odd and flat to the rest of us. Jake could barely complete a coherent utterance at all. They communicated in signs and gestures and facial expressions and perhaps even on a level that superseded the physical plane. With everyone else except her brother and Jake, Lise could be difficult. I believe now that it may have been a form of autism but in those days she was called touched. People thought of her as slow or simple because she would not look at them directly when she spoke, and on those rare occasions when she was forced to leave the safety of her yard and enter town, she would cross the street to avoid contact with someone approaching her on the sidewalk.

Mostly she stayed inside the white picket fence and took care of the flowers and the garden and her brother.

"Lise is fortunate to have Jake as a friend," Brandt said. "N takes B-five."

"Jake seems pretty happy with the arrangement. C takes B-five."

"Lise has no other friends. Really she has no one but me. And I rely on her for so much. I wonder sometimes what will happen to her when I'm gone. B takes B-five. Check."

"That's years away, Emil. And she has family besides you."

"They ignore her. They've ignored her all her life. Sometimes I think that when I came home blind they were ecstatic. It created a situation that bound their two misfits together in a controllable fashion. Here we reside inside this fence, which, for all intents and purposes, is the extent of our world. And you want to know the odd part of it, Nathan? We're happy. I have my music and Lise. Lise has her garden and me."

"I thought you said happiness was fleeting."

Brandt laughed and said, "Trapped with my own words. But if you look at the board carefully, Nathan, I think you'll see that I have laid a trap for you there."

My father spent a few moments studying the game and then said, "Ah, I see what you mean. Clever, Emil. I resign."

They continued to talk and I watched Jake and Lise in the garden and listened to Ariel clicking away on the typewriter in the study, and the world inside that picket fence seemed like a good place, a place in which all the damaged pieces somehow fit.

In the early afternoon my father got himself ready for the burial of the man we'd all begun calling simply the itinerant and I told him I wanted to go along. He asked my reason and I tried to articulate my thinking although the truth was that I didn't really know. It simply felt right. I had been the one to bring the body to light and it seemed fitting that I be there when it was delivered into a darkness eternal. I tried to say as much but knew even as I spoke that I was saying it all wrong. In the end my father studied me a long time and finally

allowed as he saw no reason for me not to be there. His only require-
ment was that I dress as I would for the funeral of someone we knew
which meant my Sunday best.

Jake was odd about the dead man. He wanted nothing to do with
the burial and went so far as to accuse me of using the whole episode
to my advantage. "You just like being a big man," he said looking up
at me from the card table he'd set up in the living room where he was
at work on a paint-by-number. The picture on the box cover showed
a rocky beach in an idyllic place that was maybe Maine and looked
inviting but it was clear that Jake's rendering, despite the guidance of
lines and numbers, would end up a good deal less than he or anyone
but a moron or a monkey would have hoped for.

"Fine," I said and I dressed alone.

My father drove the Packard to the cemetery which was set on a
hill on the east side of town. The hole was already dug and Gus was
waiting and Sheriff Gregor was there though I didn't know why and
moments after we arrived Mr. van der Waal drove up in the hearse and
my father and Gus and the sheriff and the mortician slid the coffin
from the back. It was a simple box of pine planed and sanded smooth
and it had no handles. The men lifted and carried it on their shoulders
to the grave. They laid it on wooden two-by-fours that Gus had arranged across the opening along with canvas straps for the eventual
lowering into the earth. Then the men stood back and I with them
and my father opened his Bible.

It seemed to me a good day to be dead and by that I mean that if
the dead cared no more about the worries they'd shouldered in life
and could lie back and enjoy the best of what God had created it
was a day for exactly such. The air was warm and still and the grass
of the cemetery which Gus kept watered and clipped was soft green
and the river that reflected the sky was a long ribbon of blue silk and
I thought that when I died this was the place exactly I would want
to lie and this was the scene that forever I would want to look upon.
And I thought that it was strange that a resting place so kingly had
been given to a man who had nothing and about whom we knew so
little that even his name was a mystery. And though I didn't know
at all and still do not the truth of the arrangement, I suspected that

laundry on the line in the backyard. She was a small woman not much taller than I with black hair and almond eyes and the shading and bone structure of the Sioux. Although Danny never talked about his lineage I'd heard that his mother came from the Upper Sioux community, which was along the Minnesota River well to the west. She wore tan Capris and a sleeveless green top and white sneakers. She was a teacher. I'd been in her fifth-grade classroom and I liked her. As I came into the yard she was bending to her laundry basket.

"Hi, Mrs. O'Keefe," I said cheerfully. "I'm looking for Danny."

She lifted a blue towel and pinned it to the line. She said, "I sent him to find his great-uncle."

"I know. I came to help."

"That's very nice of you, Frank, but I think Danny can handle it."

"My brother's with him."

I could tell that surprised her and for some reason didn't seem to please her.

I said, "Do you know which way they went?"

She frowned and said, "His uncle likes to fish. I sent him to look along the river."

"Thank you. We'll find him."

She didn't look particularly encouraged.

I ran off and in a couple of minutes I was walking the river's edge.

I didn't much like fishing but I knew a lot of guys who did and I knew where they fished. There were a couple of favorite places depending on what you were after. If it was catfish there was a long deep channel that ran behind an old lumberyard. If it was northern pike there was a sandbar a quarter mile farther on that half dammed the river and created a pool favored by those big fleshy fish. And of course there was the trestle half a mile outside of town. The north side of the river opposite the Flats was all cultivated fields with farmhouses hunkered in the shade of cottonwoods and poplars. At a distance ran the highway that connected the valley towns with the city of Mankato forty miles to the east. Beyond the highway rose the hills and bluffs that marked the extremes of the ancient Glacial River Warren.

I rounded a bend and heard voices and laughter and on the other side of a stand of tall bulrushes I found Jake and Danny skipping rocks. The stones as they touched the brown water left rings on the surface like a series of copper plates. When they saw me Danny and Jake stopped what they were doing and stood with their backs to the sun and squinted at me from the shadows of their faces.

"Find your uncle?" I asked.

"Naw," Danny said. "Not yet."

"Won't find him standing here throwing rocks."

"You're not our b-b-b-boss," Jake said. He picked up a flat stone and flung it angrily. It bit the water at an angle and slid beneath without skipping once.

"Why are you so mad at me?"

"B-b-b-b . . ." His face twisted painfully. "B-b-b . . ." He squeezed his eyes shut. "Cuz you're a liar."

"What are you talking about?"

"You know." He eyed Danny who stood fingering a stone that he did not throw.

"Okay, I'm a big fat liar. Happy? We should find your uncle, Danny." I pushed past them and kept walking downriver.

Danny caught up and sauntered beside me and when I looked back I saw Jake still standing where we'd left him, sullenly considering his options. Finally he followed but he stayed behind us at a distance. As much as possible we kept to the sand beaches and to the bare clay flats that had baked and cracked in the heat. Sometimes we had to break our way through stands of tall reeds and brush that grew right to the edge of the river. Danny told me about a book he'd just read in which a guy bitten by a vampire bat was the last human on earth. Danny read a lot of science fiction and he liked to tell you the whole story. He told it pretty well and just as he was finishing we beat our way through a stand of bulrushes covering a stretch of sand where we stumbled into a little clearing with a lean-to at its center. The structure was made of driftwood lashed into a frame with scavenged pieces of corrugated tin as roof and siding. A man sat in the deep shade created by the lean-to. He sat erect with his legs crossed and he stared at us where we stood on the far side of the clearing.

"That's my uncle Warren," Danny said.

I looked at Jake and Jake looked at me because we both recognized Danny's uncle. We'd seen him before. We'd seen him with the dead man.

Danny's uncle called out from the shade, "Your mother send you after me?"

Danny said, "Yeah."

The man's hands were laid flat on his bent knees. He nodded thoughtfully. He said, "Any chance I could bribe you to tell her you couldn't find me?"

Danny walked across the sand leaving the prints of his sneakers behind him. I followed Danny's prints and Jake followed mine.

"Bribe me?" Danny said. He seemed to think about it seriously. Whether he was seriously considering the offer or considering whether the offer was serious I couldn't say. In any event he shook his head.

"Didn't think so," his uncle said. "How about this then? How about you tell her I'll be around for dinner. Until then, I'm fishing."

"But you're not."

"Fishing, Danny boy, is purely a state of mind. Some men when they're fishing are after fish. Me, I'm after things you could never set a barbed hook in." He looked up at Jake and me. "I know you boys."

"Yes, sir," I said.

"I heard they buried Skipper."

"Yes, sir. Today. I was there."

"You were? Why?"

"I don't know. It seemed kind of right."

"Kind of right?" His lips formed a grin but his eyes held no humor. "Was anybody else there?"

"My father. He's a minister and said the prayers. And our friend Gus. He dug the grave. And the sheriff. And the undertaker."

"Sounds surprisingly well attended."

"It was fine. They buried him in a real nice place."

"No kidding? Well, I'll be. A lot of kindness shown there. A little late, though, don't you think?"

"Sir?"

"You boys know what *itokagata iyaye* means? You, Danny?"

"Nope."

"It's Dakota. It means the spirit has gone south. It means that Skipper's dead. Your mom or dad ever try to teach you our language, Danny?"

"Our language is English," Danny said.

"I suppose it is," his uncle said. "I suppose it is."

"You got a letter," Danny said. He pulled it folded from his back pocket and handed it to his great-uncle.

The man took the envelope and squinted. He reached into his shirt pocket and drew out a pair of glasses with thick lenses and with rims that looked made of gold. He didn't put them on but used the lenses instead in the way you might use a magnifying glass and painstakingly read the return address. Then he slid his finger under the flap, carefully tore it open, pulled out the letter, and read it with the glasses in the same slow fashion.

I stood uncomfortably waiting to be dismissed. I was eager to be gone.

"Shit," Danny's uncle said at last and crumpled the letter and threw it into the yellow sand. He looked up at Danny. "Well, didn't I tell you what to say to your mother? What are you waiting for?"

Danny backed away and turned and hightailed it out of the clearing with Jake and me at his heels. When we were a good distance away and the wall of bulrushes blinded his uncle to us I said, "What's with him?"

Danny said, "I don't know him very well. He's been gone a long time. There was some kind of trouble and he had to leave town."

"What kind of trouble?" Jake asked.

Danny shrugged. "Mom and Dad don't talk about it. Uncle Warren showed up last week and my mom took him in. She told my dad she had to. He's family. He's not really so bad. Sometimes he's kind of funny. He doesn't like staying in the house though. He says walls make him feel like he's in jail."

We walked back to where the river ran near Danny's house and we climbed the bank and Jake and I went our way toward home and Danny went to deliver his uncle's message to his mother. I wondered what exactly he would tell her.

We reached our yard and Jake started up the front steps but I hung back.

Jake said, "What's wrong?"

"Didn't you see?"

"See what?"

"Those glasses Danny's uncle had."

"What about them?"

"They don't belong to him, Jake," I said. "They belonged to Bobby Cole."

Jake stared at me a moment dumb as a brick. Then the light came into his eyes.

8

That evening my grandfather came to dinner. He brought his wife, a woman who was not my mother's mother, a woman named Elizabeth who'd been his secretary and then became more to him. My real grandmother had died of cancer when I was too young to remember her, and Liz—she insisted we call her Liz, not Grandma—was the only grandmother I knew. I liked her and Jake and Ariel liked her too. Though my father wasn't fond of my grandfather it was clear that he felt differently about Liz. Only my mother had problems with her. With Liz she was polite but distant.

My mother fixed cocktail martinis which my father, as always, declined and we all sat in the living room and the adults conversed. My grandfather spoke of the influx of Mexican farmworkers and how it was bringing an unwelcome element to the valley and my father asked how the farmers were supposed to get the work done without the help of the migrants. Liz said that when she saw the migrant families in town they were always clean and polite and the children well behaved and she felt bad that often the entire family, young children and all, had to labor in the fields to earn a living. My grandfather said, "If they'd just learn to speak English."

Jake and I often suffered through this kind of discussion in silence. No one asked our opinion and we didn't feel obliged to offer it. My mother had prepared roasted chicken and stuffing and mashed potatoes and asparagus. The chicken was burned and dry and the gravy lumpy and the asparagus tough and stringy but my grandfather raved. After dinner he took Liz home in his big Buick. My mother and Ariel went to practice with the New Bremen Town Singers, a vocal group my mother had formed two years earlier. They were going to sing the chorale that Ariel had composed for the Fourth of July celebration. My father went to his office in the church and Jake and I were left to do the dishes. I washed and Jake dried.

"What should we do?" Jake stood with a clean plate dripping water onto the old linoleum.

"About what?"

"Bobby's glasses," Jake said.

"I don't know."

"Maybe he found them. You know, just found them by the tracks where Bobby got hit."

"Maybe. If you don't hurry up and dry that damn plate there's going to be a lake on the floor."

Jake commenced to wiping with his dish towel. "Maybe we should tell somebody."

"Who?"

"I don't know. Dad?"

"Yeah and we'll have to tell him we lied about how we found the body. You want to do that?"

Jake looked sullen and then he looked at me as if I was responsible for the tough position we were in. "If you'd told the truth to begin with."

"Hey, you were the one who didn't say anything about Danny's uncle. I just played along. Remember?"

"If we'd left when I wanted to, I wouldn't've had to lie."

"Yeah, well, you did lie. And funny thing, you didn't stutter at all while you were doing it. What do you think that means?"

Jake put the dried plate on the counter and took the next in the drainer. "Maybe we could tell Ariel."

I worked an S.O.S pad over the bottom of the roasting pan my mother had used to cook the chicken and on which she had, in the process, grafted blackened skin. "Ariel's got enough to worry about," I said.

I didn't even think about telling my mother nor did Jake. She was a woman much consumed by the fiery passions of her own life and the truth anyway was that Ariel was her favorite and generally my mother left the business of dealing with her sons to their father.

Jake said, "What about Gus?"

I stopped scrubbing. Gus wasn't a bad suggestion. He'd been kind of strange on Saturday in the back of Halderson's Drugstore but that had been the effect of the beer and the other odd circumstances of that horrible moment which I would gladly have forgotten if I could. Maybe enough time had passed that Gus would be able to offer counsel that was more considered. "All right," I said. "Hurry up and finish and let's go see him."

By the time we crossed the street and approached the side door that led to the church basement and to the room where Gus slept it was twilight and the tree frogs and the crickets were kicking up a pleasant racket. Gus's Indian Chief was parked in the church lot along with a couple of cars that I didn't recognize. The light was on in my father's office and through the window came the beautiful sweep of Tchaikovsky's Piano Concerto No. 1. My father kept a record player in his office and a shelf of recordings that he often listened to as he worked. This piano concerto was one of his favorites. We went in the door and at the bottom of the stairs we stopped cold. In the center of the basement under the glare of the unshielded bulb a card table had been set up and around it were Gus and three other men. There were cards on the table and poker chips and the air was full of cigarette smoke and beside each man's stack of chips there was a bottle of Brandt beer. I knew all the men. Mr. Halderson, the druggist. Ed Florine, who delivered mail and was a member of my father's congregation. And Doyle, the cop. The play stopped the moment the men saw us.

Doyle smiled big. "Busted," he said.

"Come on in," Gus said and beckoned us with his hand.

I went right away but Jake hung back on the stairs.

"Just a friendly poker game," Gus said. He put his arm around me and showed me his cards. He'd taught Jake and me about poker and I could see that he had a good hand. A full house, deuces over queens. "No big deal," he said, "except that it might be best if your father didn't know about it. Okay?"

He spoke quietly and I understood why. The furnace in the corner of the basement was in need of repair. Gus had been charged with fixing it but because we were in the middle of summer he was in no hurry. The ducts had all been disconnected and stuffed with rags to prevent basement noise from channeling into the sanctuary and community room and my father's office. Between the rags and the Tchaikovsky the sound of the card game wouldn't have reached my father but it was clear to me that Gus didn't want to take chances.

"Sure," I said quietly.

Gus looked at Jake. "How about you, buddy?"

Jake didn't reply but he gave a shrug that signaled his reluctant consent.

Gus said, "Did you need something?"

I looked at the men around the table who composed almost the same group as had been present in the drugstore the day we found the body and who seemed no more attractive to me as confidants now than they did then.

"No," I said. "Nothing."

"In that case best get along. And remember this game is between us. Hey, care for a sip of Brandt's best brew?" The alliteration seemed to tickle Gus and he laughed.

I took a swallow of the beer which was warm. It wasn't the first time I'd tasted alcohol whose attraction I had yet to understand. I wiped my mouth with the back of my hand and Doyle clapped me on the back and said, "We'll make a man of you yet, kid."

The sound of a knock on my father's office door came to us. It must have been a loud knock to have carried to us below and was probably done so boldly in order to be heard above the strains of Tchaikovsky which ended abruptly. We heard the creak of the floorboards as my father crossed to the door.

Gus put a finger to his lips, got up from the table, went to the heating duct that ran to my father's office, and pulled out the rags. Very clearly we heard my father say, "Why, good evening. What a pleasant surprise."

"May we come in, Reverend?"

I recognized the voice. It was Edna Sweeney whose amazing underwear Jake and I had admired on the line in her backyard the day Bobby Cole was buried.

"Of course, of course," my father said. "How are you, Avis?"

Though he replied "Fair to middlin'," Avis Sweeney didn't sound so good.

"Please, sit down."

Gus stuffed the rags back into the duct and said quietly, "Going to see a man about a horse," and he headed to the bathroom. Above us chairs scraped the bare wood floor. Doyle put down his cards and got up from the table and went to the duct and removed the rags.

My father said, "What can I do for you folks?"

Quiet followed and then Edna Sweeney said, "You counsel married couples, right?"

"I do under certain circumstances."

"We need to talk to you about a marital problem, Reverend."

"What sort of problem?"

Another quiet and I heard Avis cough.

"We need to talk about our sexual intimacy," Edna Sweeney said.

"I see." My father spoke with the same calm he might have employed if Edna had said, "We need to talk to you about prayer."

I thought I should do something. I thought I should go over and grab the rags from Doyle's hand and stuff them back into the duct but I was a boy in the company of men and afraid to cross them.

"I mean," Edna Sweeney went on, "we need some marital advice about sex. In a Christian way."

"I'll see what I can do," my father said.

"It's just this. Avis and me we don't always see eye to eye about our physical relationship. The truth, Reverend, is that I want intimacy more often than Avis seems prepared to offer it. And Avis thinks that somehow my desire is an abnormality. That's the word he used. Abnormality. Like I'm a freak or something." Edna Sweeney had started the discussion in a moderate tone but her voice had rapidly intensified, especially when she spoke that final statement.

Doyle shoved the rags back into the duct momentarily and

whispered to the others, "If my ex had been that eager I'd still be married." The others stifled laughs and Doyle once again removed the rags.

"I see," my father said. "And, Avis, would you like to say something?"

"Yes, Reverend. I work hard at the grain elevator all day and I come home beat like a rug. I drag my ass—excuse me—I come in the house and there's Edna all hot to trot when I ain't got but two thoughts on my mind and that's a cold beer and putting my feet up. I think she expects I'll perform like a trained dog or something."

I imagined Avis Sweeney sitting there, toothpick thin, his big Adam's apple bouncing up and down as if riding a pogo stick. Maybe the druggist imagined it too because he laughed quietly and shook his head. I knew we shouldn't be listening and I thought that if Gus were there he would have stopped them. I knew if not Gus then the responsibility should have fallen to me but the truth was that I wasn't just afraid of saying something to the men, I was also fascinated with the discussion taking place in my father's office and so I held my tongue.

"Just a little affection, Avis," Edna Sweeney said. "That's all I'm asking."

"No, Edna, you're asking for a pony can do a trick when you snap your fingers. That ain't me, woman. Now, Reverend, understand I'm as interested as the next guy but Edna she comes on like a she-bear in heat."

"There are men who'd value that in a woman," Edna shot back.

"Well, you ain't married to one."

"Well, I wish to God I was."

"All right," my father said calmly. He allowed a few moments of judicious silence to pass, then said, "The physical intimacy between a man and a woman is a delicate balance of needs and temperaments, and seldom do all the elements align easily. Edna, are you hearing Avis? He's asking for a little time to relax at the end of a hard day before you engage in lovemaking."

"Relax? Hell, Reverend, he drinks his beer and nods off and he's no good to me then."

"Avis, instead of a beer how about a glass of iced tea?"

"Sometimes, Reverend, when I'm slaving away in the hot afternoon sun, all that gets me through the day is the idea of that cold beer sitting in the fridge with my name wrote all over it."

Edna Sweeney said, "And some men would be thinking about what's waiting for them in bed."

"We been married thirteen years, Edna. Believe me, there ain't no surprises waitin' for me in bed."

"Thirteen years," my father said. "That's quite a history together. Tell me how you met."

"What's that got to do with anything?" Avis Sweeney said.

"We met at a picnic," Edna said. "Out at Luther Park. I knew some of the people Avis works with and they invited us both. Kind of a setup, although we didn't know it."

"What attracted you to Avis?"

"Heck, he was so damn cute and kind of cocky. And we ended up talking while the others played softball, and at the end of the evening, when we were all getting ready to leave, he opened the car door for me. Like a real gentleman." Edna Sweeney stopped talking for a few moments and when she began again I could hear that her voice was choked. "And I looked into his eyes, Reverend, and I saw a kindness there that I hadn't seen in other men."

"That's lovely, Edna. Avis, what made you fall in love?"

"Hell, I don't know."

"Take your time."

"Well. She was a damn fine looking woman. And she didn't talk a lot of nonsense. I remember she talked about her family and especially about her mother, who was sickly. And I could tell she had a lot of heart to her. And then I got sick, too. Came down with a bad flu, and there she was every day on my doorstep with some kind of soup she'd made. She's a real good cook, Reverend."

"So I've heard, Avis. It's clear to me that you love each other and, as long as you have that love, everything else can be worked through. I'll tell you what. I have a good friend. His name is Jerry Stowe. He's also clergy but he specializes in counseling couples who are having difficulty with the physical intimacy in their relationship. He's very good and I'm sure he could help you. Would you be willing to let me talk to him and set up a counseling session for you?"

Avis said, "I don't know."

My father said, "In coming to me, you've already taken the hardest step."

"I'd be willing," Edna said. "Please, Avis."

At the card table the men sat stone still.

"All right," Avis finally said.

I heard the toilet flush in Gus's bathroom and a moment later the door opened and Gus came out buckling his belt. He looked up and spent a moment comprehending the situation.

Upstairs my father said, "I'll call him first thing tomorrow and then we'll work out a time with you. Avis, Edna, I often see couples who are in real trouble, who've lost the strong foundation of their love. Clearly you're not among them. Avis, take Edna's hand. Let's pray together."

Gus went quickly to where Doyle stood and grabbed the rags and stuffed them into the duct. In a harsh whisper he said, "What the hell are you doing, Doyle?"

Doyle easily shrugged off Gus's anger. "Just curious," he said and sauntered back to the card table.

We heard chairs scrape above and footsteps heading to the door and a minute later Tchaikovsky began again.

Halderson shook his head. "Who would've thought being a preacher could be so interesting?"

Doyle said, "Mark my words, boys. Avis doesn't jump that woman's bones, somebody else will."

Halderson asked, "You got a candidate in mind?"

"I'm always thinking," Doyle said. "Always thinking."

Gus returned to the table but didn't immediately pick up his cards. It was clear he was still upset with Doyle. He looked at me and Jake and his anger seemed to spill out at us and he said, "Thought you two were leaving."

We started to back away.

"Hey, boys." Doyle held up his cards. "Like we said, all this is between you and us, okay? No sense getting your old man worked up over a friendly game. Ain't that so, Gus?"

Gus didn't reply but his look told us it was so.

We walked back to the house and went inside and said nothing. In terms of what to do about Bobby Cole's glasses we were no better off than we'd been before. But something amazing had happened in the basement of my father's church. We'd been among men and shared something with them that felt illicit and although I understood that it was somehow at the expense of my father I was thrilled to have been included in that confidence, to be part of that brotherhood.

When Jake finally spoke it was clear that he had a different view.

"We shouldn't've been listening. That was private stuff," he said. He was sitting on the sofa staring at a blank television screen.

I was standing at a back window staring across the dark empty pasture at the Sweeneys' house. There was a light in a back room which I thought might be the bedroom. "We didn't mean to," I said. "It was sort of an accident."

"We could've left."

"Why didn't you then?"

Jake didn't answer. The light went out at the Sweeneys' and after that the house was totally dark.

Jake said, "What do we do about Danny's uncle?"

I dropped into the easy chair my father usually occupied when he read.

"We keep it to ourselves," I said.

My father came home soon after. He poked his head into the living room where we sat watching television. "I'm going to dish up some ice cream for myself," he said. "You guys want any?"

We both said yes and a few minutes later he delivered bowls with a mound of chocolate in each and sat with us and we ate in silence watching *Surfside 6*. When we were finished Jake and I took our bowls to the kitchen and rinsed them out and set them beside the sink to be washed and headed toward the stairs to go to bed. My father had set aside his empty bowl and turned off the television and moved to his easy chair. In his hands he held an opened book and when we passed through the living room and trooped toward the stairs he looked up from his reading and eyed us curiously.

"I saw you two come over to the church earlier. I thought maybe you wanted to talk to me."

"No," I said. "We just wanted to say hi to Gus."

"Ah," he said. "And how was Gus?"

Jake stood with one hand on the banister and one foot on the first stair. He gave me a worried look.

"He was fine," I said.

My father nodded as if I'd offered a piece of sobering news then he said, "Was he winning?"

His face was a stone tablet absolutely unreadable to me.

If I'd been Jake I'd have probably stuttered to beat the band. As it was I collected myself and swallowed my surprise and said, "Yes."

My father nodded again and went back to his reading. "Good night, boys," he said.

9

The Fourth of July was my third favorite holiday. Immediately ahead of it was Christmas which took second place to Hallow-een. What made the Fourth special was what makes the Fourth special for any kid: fireworks. Today in Minnesota most fireworks with any real bang to them are illegal, but in 1961 in New Bremen, pro-vided you had the money, you could purchase anything your heart desired. In order to buy fireworks I'd been saving everything I could of my earnings from the yard work I did for my grandfather. A couple of weeks before the Fourth a number of stands appeared in town fes-tooned with red, white, and blue ribbons and selling a tantalizing array of explosives and every time I passed one of them and saw all the pos-sibilities laid out on the plywood counters or in the boxes stacked in the shade of the canvas tents I grew eager with anticipation. I couldn't purchase anything without my father being present to approve each item and I didn't want to buy too early because the temptation to blow up my arsenal would be too great, so I window-shopped the stands and made a mental list of everything I desired, a list I revised a hun-dred times as I lay in bed at night imagining the big day.

Fireworks were an issue with my parents. My mother would have preferred that her sons have nothing to do with bottle rockets and firecrackers and Roman candles. She had a very real concern for our safety which she expressed to us and to our father in no uncertain terms. My father countered with the mild argument that fireworks were a part of the culture of the celebration and that as long as Jake and I set off our explosives under proper supervision our safety wasn't terribly compromised. It was clear to us that my mother didn't buy it but she understood that without my father's full support she couldn't stand against the uproar Jake and I would raise if she put her foot down absolutely. In the end she settled for a dour admonition directed at my father. "Nathan," she said, "if anything happens to them, I'm holding you responsible."

During the week preceding the Fourth of July my father was usually a wreck. The truth was that he hated fireworks even more than my mother did. As the Fourth approached and the occasional early report of a detonated cherry bomb or the rattle of a string of firecrackers broke the quiet in our neighborhood my father would become visibly upset. His face took on an expression that was tense and watchful, and if I was with him when a sudden pop of gunpowder occurred I saw his body go instantly rigid and his head jerk left or right as he sought desperately to locate the source. But he nonetheless defended his sons' right to celebrate the holiday in the generally accepted manner.

Ten days before the Fourth, on Saturday when Jake and I had finished our yard work and received the two dollars each that was our due, we headed to Halderson's Drugstore to slake our thirst with root beer. As we stepped into the shade of the awning above the front plate-glass window the door opened and Gus came out followed by Doyle. They were laughing and almost bumped into us and I could smell beer.

"We're going to get some fireworks, boys," Gus said. "Want to come along?"

My week of being grounded was over and I eagerly accepted the offer. But Jake looked at Doyle and shook his head. "No th-th-thanks."

"Come on," Gus said. "I'll buy something for each of you."

"No," Jake said. He shoved his hands into his pockets and dropped his eyes to the sidewalk.

"Let him go," I said.

Gus shrugged. "All right then. Come on, Frankie." He turned and headed toward Doyle who was waiting behind the opened door on the driver's side of a gray Studebaker parked at the curb.

Jake grabbed my arm. "Don't g-g-go, Frank."

"Why not?"

"I've got a b-b-bad feeling."

"Forget it. It'll be all right. You go on home." I shook loose his hand and climbed into the backseat of the Studebaker.

Doyle pulled away from the curb and Jake watched us from the shadow of the drugstore awning. Up front Gus banged his fist against the dashboard and said, "Boys, we're going to have us one hell of an afternoon."

We stopped first at the Freedom Fourth Fireworks stand which was set up in a vacant lot across the street from the Texaco gas station. There were a lot of people at the stand and Doyle called out their names and shook hands all around and before he let go he said, "Hope you still got all your fingers come July fifth," and he laughed. Gus and Doyle bought a bunch of fireworks which the people at the stand put into a couple of big brown paper bags. At the end Gus turned to me and said, "What do you want, Frankie?"

I looked at the box of M-80s which were firecrackers powerful enough to blow your fingers off and which my father would never have allowed me. I pointed and said, "One of those."

Gus said, "I don't think Nathan would like that."

But Doyle said, "Hell, I'll pay for it." And he grabbed a handful of the explosives and laid down money on the plywood counter and we left. We made one more stop, this at a liquor store where Doyle bought beer in cans, then we drove to Sibley Park on the river just outside of town. It was a few hundred yards beyond the home of Emil Brandt and as we passed I saw Ariel sitting on the porch with Brandt. She had papers in her hands and I figured she was working on his memoir. Lise was watering the flowers along the fence with a hose. She had on dungarees and a sleeveless green top and wore a big straw hat and gardening gloves and looked almost pretty. None of them paid any attention as I sped past in Doyle's Studebaker. At the park there was a ball field and a playground of ugly metal structures—a jungle gym and a long slide and three swings and a rusty merry-go-round—that on a hot summer day could burn you like a lit match. A few weathered picnic tables stood in grass that went unwatered and was always completely dead by late July. Doyle's Studebaker when he pulled into the gravel lot was the only vehicle in sight and the park was empty. We piled out and I followed the two men across the field of unkempt grass. They headed toward the river, crossed the railroad tracks that ran alongside the park, took a path through the cottonwoods, and emerged on a long sandy flat where high school kids sometimes built bonfires and drank beer. The char from those fires spotted the sand like black lesions. In the shade of a cottonwood Doyle and Gus set down the paper bags full of fireworks and Doyle took a church key from his pocket and punched holes in a can of beer which he handed to Gus. Then he punched open a can for himself. They sat and drank and talked and I sat with them and wondered when the fun would begin.

They talked baseball. It was the first season for the Minnesota Twins who'd been the Washington Senators the year before. The names of Harmon Killebrew and Bob Allison and Jim Lemon were on everyone's lips.

Doyle addressed me. "What do you think, Frankie? Think Minnesota's got itself a good ball club?"

I was surprised at Doyle's question because not many adults asked my opinion of things. I tried to speak knowledgeably. I said, "Yeah. Their bull pen's a little weak but they've got strong hitters."

"That they do," Doyle said. "Gus tells me you're a good ballplayer yourself."

"I'm okay," I said. "I'm a pretty fair hitter."

"Play on a team?"

"No. Just pickup games down on the Flats."

"Want to be a ballplayer when you grow up?"

"Not really."

"What? A preacher like your old man?"

He laughed when he said this as if being a minister was a joke of some kind.

Gus said, "His father's a good man and a hell of a preacher."

"Scared of fireworks though," Doyle said.

I wondered how he knew but when I looked at Gus's face I understood where the information had come from.

Gus said, "It was the war. Did that to a lot of men."

"Not me or you," Doyle said.

"Every man's different."

Doyle drank his beer and said, "Some men they just didn't have the stomach."

"That wasn't the Captain," Gus said and there was something angry in his voice.

Doyle caught the tone and grinned. "You still call him Captain. Why's that?"

"That's how I first knew him. A damn fine officer."

"Yeah?" Doyle looked at Gus slyly. "I heard he cracked."

Gus glanced at me and then said, "Doyle, you listen to too much gossip."

Doyle laughed. "Maybe so, but I know things because of it, Gus. I know things."

Gus turned the talk to politics and they discussed Kennedy and I lost interest and began thinking about all those fireworks in the paper bags and especially about that big M-80 with my name written all over it. Then I realized the talk had swung around to a subject that concerned me.

Gus was saying, "I've seen him down on the Flats a few times. Just wondered about him."

"His name's Warren Redstone," Doyle said. "Soon as he showed up in town the chief told us to keep an eye on him. Troublemaker from way back. He tried to start some kind of Sioux uprising here in the valley a bunch of years ago. Got into trouble with the Feds and vamoosed. The chief's in touch with the FBI, but I guess they got no interest in him now. He's got a rap sheet, but he's never done serious time. He's staying with his niece and her husband. The O'Keefes. When I'm on duty, I roll my cruiser down to the Flats pretty regular just to let him know I'm around."

Gus said, "Is that why I see you in the neighborhood so much? I could've sworn it was because of Edna Sweeney."

Doyle threw his head back and howled like a wolf. He crushed his beer can and threw it onto the sand. "Come on," he said and reached for one of the paper bags. "Let's have us some fun."

Doyle set up some skyrockets and lit three punks and each of us touched a fuse at the same time and the rockets shot high and went off almost simultaneously in explosions of dark smoke that were like splatters of mud thrown against the blue wall of the sky. We set off strings of firecrackers and Doyle put a cherry bomb in Gus's empty beer can and the can exploded and jumped as if it had been blasted by a shotgun. He pulled out three of the M-80s and handed one to each of us. He lit his and threw it into the air. The crack of the explosion so near to us was like a gun fired into our faces and I recoiled. But Gus and Doyle didn't seem bothered at all. Gus lit and threw his M-80 and I squeezed my eyes in anticipation but nothing happened.

"Dud," Doyle said. "The son of a bitch didn't go off. Heard that's a problem with you sometimes, Gus." He laughed and I had no idea what he was talking about. "Go on, Frankie," he said. "Your turn."

I didn't want to light the M-80 in my hand. Although fireworks excited a measure of recklessness in me I still carried a healthy regard for the strictures my father had laid down and holding a lit firecracker, especially one that could blow my fingers off, wasn't something I was inclined to do. Instead I mounded some sand and stuck the M-80 in it like a candle on a birthday cake and lit the fuse and stepped back. A moment later the blast obliterated the mound peppering us with stinging grains of sand.

Doyle danced away and I thought maybe he'd been hurt by something flung at him in the explosion. He split off from us and ran across the sand flat toward the river dodging left and right and finally threw himself down with his arms stretched out ahead. He came up on his knees clutching his hands to his chest and rose to his feet and walked back to us with a big stupid grin on his lips. He held out his arms toward us with his hands cupped together and from the small hole ringed by his thumbs a big bullfrog peered out.

"Give me one of those M-80s," he said to Gus.

Gus reached into one of the paper bags and brought out another of the big firecrackers. Doyle gripped the frog in one hand and with his other pried its lips apart.

"Stick it in there," he said.

Gus said, "You're going to blow up that frog?"

"Damn right I am."

"I don't think so," Gus said.

I stood paralyzed and disbelieving as Doyle snatched the M-80 from Gus. He stuffed it into the frog's mouth with the fuse extended and reached into his pants pocket and pulled out a cigarette lighter. He flipped the lid and thumbed the striker and touched the flame to the fuse and pushed the explosive deep into the frog's throat. Then he threw the frog into the air. The poor creature exploded not five feet from our faces spattering us with its blood and entrails. Doyle bent backward laughing toward the sky and Gus said, "Damn it," and I wiped at the viscera on my face and felt sick to my stomach.

"Whoo-eee," Doyle cried out. With his index finger he wiped a piece of frog gut from his cheek. "That critter blowed up good."

"You okay, Frank?" Gus reached out and put his hand on my shoulder and tried to look into my face but I turned away.

"I better be going," I said.

"Come on," Doyle said. "It was only a frog, for God's sake."

"I gotta get home anyway," I said not looking back.

"We'll give you a lift, Frank," Gus said.

"No, I'll walk," I said. I headed away on the path that threaded through the cottonwoods and that led across the railroad tracks to the park.

"Frank," Gus called.

"Hell, let the kid go," I heard Doyle say. "And give me another beer."

I stomped across the dry grass of Sibley Park. My shirt was spotted with frog gut and blood. It was in my hair and dripping along my jawline. I wiped at my face and looked down at my ruined clothing and I was angry with myself and with Doyle and, although he'd done nothing to deserve it, angry with Gus as well. I'd had a vision of what that afternoon could be and the vision had become ruined by mindless cruelty. Why hadn't Gus stopped Doyle? Why hadn't I? I was crying and for that weakness too I hated myself. I started up the road but realized that I'd have to pass the home of Emil Brandt and then walk the streets of town and I didn't want anyone to see me looking like I did so I returned to the railroad tracks and followed them to the Flats.

I was cautious approaching the house. If my parents saw me covered in the drying darkened remains of a dead bullfrog, how could I explain this most recent trespass? I slipped through the back door and into the kitchen and listened. The house was cool and, I thought at first, silent. Then I heard the sound of crying soft and broken and I poked my head into the living room. Ariel sat on the bench of our old upright piano. Her arms were laid across the keyboard and her head was laid upon her hands. Her body shook and her breath between her sobs came in airy little gasps.

I said, "Ariel?"

She sat up quickly and straightened her back. Her head turned and she looked at me and for a moment it was not Ariel but a creature much afraid and I thought of that frog in the moment when the explosive was shoved down its throat. Then she saw my soiled shirt and the splatters of viscera dried on my cheeks and in my hair and her eyes went wide with horror.

"Frankie," she cried leaping from the bench. "Oh, Frankie, are you all right?"

She forgot in an instant whatever was the source of her own suffering and she turned all her attention on me. And I, in my selfish innocence, allowed it.

I told her what had happened. She listened and shook her head sympathetically and in the end she said, "We've got to get you out of those clothes and wash them before Mom gets back. And you need to take a bath."

And Ariel who was an unjudging angel set about saving me.

That evening after dinner I got together a pickup game of softball with some of the other kids in the neighborhood. We played until the evening light turned soft blue and we couldn't see to hit or to field anymore and suggestions were made of other games we could play that would prolong our easy camaraderie. But some had to go and so our gathering dissolved and we drifted away each of us to our own home. Jake and I walked together. With every step he slapped his ball glove against his thigh as if beating time with a drum.

"You still got all your fingers," he said.

"What?"

"I figured you'd blow yourself to kingdom come."

I knew what he was talking about. I thought of telling him the story of the exploded frog but I didn't want to give him the satisfaction of knowing that he'd been right in believing I had no business going with Gus and Doyle.

I said, "We had a good time. I set off some M-80s."

"M-80s?" Even in the dark I could see that the huge pools of his eyes reflected both envy and censure.

When we reached the house my father was standing on the porch smoking his pipe. The ember in the bowl glowed brightly as he drew on the stem and I smelled the sweet drift of Cherry Blend. Gus was with him. They were talking quietly as friends do.

My father called to us as we came up the walk. "How'd the game go, boys?"

"Fine," I said.

Gus said, "You win?"

"We played workup," I replied in a cold tone. "Nobody won."

"Hey, Frankie," Gus said. "Could we talk? I told your dad about this afternoon."

I looked at my father for any sign of reproof but in the shadow of approaching night with the warm light through the windows at his back he looked unconcerned. He said, "It would be a good idea."

"All right," I said.

Jake had paused on the steps and his eyes skipped back and forth between Gus and our father and me, and his own face was clouded with confusion.

Gus said, "Let's take a walk."

My father said, "How about a game of checkers, Jake?"

Gus left the porch and I turned from the house and side by side we walked into the twilight beneath the limbs of the elms and maples that arched the unlit and empty street.

We walked for a while before Gus said anything. "I'm sorry, Frankie. I shouldn't have let that happen today."

"It's okay," I said.

"No, it isn't. Doyle, he's a certain kind of man. Not a bad man really but an unthinking man. Hell, so am I for that matter. The difference between us is that I have some responsibility for you and I let you down today. That won't happen again, I promise."

The crickets and the tree frogs had started to clip at the silence that came with the evening and above us through the breaks in the canopy of leaves the sky had begun to salt with stars. The houses set back from the street were charcoal gray shapes with windows like uninterested yellow eyes observing our passing.

I said, "What did Doyle mean, Gus, that Dad cracked during the war?"

Gus stopped and eyed the sky then tilted his head as if listening to the growing chorus that accompanied the approach of night. He said, "You ever talk to your dad about the war?"

"I try sometimes. I keep asking him if he killed any Germans. All he ever says is that he shot at a lot of them."

"Frank, it's not my place to talk to you about what your father experienced in the war. But I'll tell you about the war in general. You talk to a man like Doyle and he'll tell you a lot of bullshit. You watch John Wayne and Audie Murphy in the movie house and it probably seems easy killing men. The truth is that when you kill a man it doesn't matter if he's your enemy and if he's trying to kill you. That moment of his death will eat at you for the rest of your life. It'll dig into bone so deep inside you that not even the hand of God is going to be able to pull it out, I don't care how much you pray. And you multiply that feeling by several years and too many doomed engagements and more horror, Frankie, than you can possibly imagine. And the utter senselessness and the total hopelessness become your enemy as much as any man pointing a rifle at you. And because they were officers, some men like your father were forced to be the architects of that senselessness, and what they asked of themselves and of the men they commanded was a burden no human being should have to shoulder. Frankie, your father someday may tell you about the war or he may not. But whatever you hear from Doyle or from anyone else will never be your father's truth."

"You're not afraid of fireworks," I said.

"I've got my own devils. And Doyle, he's got his."

We'd walked to the end of a street with a guardrail and thirty yards beyond it ran the river. In the pale thin light that was all that was left of the day the water had become blue-black and looked like a satin ribbon torn from a dress. Far off along the highway to Mankato car headlights flew across the face of the hills and blinked off and on as they were obscured occasionally by trees and barns and outbuildings and they reminded me of fireflies. I sat on the guardrail and looked back at the Flats where the lights of the homes held constant.

"I've got twenty-seven dollars saved, Gus. I was going to buy a bunch of fireworks. I don't want fireworks anymore."

Gus sat down beside me. "I'm guessing you'll find something to spend it on, Frankie. Hell, if you can't think of anything else, I could always use a loan." He laughed and bumped my leg playfully with his own and then he stood. He glanced back at the river where bullfrogs sang a chorus so loud you could barely hear yourself think. "We'd best be getting home," he said.

10

On Sunday morning Jake complained that he wasn't feeling well and asked if he could stay home. For me skipping church was always a delightful daydream. The idea of missing out on three services and lounging around the house in my pajamas was enough to make me drool. If the request had come from me my mother would have suspected something but my brother didn't fake things. She felt his head with the back of her hand then used a thermometer. He didn't have a fever. She gently probed his neck feeling for swelling and found none. When she asked him what specifically were his symptoms he gave her a lackluster stare and said that he just felt really lousy. She talked it over with my father and they agreed that he should stay in bed. The plan was that we'd do the service in Cadbury and check on him when we came back for the worship in New Bremen.

During the service in Cadbury I sat with Peter Klement. He came with his mother who sang in the choir. The black eye that he'd sported the afternoon we visited his house was little more than a shadow now and neither of us said anything about it. During the social time after church we chucked rocks at a telephone pole where someone had stapled a poster for a circus coming to Mankato and we talked about the Twins. Ariel finally called to me and I left with my family to return to New Bremen for the second service of the morning.

When we pulled up to the house Jake was waiting on the front porch and Gus was with him. They hurried down the steps and it was clear something was wrong.

"You better get up to the hospital, Captain," Gus said. "Emil Brandt tried to kill himself this morning."

I got the details from Jake who stayed behind with me while my father and mother and Ariel drove to the hospital. It had happened like this.

Jake had been in bed and trying to sleep. We hadn't been gone fifteen minutes when there was a furious pounding at the front door. He got up and went downstairs and found Lise Brandt on the porch. He said her face looked like something out of a monster movie it was so distorted and frightening. She babbled and gesticulated and he stepped outside and told her to calm down even though his own heart was galloping because he could see that whatever she was trying to communicate, it was something horrific. She gripped his head in her hands and squeezed so hard that he thought his eyes would pop out. It took him a few minutes but in the end he understood. Emil was in trouble. Emil was dying.

He'd run across the street to the church with Lise at his side and he'd gone downstairs where Gus was sitting on the toilet. Gus had sworn at them and reached out and slammed shut the door to his little bathroom and Jake had knocked on it hard and hollered that Emil Brandt was dying and they needed Gus's help. Gus was out quickly and ushered them back to the house and grabbed the phone and called the fire department and told them to get their asses to Emil Brandt's place, the man was dying. Then he mounted his motorcycle with Jake behind him and Lise in the sidecar and they shot up the road to Brandt's house. By the time they got there the fire department ambulance was parked in front.

One of the firemen told Gus that it looked like Brandt had swallowed a bottle of sleeping pills. They were pumping his stomach. They wouldn't let Lise into the bedroom but she tried to shove her way inside and the fireman who'd talked to Gus held her back. The moment he touched her she went berserk. It was as if his hands were fire. She leaped back and folded herself into a corner of the living room and began to scream uncontrollably. The fireman reached out to her again but Jake told him no, don't touch her, she can't stand being touched by strangers. He told the fireman to wait and she would calm down eventually. Brandt was brought out on a gurney while Lise screamed in her corner and they loaded him into the ambulance and they rushed him to the hospital. When Lise calmed down as Jake had predicted he made her understand what had happened and although she was frantic about her brother she didn't commence again to screaming.

Someone had called Axel Brandt and he arrived minutes after the firemen had sped away with Emil. Gus explained things to him and he signed to his sister and told Gus they were going to the hospital. And when they were gone the house was silent and empty, a place that felt as if a tornado had swept past and sucked out the air and neither Gus nor Jake wanted to linger. They came back on the motorcycle to wait for my parents and to deliver the news.

My father charged Gus with the responsibility of explaining the situation to Albert Griswold, a deacon who usually came early to help set up the worship. Griswold was a town councilman who could talk your brain numb. When Gus laid things out for him and made it clear that he needed to conduct the service, I saw the man puff up with pleasure at the opportunity. His wife was in the choir and was a fair organist and my mother left instructions with Gus that Lorraine Griswold was to lead the music for the service.

Whatever illness had afflicted Jake seemed to have been cured by the events of that morning and after my parents left he dressed in his Sunday clothes and was prepared to attend church. For a brief time I weighed the delicious possibility of skipping the service. In all the confusion who would notice? But under the circumstances it seemed that my presence and Jake's would be judicious and I steeled myself for what I knew would be a long grind. Jake turned out to be a bit of a celebrity and much to his dismay he was assaulted with questions about what had happened. He tried to answer but his stutter was painful to him and to everyone listening and he looked to me for help. I was only too happy to oblige and in the story I told I made him a hero, insisting that it was only because of Jake's quick action that our most famous citizen was saved from death by his own hand.

People looked aghast. "His own hand? He tried to kill himself?"

"That's certainly how it looked," I told them. "If Jake had come a few minutes later, Mr. Brandt would have been dead."

Their eyes were full of amazement at both Brandt's unthinkable behavior and young Jake's valiant action.

I thought I might in this way, making him a hero, redeem myself in my brother's opinion for turning him into such a vague and unimportant figure in my telling of the story of our discovery of the dead man. Not so. As I told and retold the events of that morning, each time inflating just a bit more the importance of Jake's role, his scowl grew more profound and he finally grabbed the sleeve of my suit coat and pulled me out the church door and stuttered at me, "Just st-st-st-stop it."

"What?" I said.

"Just t-t-tell the tr-tr-truth."

"I am."

"Bullshit, goddamn it!"

The sun stopped in its rising. The earth ceased to turn. I stood dumbfounded, staring at Jake, amazed at this blasphemy there on the very steps of the church and said with such clarity and power and without stumble that everyone inside could have heard. I felt the eyes of my father's entire seated congregation shift to the church steps where we stood and I felt the wave of censure roll out from the sanctuary. Jake's own eyes grew huge with fear and shame at the realization of what he'd just done and they held on my face and I knew he was terrified to look through the door at the people gathered inside who'd been stunned to silence.

Then I laughed. Oh, Christ, did I laugh. I couldn't help myself it was all so unexpected and surreal. Jake fled, running from the church to our house across the street. And I turned back and entered the shadow of the sanctuary still smiling and suffered the glaring condemnation of the congregation and sat through the long service in which Albert Griswold held forth in his impromptu and interminable sermon about the need to impress godly values on the youth of the day and when it was over I walked back to the house and found Jake upstairs in our room and I apologized.

He stared sullenly at the ceiling and didn't answer.

"It's okay, Jake. It's no big deal."

"Everyone heard."

"So?"

"They'll tell Dad."

"He won't care."

"He should. It was awful. And it was all your f-f-fault."

"Don't get mad at me. I was just trying to help."

"I don't n-n-need your help."

I heard the creak of the floorboards just outside our room and when I turned there was Gus leaning against the doorway eyeing Jake with a grim countenance. "Bullshit, goddamn it," he said repeating the words that were Jake's transgression. "Bullshit, goddamn it, right there in the church doorway." His lips went into a thin line like a little whip and he said again, "Bullshit, goddamn it." He shook his head then a broad grin broke across his face and he laughed mightily. "Jakie, I can't remember enjoying a moment in church more. No, sir, I can't. You punched 'em square in the face of their piety. Bullshit, goddamn it."

Jake's mood didn't improve much. "Dad'll be mad," he said.

"I'll talk to your dad," Gus said. "And, Jake, there's going to be lots in this world you're going to feel bad about. Save your regret for the important things, okay?"

Gus turned around and I heard the dance of his footsteps down the stairs and the last of his laughter and when he was gone the blessing that had been the lightness of his spirit seemed to have brightened Jake's mood a bit and my brother looked like a man reprieved.

In the late afternoon my father came home from the hospital looking for Jake. He found us together in our room. Jake was reading one of his comic books and I was reading the book that Danny O'Keefe had told me about, a book called *I Am Legend*. My father had long ago made a purchase that did a good deal of damage to his chronically battered bank account. He'd invested in a fifty-four-volume set of books published by Encyclopaedia Britannica and called Great Books of the Western World. It included the works of Homer and Aeschylus and Sophocles and Plato and Aristotle and Thomas Aquinas and Dante and Chaucer and Shakespeare and Freud. It offered much of the most enlightened thinking by the greatest Western minds of the last two or three thousand years. When he walked into our room that afternoon and saw us reading instead comic books and pulp novels, he may well have been disappointed but he said nothing. He addressed Jake: "I need your help, guy."

Jake put down the comic book and sat up. "What with?" he said.

"Lise Brandt. She won't leave the hospital without Emil and they want to keep him for a while. She won't listen to him or Axel or be reasoned with. Emil suggested that she might listen to you, especially if you were willing to stay with her until he could come home. What do you say?"

"All right." Jake scooted off his bed.

"Can I come too?" I asked.

My father nodded and motioned for me to be quick about it.

The Minnesota Valley Community Hospital was a new structure of stunningly red brick built on a hill overlooking New Bremen. Its construction had been largely underwritten by the Brandt family. Emil's room was on the second floor and the waiting area of that level was crowded. Brandt's immediate family was there: his brother, Axel; Axel's wife, Julia; his nephew, Karl, who sat with his arm protectively around Ariel's shoulders. Some people had come from the small college on the hill where Emil was the crown jewel of the music faculty. My mother was there sitting on a windowsill smoking a cigarette in her Sunday finery and looking pensive. The only one I expected to see and did not was Lise.

Axel strode forward the moment Jake appeared. He was a tall handsome athletic man with thinning blond hair and eyes whose blue was so intense it was as if he'd purchased pieces of the sky for their making. He possessed an overall countenance that every time I saw him struck me as regretful.

"Thank you, Jake," he said with great sincerity.

Jake nodded and I understood that in this gathering he was reluctant to speak.

My father said, "Where is she?"

"In Emil's room. I can't go near her. Nobody can. Jake, she won't leave. But it's important that she does. Emil badly needs rest. Will you talk to her?"

Jake looked down the corridor which at the moment was empty.

"We could remove her forcibly," Axel went on, "but it would create such a scene and upset Emil further and I don't want that. Please, will you talk to her?"

Jake looked up at Brandt and nodded.

Ariel left Karl and came to Jake and knelt down. Her eyes were feverish looking. "Oh, Jakie, please get her out of there without a scene. He needs his rest so."

I heard him whisper, "I'll try."

Ariel kissed his cheek and he turned and walked away and on either side of him walked my father and Axel Brandt. I watched him keeping pace between those two men who towered above him and although it wasn't as if Jake was walking toward a firing squad I understood nonetheless that a heavy yoke had been laid upon his small shoulders. I had tried that morning to make my brother out to be a hero and in doing so had stretched the truth. As he disappeared into Emil Brandt's room I understood with great affection that I needn't have done so.

I sat beside my mother on the windowsill which had a marvelous view of the town. The hill was high and steep and below us New Bremen lay quiet on that Sunday afternoon. The streets platted so carefully by those early German immigrants reminded me of the squares on the chessboard that my father and Emil Brandt used for their weekly game which would probably not be played this Monday. My mother put her hand on my leg and squeezed. She didn't look at me and I wasn't sure if it was some kind of nonverbal signal or if I was simply a touchstone that helped to ground her in the face of the uncertainty at hand.

After a moment she asked, "Did the music go well at church?"

"Yes," I said. "But not as good as when you're there."

She nodded and although she didn't smile I could tell she was pleased.

"Is he going to be okay? Mr. Brandt, I mean."

She stubbed out her cigarette in a square glass ashtray beside her and stared at the black smudge and answered slowly, "Emil is complicated. But I'm sure he'll recover."

"Why'd he do it?" I spoke quietly so that the others wouldn't hear. "I mean, he's famous and everything. Is it because of his face?"

"He's a beautiful man, Frankie," she said. "His face isn't important." *Maybe to him it is,* I thought but didn't say.

Julia Brandt stood up and walked toward us. She wore a pink dress with black piping and her high heels were black and pink to match. Around her neck was a string of pearls and her earrings were pearl too. Her hair was as black as a moonless night and her eyes dark as cold cinders. I didn't like Julia Brandt and I knew my mother didn't like her either.

"Ruth," Mrs. Brandt said looking pained, "this is all so horrible."

"Yes," my mother said.

Mrs. Brandt reached into the purse she carried and pulled out a gold cigarette case and snapped it open. She held it out to my mother in offering and my mother shook her head and said, "No thank you, Julia." Mrs. Brandt slipped a cigarette free and tapped it on the lid of the gold case and put the case away and brought out a gold lighter with a little sapphire in the center. She slid the cigarette between her rubied lips and flipped the lighter open and thumbed the striker and touched the flame to the tip of her cigarette and lifted her head high like a wild animal about to howl and blew out a flourish of smoke.

"Tragic," she said. She looked toward the corner where Karl and Ariel sat together, and deep in the dark cinders of her eyes little flames seemed to have been kindled. She said, "Though it's fortunate in a way."

"Fortunate?" My mother's voice and face were taut.

"For Ariel and Karl, I mean. That it's happened now while they still have each other for comfort. In a few weeks, they'll be off in different worlds, very far from each other."

"Julia," my mother said, "there is nothing fortunate about this except that Emil didn't succeed."

Mrs. Brandt drew on her cigarette and smiled and smoke escaped slowly from her lips. "You and Emil have always been close," she said.

"I remember when we all thought you might marry. We might have been sisters." She carefully eyed my mother's Sunday dress and shook her head. "I can't imagine being married to a minister, always having to dress so . . ." She drew on her cigarette again, let out a billow of smoke, and finished, ". . . sensibly. But then you have a wonderful life, a very spiritual life, I suppose."

"And I'm sure you have a very different life, Julia."

"It can be a trial, the responsibility of being a Brandt, Ruth."

"A terrible burden," my mother agreed.

"You have no idea," Mrs. Brandt said with a sigh.

"Oh but I do, Julia. It's clear from all those worry lines on your face. Excuse me," she said sliding from the sill. "I need to get some air."

My mother walked from the waiting area and Mrs. Brandt took another long draw on her cigarette and said under her breath, "You perfect bitch." Then she looked down at me and smiled and turned away.

11

Jake succeeded in coaxing Lise from her brother's hospital room and Jake and my father and Axel all drove her home together in Mr. Brandt's Cadillac. My mother followed in the Packard along with Ariel and me. In his sports car Karl returned his mother to her big mansion. Emil was left alone to get the rest everyone said he needed.

Because Ariel and Jake were familiar visitors to the house and because they were willing it was decided that they would stay with Lise until Emil was able to return home. My mother said she'd pack overnight bags for them. When everyone left I stuck around to keep Jake and Ariel company for a while.

There were curtains over the windows but the interior walls of Emil Brandt's home were basically bare. The blind man, I figured, cared not at all about appearance and Lise Brandt was such a mystery to me that I didn't know what to think about her. There was little furniture and it was placed far apart and Ariel had told me that because of Mr. Brandt's blindness it was never moved. There were no bookshelves, no books. But there were flowers, a profusion of flowers arranged beautifully in vases set about every room. The center of the house seemed to be the grand piano that took up the entire space of what had probably once been the dining room. Ariel had told me this was where Emil Brandt practiced and composed. Near the piano sat expensive-looking reel-to-reel recording equipment which, according to Ariel, Brandt used while composing since he couldn't see to write on a score sheet. There was a fine hi-fi system in the living room with enormous speakers and a whole wall of shelves filled with records. I considered the spare look of the house, and thought about the texture of the furniture upholstery which was soft as a flower petal, and about the fragrance of the flowers that perfumed the rooms, and about the piano and the stereo speakers that filled the house with music, and I realized that Emil Brandt had constructed a world of those senses he still possessed.

The kitchen was different from the rest of the house. This was Lise's territory. It was large and neatly arranged and colorful and had a wide sliding door along the back wall that opened onto a beautiful deck that overlooked the gardens and the river.

It was late afternoon by the time we were settled and Lise Brandt set about making dinner. Ariel asked if she could help, facing Lise and enunciating clearly so Lise could read her lips. Lise shook her head and motioned Ariel out but she beckoned Jake to come and give her a hand. We ate at a table in the kitchen, ate a better meal than my mother had ever put together. Fried chicken, mashed potatoes and gravy, buttered carrots, baked squash, all of it delicious. I thought that despite his blindness Emil Brandt was a lucky man. After dinner Ariel offered to do the dishes but once again Lise shooed her away and accepted help only from Jake.

It was nearing sunset when Lise put on her overalls and signed to Jake that there was still work to be done in the garden. I could tell he was not inclined but he said okay. He also asked if it would be all right if I helped and after a few moments of consideration Lise nodded. Ariel stayed inside and the music she played on the grand piano flowed out the windows of the house. From what I knew of the music of Emil Brandt I was pretty sure she was playing one of his compositions, a piece in a minor key, sad and beautiful. In the large toolshed Lise took a pick, a shovel, and a crowbar from where they hung on a wall and handed a tool to each of us. I got the pick, Jake the shovel, and Lise kept the crowbar. She led us to an area of recently turned earth along the back picket fence. It was clear she was expanding her garden but she'd encountered an obstacle, a rock the size of a prizewinning pumpkin near the center of the new plot. It was deeply embedded in a layer of clay and probably had been there since the Glacial River Warren tumbled it down from the Dakotas. We stood for a minute eyeing it from all angles.

I lifted my hand to get Lise's attention. "Maybe you could just plant around it," I suggested, speaking carefully so that she could read my lips.

She shook her head furiously and pointed at my pick and mimed digging.

"All right then," I said. "Stand back."

I hoisted the pick and chopped into the clay beside the boulder. Lise and Jake stood back and let me work. I broke the ground and worked my way completely around the stone and afterward Jake followed with his shovel and cleared away the big loose clods. We worked in this way for nearly half an hour while Lise stood by and watched. I was beginning to resent all this labor while she did nothing except shake her head as if our efforts didn't meet with her approval. I was about to step away and say something when she tapped Jake's shoulder and motioned us to stop. She laid her crowbar down and went to the shed and from a pile of rocks on the east side she took one that was roughly the size and shape of a loaf of bread. She brought it back and set it six inches from the boulder. She took up her crowbar and jammed the chiseled end under the big stone and using the smaller stone as the fulcrum of her lever she put the force of her whole body into prying the obstacle loose from the grip of the hard clay. Her face squeezed into intense lines of determination and I looked at her bare arms and marveled at how muscled they were and how the veins there ran in long thick tendrils under her skin. Jake and I dropped our tools and knelt on either side of the stone and gripped it and pulled with all our might. And finally the rock broke free. It was too heavy for us to lift so Jake and I slowly rolled the great pumpkin of a rock across the yard to the shed where it joined all the other rock and stone that Lise Brandt had cleared to have her gardens. When it was settled there Jake leaped up and cried out victoriously. Lise gripped her crowbar in one hand and shot her other hand into the air in a sign of triumph and sent forth a prolonged guttural intonation that sounded not at all human and that if I'd heard it alone at night would have made me freeze in my steps. But I understood what it was about and I joined in the celebration.

And that's when I made my mistake.

In my excitement I clapped Jake on the shoulder in the way of comrades and then I did the same to Lise Brandt. The moment I touched her she swung around with the crowbar in her hand. If I hadn't been so quick and leaped back out of reach, that iron bar would have crushed my skull. The sun in its setting had gone red and a long beam shot through a break in the branches of an elm and lit her face with a demon light. Her eyes held a wild look and she opened her mouth and began to scream in the way she had earlier when the fireman had restrained her.

I looked desperately to Jake and shouted above the screams, "What do we do?"

"There's nothing we can do," he said. He looked in pain himself as if Lise Brandt's unfathomable misery were his own. "Just leave her alone and she'll stop."

I pleaded with her, saying desperately, "I'm sorry, Lise. I didn't mean anything." But she didn't hear. I put my hands over my ears and backed away.

Ariel rushed from the house calling as she came, "What happened?"

"Nothing," Jake said. "Frank touched her, that's all. It was an accident. She'll calm down in a while. She'll be fine."

"I've got to get out of here," I said.

"Go," Jake said. "Go." And he furiously motioned me away.

There was a gate in the back fence and I pushed through it. Beyond was the thread of a path that ran down the hill toward the railroad tracks that lay between the Brandt property and the river. I fled the screaming but it followed me all the way down the slope and across the tracks and through the cottonwood trees and it wasn't until I slid down the riverbank and was on the sandy flat that the terrible sound finally ceased. My heart beat wildly, not just from the running but from the panic of Lise's awful scream, and I understood only too well why Axel and Julia Brandt had sent her into exile in a place that was far beyond the hearing of most people in New Bremen.

In the blessed quiet of evening I walked along the river toward home. Black terns cut sharp curls above the channel, snatching insects from the air. In the sky the clouds had gone the color of flamingo feathers. I came to the first houses of the Flats and heard Danny O'Keefe and some other kids calling out to one another beyond the cottonwood trees but I didn't want to join them. I made my way across the dry mudflats and approached the sandy area covered with bulrushes where Danny's uncle had built his lean-to. From deep in the tall reeds came the rustling of someone headed my way and I slipped into the cover of the bulrushes and laid myself down trying to be inconspicuous. In a few moments a figure passed a dozen feet from where I lay. I saw that it was Warren Redstone. He walked slowly toward Danny's house, climbed the riverbank, and disappeared. I waited a little while to be sure he was gone for good then stood up and began to make my way through the bulrushes trying to move more quietly than Danny's great-uncle had. Which turned out to be a good idea because when I reached the clearing where Warren Redstone had built his little lean-to I caught sight of a dark shape lurking at the makeshift structure. I crept forward and once again lay on the sand among the reeds, and in the fading light of evening I watched.

A man was crouched on all fours with his torso deep in the lean-to and his rear end outside. He spent a moment rummaging in the inner shadow then backed out and stood up. The light was dim and he kept his back to me and I couldn't see who he was. It seemed to me that he was studying something he held cupped in his hands. He knelt again and crawled back inside and this time the beam of a flashlight shot into the dark there. I still couldn't see exactly what the man was doing but after a couple of minutes he backed out and stood and brushed sand from his hands and from the knees of his trousers. He broke a few of the bulrushes and gathered them into a kind of broom and swept away all sign of his presence and kept sweeping as he backed to the reeds. He reached to his belt and a moment later the beam of the flashlight shot out and played across the sand as if to be certain he'd erased all evidence of his presence there. Then he turned and disappeared in the direction of town.

In the wash of the flashlight beam I'd seen his face. It was Gus's friend Officer Doyle.

By the time I left my hiding place night was almost upon me. I went to the lean-to and tried to see inside but the dark was nearly absolute now and whatever it was that had so intrigued Doyle was hidden to me. I thought about erasing my tracks in the way Doyle had done but didn't see any reason and as the bullfrogs began their deep-throated courting I headed home.

12

E mil Brandt didn't return until the following Saturday, three days before the Fourth of July. He came from the Twin Cities where he'd been transferred to a private hospital for rest and care. Axel drove him to the farmhouse beyond the edge of town. My father was there to meet them and so was I. Emil's eyes were sunken and his face drawn but he was smiling and Lise made a huge fuss over him and despite her own abhorrence at being touched she touched him lightly several times, her hands like butterflies lighting on his arms and shoulders. Ariel embraced him and held to him a long time and wept.

"I'm fine," he said to her. And to us all he said, "I'm fine."

Once he'd delivered his brother Axel didn't linger. He thanked Ariel and Jake for all their help and then drove away in his big black Cadillac and I thought he seemed greatly relieved to be finished with his part in the drama. My father and Ariel told Emil to rest but Brandt insisted that life resume in its normal way and he signed to Lise giving her instructions to get the chess set and he and my father prepared to play a game.

Brandt said to Ariel, "This will be an interesting chapter in my memoir, don't you think?"

"Please don't joke about it, Emil," Ariel replied.

He reached out and when she took his hand he said gently, "It was an accident. A terrible accident that's all. It's finished. Now you should go home. You've done enough for me here."

"No," Ariel said. "I'd like to stay."

He nodded and his eyes though sightless settled on her face in a way that made me believe he saw her perfectly. "Very well," he said. "There's work to be transcribed."

Ariel left and a few minutes later from the window of the study came the sound of her fingers dancing over the keys of the typewriter.

My father and Emil set about their game and my father asked me to go inside and see if Lise needed my help.

"Jake's helping her," I said.

"I'm sure there's something you can do," he replied and it was clear my presence was not wanted.

I went inside and stood in the kitchen doorway. Jake and Lise were busy pulling things from shelves. I offered to help but Jake said they were fine and Lise, when she saw me, made a peeved shooing gesture with her hands and I left. I wandered to the living room and stood looking at a fancy plaque hanging on the wall. It was from a music festival in Vienna and Emil Brandt's name was inlaid in silver in the center. Through the living room window that overlooked the front porch came Brandt's voice delivering a chess move which my father countered. Then Dad said, "Not long ago you told me you were happy, Emil. What happened?"

"Happened? I drank too much scotch and ingested too many sleeping pills. An accident, I swear."

"I don't believe that. Nobody believes that, Emil."

"What you or anybody else believes, Nathan, troubles me very little."

"We're people who care about you."

"If that's true then you'll let the issue drop."

"And if you accidentally ingest too many sleeping pills again?"

Brandt was silent for a long time and all I could hear was the sound of Jake laughing in the kitchen and Ariel's fingers on the typewriter keys and in the distance the deep rising rumble of a train approaching on the tracks along the river. The train came and the house shook just a little with its passing and when it was gone Emil Brandt said, "I don't have the courage to try again, Nathan."

"But why, Emil? Why try at all?"

Brandt laughed bitterly. "You have such a rich life. How can you possibly understand?"

"You have your own riches, Emil. Your music for example. Isn't that a great blessing?"

"In the balance it has come to have little weight."

"And what is it that weighs so heavily on the other side of the scales?"

Brandt didn't reply. Instead he said, "I've had enough chess for today. I want to rest now."

"Emil, talk to me."

"I said I've had enough."

I heard Brandt rise and move toward the door.

Quickly I went to the kitchen and found Jake covered in flour and Lise rolling out dough on a large breadboard. From the living room came my father's voice calling to us, "Boys, it's time to go home."

Jake gestured to Lise and she looked disappointed but she nodded that she understood and accepted. He brushed the flour from his clothing and joined me at the kitchen door.

Emil Brandt stood in the living room with his arms crossed over his chest, looking eager to be free from us all. Jake and I bid him goodbye and in return he offered only a terse nod. We walked to my father who stood holding the screen door open.

"I'll pray for you, Emil," he said.

"About as useful as throwing a penny down a wishing well, Nathan."

We all trudged to the Packard where I said, "Dad, is it okay if Jake and I walk home?"

Jake shot me a questioning look but kept quiet.

"All right," my father said in a distracted way. He was gazing back at the Brandt house and I'm sure he was thinking hard about the disturbing conversation he'd just had with his good friend. "Don't dawdle," he said and got into the car and drove away.

"Why are we walking?" Jake complained.

"Something on the river I've been wanting to look at. Come on."

The day was hot already and humid and as we kicked through the weeds on our way down the slope toward the railroad tracks the grasshoppers flew up before us in a buzz of complaint. Jake complained too. "Where are we going, Frank?"

"You'll see in a minute."

"This better be good."

We crossed the tracks and slipped through the cottonwoods and hit the river and started toward the Flats. When we came in sight of the stretch of sand covered with bulrushes Jake began to angle toward the riverbank. I kept walking straight ahead.

Jake said, "Where are you going?"

"I told you, you'll see."

Jake suddenly understood my destination and he shook his head feverishly. "Frank, we shouldn't go there."

I put my finger to my lips to signal silence and began as quietly as possible to thread my way through the bulrushes. Jake hesitated and started for the riverbank, paused again, and finally followed me. Near the clearing I went down on all fours and approached in the creep of an animal stalking and Jake did the same. The clearing was empty and the lean-to deserted. For a full minute I watched and waited while dragonflies shot through the heavy morning air around us. At last I stood.

Jake said, "We shouldn't be doing this."

"Quiet," I said.

At the lean-to I knelt and crawled into the shade inside. I wasn't sure what I was looking for and at first there seemed to be nothing to see. Then I spotted a slight mounding of the sand in one corner and began to dig and quickly uncovered a large tin can that stood a foot high and was maybe eight inches in diameter. It was covered with a white rag that was secured with a rubber band. I pulled the can from the sand and brought it into the sunlight where Jake stood looking on unhappily. I popped the rubber band free and drew off the rag and peered inside. In the can were many items. The first thing I pulled out was a rolled-up magazine. *Playboy*. I knew about this publication but I'd never seen a real issue. I spent a few minutes going through it with my mouth wide open and Jake leaning over my shoulder so he could see too. Finally I laid it aside and dug in the can again. There was a Mickey Mouse wristwatch with one of Mickey's hands missing. There

was a ceramic frog no larger than my thumb. There was a little Indian doll dressed in buckskin and a comb that was carved from ivory
and decorated with scrimshaw and a military medal, a Purple Heart.
Among these and the many other small items were the glasses that
had once been Bobby Cole's and the photograph that had belonged
to the dead man. I didn't understand the importance of most of these
things but to Danny's uncle they clearly held value. I wondered what
interest Doyle had in the contents of the can.

"What is all that stuff?" Jake asked.

"I don't know."

"Did he find those things, you think?"

"Or stole them, maybe. Get me some of those reeds," I said nod-
ding toward the bulrushes.

"What for?"

"Just get them."

While Jake did as I'd asked I put everything back in the can, returning the *Playboy* with great reluctance, and lidded the tin with the
rag and slipped the rubber band into place and set it all back in the
hole in the corner of the lean-to and covered it with sand just as I'd
found it. Jake brought me half a dozen reeds which I clumped together so their bushy ends formed the kind of broom I'd seen Doyle
create many days earlier.

I said to Jake, "Follow our tracks back the way we came."

He went and I went after him, trying to sweep from the sand any
sign that we'd ever been there.

13

Jake and I did our Saturday yard work at my grandfather's house and when we got home Danny O'Keefe called and asked if we wanted to come over to his house to play Risk. Danny was there and another kid named Lee Kelly who was okay but never brushed his teeth so his breath always smelled like sour cabbage. We played at the dining room table which was unusual. Usually we played in the basement. In Risk, Jake always conducted himself with conservative fervor, holing up in Australia and stacking an Everest of armies on Indonesia so that only the very foolish would attempt to take his continent. That would be me. I spread myself over Asia and then viciously tried to breach Jake's stronghold. I didn't succeed and the next turn he decimated me before retiring to his little Australian sanctuary. After that Danny and Lee attacked me from America and Africa and less than half an hour later I was out of the game and Jake got all my cards. I generally played a little fast and loose with my resources but I figured hell, a man's reach should exceed his grasp, especially in a stupid board game.

I hung around for a while watching the others play then asked Danny if I could get a grape Nehi out of the refrigerator. When I got the bottle of soda pop I heard the broadcast of a Twins game coming up the basement stairs and I drifted that way. The basement of the

O'Keefes' house had been finished in dark wood paneling. There was a sofa and some end tables that looked as if they'd been reconstructed from old wagon wheels and a couple of lamps with shades that turned and had pretty women on them in skimpy clothing, one of the reasons we liked playing Risk and other games down there. Seated on the sofa watching the ball game on television was Danny's great-uncle. His hair was neatly combed and he was dressed in a clean plaid shirt and chinos and loafers. He looked very different from the day I'd seen him sitting beside the dead man.

When I hit the bottom of the stairs he glanced away from the screen and said, "Twins are getting shellacked." There was no emotion in his dark eyes, no sign of recognition.

"What inning?" I asked.

"Bottom of the eighth. Barring a miracle it's all over." He was holding a can of Brandt beer and he took a sip. He didn't seem to mind me being there, busting in on his solitude. He said, "What's your name?"

"Frank Drum."

"Drum." He took another sip of beer. "What kind of name is Drum? Sounds like it could be Indian."

"It's Scottish."

He nodded then Killebrew hit a home run and Danny's great-uncle seemed to forget about me.

I waited until the excitement in the ballpark had passed then I said, "What did you do with the picture?"

"Picture?" He squinted at me.

"The one we found on the dead guy."

"What difference does it make to you?"

"I just wondered. When we buried him nobody knew his name. I thought maybe the photograph might help."

He put his beer down. "Did you say anything to anyone about it? About me?"

"No, sir."

"Why not?"

"I don't know."

"You think I had something to do with that man dying?"

"No."

He stared at me and I stood there with the grape Nehi growing warm in my hand. He finally asked, "Do you want the photograph?"

"Maybe."

"What would you do with it? Give it to the police?"

"Maybe."

"And when they ask where you got it what would you say?"

"I found it. Down by the trestle."

"In a place you're not supposed to be?"

"I can be there."

"That's not what Danny tells me."

I thought about Danny reporting my activities to his great-uncle. It gave me the creeps.

"I heard you were in jail," I said.

"Who told you that?"

"I just heard. Is it true?"

"Only part of the truth."

"What's the rest?"

"Did you hear why I was in jail?"

"No."

"The rest of the truth is why."

"Okay why?"

"*Wo iyokihi.*"

"What's that?"

"It means responsibility. We who are Sioux have a responsibility to make sure the past isn't distorted by the lies whites tell each other and try to tell us. Do you know about the war the Dakota fought against the white people here in eighteen sixty-two?"

"Sure. Your people attacked New Bremen and killed a bunch of settlers."

"Do you know why our people did that?"

The truth was I didn't. I pretty much figured that's just what Indians did, but I didn't say that.

"Our people were starving," Redstone said. "The whites trespassed on our land, feeding our grass to their animals, cutting our trees for their houses, shooting what little game we still had. Our crops failed, and the winter was hard, hard. We asked for the food the whites had promised us in the treaty we'd signed. Know what they said to our starving people? They said, 'Let them eat grass.' Sure we fought. We fought for food. We fought because promises were broken. We fought because we refused to be crushed under the boots of the whites. The man who told us to eat grass, he was killed, and our warriors stuffed grass into *his* mouth. It was a hopeless thing we tried to do, because the whites, they had soldiers and guns and money and newspapers that repeated all the lies. In the end, our people lost everything and were sent away from here. Thirty-eight of our warriors were hung in one day, and the whites who watched it cheered."

I didn't know what to believe. I'd heard a different spin in school when they taught us about the uprising but I was always ready to discount what was fed to us in the classroom. School had never been my favorite place and I'd never been a favorite of my teachers many of whom said I asked too many questions and asked them in a way that sometimes sounded disrespectful. Parent-teacher conferences could be dicey. Ariel and Jake were different. All they ever got was praise.

"What does that have to do with you and jail?" I asked.

He finished his beer, stood up, and went to a small refrigerator in the corner where he pulled out another can of Brandt which he opened with a church key. He took a long draw. It was the first time I'd seen him up close standing to his full height and I suddenly realized how tall he was and how despite his age which must have been at least sixty he looked powerful. He wiped his mouth with the back of a huge hand the color of faded red brick.

"I spoke the truth. And for that I was labeled a troublemaker and put in jail."

"In America, people don't get thrown in jail just for being trouble-makers," I shot back.

He stared down at me and I thought I understood how discon-certing it must have been for one of those slaughtered settlers to have faced an angry Sioux warrior. He said in a flat voice, "That's how they get away with it."

Danny called from upstairs, "Hey! Game's over. Want to go swimming?"

Warren Redstone held me paralyzed for a moment with the anger in his dark stare. Then he said, "Go on and play, white boy." And he turned his back to me.

14

I n New Bremen there were three places to swim. One was the public pool which was crowded and loud and the lifeguards were always blowing their whistles at you. The second was the country club but you had to have money or be friends with people who did. The third was an old stone quarry south of town which had been abandoned years before when an underground spring filled the great gaping hole with water so quickly that much of the equipment had to be left in place. Word was that if you swam deep enough you could still make out the vague disturbing shapes of massive machinery like monsters asleep on the bottom. The quarry was fenced and posted against trespassing but no one paid any attention. Though it was a place our parents warned us away from it was one of our favorite destinations on hot summer days. Even Jake so pure of heart ignored my folks' stricture and always tagged along with the rest of us.

We rode our bikes through New Bremen, Jake, Danny, Lee, and I, past the town limits, and in another mile turned west along a couple of dirt ruts overgrown with weeds. The quarry was on the far side of a line of birch trees that isolated the area even further. The rock that had been taken was red granite and the area around the quarry was littered with great jumbles of red spoil unsuitable for construction. To this day whenever I think of that quarry I have the sense of a place of deep and mindless wounding. When we pulled up I was dismayed to find a black '32 Deuce Coupe parked near the break in the Cyclone fence which everyone used to access the quarry. The shattered headlights and taillights had been replaced.

"Morris Engdahl's car," Danny said.

"He's probably out here torturing ducks," I said.

Jake turned back disappointed. "Let's go home."

Danny and Lee turned their bikes with him.

"Not me," I said. "I came here to swim." I walked my bike to the fence and popped the kickstand down.

Jake opened his mouth then closed it then opened and closed it again and not a word came out. Like a fish trying to suck air.

"I don't know," Danny said. He sat astride his bike and looked with great uncertainty at the others.

Lee said, "You're really going?"

"Hell, just watch me." I ducked through the break in the fence and walked along a path worn in the weeds, walked slowly. In a minute I heard the sound of the others running to catch up.

At the western edge of the quarry was a large flat table of red rock that stood half a dozen feet above the water and was surrounded by willows that curtained it from view. This was the favorite place for swimming because the water dropped immediately and deeply and you could jump and dive from the rock without worrying about what might be under the surface and when you were ready to climb out there were natural steps and handholds in the face of the rock. I heard music coming from the willows, the tinny sound of a transistor radio on which Roy Orbison was singing *Running Scared*. We walked silently and in single file along the trail and when we reached the willows I held up my hand signaling the others to stop and I crept forward.

They lay on a big blanket that had been spread over the wide flat ledge of rock. Morris Engdahl in his white swimming trunks had pretty much glued himself to a girl who wore a red bathing suit and had long blond hair. On top of a cooler sat a couple of bottles of beer and the transistor radio which was now playing Del Shannon's *Runaway*. While I stood watching from the shadows of the willows Morris Engdahl's left hand crawled over the girl's right breast like a big white spider and began to knead the fabric of her suit. In response she arched her back and pressed harder against him.

Though we were trying to be quiet Engdahl must have heard us because he turned his head in our direction. "Jesus, if it ain't Frankfarter," he said. "And Howdy D-D-D-Doody. And a couple of Mouseketeers. Getting a good eyeful?"

"We just came to swim," I said.

Morris continued to lie atop the girl. "Yeah well we were here ahead of you," he said. "So beat it."

"There's lots of room."

"Let's g-g-g-go," Jake said.

"That's a g-g-g-good idea," Engdahl said with a laugh.

"Come on, Frank," Danny said.

"No. We can swim here. There's lots of room."

Engdahl shook his head and finally rolled off the girl. "Not the way I see it," he said.

I gestured to the others to follow me. "We'll go around to the other side," I told them.

"I don't want them here at all, Morrie," the girl said. She sat up and her breasts in her red suit stuck out big as traffic cones. Her lips were a ruby pout. She reached for one of the beers on the cooler.

"You heard her," Engdahl said. "Get lost."

"You get lost," I said. "It's a free country."

"Who are these little creeps, Morrie?"

"His sister is Ariel Drum."

"Ariel Drum?" The girl's face took on a look as if she'd just bit into a sandwich made of cow dung. "God, what a skag."

"She's not a skag," I shot back brilliantly, not entirely sure what the word even meant.

"Listen, you little shit," Engdahl said. "Just because it's a rich boy putting it to your sister, that don't mean she ain't a skag."

"Nobody's putting it to her," I said and stepped toward Engdahl with my hands fisted. I spat out at the girl, "You're the skag."

"You going to let him call me that, Morrie?"

Engdahl got to his feet which were bare. He was a thin guy and white as biscuit dough but he was a head taller than me and had probably been in his share of fights and he didn't look at all reluctant to bust my face wide open. In a swift panic of thought I figured I had two choices. One was to run. The other was to do what I did, which was to lower my shoulder and charge Morris Engdahl. I hit him square in the stomach, putting behind it the full force of my hundred and thirty pounds. I caught him off guard and together we tumbled into the water. I came up sputtering and swam fast back to the rock and climbed up before Engdahl had a chance to get his hands on me. I danced back to where the others stood and I spun around expecting Engdahl to be right behind me. He wasn't. He was still in the water, flailing desperately.

"He can't swim," the girl cried at us. She was on her knees, bent low toward the water, and I could see a good deal of her breasts and for a moment that view was far more riveting than the question of Morris Engdahl's fate. In the next moment Jake was shaking a dead willow branch that was a good eight feet long in my face. I grabbed it and leaped to the edge of the rock and extended the end toward Engdahl.

I yelled, "Grab it!"

His eyes had gone mostly white and his arms beat at the water around him shattering the surface into flying diamonds and he was coughing hard and I was afraid he was beyond having sense enough to save himself. But he managed to grasp the end of the branch. I pulled and the girl grabbed the branch too and pulled with me and together we hauled Engdahl back to the rock where his hands found purchase. He held to the stone a long time with most of him still in the water while he caught his breath then he began a slow climb out. He reached the top of the rock where I stood dripping wet in my shorts and T-shirt and sneakers. All of us stared at him in wordless fixation. His breathing was deep and raspy and his eyes held a desperate look. He brushed the long black hair out of his face.

He sprang forward and grabbed me. He took two big fistfuls of my T-shirt, squeezing the thin cotton so viciously that he wrung out water. His lips were pressed tightly together and I was amazed he could speak through them but he did. He said, "I'm going to kill you."

I looked into his face, into eyes that were a dark menacing blue and so completely abandoned to anger that there was in them not the slightest glimmer of reason and I knew I was dead.

"Let him g-g-g-g-go!" Jake yelled.

And my friends echoed, "Let him go!"

The girl with the mesmerizing breasts cried, "Morrie, don't!" When he didn't respond she stepped close and pushed herself against us both in a kind of wedging maneuver meant, I suppose, to separate Engdahl's hands from my shirt. It was a surreal moment. Death looked me in the face but all I could feel was the warm press and yield of that girl's breast against my shoulder. It was as if in the second before dying I'd been allowed to glimpse heaven and I was almost okay with my fate. "Morrie," she purred in a deep-throated way that spoke to something instinctive and sexually primal in every male there. "Morrie, baby, let him go."

Engdahl was many things. Crude. Ignorant. Callous. Self-absorbed and at the moment embarrassed and angry. But he was also nineteen and one element of his being topped all others and with it the blonde had him hooked. I felt his fists soften and then release their grip on my T-shirt. He shot out a deep final breath like a horse clearing its nostrils and he stepped back. The girl stepped away too and stood in such an enticing pose that Morris Engdahl couldn't take his eyes off her.

That was my opening. I charged him again and shoved him brutally. He stumbled back and once more toppled from the rock into the water below. I stood at the edge looking down as he sputtered and splashed and this time was able on his own to grasp the safety of the rock and begin to pull himself out.

I yelled, "Run!" and turned and fled from the quarry with the others at my heels. We raced as if the Devil himself was in pursuit. We pounded the worn path to the fence, squeezed through the breach, leaped onto our bikes, and shot down the ruts toward the main road to town.

"He'll catch us!" Danny shouted as he pedaled for his life. "He'll run us down!"

Which was probably true. In his Deuce Coupe Engdahl would be on us within minutes.

"Follow me!" I yelled and veered out of the ruts and bounced through the tall wild grass of the field that lay between the quarry and the road. I made desperately for one of the piles of spoil rock that had been dumped in the empty acreage and I shot behind it and threw my bike down so that it was hidden in the grass. After me came Danny and Lee and Jake all of whom did as I'd done and together we hunkered behind the jumble of stone blocks with our hearts kicking at our sternums. In a minute we heard the roar of the Ford engine from behind the line of birch trees. The Deuce Coupe shot past with Engdahl at the wheel and the blonde at his side. The black hot rod with fire painted along its length hit the pavement, squealed left toward town, and disappeared with Engdahl in pursuit of four boys he would not find that day.

We looked at each other and allowed ourselves at last to breathe and then we began to laugh and fell onto our backs in the grass and howled in relief and triumph. We'd bested Morris Engdahl who was many things. Tough. Mean. Vengeful. And, most important to us that summer afternoon, blessedly stupid.

15

That evening my mother and Ariel left the house in the Packard to attend the final rehearsal of the chorale that Ariel had
composed and that was intended to be the highlight of the
Independence Day celebration in Luther Park. Dad had played tennis
that afternoon with one of his fellow clergy in town, a Catholic priest
named Father Peter Driscoll. My father called him Pete. The rest of
us called him Father Peter. Dad had invited him to dinner after their
match and because my mother and Ariel were not home he'd bought
broasted chicken and French fries and coleslaw at the Wagon Wheel
Drive-In and all the males of the household along with Father Peter
dined informally at the kitchen table.

I liked Father Peter. He was young and told a lot of jokes and
was good looking. With his red hair he reminded me of a picture I'd
seen of President Kennedy on the cover of *Life*. He'd gone to Notre
Dame where he'd played shortstop for the university baseball team
and he talked knowledgeably about the game and was excited about
the Twins. At the end of the meal, Jake and I were put to work doing
the dishes while Dad and Father Peter still dressed in their tennis
whites went out to the front porch where they both packed pipes and
sat and smoked.

When we finished the dishes, Jake said, "What do you want to do?"

"I don't know," I said. "Nothing I guess."

Jake went upstairs to work on a model airplane he was building. I figured maybe I'd talk to Gus about Danny's uncle and maybe about Morris Engdahl while I was at it. There was something else I wanted to talk to somebody about, something that since the episode at the quarry had been bothering me, but I wasn't sure Gus was the guy. It didn't matter because I looked out the front window and saw that his motorcycle wasn't in the church parking lot. Through the screen I could hear Dad and Father Peter talking. The priest was saying, "I'm just telling you what I've heard, Nathan. New Bremen's a small town. People talk."

"Your Catholic congregation talks about the wife of the Methodist minister?" My father sounded slightly amused.

"My parishioners talk about everything and everyone, Nathan. Some of them grew up with Ruth and frankly they were surprised when they learned she'd married a preacher. She was, I understand, pretty fierce and wild in her youth."

"Still is, Pete. But when she married me I wasn't a minister. She married a cocky law student who thought he was going to set the courtroom on fire and make millions in the process. The war, well, that changed things. She didn't sign on for the job she has now. But she does it to the best of her ability."

"She drinks, Nathan."

"In the privacy of her own home."

"She smokes cigarettes."

"Every woman in every movie I've ever seen has smoked cigarettes. A good many of the women in my own congregation smoke in private. Ruth simply chooses not to hide it."

"Worst of all, they say she shuns the activities of the WSCS."

The WSCS, the Women's Society of Christian Service, was an important organization in the church, and the women of my father's congregations took great pride in their work on its behalf.

"She puts all her energy into the music programs for three churches," my father said. "That's where her heart is."

"You don't have to convince me, Nathan. I like Ruth and I love her spirit and I think what she's achieved musically for this community and for the churches you serve is nothing short of miraculous. But I'm not a member of your congregation and I'm not the one bending your district superintendent's ear."

There was quiet on the porch. Then I heard a train horn blare a warning and for a full minute after that a loud freight rumbled through on the tracks a block away and when it had passed my father said, "She won't change. I wouldn't ask her to."

"I'm not advising that you should. I just thought you might want to know what folks are saying."

"I know what they say, Pete."

"Ah, Nathan, it's so much easier to be married to the Church."

"But the Church won't scratch your back when it itches or snuggle up to you on a cold night."

Both men laughed and Father Peter said, "Time to go. Thanks for dinner."

Later that evening I told my father I was going to the Heights but I didn't tell him why. He looked up from his reading and said, "Be home before dark."

I left the house and walked up Tyler Street and a minute later I heard the slap of sneakers on the pavement behind me and Jake ran to my side.

"Where you going?" he said a little out of breath.

"Uptown," I said. "Looking for Gus."

"Can I come?"

"I don't care."

Jake fell in step beside me. He said, "Are you going to tell Gus about Morris Engdahl?"

"Maybe."

"I've been thinking, Frank. Maybe you should tell him you're sorry."

"Engdahl? Fat chance."

"If he catches you he might hurt you or something." Jake was quiet for a moment then he said, "Or me."

"You don't have to worry," I said. "I'm the one who pushed him in the water."

We crossed the tracks and Jake picked up a rock and threw it at the crossing sign and it hit with a crack like a small gunshot. "I hate it when he calls me Howdy Doody," he said.

We were both silent after that, thinking our own thoughts. I was thinking that although I'd shrugged off Jake's concern for his safety it was not an unreasonable fear. Morris Engdahl struck me as exactly the kind of guy who if he had a grudge against you would gladly beat up your brother. We turned off Tyler onto Main Street and headed toward the shops of town. It was a few minutes before eight o'clock and the sun was caught in the branches of the trees and the light across the lawns was yellow-orange and broken. From down the streets that we crossed came the occasional rattle of firecrackers and the pop of bottle rockets but otherwise the evening was calm and quiet. I wasn't thinking only about Morris Engdahl but also about his accusation and that of his girlfriend, that Ariel was a skag. I didn't like the word. I didn't like the sound of it or the feel as it had leaped off my own tongue that afternoon or the place in my head that it had unlocked. As nearly as I could figure, *skag* referred to a girl who had sex with guys, maybe especially creepy guys like Morris Engdahl. Tying that particular activity to Ariel in that particular way wrenched my gut.

I was not ignorant of sex. I simply associated it with married people and I understood that men and women who indulged in sexual intercourse before marriage were doomed in many ways and I couldn't imagine Ariel doomed in any way. Yet in the dark corners of the place so newly opened to my thinking there were already items I'd thoughtlessly stored there. Ariel's late night rendezvous. Her sudden reluctance to leave New Bremen for Juilliard which had been the dream of her life. Her inexplicable tears when I'd caught her alone recently. In the hours since I'd left the quarry I'd come to realize that not only was she in love with Karl Brandt but she'd probably been sleeping with him as well. At thirteen I had no idea what to do with that.

Then as if conjured by the devil of my own thinking Karl Brandt pulled alongside us in his red Triumph with the top down.

"Hey, you two goofballs," he cried with friendly familiarity, "where you going?"

I stared at him, trying to fix in my understanding the new contours of his existence in my family's life. What I knew without doubt was that I liked Karl Brandt. I liked him still. I'd seen no arrogance in him, had never felt patronized by him, and in all the times I'd been around him when he was a guest in our home I hadn't once sensed in his feelings for Ariel anything but genuine affection. But what did I know?

"Looking for Gus," Jake said.

"Haven't seen him," Karl said. "But I'm headed up to the college to pick up Ariel after the rehearsal. You guys up for a spin in my little red demon here?"

"Heck, yes," Jake said.

Karl leaned over and popped the door.

There was no backseat so Jake and I were forced to squeeze into the passenger's seat together.

Karl said, "All set?"

He shot away from the curb and almost immediately the wind was a fury all around us.

We didn't go directly to the college which was on the hill not far from the hospital that overlooked Luther Park. Karl zipped all over New Bremen for a while and then hit a couple of the back roads beyond the town limits where he really leaned on the accelerator. The wind howled and Jake like a madman howled with it and Karl's gold hair flew around like corn silk in a tornado and he laughed with genuine pleasure but I found myself holding back as I looked at him, marveling at the ease of his life and at the same time feeling the slow invasion of a resentment that had never been there before.

As we pulled back into town and Karl braked to a reasonable speed and the wind died around us I asked, "Are you going to marry Ariel?"

It took a moment for him to swing his gaze toward me and I thought I sensed in his hesitation something that had nothing to do with careful driving but was born of a reluctance to look me in the eye.

"We haven't talked about marriage, Frankie."

"You don't want to marry her?"

"We both have other plans right now."

"College?"

"Yeah, college."

"Ariel doesn't want to go to Juilliard."

"I know. She's told me."

"Do you know why?"

"Look, Frankie, this isn't a discussion I want to have with you. This is between Ariel and me."

"Do you love her?"

He looked at the road and I knew it was because he could not look at me.

"She loves you," I said.

"Frankie, you've got no idea what you're talking about."

"She told me love is complicated. It seems easy enough to me. You love each other and you get married and that's how it works."

"Not always, Frankie. Not always." He said this with such heaviness that he sounded crushed.

The college was small and its primary purpose was to turn out Lutheran ministers. It had an excellent music program and a fine auditorium which was where we found my mother and Ariel and to my great surprise Emil Brandt. The rehearsal was just ending when we arrived and the singers who were a mix of college students and townspeople were dispersing. My mother and Ariel and Brandt all stood together at a baby grand piano that had been set on the stage. I knew that Brandt had agreed to play for the chorale and that his participation had been a huge part of the publicity for the event but I figured that considering his recent brush with death the idea had been scrapped. Not so, it appeared.

Karl bounded up the steps and greeted his uncle and my mother and gave Ariel a peck on the cheek and said to her, "All set?"

"You two go on," my mother told them. "I'll drive Emil home."

Karl took Ariel's hand and drew her off the stage. As he passed where we stood in the aisle he said, "You guys are on your own getting home."

On the stage my mother and Brandt stood together and I had the sense that she was waiting for her sons to leave so that she could be alone with him. She wore a pair of dungarees and a blue denim shirt over a white top and she'd bunched the shirttails around her waist and tied them in a loose knot in a way that I'd seen Judy Garland do in a movie about show people.

"Frank," she said to me in a dramatic tone, "you and Jake better get started if you're going to make it home before dark."

Jake in obedience turned without a word and started out of the auditorium. The lights had begun to wink off leaving the seats in darkness. I remained a moment longer, certain that something in that auditorium was unfinished.

From the stage my mother said, "Go on, Frank."

I followed Jake into the lobby which was lit now by only a few dim overheads. My brother said, "I have to go to the bathroom."

I pointed down the hall. "That way," I told him. "I'll wait here."

The door to the auditorium stood open and the acoustics inside were excellent. My mother and Emil Brandt were in deep conversation on the stage and even in the lobby where I stood waiting for Jake I could hear every word.

Brandt said, "It's a beautiful piece she's composed, Ruth."

"She's learned a great deal from you, Emil."

"She was born with talent. Yours."

"She'll do a lot more with hers than I ever did with mine."

I heard a simple melody tapped out on the piano and then Brandt said, "Remember that?"

"Of course. You wrote it for me."

"A present for your sixteenth birthday."

"And two days later you were gone to New York without a word of good-bye."

"If I knew then what I know now maybe I'd have made different decisions. Maybe I wouldn't have this face of mine and I would still have eyes and I would have children like yours. She's so much like you, Ruth. I hear you in her voice, I feel you in her touch."

"She adores you, Emil. And I will always love you."

"No, you love Nathan."

"And you."

"Differently."

"Yes. Now."

"He's a lucky man."

"And you, Emil, are a man much blessed too. Can't you see that?"

"I have moments of such darkness, Ruth. Such darkness you can't imagine."

"Then call me, Emil. When the darkness comes, call me. I'll be there for you, I swear it."

In the course of their conversation I'd drifted slowly to the auditorium door and I could see them on the stage. They sat together on the piano bench. My mother's hand was pressed to Brandt's left cheek, the one bubbled with thick scar tissue. As I watched, Brandt's own hand rose and covered hers.

"I love you," he said.

"You look so tired," she replied, then took his hand and kissed it gently and said, "I should get you home."

She stood up. Like a man old beyond his years, Emil Brandt rose with her.

"What's it mean? Skag?"

Jake lay in his bed in the dark on his side of the room.

"It doesn't mean anything," I said. I'd been lying there awhile in my own bed with my hands behind my head staring up at the ceiling and thinking about the blonde with the red bathing suit and trying my best to recall exactly the image of her breasts when she bent over on the rock that afternoon.

"Is it something bad?"

"It's nothing."

"The way that girl at the quarry said it it's something."

I was surprised that Jake brought it up. Except for being worried about what punishment Morris Engdahl might be contemplating for us he hadn't talked about the incident at the quarry. In a way I'd been glad. I'd been hoping the whole skag thing had gone over his head. It hadn't.

I considered trying to detour his wonderment but I knew that when Jake was after something he stuck with it until he was satisfied and I was concerned that he might try getting the answers from our parents and that would be disastrous on so many levels that I finally settled on dishing him the truth. Or as much of the truth as I understood.

"It's a girl with loose morals," I said trying, I suppose, to frame it in a kind of Victorian way because it sounded not so terrible.

"Loose morals," Jake said. He was quiet for a while then asked, "What did he mean when he said the rich boy was putting it to her?"

What the words brought to my mind was an incident I'd observed earlier that spring when I'd gone with my father to visit a member of his congregation, a man named Kaczamarek who had a large farm with lots of livestock. While my father stood in the yard and spoke with Kaczamarek, I wandered down to the pasture where there were horses grazing. As I watched, a roan stallion approached and mounted a black mare. His penis was the size of my forearm and it disappeared entirely inside the rear of the mare. When the mating was finished he slipped from her back and returned to his grazing as if what had occurred was of no great importance.

I tried to wipe that image from my mind.

"He meant they were making out," I said. "You know, kissing and stuff."

"Kissing's not bad, is it?"

"No," I said. "It isn't."

"Have you ever kissed a girl?"

"Yeah. Well, actually no. She kissed me."

"Who?"

"Lorrie Diedrich."

"What was it like?"

"It was quick. I didn't feel much."

"You didn't kiss her back?"

"It was at the fair last year," I explained. "She'd been licking a licorice ice cream cone and she had this black mustache. She looked like Groucho Marx."

Downstairs I could hear my mother playing the piano, going over and over the music for Ariel's chorale on the Fourth. She always got nervous before the performances she directed and playing seemed to help.

"That girl," Jake said. "The one with Morris Engdahl. She was pretty. They were kissing like crazy. Is she a skag?"

My mother finished playing and the house lapsed into silence and the only sound came from outside where the crickets chirred a chorus that was probably part of some crazy bug mating ritual.

"Yeah," I said trying to rid myself of the image of her breasts. "She's a skag."

16

ndependence Day arrived with the concussion of early fireworks as if a great battle had begun. When I got up my father had already breakfasted and gone to his office in the church where he kept the windows closed and the volume on his phonograph turned up high so the music would drown out much of the boom and rattle. My mother was up earlier than usual, the result of her anxiety about the chorale performance that evening. She was pacing the floor in the living room with a cigarette wedged between her fingers and trailing smoke behind her. When she saw me come down the stairs she stopped and her blue eyes locked on me.

"Frankie," she said. "I need you to go to Emil Brandt's house. Ariel's there. Tell her I have to talk to her right away."

"Can't you call?"

"I've tried. No one answers. I need you to go."

"Can I eat something first?"

"Yes but quickly," she said.

I heard the stairs above me creak and I looked back and saw Jake in his pajamas coming down after me. "I'll go too," he said.

"No, I need you to do something else for me, Jake." She went to the dining room table and picked up a sheaf of papers. "Take these to Bob Hartwig's house. He's expecting them."

Hartwig was the editor of the weekly *New Bremen Courier*.

"They're the names of everyone performing tonight," she said, "and a little bit of history about the piece and about Ariel and, oh, well, everything. I was supposed to have them to him yesterday but simply forgot. He'll need them for the article he's writing about all the celebrations today."

"I'd rather go get Ariel," he said.

"You'll do what I've asked."

My mother when she gave a directive was not inclined to look kindly on objection. Her accomplishments with the choirs in our churches and with the summer musicals in the park had become nearly legendary but they were achieved in large measure because she ruled with an iron fist. When Jake pouted at her order she leveled on him a death-dealing look.

I knew Jake was pissed and that later he would bitch and moan to me but to my mother he simply replied, "Yes, m-m-ma'am."

We fixed ourselves cereal and Jake ate silently and glowered at me though I had nothing to do with his situation. For my part I kind of enjoyed his misery.

We got dressed and headed up to the Heights. It was a great day for the Fourth, sunny and with the promise that it would stay that way and already it was hot. At the old Sibley Road I turned to the right and separated from Jake to head toward the Brandts' house which was half a mile distant. Jake slogged on up the Heights toward Austin Street where Mr. Hartwig lived. When I looked back he'd stopped and was throwing rocks angrily at a telephone pole and I figured that in his mind it was probably our mother.

Ariel had taken the Packard but when I arrived at the Brandt house I didn't see it parked anywhere. I went to the garage and peeked through a window. The only automobile inside was the black Chrysler that nobody ever seemed to drive. I mounted the steps of the front porch and knocked on the door. No one came. I called out, "Ariel! Mr. Brandt!" I received no answer and stood on the porch deep in indecision. Considering the state my mother was in I knew that if I returned home without Ariel I'd be eaten alive. I knocked again and called once more and then thought that even if Lise couldn't hear me she probably knew where her brother was and my sister. I realized that it would have been better for Jake to have come instead because Lise would be able to communicate with him more easily. But I was the one who was there so I opened the screen door and, entering the Brandt home, I stepped into one of the most bizarre moments of my life.

I hadn't been inside the house enough to know it well and I found myself prowling like a burglar. I crept to the kitchen which was far cleaner and more orderly than the one my mother kept. I looked through the screen door into the backyard at the large lovely garden but no one was there. I returned to the living room and stood a moment knowing I should check the back room where Ariel transcribed the life story of Emil Brandt but feeling more and more certain that I was trespassing in an unconscionable way. I'd almost decided to leave and take my chances with my mother when I heard an odd utterance from one of the rooms far down the hallway. It was a soft guttural cooing and I wondered if maybe the Brandts had some bird in a cage somewhere.

"Is anybody there?" I called.

The cooing went on a moment or two more then stopped and I thought someone would answer but no one did and the gentle dove-like song began again.

I've compared the sound to that of a bird but in truth it wasn't like any bird I'd ever heard before, or any animal for that matter, and once the mystery had presented itself I was a goner. I had to know.

I eased my way down the hall one soft and utterly silent step at a time keenly aware that the Brandts' farmhouse though renovated was still an abode of ancient construction, like the house that served as our parsonage, and at any moment my foot could hit a loose board that would cry out like a kicked cat. There was a beautiful runner over the floor into which had been woven an Oriental scene of trees with bare black branches where bluebirds sat and I tiptoed on those thin branches and on the mute bluebirds toward a door that was slightly ajar at the end of the dark hallway. I put my eye to the gap in the doorway and saw half a bed neatly made and on the far wall a window with gauzy curtains that muted the morning sunlight but I couldn't see the source of the noise. I reached out and nudged the door open farther.

I had never before seen a fully naked woman in the flesh. Not even the photographs I'd ogled in *Playboy* a few days earlier prepared me for what I beheld in Lise Brandt's bedroom on Independence Day in 1961. The room was a glory of flowers cut from her garden and bursting from vases set on every flat surface and the air was powerfully redolent with their fragrance. Her back was to me. She'd let her hair down and it fell in a long brown flow over her shoulders. She stood at an ironing board with a hot iron in her hand and she bent to the work of pressing her brother's freshly laundered clothing which was in a basket near her feet. She was the source of the cooing, a sound full of contentment as if the hot tedious labor in which she was engaged was the most delightful pastime imaginable. With each stroke of the iron she swayed dramatically as if to music only she could hear. I watched the strong muscles of her shoulders and back and buttocks tense and release and every part of her body seemed alive in itself and not just an element of some larger configuration of flesh.

I was stunned but not senseless and I knew that any moment I might be discovered. I remembered well the near-catastrophic incident in the garden only a few days earlier when I'd accidentally touched her. I backed out of the room and crept silently down the hallway though I could have screamed bloody murder and it would have made no difference. I stepped outside onto the front porch where I sat with my hands on my lap waiting for Ariel's return.

Twenty minutes later Lise Brandt appeared at the screen door fully clothed. She'd tied her hair back in a ponytail. She eyed me suspiciously and using that voice I knew she hated she asked, "Wha you wan?"

"I came for Ariel," I said facing her so that she could read my lips.

"Gone. Driving with Emil," she said in a flat voice and slurring the words she could not hear.

"Do you know where they've gone?"

She shook her head.

"Do you know when they'll be back?"

Another shake. Then she asked, "Where's Jake?"

"On an errand for my mother."

She stared at me. Then she said, "Wan lemonade?"

"No thanks. I'd better be going."

She nodded and, finished with me, turned away.

I walked home trying to set in my mind so that they would be there forever every detail of Lise Brandt naked and ecstatic at her ironing board. My mother when she did the ironing at our house did it grudgingly and was always in a foul temper. But she did it fully clothed and I couldn't help wondering if that made a difference.

Ariel had been driving with Emil Brandt at his request. She'd taken him on a long swing that morning through the river valley with the windows of the Packard down so that he could absorb the summer day. He was, he told her, ripe for inspiration. He needed the feel of the country air in his face, the smell of the land in his nostrils, the sound of the birds and the rustle of the cornfields singing in his ears. Emil Brandt who'd written no music in a long time claimed he was ready to create something great, a celebration of the Minnesota River valley. His brush with death, he told Ariel, had changed his outlook. He was more inspired than he'd been in years. He was ready to knuckle down and compose again.

She related this to us all at lunch around the kitchen table while we ate fried bologna sandwiches with chips and cherry Kool-Aid. My father said, "That's wonderful to hear."

But my mother was skeptical. She said, "Just like that?"

My father put down his glass and shrugged. "Like he says, Ruth, a brush with death. It can change a man dramatically."

"When we last talked, it was clear to me he's still struggling with that darkness of his."

"Work is what he needs to bring him back to happiness," Ariel said.

My mother looked at her. "Is that your opinion?"

"It's what Emil says."

"Can I have another sandwich?" I asked.

"Fry yourself up a slice of bologna," my mother said.

"Me, too," Jake said.

I threw two slices into the frying pan which was still on the stove and started the burner.

"I don't know," my mother said.

"You don't know him," Ariel said.

My mother shot Ariel a look I'd never seen before, edged with meanness. "And you do?"

"Sometimes I think I'm the only one who does," Ariel said. "He's a genius."

"I won't dispute that," my mother said. "But he's a great deal more. I've known him all my life, Ariel. He's a very complicated man."

"Not really," Ariel said.

My mother said, "Oh?" That one word. Like an ice cube against bare skin. I glanced at Ariel who clearly was not about to back down.

"I've put his life story onto paper," Ariel said. "I know him."

My mother propped her elbows on the table and folded her hands beneath her chin and stared at Ariel and asked, "And who, pray tell, is Emil Brandt?"

"A wounded man," Ariel replied without hesitation.

My mother laughed but there was a chill to it. "Ariel, dear, Emil has always been a wounded man. He's always been a man too misunderstood, too little appreciated, too bound by our provincialism here, too everything that did not advance the wants, needs, and desires of his own often selfish heart."

Jake left the table and came to the stove. I figured he was moving to safety.

"You told me once that greatness demanded selfishness," Ariel shot back. "And anyway he's not selfish."

"He's simply great?" Mother laughed again. "Oh, sweetheart, you're so young. You have so much to learn."

"You throw my age at me like it was some kind of handicap."

"It is in a way. Someday you'll see that."

My father held up his hand as if to make peace, but before he could speak Ariel said angrily to my mother, "I thought you were his friend."

"I am. I have always been. But that doesn't mean I don't see him as he is. He has many faults, Ariel."

"Who doesn't?"

"I've seen him in moods so dark I've wondered if he would ever come out into the light again. It's amazing to me that he hasn't tried suicide before."

"He has," Ariel said.

My mother looked at her in a startled way. "You know this how?"

"It's in his memoir."

"He's never said anything to me about it."

"And maybe there's a reason for that." Ariel's eyes were hard and sharp in the way of railroad spikes. She scooted her chair back and rose to leave the table.

My mother said, "Where are you going?"

"I don't know. For a walk."

"Good. You need to cool off. You have an important performance tonight."

"Fuck the performance," Ariel said and turned and stormed out the door.

Ariel had never sworn that way before, never with that particular word anyway, and it seemed to have stunned us all. The only sound was the sizzle of the bologna in the frying pan.

Then my mother shot back her own chair and stood as if to go after Ariel.

"Don't, Ruth," my father said and laid a hand on her arm. "Let her walk it off."

"I won't tolerate her disrespect, Nathan."

"There will be time for her to apologize and she will, Ruth. You know it. There's a lot of pressure on her today, on both of you."

My mother stood looking at the screen door and her mouth was a line stitched across her face. Then I saw her relax. "You're right," she said. She looked down at my father. "You're right." Then she said with a whisper of astonishment, "Emil tried to kill himself before."

She left the table and went to the living room and a moment later the sound of the piano filled the house.

17

There was a parade that afternoon as there was every Fourth of July. The high school band marched in their braided uniforms and so did members of the VFW, many of them dressed in the military finery in which they'd served. The firemen drove their trucks, and the mayor and other city politicians rode in cars and waved, and there were flatbeds made into floats and hauled behind pickups cleaned and waxed for the day, and the Highsteppers rode their beribboned show horses, and even kids joined in the parade, pulling their pets or small siblings behind them in Radio Flyer wagons decked out in crepe of red, white, and blue. The procession marched along Main Street between cheering throngs and turned at Luther Avenue and continued a quarter mile to Luther Park which was full of vendors selling cotton candy and hot dogs and bratwurst and mini-donuts and helium-filled balloons. Every organization in town seemed to have a table where they hawked homemade pickles or baked goods or beautifully crocheted antimacassars and pot holders. There were games with prizes and there were polka bands and a temporary dance floor that had been laid out on the grass. There were shows in the band shell that included local musicians and storytellers and performers of odd feats. And there was a beer tent courtesy of the Brandt brewery.

Jake and I watched the parade and with some of the money

we'd earned mowing my grandfather's lawn we bought stuff to eat and tried our hands at ring toss and knocking down milk bottles in hopes of winning a stuffed toy that we really didn't want. We ran into Danny O'Keefe and he joined us. When the sun dropped from the sky and evening settled over the park the crowd drifted to the band shell behind which had been set the fireworks for a huge display that would follow the performance of Ariel's chorale and crown the day. All the folding chairs were occupied by the time Jake and Danny and I arrived and we leaned against the trunk of a big elm on the periphery but still with a good view. Stage lights came on and the mayor stepped to a podium and gave a brief speech and then a girl named Cindy Westrom came up to read an essay about freedom that she'd written for a contest sponsored by the VFW and that had won her twenty-five dollars. I said I had to go to the bathroom and left Jake and Danny and headed toward the portable toilets that had been set up near the beer tent.

I waited in a short line and while I stood there I saw Morris Engdahl come out of the tent. He was alone and sipping his beer, eyeing the crowd over the lip of the cup as if he expected to fight us all. I turned my back and a moment later a toilet became free and I shot for it. I took care of business and even though it smelled pretty bad in there I lingered inside for a couple of minutes more to give Engdahl a chance to move on. When I stepped out a man shoved past me into the toilet dragging a kid of about five who was holding his crotch in desperation. I looked around carefully, relieved to find no sign at all of Morris Engdahl.

Back at the elm tree I found that Jake and Danny had been joined by Warren Redstone. They weren't talking, just standing there together staring at the stage of the band shell where a girl in a drum majorette outfit was twirling a baton that had flames at both ends. It was a pretty good trick and when I joined the group I watched the girl too and didn't feel like I needed to say anything. The flaming baton was followed by a banjo player who plucked out a rousing rendition of *Yankee Doodle* while another guy tap-danced like crazy. We all applauded wildly. Then a woman who taught drama at the high school got up and read the whole Declaration of Independence and right in the middle of it someone grabbed my arm and swung me around and I found myself staring into the angry besotted eyes of Morris Engdahl.

"I knew I'd find you, you little shithole," he said and tried to pull me into the gathering dark beyond the edge of the crowd.

A huge hand shot out and wrenched Engdahl's grip from my arm and Warren Redstone stepped between Engdahl and me. He said, "Are you the kind of man who fights only boys? Or would you be interested in fighting a man?"

Danny's great-uncle may have been old but he was tall and powerful looking and he glared down at Morris Engdahl with a look hard and pointed enough to split rocks. Engdahl took a step back as if he'd already been struck a blow and he stared up into Redstone's dark unblinking eyes and it was clear that he had nothing in him to match the old man's grit. He said, "This is between me and the kid."

"No, I'm between you and the kid. You want to get to the kid, you come through me."

For a moment I thought Engdahl might do something stupid. At least it seemed to me that taking on Warren Redstone would be stupid. But Engdahl's cowardice was greater than his stupidity. He backed up a few steps and pointed a finger at me. "Dead," he said. "You're dead." Then he turned and vanished into the dark in which he'd sought to drag me.

Redstone watched him go. "A friend?" he said.

"He wouldn't let us swim in the quarry," I replied, "so I shoved him in. Pissed him off pretty good."

"You shoved him in?" Redstone looked at Danny. "You were there?"

"Yes, sir," Danny said.

He looked me over again, differently this time. "Drum," he said as if my name pleased him. "You sure you don't have any Sioux in you?"

Fifty yards away the singers began to mount the stage of the band shell and take their positions on the risers. I didn't do an exact count but there were easily three dozen. The crowd started to quiet and a few seconds later my mother led Emil Brandt by the hand up the steps to the grand piano placed there for him. This was a true rarity, Emil Brandt in a public performance, and the crowd broke into applause. He kept the scarred side of his face turned away from the audience and seated himself at the piano and my mother went to the center of the stage and everything grew quiet. I could still hear people laughing faintly at the food stands and someone shouting along Luther Avenue and from the Flats in the distance the howl of a horn as a train approached the crossing on Tyler Street but my mother's voice rose above them all.

"Thank you for turning out today to celebrate our nation's birth. The history of this country has been written with the blood of patriots and the sweat of farmers and laborers and men and women no different from all of us here this evening. It began with a dream conceived by our forefathers, a dream every bit as alive and vibrant and promising today as it was to those brave patriots one hundred and eighty-five years ago. To celebrate that dream and the nation built upon it, my daughter Ariel has composed a chorale titled *The Freedom Road*, which the New Bremen Town Singers, accompanied by our town's world-famous composer and piano virtuoso Emil Brandt, are proud to perform for you for the first time anywhere this evening."

My mother turned to her singers and raised her hands and held them poised a moment, then called out to Brandt, "Now, Emil." The chorale began with Brandt doing a slow gallop of his fingers on the keyboard that gradually increased in tempo until it was a furious flight and the singers chimed in with the urgent cry, "To arms, to arms!" Ariel's chorale covered the history of the nation from the Revolution through the Korean conflict and celebrated the pioneers and soldiers and visionaries who created a nation from, as Ariel had written for the chorus, the raw dirt of God's imagination. My mother conducted with dramatic flourish and the music was electric and Brandt on the piano was inspired and the voices of the singers pouring from the white cup of that band shell made the whole thing intoxicating. It lasted twelve minutes and when it was finished the audience went crazy. They stood and applauded and added their cheers and whistles and the sound was like thunder off canyon walls. My mother signaled to Ariel who'd been standing with my father and Karl at the bottom step of the band shell. Ariel climbed the steps and took Emil Brandt's hand to lead him to the center of the stage but he pulled back and remained seated at the piano with his smooth cheek to the audience and he spoke something into Ariel's ear and she went on without him and stood with my mother and together they took their bows. That evening Ariel had worn a beautiful red dress. She wore a gold heart-shaped locket inset with mother-of-pearl and a mother-of-pearl barrette, both of which were heirlooms. She wore a gold watch that had been a graduation gift from my parents. And at that moment she wore a smile that could have been seen from the moon. I thought my sister must be the most special person on earth and I knew absolutely she was destined for greatness.

Warren Redstone touched my arm. "That girl's name is Drum," he said. "Any relation?"

"My sister," I called above the din.

He looked at her keenly and nodded. "Pretty enough to be Sioux," he said.

After the fireworks had ended we drifted home, Jake and I. All over New Bremen the celebration continued and the sky was alive with burning blooms of color and from the dark down the cross streets came the rattle of strings of firecrackers. Gus's motorcycle was gone and I suspected he would finish celebrating Independence Day in a bar. The light in my father's church office was on and his windows were closed and the sound of Tchaikovsky bled through the glass. The Packard was not in the garage and I knew that my mother was at a post-chorale celebration with Ariel and Brandt and the New Bremen Town Singers and would not be home until late.

We'd been instructed about our bedtime and we got into our pajamas and hit the sack at ten-thirty. Through the screen of our bedroom window I listened as the sounds died to an occasional distant pop or crackle and I heard my father return from the church and much later through the dim veil of sleep I dreamed the sound of the Packard crushing gravel in our drive and a car door slamming closed.

And even later I woke and heard my father on the telephone and my mother's worried voice prompting him and the dark outside was thick as tar and not even the crickets chirred. I got up and found them downstairs with their faces pinched and tired. I asked what was

wrong and my father said that Ariel had not yet returned and go back
to bed.

Because of my father's occupation I was used to late night urgen-
cies and because I'd witnessed her comings and goings that summer
I was used to Ariel sneaking off in the dark and returning safely before dawn and because I was little more than a child still wrapped in
a soothing blanket of illusion I trusted that my mother and father
together could handle anything and I went back to my bedroom and
drifted selfishly into sleep listening to the distant distraught voices
of my parents while they continued their telephone calls and waited
anxiously for word of their daughter.

18

The next morning I woke to the threat of rain.

I found my parents downstairs in the kitchen with Karl Brandt and Sheriff Gregor and a deputy named Zollee Hauptmann. The sheriff was dressed in jeans and a short-sleeved blue work shirt and his cheeks were red and shiny as if he'd just finished shaving. The deputy wore a uniform. They were drinking coffee at the table and Gregor had a small notebook in front of him, writing as my parents talked. I stood in the doorway to the dining room and they barely noticed me.

Ariel had been with Karl Brandt, I learned as I listened, and with other friends who'd gathered on the river at Sibley Park and built a bonfire on the same stretch of sand where Doyle had blown up the frog with an M-80. There'd been alcohol and everyone was drinking and somewhere along the way they'd lost track of Ariel and no one knew, not even Karl, when she'd gone or where. She'd simply vanished.

Gregor requested the names of the other friends and Karl gave him ten or twelve.

"Was Ariel drinking too?" Gregor asked.

Karl said, "Yes."

"You took her there? To the river?"

"After the party," he said.

"The party with the New Bremen Town Singers?"

"Yes, that one."

"But you didn't bring her home from the shindig at the river. Why not?"

"She wasn't around when I was ready to go."

"Did that concern you?"

"Yes. But I just figured she got a ride with someone else. I was pretty drunk by then."

"You're not old enough to be drinking," Gregor said.

"Yeah, well kind of late to worry about that now."

"Maybe if you hadn't been drinking you'd know where Ariel is."

Karl looked guilty and clammed up.

"Any of your friends that you also noticed gone?"

Karl thought, then shrugged. "People were coming and going all night."

"And she said nothing to you before she left?"

"No," Karl said. "Not about leaving anyway."

"What time did you leave the party?"

"I don't know exactly. Two, two-thirty."

"Did you go straight home?"

"Yes."

From his little notebook Gregor tore out the list he'd made of the names Karl had given him and he handed the sheet to Hauptmann. He said, "Start calling, Zollee."

Hauptmann went outside through the screen door and I heard the engine of his cruiser turn over and he left. To my parents Gregor said, "Does your daughter have any special friends she might have stayed with last night?"

"Yes," my mother said. "We've called them all. No one's seen her."

"Could you give me their names? I'd like to talk to them myself."

"Of course." My mother rattled off six names which Gregor wrote down.

My father got up and went to the coffeepot on the stove and poured himself another cup. He saw me in the doorway and said, "Why don't you go upstairs and get dressed, Frank."

I said, "Where's Ariel?"

"We don't know."

"Hello, Frank," Sheriff Gregor said to me like we were old friends and like he kind of meant it.

"Hi," I said.

"Ariel didn't come home last night," he said. "Your folks are a little worried. Do you have any idea where your sister might be if she's not at home?"

"Mr. Brandt's," I said without even thinking.

"Emil!" My mother said this as if it was a revelation. She jumped up and hurried past me to the telephone in the living room.

"Why Mr. Brandt?" The sheriff looked at me and then at my father.

"They're good friends," my father said. "And he lives very near Sibley Park."

My father sounded hopeful. With his coffee cup in his hand he came to where I stood and looked beyond me to the living room and listened to the telephone conversation my mother had with Emil Brandt.

"She didn't come home last night, Emil," my mother was saying. "I thought maybe she'd stayed at your place." My mother listened and looked down at the floor. "No, no, Karl doesn't know either. They were at Sibley Park, a bonfire on the river. She left and no one knows when or with whom." Mother listened some more, this time with her eyes closed, and when she spoke there was a tremble to her voice that I was pretty sure would lead to tears. "I will, Emil," she said. "When we know something." She hung up and saw my father watching and shook her head and walked to him and laid her cheek against his shoulder and began to cry.

Sheriff Gregor stood up and slipped his notebook into his shirt pocket. He said, "I'll take a couple of men and go on down to Sibley Park and have a look around. Karl, I want you there to point out where all the activity took place. I'll also talk to Ariel's friends my-self and see if they tell me anything different from what they've told you folks. And, listen, in my experience kids turn up. They've done something they're ashamed of or something stupid or they just up and decide on the spur of the moment to drive to the Twin Cities and they come back. Honestly, they come back." He offered us a smile meant to reassure.

"Thank you," my father said. Then he said, "Would you mind if I joined you at the river?"

The sheriff said, "Fine by me. I'm going to stop by my office first. I'll meet you at Sibley Park in half an hour. You too, Karl."

He left and Karl said to my parents, "I'm sorry. I'm really sorry. I should have, I don't know, been more responsible, I guess. I just don't know where she would have gone."

"We'll start at the river," my father said.

I took a step into the kitchen. "Can I go, too?"

My father considered the request, but distractedly. To my surprise he said, "All right."

My mother was drying her eyes and looking lost. "I don't know what to do," she said.

"Pray," my father advised. "And stay here by the phone in case she calls."

Upstairs I found Jake awake but still lying in bed. "What's going on?" he asked.

I slipped out of my pajamas. "Ariel's gone," I said.

"Gone where?"

"Nobody knows." I began dressing from the pile of clothes I'd worn the day before and had left on the floor.

Jake sat up. "Where are you going?"

"Sibley Park. That's where Ariel was last night."

Jake scooted off the bed and shed his pajamas and began to pull on clothes. "I'm coming too," he said.

There was no sun or any promise of sun. The clouds lay thick and gray and gave the sky the feel of a flat rock pressing on the valley. We got to Sibley Park before the sheriff and we stood at the edge of the river where Ariel had last been seen. The sand was spotted with the cold black char of many previous fires. The one that had been kindled the night before was still smoldering. All around it the sand was pitted where people had sat and was littered with empty beer cans and beer bottles and looked like a place of wild revelry.

"Quite a party," my father said.

Karl Brandt put his hands into his pockets and hung his head and didn't reply.

Me, I couldn't conceive that Ariel might be gone for good and I still thought in the way of a child that we were part of an adventure whose end at the moment was a curtain of smoke from which Ariel would somehow emerge and return to us. I stood under that oppressive sky and eyed the disheveled sand and the smoldering char and knew we'd find something that would guide us to an answer. I knew this absolutely and I was eager to begin. I started to walk toward the fire and Jake followed, asking, "What are we looking for?"

"Stop, boys," my father said. "We're not looking for anything yet. We wait for the sheriff."

Which seemed like a waste to me but my father had spoken and Jake and I obeyed.

The sheriff came ten minutes later with two men. One wore a deputy's uniform. The other was a town cop: Doyle. They strode down the path through the cottonwood trees and stood with us on the sand and surveyed the scene.

"Christ, what a mess," the sheriff said. He gave Karl Brandt a look of severe disapproval. "What were you kids thinking?"

Karl shrugged. "It was a party."

"More like a rampage. When we're finished, this gets cleaned up. You and your friends, understand?"

"Yes, sir."

"All right," the sheriff said. "Let's just take a look around the fire first, then we'll spread out and see what we can find on the perimeter. Don't disturb anything. If you find something of interest, give a holler but don't touch it. Clear?"

Everyone nodded including me and Jake.

"Boys," the sheriff said, "stick with your dad. Do what he tells you."

"Sure," I said. And Jake's head bobbed as if on a spring.

For thirty feet in all directions of the burned-out fire the scene was basically the same. I could see where butts had nestled in the sand and feet had dragged and in one spot everything was kicked all to hell like there'd been a fight.

"Morris Engdahl and Hans Hoyle," Karl said when the sheriff asked him about it. "They traded blows over cars."

"Cars?"

Karl shrugged. "Important to them, I guess. They didn't do any real damage."

At the mention of Morris Engdahl, Jake gave me a piercing look. "Tell them, Frank," he said.

"Tell me what?" the sheriff said.

I didn't want to say anything because I figured I'd have to go all the way back to the quarry incident and tell my father that we'd gone to a place we weren't supposed to go but Jake gave my shoulder a nudge and my father and Doyle and the other two men stood looking at me and I knew there was no way around it so I told them pretty much everything. About the quarry and Engdahl chasing us and how at the celebration in Luther Park he'd tried to drag me off into the dark and for a reason I couldn't explain I said, "He didn't like Ariel."

"How do you know that?" the sheriff asked.

"He called her names."

"What did he call her?"

"Skag."

"Anything else?"

"Harelip."

"All right," the sheriff said.

My father spoke to me from the other side of the fire char. "Frank, he said these things to you?"

"Yeah. Me and Jake."

"Engdahl's scum," Doyle said.

The sheriff said, "Let's finish here, then we'll worry about Morris Engdahl."

We fanned out and spread the search in a loose circle that reached the river and extended a hundred yards in both directions along the banks but found nothing the sheriff thought significant. We gathered back at the fire and the sheriff said, "Okay. I'm going to get Morris Engdahl down to my office and ask him a few questions. Mr. Drum, I'd like you there for that."

"All right," my father said.

"And your two boys as well," the sheriff added, "if that's all right with you. I'd like to get a complete statement from them about their altercations with Engdahl. And I think we'd all be interested in hearing what Engdahl has to say for himself. On a lot of fronts."

We started up the trail that led through the cottonwoods but Doyle hung back. The last I saw of him that morning he was headed downriver toward the Flats.

19

At home we found Gus with my mother which was odd. Though she tolerated his presence my mother didn't care much for Gus. She often told my father that his friend was crude and vulgar and an influence on us boys that we would all come to regret. My father acknowledged the truth of much of what she said but in the end always defended Gus. I owe him my life, Ruth, he would say but I never heard him say why.

They sat at the kitchen table both of them smoking and when we walked in my mother stood and looked with hope toward my father. He shook his head. "We didn't find anything," he said.

"They're looking for Morris Engdahl," I said.

"Engdahl?" Gus swung around and eyed me. "Why Engdahl?"

I told him about the quarry and about Luther Park.

My mother put a hand to her mouth and spoke from behind her fingers. "You think he might have done something to Ariel?"

"We don't know anything," my father said. "They just want to talk to the boy."

We ate. Cold cereal with slices of banana chewed and swallowed in an awful silence. Near the end the telephone in the living room rang and my father leaped to answer.

"Oh," he said. "Hello, Hector." He bowed his head and closed his eyes and listened, then said, "We have a situation here, Hector, and I can't make the meeting. Whatever the group decides is fine with me." He hung up and came back to the kitchen. "Hector Padilla," he said. "There's a meeting this morning to talk about the migrant worker shelter."

The phone rang again and this time it was Deacon Griswold calling to say he'd heard about Ariel and if there was anything he could do just let him know. And it rang again a few minutes later and it was Gladys Rheingold saying that if Ruth wanted company she'd be happy to come over. And it rang and rang after that with offers from townspeople and neighbors who'd heard about Ariel and wanted to know if they could help. And finally it was the sheriff saying he had Morris Engdahl at his office and would Dad and we boys come down there.

"Mind if I tag along?" Gus said.

"I don't suppose it'll do any harm," my father replied. Then to my mother he said, "Would you like me to call Gladys?"

"No," she said. "I'll be fine."

But it was clear to me that she wasn't fine. She looked sick, her face drawn and ashen, and she was smoking one cigarette after another and drumming her fingers on the table.

"All right," my father said. "Frank, Jake, let's go."

We left, all of us except my mother, who sat staring at the kitchen cupboard with cigarette smoke above her head as thick as if she herself was on fire.

The sheriff sat with his arms folded on the table. Engdahl sat across from him slumped in a chair in a manner that was clearly meant to communicate his disrespect. He looked bored in a calculated way.

The sheriff said, "Is it true you threatened these boys?"

"I told them I'd kick their asses, yeah."

"I understand you assaulted Frank last night."

"Assaulted? Hell, all I did was grab the little puke's arm."

"And might have done more if Warren Redstone hadn't been there?"

"Redstone? I don't even know who the hell that is."

"Big Indian."

"Oh. Him. We had some words, and I left. That's all."

"Where'd you go?"

"I don't remember. Around."

"Alone?"

"I ran into Judy Kleinschmidt. We kind of made a night of it."

"Did you go to Sibley Park and do a little partying with some kids there?"

"Yeah."

"Did you see Ariel Drum?"

"I saw her, yeah."

"Talk to her?"

"I might have said something. Hell, I talked to a lot of people there."

"I heard you got into a tussle with Hans Hoyle."

"Yeah. Traded a couple of punches, nothing serious. He called my car a piece of shit."

"Watch your mouth, Morris. What time did you leave the party?"

"I don't remember."

"Did you leave alone?"

"No. Judy was with me."

The sheriff nodded to one of his men and the deputy left.

"Did you go straight home?"

"No."

"Where'd you go?"

"I'd rather not say."

"I'd rather you did."

Engdahl thought a moment then shrugged in a what-the-hell way. "I went to the old Mueller place out on Dorn Road," he said.

"Why?"

"The place is empty and there's a big pile of hay in the barn and I had a blanket in my car. See?"

The sheriff took a moment to put two and two together. "You and the Kleinschmidt girl?"

"Me and Judy, yeah."

"How long did you stay?"

"Long enough." Engdahl grinned and showed his teeth.

"Then what?"

"I took her home. Then went home myself."

"What time was that?"

"I don't know. The sun was about to come up."

"Anybody see you arrive?"

Engdahl gave a quick shake of his head. "My old man had a snootful last night and was sawing logs on the sofa. Wouldn't've heard a bomb go off."

The sheriff leaned back and crossed his arms over his chest and for a full minute sat in silence and appraised Morris Engdahl. Over the course of that minute Engdahl went from his slouch to an erect posture and then to a twitching of his shoulders in a nervous way and finally said, "Look I told you everything. I don't know anything about Ariel Drum. I saw her at the party on the river, that's all. Hell, I don't think I even said a word to her. She was sitting on the other side of the fire and just staring into it like maybe she was too good to talk to the rest of us. She's like that. Doesn't matter she's got a harelip." He stopped blathering and shot my father a guilty look.

The sheriff waited but once Engdahl had embraced silence he held to it.

"All right, Morris. I'd like you to stick around until we find Judy and talk with her."

"Stick around? I gotta be at the cannery at four for my shift."

"We'll do our best to get you there on time."

"Christ, you better."

"Say, Lou," the sheriff said to the deputy who'd been with us on the river. "Put Morris in a cell so he can lie down. He looks like he could use twenty winks."

"You're locking me up? I didn't do anything. You can't arrest me."

"I'm not arresting you, Morris. Just offering you our hospitality for a while. Just until we talk to Judy Kleinschmidt."

"Shit," Engdahl said.

"Watch your language," the sheriff snapped. "Impressionable boys here."

Engdahl looked at me and if looks could kill I'd've been dead a dozen times.

We headed home and when we arrived we found a cruiser from the New Bremen police department parked in our gravel drive. My father pulled up next to it on the grass and we went inside where Doyle sat at the kitchen table with my mother.

"Nathan," she said looking up at him lost and frightened.

Doyle stood and turned to my father and held out his left hand. "Mr. Drum, I just want to show you something. Is this your daughter's?"

Doyle's big palm cradled something wrapped in a clean handkerchief. With his right hand he drew back the corners of the handkerchief and revealed a gold necklace with a heart-shaped locket inset with mother-of-pearl.

"Yes," my father said. "She was wearing it last night. Where'd you get it?"

Doyle's face was cold as winter concrete. He said, "It was in the possession of Warren Redstone."

20

Gus went with my father and Doyle to the sheriff's office to discuss the locket. Jake and I stayed with our mother which was difficult. She communicated her fear through silence and random movements. She sat at the kitchen table and smoked for a minute then stood and paced and ended up in the living room where she picked up the phone as if to make a call but put the receiver back down and crossed her arms and stared through a window while the cigarette smoldered in her hand. From the kitchen I watched the ember crawl toward her fingers as she stood frozen in terrible thought or speculation.

"Mom," I said when I couldn't stand it anymore and I was sure she would be burned.

She didn't look away from the window.

"Mother!" I said. "Your cigarette!"

She didn't move or acknowledge my words in any way. I rushed across the room and touched her arm and she looked down and suddenly realized what was about to happen and dropped the cigarette and stamped the ember out leaving a black smudge on the honey-colored floorboard.

I glanced back at the kitchen. Jake had been watching and I saw the frightened look on his face. It was clear that the house with Mother in it was a place oppressed by desperate worry and I didn't know what to do or how to help.

Then I heard the crush of gravel in the driveway. I went to the kitchen and looked out the window. Karl had pulled up in his little Triumph with Emil in the passenger seat. Above them loomed a brooding sky. Karl helped his uncle out of the car and led him to the kitchen door.

"Mr. Brandt's here!" I called.

"Oh, Emil," Mother said sweeping into the kitchen and drawing Mr. Brandt into her arms. "Oh, Emil. I'm so glad you came."

"I couldn't stand waiting this out alone, Ruth. I had to be here."

"I know. I know. Come and sit with me."

She led him into the living room where they sat together on the sofa.

Karl hung back with me and Jake. He asked, "Any word?"

"They found her locket," I said.

"Who?"

"Officer Doyle. Warren Redstone had it."

"Who's Warren Redstone?"

"Danny O'Keefe's great-uncle," Jake said.

"How'd he get it?"

"I don't know," I said. "My dad and Gus and Officer Doyle went to the sheriff's office with it."

"How long ago?"

"Half an hour maybe."

Karl stepped into the doorway to the living room. "I'm leaving for a little while, Uncle Emil," he said. "I'll come back for you."

He took off in a hurry. He leaped into his red sports car and shot from the drive and sped up Tyler Street toward town. With my mother and Brandt in the living room and my father and everyone else gone to the sheriff's office, Jake and I were left alone with our own concerns.

"You hungry?" I asked.

"No," Jake said.

"Me neither." I sat down at the table and ran my hand across the smooth Formica. "How'd he get it?"

"Get what?"

"Ariel's locket."

"I don't know." Jake sat down too. "Maybe she gave it to him."

"Why?"

"I don't know."

"Maybe he found it."

"Where?"

"I don't know," I said.

"You don't think he hurt her or anything?"

I thought about Warren Redstone and about how when we'd met him for the first time under the trestle with the dead man I'd been afraid for Jake. I thought about how we'd stumbled across him at his lean-to on the river when Danny was with us and how Danny had fled. I thought about his cold dismissal of me in the basement of Danny's house just before we went to the quarry. And I thought about how, when he'd interceded for me the night before, there was something in him that had frightened even Morris Engdahl.

I stood up. "I've got to get out of here," I said.

Jake stood up too. "Where are you going?"

"The river."

"Me, too," he said.

I went to the doorway and saw my mother and Brandt in deep urgent conversation. "Jake and me are going out for a while," I told them.

Mother glanced in my direction and then went back to talking with Brandt. Jake and I left the house through the kitchen door.

The sky had changed. The gray had deepened to the color of charcoal and the clouds had begun to boil. An erratic wind had risen and within its gusts was carried the sound of distant thunder from the west. We crossed the backyard and the pasture where the wild grass and daisies rippled as if the skin of the earth was alive. We skirted the Sweeneys' house where laundry hung on the line and I could hear the pop of bed linen snapping in the wind. We crossed Fourth Street and threaded our way between two fenceless houses and across Fifth. On the far side the ground sloped immediately toward the river. The slope was covered with bramble but a path had long ago been worn through the tangle of thorny vines and we followed it to a dry mudflat that edged the brown water and we turned northwest where two hundred yards away lay the long reed-covered stretch of sand on which Warren Redstone had constructed his lean-to.

"What are we doing?" Jake asked.

"Looking," I said.

"For what?"

"I don't know."

"What if he's there?"

"Then he's there. Are you afraid?"

"No."

"Then come on," I said and quickened my pace because I'd felt the first drops of rain.

We didn't bother trying to hide our approach but plunged recklessly through the reeds that grew higher than a man's head. We emerged to find the clearing vacant. I went straight to the lean-to and ducked inside and saw immediately that the buried can had been removed. What remained was a small mound of sand beside an empty hole.

"It's gone," I said and backed out and stood and turned and found Jake terrified and mute in the grip of Warren Redstone.

"Little thieves," the man said.

"We're not thieves," I shot back. "You're the thief. You took my sister's locket."

"Where's my can?" Redstone said.

"We don't have your can. The police do. And they have Ariel's locket and they're going to arrest you."

Redstone said, "What for?"

"Let Jake go," I said.

Redstone did as I'd demanded, released Jake with a rough little shove in my direction. My brother stumbled to my side and turned and we both faced Danny's great-uncle.

"Where's Ariel?" I said.

He looked at me and I could not read his face. He said, "Your sister?"

"Where is she?"

"I haven't seen her."

"You're a liar. You had her locket."

"I found that locket."

"Where?"

"Upriver."

"I don't believe you."

"I don't give a rat's ass whether you believe me or not. I just want my can."

"The police have it and they're going to put you in jail until you tell them what you did with Ariel."

"Christ, boy, the only thing in that can are bits and pieces of my life. Nothing important to anyone but me. Everything in there I found somewhere or someone gave me. I'm not a thief. And I sure as hell don't know anything about your sister."

Redstone stared at me and I stared back and if there was any fear in me at all it lay so deep beneath my boiling anger that it had no effect. If Redstone at that moment had attacked I'd have fought him tooth and nail.

Rain began to fall in drops so large and heavy they left dents in the sand. The wind was fierce and steady and the thunder that had been distant broke now above the town and although I couldn't see the lightning I could smell the electricity of the storm. Rain ran down Redstone's face like water down a rock and still he did not look away from me or move. I stood as unyielding as he although I knew that with his huge hands he could at any moment destroy me.

Then we heard the sirens approaching.

Redstone cocked his head and listened. From the direction of the slope along Fifth Street I heard the sound of car doors slamming and men shouting.

I hollered, "Here! He's here!"

Redstone swung his dark eyes back to my face and there was in them at last something that I understood and that to this day makes me ashamed.

He said calmly and without hate, "You've just killed me, white boy."

He turned and began to run.

21

The bulrushes shook as if a herd of elephants raged through and in a moment a group of men burst into the clearing. My father and Karl and Gus were among them and the sheriff was there and Doyle and a couple of deputies. They halted when they saw Jake and me at the lean-to. Halted all except my father who strode straight to us and stood eyeing us with confusion and concern.

"What are you boys doing here?"

"Looking for Warren Redstone," I said.

The sheriff came and stood beside my father. He said brusquely, "Where did he go?"

I thought about Redstone's parting words: *You've just killed me, white boy.* And I recalled the afternoon in the back of Halderson's Drugstore and the drunken men with the look of murder in their eyes. I stared into my father's face where rain ran off his brow in clear rivulets and I saw a fearful desperation there. I looked into the sheriff's face and was met with a coldness, a hard determination empty of compassion, and although I didn't see murder in either of these men what I did see was disturbing enough to make me hold my tongue.

"That way," Doyle shouted and pointed downriver toward the path Jake and I had hastily broken through the reeds and Warren Redstone in his own flight had followed.

"How long ago?" the sheriff demanded.

"A couple of minutes," I said.

All the men began a footrace except my father who hesitated a moment and pointed toward the slope of the riverbank and said, "Go on up to the car and stay there, do you understand?" And without waiting for us to reply he joined the others in pursuit.

I stood in the rain and looked down the ragged empty way we'd torn through the reeds.

Beside me Jake said, "Is it true?"

"Is what true?"

"That he's as good as dead? That they'll kill him?"

"He thinks it's true," I said.

"Do you think he hurt Ariel?"

"I don't know."

"I don't think he did, Frank."

The moment of my own anger had passed and in the quiet of the regret that followed I thought Jake was right.

"Come on," I said and began to run in the direction Redstone and the men had gone.

Thunder broke again and again over our heads and in those moments lightning whitened the gray curtain of the rain. The downpour was so heavy I couldn't see more than thirty yards ahead and the men were not there. We raced as fast as our legs would carry us but the men's legs were twice as long and took them away at twice the speed and I was sure that catching them was hopeless. Jake at the beginning was by my side but he gradually fell back and though he called to me to wait I ran on alone. Past the place where only fifteen minutes earlier we'd come down from the Flats, past the last of the houses along Fifth Street, and finally to the trestle across the river where my history with Warren Redstone had begun.

I'd run myself out. I stood dripping wet in the shelter of the trestle in the same place where the dead man had lain and Redstone had sat beside him. I breathed in gasps and my side hurt. The riverbank had become slick from the rain and in the mud there I could see tracks where the men in front of me had run in their pursuit. I thought I might even have heard them calling to one another though I couldn't be certain because the roar of the wind and the pounding of water out of the sky drowned out almost all other sounds. I lifted my face in the same way Warren Redstone on that first encounter had lifted his and had caught Jake and me spying on him through the crossties of the trestle. And there above me between the crossties was the face of Redstone staring down.

He didn't move. He didn't speak. He simply lay flat on the trestle and looked at me with eyes as brown and old and worn down as two stones that had tumbled along the glacial river over ten thousand years ago, a river that had been given the same name as he: Warren.

I remembered what he had said to Jake on our first meeting, that the tracks were like a river, a steel river, always there but always moving, and I realized that the river Warren Redstone intended to follow was not one of water.

He stood. I saw his body in flickers between the crossties as he started across the trestle. I left the shelter of the railroad bridge and walked out along the riverbank and watched him moving quickly and carefully from crosstie to crosstie with his head down so that he would not misstep and fall. He looked back at me once as if gauging my intent then returned his attention to making his escape.

The last I saw of him he'd crossed the trestle and slipped behind the veil of the heavy rain.

22

The sheriff's people finally got around to searching the railroad tracks on the other side of the river but by then Warren Redstone was long gone. I never said a word to anyone about seeing him. How could I possibly explain my silence, my complicity in his escape, things I didn't really understand myself? My heart had simply directed me in a way that my head couldn't wrap its thinking around and the deed once done was impossible to undo. But it weighed on me heavily. And with all that was about to occur, that guilt over my silence would finally come near to crushing me.

In the driving rain that afternoon a search was conducted along both sides of the river from well above Sibley Park to well beyond the trestle. It turned up nothing. The sheriff's people also carried out a search of the O'Keefes' basement where Warren Redstone had been staying. They'd hoped to discover something that might further connect the man to Ariel, maybe even the mother-of-pearl barrette that matched her locket or the gold watch she'd worn that night, but they came away empty-handed. The sheriff told us that he'd notified authorities in all the adjoining counties and assured us that Redstone would be caught. In the meantime, he would continue his search for Ariel.

Judy Kleinschmidt finally confirmed Morris Engdahl's story and so gave him the alibi that freed him from the cell where for several hours he'd remained the guest of the sheriff's department. The sheriff confided to my father that he didn't necessarily believe Engdahl's story or the girl's confirmation of it but he had no choice at the moment except to release the kid, especially in light of the locket that had been in Warren Redstone's possession.

By that evening our situation was well known in New Bremen. My grandfather and Liz arrived and Liz took charge of feeding us which was its own blessing since she was a wonderful cook. Emil Brandt had gone home and then returned because, he told my mother, he couldn't wait this out alone. Karl, who'd brought him, looked uncomfortable in our presence and in the presence of our misery and he quickly left. The downpour continued and brought an early dark and after dinner the adults sat in the living room and Jake and I sat on the front porch, barely talking, and watched the rain fall so hard it threatened to beat the leaves from the trees.

Time in the Drum household changed that night. We entered a period in which every moment was weighted with both the absolute necessity of hope and a terrible and almost unbearable anticipation of the worst. My father's response was to pray which he did often and fervently. He prayed alone and he prayed in the company of his family. I sometimes prayed with him and so did Jake but my mother didn't and usually stared straight ahead with a look that seemed to vacillate between bewilderment and rage.

On Thursday morning the visitors began to arrive. Neighbors and members of my father's congregation dropped by, staying only a moment, just long enough to deliver their good wishes along with a casserole or a loaf of homemade bread or a pie in order to free my mother from the responsibility of the kitchen. My grandfather and Liz came early and Liz prepared our meals from the delivered food and my grandfather greeted the visitors at the door and thanked them on my parents' behalf and in between the visitations he and Liz sat with my mother and with Emil Brandt who was always present. The Methodist district superintendent, a man named Conrad Stephens, drove over from Mankato and offered to cover the Sunday services for the churches in my father's charge. My father thanked him and said he would think about that.

Gus was in and out. I heard the growl of his motorcycle arriving and leaving. He was in touch with Doyle who was deeply involved in the effort to locate Ariel and he often slipped into the house and spoke with my father in low tones and then left without a word to the rest of us. I found out later he was bringing my father information about the reports the sheriff's people and the town's chief of police were receiving concerning Ariel's disappearance. A girl fitting her description had been seen in the company of some boys down in Blue Earth or someone thought they saw her walking along the road near Morton or she'd been spotted at a truck stop in Redwood Falls.

It was an awful time and Jake and I frequently sought sanctuary in our room. Jake would lie on his bed with one of his comic books open but more often than not instead of reading he stared silently at the ceiling. Or he sat at his little workbench and tried to focus on his plastic airplane models and our room was filled with the dizzying smell of glue. Much of the time I sat on the floor by the window looking at the church across the street and wondering about my father's God. In his sermons my father often talked about trusting God and trusting that no matter how alone we might feel God was always with us. In all that terrible waiting I didn't feel the presence of God, not one bit. I prayed but unlike my father who seemed to believe that he was being heard, I felt as if I was talking to the air. Nothing came to me in return. Not Ariel or any relief from the worry about her.

All day the rain continued and the hours passed in a deep fog of fear and waiting. Since Ariel had gone missing my parents had had almost no sleep and they looked terrible. That night as Jake and I lay in bed my father received a telephone call from the sheriff. He took the call in the hallway outside our room and I got up and stood in the doorway and listened to his end of the conversation. He was grim and clearly upset. When the call was finished he told me to go back to bed and he went downstairs where my mother and Emil Brandt and my grandfather and Liz sat together in the living room. As quietly as I could I crept to the top of the stairs and listened.

We were not the only family suffering in the wake of Ariel's disappearance, my father reported. Because of Warren Redstone, Danny O'Keefe's family was being harassed. They'd received a number of threatening calls and had stopped answering their telephone. That very night their living room window had been shattered by a rock thrown from the dark outside. My father said he was going to the O'Keefes' house and apologize to them.

"Apologize for what?" my grandfather asked.

"For the ignorance of others," my father said.

"What ignorance?" my grandfather persisted. "Those people housed and fed Redstone. My god, Nathan, do you believe that they didn't know what kind of man he is?"

"And what kind of man is he, Oscar?"

My grandfather sputtered. "He . . . he . . . well he's a troublemaker."

"What kind of trouble?"

"Well," my grandfather said, "it was a long time ago."

"Oscar, the only thing I know for sure about Warren Redstone is that he intervened when Morris Engdahl tried to hurt Frank."

"He had Ariel's locket," my mother said in a stone voice.

"Yes," my grandfather chimed in. "What about that?"

"Frank says Redstone claimed to have found it."

"And you believe the lies of an Indian?" my grandfather shot back.

"An Indian." My father's voice was stern but not cold. "If you ask me, Oscar, I'd say that's the whole point of this harassment. It has nothing to do with Ariel. Ariel is simply the excuse some people are using to let loose their prejudice and their cruelty. So I'm going to the O'Keefes' and I'm going to tell them I'm sorry for their ordeal."

My grandfather said bitterly, "And if Mr. Redstone is responsible for Ariel being missing?"

"There's a good explanation why Ariel is gone," my father replied. "I truly believe that. And I believe she'll be coming back to us. There's no reason in the world why the O'Keefes should have to suffer."

I heard him cross the room and from the dark at the top of the stairway where I sat hidden I caught a glimpse of him as he left through the front door.

"A fool," my grandfather said.

"Yes, but a great one," Emil Brandt replied.

Loss, once it's become a certainty, is like a rock you hold in your hand. It has weight and dimension and texture. It's solid and can be assessed and dealt with. You can use it to beat yourself or you can throw it away. The uncertainty of Ariel's disappearance was vastly different. It surrounded us and clung to us. We breathed it in and breathed it out and we were never sure of its composition. We had reason to be afraid yes, but without any real idea of what had happened or was happening to Ariel we had every reason to hope as well. Hope was what my father held to. My mother chose despair. Emil Brandt was a constant presence and a great comfort to her and was sometimes able to discuss with her in a way my father could not the darker possibilities of the situation. Jake turned to silence which because of his stuttering was a familiar shelter for him. Gus just looked grim all the time.

Me, I dreamed the best of scenarios. I imagined Ariel sick of life in the valley and eager for experience and I saw her on the seat beside a friendly trucker rolling across the high plains with her eyes on the Rocky Mountains that rose like a dark blue wave out of yellow wheat fields and somewhere beyond those mountains was Hollywood and greatness. Or I saw her bound for Chicago or New Orleans where she would also make a name for herself. Sometimes I saw her frightened and desperate in her flight which in a way was hopeful because it meant that we would get a call from her from a phone booth in the middle of somewhere she didn't want to be asking my father to please come and bring her home. I believed that one way or another we would hear from her and she would return. I believed it with all my heart and when I prayed that was my prayer.

For two days the sheriff's department and the town police conducted dozens of interviews with the kids who'd been at the party on the river and with Ariel's friends but they learned nothing that helped clear up the mystery.

By the third afternoon the atmosphere of our house so oppressed me that I began to think I would suffocate or go crazy. My father had gone to a meeting with the other clergy in town to discuss the concern about the possibility of violence, not just against the O'Keefes but also against several Sioux families in the area who'd received overt threats though they had nothing to do with my sister. I'd heard that the other kids on the Flats were keeping away from Danny and I thought that was wrong and I wanted to show him that as far as I was concerned there was nothing between us but the friendship that we'd always shared. I told Jake I was going to Danny's house and he said he wanted to go along and I said that was okay by me. My mother was with Brandt in the living room where the drapes were drawn and I spoke into the cool dark there. "Jake and me are going to Danny O'Keefe's house," I said. "He's been having a tough time, I heard."

"Just like your father," my mother said. I couldn't see her face but her voice sounded displeased.

"Can we go?"

She didn't answer immediately but Emil Brandt whispered something and she said, "Yes, but be careful."

The rain had stopped sometime in the night and was followed by a hot and windless summer day. Everything was soaked and the ground was soggy and because of the humidity the air we breathed sat heavy in our chests. On the Flats nothing moved. The drapes were drawn against the heat and nowhere did we hear the sound of kids at play. My father said that parents were watching their children carefully, keeping them close to home until the mystery of Ariel's disappearance was solved. It felt like an episode from *The Twilight Zone* in which everyone except Jake and me had vanished from the world.

Danny's mother answered the door. She looked at us with wonderment but not unkindly. Then she looked beyond us at the street and I understood that she was afraid.

"Is Danny home?" I asked.

She said, "Why are you here?"

"I was just wondering if Danny wanted to come out and play."

"Danny's gone to stay with relatives in Granite Falls for a few days," she said.

I nodded and then said, "I'm sorry, Mrs. O'Keefe."

"For what, Frank?"

"For your trouble."

"And I'm sorry for yours."

"Yeah. Well, good-bye, I guess."

"Good-bye, Frank." She looked at Jake and I thought she was going to say good-bye to him as well but she didn't and I realized that she probably couldn't remember his name which was a common result of Jake's tendency toward silence in the company of others.

We stepped away from the front porch and Jake said, "What do we do now?"

"Let's go down to the river," I said.

In those days the Flats ended at the O'Keefes' house. Beyond lay undeveloped marshland. We threaded our way through the tall cattails along a trail known to all the kids on the Flats and we emerged on the bank of the river. The two days of rain had swollen the flow and the water level and current were both far greater than they'd been in weeks. We began an aimless walk downstream toward our part of the Flats. The edge of the river was always changing, sometimes sand and sometimes mud, sometimes wide enough for a marching band and sometimes barely broad enough for the feet of two boys. The clearing on the stretch of reedy sand where Danny's uncle had built his lean-to was almost completely surrounded by water now and because we'd often been warned about quicksand we stayed away from it. We walked past the place where if we wanted to return home most easily we would have climbed the bank but at the moment I wasn't keen on returning to our house and to its atmosphere of dread. Not far beyond that Jake picked up a piece of driftwood as long as his arm and said, "Want to race boats?"

I found a big hunk of wood about the same size and said, "Go!" And we threw our make-believe boats into the river and the current snatched them away and we followed at a run. The boats swirled and turned and slid past submerged logs whose branches jutted above the river's surface like the fingers of water beasts trying to haul them under.

"Mine's winning," Jake hollered and laughed for the first time in days.

We raced to the trestle where so much of that summer's tragic history had already been played out. Where the water swirled around the pilings a little dam had formed of debris swept up by the powerful risen flow and our boats were caught among the branches and other detritus and the contest ended. We stood on the riverbank in the shade of the railroad bridge breathing fast and sweating profusely, with our sneakers covered in mud and our clothing snagged with burrs and our hearts lighter than they'd been since Ariel had vanished.

"Let's sit down," I said.

"Where?" Jake looked at the muddy riverbank.

"Up there." I pointed toward the crossties above us.

Jake began to protest but I'd already started up the embankment and there was nothing for him to do but follow.

My shirt stuck to my sweaty back and I took it off and threw it over my shoulder and Jake did the same. The weeks we'd spent outside in the summer sun had turned our skins the color of pecans. I walked onto the trestle just far enough to sit where my legs could dangle. Jake looked down the tracks warily and listened carefully and finally sat beside me. I'd scooped up a handful of rocks from the roadbed and I began to throw them at the branches and other debris that rode the river. Jake saw what I was doing and grabbed a handful of rocks for himself.

We sat this way for several minutes in the nearly silent swelter of that July afternoon. The sky was a cloudless blue, the cornfields on the other side of the river deep jade, the distant hills a mottled green like turtle shells, and the water of the Minnesota River the color of cloudy cider. I was so used to the fertile smell of the valley that I barely noticed the raw fragrance drawn up from the wet black earth by the heat of the sun. What I did note was how, for a moment, things felt normal again. God, I wanted that moment to last forever. And with guilty clarity I realized that as much as I wanted Ariel to return to us I wanted even more for things simply to be as they'd been before.

Jake threw a rock and said, "Every time I think about Ariel it feels like somebody punched me in the gut. Do you think she'll ever come home, Frank?"

"I don't know."

"I thought so at first but I don't think so now."

"Why?"

"I just have that feeling."

"Well get rid of it," I said and threw a rock.

"I've been dreaming about her."

"Yeah?"

"I dream about her in heaven."

I'd been ready to throw another rock, even had my arm cocked, but I stopped and looked at my brother. "What's it like?"

"Mostly she's just happy. I feel kind of good when I wake up."

"Jesus, I wish I had that dream."

"You said—" Jake began his usual complaint about my language but dropped it. He looked past me and looked down and said, "What's that, Frank?"

I turned my eyes to where he pointed at the little dam of debris the river had swept up and the trestle pilings had captured. Within the thick nesting of brush and branches which were all shades of brown and black was an undulation of bright red that couldn't be seen from the riverbank but was quite visible from above. I stood and crept farther out onto the trestle where Jake was reluctant to follow and I reached the place directly above the debris. I peered down among the debris and branches where the brown cider water rushed through and obscured everything beneath the surface. It took me a moment to realize what I was looking at. And when I did the breath went out of me.

"What is it, Frank?"

I couldn't look up. I couldn't look away. I couldn't speak.

Jake said, "Frank?"

"Get Dad," I finally managed to say.

"What is it?" Jake insisted.

"Just get Dad. Now, Jake. Go. I'll wait here."

Jake stood up and started out farther onto the trestle and I yelled at him, "Don't you come out here. Don't take another step. Just get Dad, goddamn it."

Jake stumbled back and almost fell from the trestle and picked himself up and turned and began to run along the tracks toward the Flats.

Strength deserted every muscle of my body and I collapsed and stared down between the crossties at the rippling swatch of red which I'd realized was the fabric of a dress ruffling in the current. And beside it from the obscured depth of the river a little stream of a deeper color roiled up and fluttered along the surface and I knew this was Ariel's long auburn hair.

The day was hot and windless and the sky a hard china blue and I lay alone on the railroad bridge and cried my heart out above a river that seemed to have none.

23

Knowing was far worse than not knowing.

Not knowing had offered hope. Hope that there was some possibility we'd overlooked. That a miracle might yet occur. That one day the telephone would ring and there would be Ariel's voice on the other end like a bird singing at sunrise.

Knowing offered only death. The death of Ariel and of hope and of something that I didn't see at first but whose loss would reveal itself to me more and more as time went on.

New Bremen was in Sioux County and like many basically rural counties had an elected coroner whose duty it was to certify cause of death. The coroner for our county was van der Waal, the mortician. This wasn't a piece of information most kids my age would typically have known but because my father's occupation often drew him to the deathbed I'd heard him on many occasions recount to my mother van der Waal's pronouncements. In that summer with Bobby Cole and the itinerant already in the ground van der Waal was even more darkly familiar to me.

He was tall with gray hair and a gray mustache that he often smoothed unconsciously as he talked. He spoke slowly and with great consideration in the words he chose and despite what I believed to be the gruesome nature of his occupation I thought of him as a kind man.

I wasn't allowed to be at the river when the sheriff's people re-
trieved Ariel's body for transport to van der Waal's Funeral Home. My
father was there and to this day he has never spoken of that experience.
For my part I imagined it a hundred times that summer. It haunted
me. Not Ariel's death itself which was still a mystery but her rising
from the river in the hands of my father and the other men and her
repose as I envisioned it on the clean soft bed of a satin-lined coffin
at van der Waal's. I didn't know then in the way I do now the details
of death in a river, of a body submerged for three days, of the desecra-
tion of the flesh that occurs during an autopsy, and I will not tell you
these things. I imagined Ariel as I'd last seen her, beautiful in her red
dress with her long auburn hair brushed silky and held back with the
mother-of-pearl barrette and about her throat a gold necklace with a
heart-shaped locket and on her wrist a gold watch and in her eyes a
tearful sheen of happiness as she accepted the applause for her music
that Fourth of July night at Luther Park.

When Jake asked me what I'd observed in the murky water beneath the trestle but wouldn't let him see I described to him Ariel
with her hair flowing and her dress aflutter as if she was simply standing in a strong summer breeze and he seemed satisfied with that and
relieved. I have never asked him if now he understands the distasteful
truth of what must surely have been the state of her body and I have
tried my best not to imagine it myself.

An awful hush settled over our house. My mother became nearly
mute and more often than not the only sound from her was weeping.
She kept the curtains drawn so that it felt as if permanent night had
fallen. Never much concerned anyway with her mundane domestic du-
ties she completely stopped cooking and cleaning and sat for hours in the
quiet dark of the living room. She was flesh without spirit, eyes without
sight. It felt as if I'd lost not only my sister but my mother as well.

My grandfather and Liz came and stayed for the better part of
every day. Liz took responsibility for the kitchen and for the phone
which rang often with calls of condolence and she greeted those who
came in person to offer the comfort of a few words and a prepared
casserole and our kitchen became a wondrous buffet of midwest hot
dish. Emil Brandt continued to be my mother's constant companion

but even his presence was insufficient to lift her from the dismal place into which she'd fallen.

From the moment he looked down beside me where I stood on the trestle and saw what I saw, my father became a man I didn't recognize. He had turned to me and said, "Come along, Frank," as if what we'd seen was nothing more than an unpleasantness or a discourtesy best ignored. He didn't speak to me the entire way home and once there guided me up to my room and from the telephone in the hallway called the sheriff. When he came to me afterward where I sat on my bed he said, "Not a word to your mother, Frank. Not a word until we're sure." His face was pale and stiff as if sculpted of beeswax and I knew he was just as sure as I was of what we'd seen. He left me and I heard him go downstairs and speak with my grandfather and then I heard the screen door open and close and I went to the window and although my heart had already broken for Ariel it seemed to break again as I watched him walk alone back to the trestle.

In the days afterward Jake grew sullen and kept mostly to our bedroom. Ariel's death devastated me and I broke into tears at odd moments but anger was Jake's response. He lay on his bed and brooded and if I tried to talk to him he was liable to snap at me. He cried too but they were hot tears and he wiped at them with his fists and flung them away. His anger spilled out at everyone and everything but it seemed especially directed at God. Prayers at night had been a routine all our lives yet after Ariel's death Jake refused to pray. Nor would he bow his head for grace before meals. My father didn't make a point of it. He had so much on his shoulders already I suppose that he simply decided to let Jake and God work out the trouble between them. But I tried to talk sense into my brother one night upstairs in our room. He told me just to l-l-l-leave him alone. I'd had enough of him at that point and I said, "The hell with you. Why are you so mad at me? I didn't k-k-k-kill Ariel." He looked up at me from the bed where he lay and said with what sounded like threat in his voice, "Somebody did."

Which was a possibility I'd chosen to reject entirely. In my thinking, Ariel had simply had too much to drink at the party and had stumbled into the river and drowned. She was a terrible swimmer. Her death was horrible beyond belief but it was an accident and accidents happened all the time even to the best of people. Or so I told myself. Looking back now, it's easy to see what I was really afraid of. Which was that if Ariel's death wasn't accidental, then I had let the man most probably responsible for it get away and, oh Christ, I didn't think I could live with that.

So even after Jake threw the possibility at me I continued to blind myself to it. Until Gus and Doyle opened my eyes.

Gus was a constant but quiet presence through much of the aftermath of Ariel's death. When he entered the house he never ventured into the living room which had become like a cave where my mother brooded. He kept his presence to the kitchen where he talked with my father and ate the food which Liz dished from the contributions that poured in from friends and neighbors and members of my father's congregations. I had the sense that he served as messenger and confidant and runner of errands in order to lessen my father's burden.

Late Saturday afternoon, Gus caught me alone in the front yard with a stick in my hand making life miserable for a colony of ants. He stood beside me and watched the rage I'd incited among the insects as a result of breaking open the little anthill they'd carefully constructed. "How're you doing, Frank?" he asked.

I watched the ants going berserk for a while before I answered, "Okay, I guess."

"Haven't seen you out much."

"Too hot," I said. Though the truth was that I didn't feel like seeing anybody or being seen. I missed Ariel so much, felt so empty and hurting that I was afraid I might break down and cry at any moment and I didn't want anyone seeing me if that happened.

"Bet a tall root beer in a frosted mug would cool you off. What do you say we head up to Halderson's Drugstore on my motorcycle?"

A ride on Gus's Indian Chief was always a treat and I was tired of the house and the darkness inside and Jake's sullenness and the unsettling strangeness of everything that had been so preciously familiar and I said, "Sure."

"Think Jake might want to go?"

I shook my head. "He just wants to be upstairs and be mad."

"All right if I ask him?"

I gave a shrug and went back to poking at the ant colony.

Gus returned a few minutes later without Jake. I was sure my brother had told him to get l-l-l-lost but Gus reported that Jake had just said he'd rather be alone right now. Gus lightly punched my arm and said, "Come on, Frankie. Let's ride."

We didn't go straight to Halderson's. Gus took us out of town and over back roads. We flew between fields of corn that stood as high as my waist and that stretched away to the horizon on all sides with hot silver sunlight pouring over their leaves so that they glistened like the endless water of a green sea. And we dipped into the cool shade of hollows where creeks ran beneath leafy canopies of cottonwood and hackberry and birch. We climbed to the top of the ridge that marked the southern boundary of the river valley and below us spread a land full of the promise of a good fall harvest and cut by a river that I understood was the reason for the rich life there. And although I'd been angry at the river for Ariel's death I understood the river was not to blame.

All the while I sat in the little sidecar and let the wind and the sun and the beauty of the land wash over me. I felt cleaner and better than I had since Ariel first went missing. I didn't want to go back. I wanted to stay with that big motorcycle and leave New Bremen behind forever. But eventually Gus guided us into town and pulled the Indian Chief up before Halderson's Drugstore and killed the engine and I hopped out of the sidecar and we went inside.

Cordelia Lundgren was behind the counter of the soda fountain. I knew her slightly. One of Ariel's friends. She was heavy and suffered from a bad complexion and when she saw me her face took on a look of panic as if she had no idea what to say to me. So she said nothing at all.

"A couple of root beers," Gus said as we sat down on the stools. "And make sure those mugs are good and frosty."

Halderson came from behind the pharmacy window and leaned against the counter. "Those root beers are on the house," he told Cordelia. He looked at me and said, "Frank, I'm sorry about your sister. It's a crying shame."

"Thank you, sir," I said and waited for my root beer.

"Any more word, Gus?"

"No," Gus said, and out of the corner of my eye I saw him gesture to Halderson in a way that was meant to cut off any further questioning.

"Well, I just wanted to say how sorry I am."

I studied the miscellaneous items lined up along the preparation area of the soda fountain—cherry and lime syrups for phosphates, chocolate and butterscotch and strawberry for sundaes, chopped nuts and bananas and whipped cream—and without looking at Halderson I said, "Yes, sir. Thank you."

"Anything you or your family need just let me know."

"I will, sir."

It was an awkward dance, with death calling the tune, and in a way I felt sorry for Halderson who was simply trying to be kind. I was relieved when Cordelia brought the root beers and Halderson returned to his pharmacy window.

Ten minutes later Doyle walked in. He was in uniform and he came straight to Gus and me.

"Saw your motorcycle out front," he said.

"Yeah, Frankie and me, we just had ourselves a great ride in the country."

"I'm really sorry about your sister, Frank. I promise you we'll get the bastard who killed her."

"What do you mean? I thought she drowned in the river." It was Halderson who said this. When Doyle walked in the pharmacist had come out again from behind his window.

"According to the coroner's preliminary report, there's more to it than that," Doyle said. He eased himself onto the stool next to Gus.

"Not now," Gus said and gave a nod in my direction.

"I want to know," I said.

"I don't think so," Gus replied.

Doyle said, "The boy has a right to know seems to me."

"That's not for you to say," Gus responded.

"Hell, he'll know sooner or later."

"Tell me," I said.

Doyle ignored the stern look from Gus. "The coroner says your sister drowned but it wasn't the river that killed her. He believes she was hit on the head and probably knocked unconscious and thrown in. He wants some hotshot medical examiner from Mankato to come out and do a full autopsy."

Oh, God, please no, I thought.

"Do they have any idea who might have done it?" the pharmacist asked.

"Pretty sure it was the Indian," Doyle said. "Redstone. He had her necklace."

A tidal wave of guilt swept me up and spun me around and dizzied me. *Oh God oh God oh God,* I thought. *I let him get away.*

And then because I couldn't bear the guilt I grabbed at the fading sense I'd had of Redstone that he was different from the way everyone else seemed to see him. I said almost breathlessly, "He told me he found the locket."

"And you believed him? An Indian?" Doyle looked at me like I was an idiot.

His interest was a policeman's interest. He was concerned with facts. How could he understand my own sense of Warren Redstone? Still I stumbled desperately on. I said, "Why would he want to hurt Ariel? He didn't even know her."

"I'm betting the autopsy'll tell us why," Doyle said enigmatically and I saw him shoot a knowing look at Gus.

"He didn't do it," I insisted childishly, illogically.

Maybe to save me from appearing any stupider or maybe simply to distract me from thinking too much about Doyle's veiled reference to what the autopsy might reveal, Gus said to his friend, "What if it wasn't the Indian?"

Doyle shrugged. "My next choice would be Engdahl."

Which was an enormous relief to me and I jumped on the possibility. "That girl he was with, she's a skag," I said. "I bet everything she said about that night was a lie."

"A skag?" Doyle seemed to find that amusing. He grinned briefly and said, "When the sheriff finds them, I'll make sure he knows that, Frankie."

"Finds them?" Halderson said.

"He's looking for them now," Doyle told us. "Both kids just up and disappeared, Engdahl and his girlfriend."

"That doesn't necessarily prove anything," Halderson pointed out.

"Maybe not but it sure doesn't look good." Doyle eyed me. "Your father probably knows all this. The way I understand it the sheriff's been talking to him all along. Hell, Gus probably already knew, too."

I looked at Gus and could tell from his face that he did indeed know.

I slid off the stool and left the drugstore. Gus came out behind me. "Wait, Frank."

"I'll walk home," I told him over my shoulder and kept going.

He fell in step beside me on the sidewalk. "What did you want me to do, Frank? Your father asked me not to say anything."

"He could've told me."

"He doesn't want you hurting any more than you already are."

We were passing the barbershop and through the open door came Herb Carneal's voice on the radio calling a Twins game. "We'd all know sooner or later," I said.

"Maybe later is better, Frank. You've already had your share of bad news."

I didn't agree with Gus. As bad as the knowledge might be I wanted the truth. And I was angry with my father for keeping it from me.

"He should have told me," I said.

Gus stopped and because he did I did. I turned back and found him standing on my shadow on the concrete and looking at me sternly. He said, "You think your mother is ready to hear these things? Jesus, Frankie, use your head. Your old man is shouldering so much right now you really need to give him a break. Sure it hurts you. Think he's not hurting? Christ," Gus said with final disgust. "You want to walk home, go right ahead."

He turned back toward his motorcycle and I turned toward home. I shoved my hands into my pockets and in the long slant of the late afternoon sun I walked down Main Street which should have been familiar to me but didn't feel so. I came to Cedar Street down which every weekday from September to June, Jake and I walked to school. And here was the intersection with Ash where the Guttenburgs' house stood and where Jake and Danny O'Keefe and I had built a great snow fortress last winter with Skip Guttenburg and had battled the Bradley brothers across the street. And here was Sandstone Street and a block north was the parking lot of Rosie's where Jake and I had smashed the lights of Morris Engdahl's Deuce Coupe. These streets and their memories seemed to belong to a different time and even to a different person. I felt as if Ariel's death had shoved me through a doorway into a world where I was a stranger. I wished that Gus had never brought me back from the country roads and I couldn't remember ever feeling so lost or so alone.

I heard the sound of the Indian Chief long before Gus pulled up beside me.

"Hop in," he said above the rumble of the engine and nodded toward the sidecar. "I'll take you home."

I didn't argue.

That night after Emil Brandt and my grandfather and Liz had all left and Jake was sleeping, I lay awake listening to the sound of the wind in the trees outside my window. It was a fierce wind and I heard anger in the way it shook the leaves and bent the branches. I thought that a storm might sweep in behind it but I heard no thunder and when I got up and went to the window and looked outside I found to my surprise that the sky was clear and full of stars and the moon was about to rise.

I couldn't stop thinking about Warren Redstone. The weight of my guilt over letting him go was crushing me. I tried to pray but had no idea what to say except that I was sorrier than I'd been about anything ever. I kept seeing the sweep of Ariel's hair in the river current and the flutter of her red dress and, on the trestle above, Redstone sneaking away. I balled my fists and pressed them into my eye sockets as if to push those images out of my head.

The light was on in the hallway and I heard the heavy restless tread of my father descending the stairs. I left my room and saw that although it was late my parents' bed was empty. I went to the landing. I couldn't see much of the living room below but I could tell that it was dimly lit with the glow of a single lamp. I heard my father speak.

"Would you like some company?"

He received no response.

"I should probably close the windows, Ruth. It feels like a storm."

"I like them this way."

"Would you mind if I sat here with you and read?"

"Do whatever you like."

Things were quiet. Then my mother said, "The Bible?"

"I find comfort in it."

"I don't."

"I won't read aloud."

"If you must read that book read it somewhere else."

"Is it God you're angry with, Ruth?"

"Don't use that tone with me."

"What tone?"

"Like I'm one of your flock. Lost. I don't need your help, Nathan. Not the kind of help you're going to offer from that book."

"What kind of help would you like?"

"I don't know, Nathan. But not that."

"All right. I'll just sit then."

A few moments of tense silence followed, then my mother said, "I'm going to bed." She said it in a way that made me think she was irritated with my father, with his presence, though what he'd done to make her angry I didn't know. I heard the floorboards yield under her weight and I went quickly to my bedroom and lay down with the door open. She came up the stairs and went into the bathroom and I heard water run in the sink and heard her brush her teeth and gargle briefly. She crossed the hallway and entered her bedroom and closed the door. My father didn't follow her upstairs.

I lay for a long time listening to the wind grab the trees and shake them. I was still wide awake when I heard the front door open and close. I swung my feet off the bed and hurried to the window and saw my father cross the street to the church. He went into the sanctuary and was lost to me in the darkness there.

In my pajamas and barefoot I went downstairs and out the front door and followed where my father had gone. The night was warm and the wind against my face felt fevered. I climbed the steps to the church and saw that the door had not shut completely and the wind had pried it open just enough for me to slip inside without a sound.

My eyes had already adjusted to the night and in the dark of the sanctuary which was far from total I saw the black shape of my father at the altar. His back was to me. He struck a match and put the flame to the wicks of the candles that flanked the altar cross on either side. He blew out the match and knelt before the altar and bent himself so low that his forehead touched the floor. He stayed that way a long time and was so silent I thought maybe he'd fainted.

"Captain?"

Gus stepped in from the doorway that led to the basement stairs. My father rocked back and came upright. "What is it, Gus?"

"Nothing. Heard someone up here, thought it might be you. Thought maybe you'd like some company. Was I wrong?"

"No, Gus. Come in."

I sank quickly to the floor and made myself small in the shadows near the front door. My father put his back against the altar and Gus joined him and leaned back too in a way that seemed familiar and relaxed.

My father said, "I did come looking for company, Gus. I hoped God might have something to say to me."

"Like what, Captain?"

My father was quiet and because the candles were on the altar behind him his face was in shadow and lost to me. Finally he said, "I've been asking the same questions of him over and over. Why Ariel? Why not me? The sins are mine. Why punish her? Or Ruth? This is killing her, Gus. And the boys, they don't understand, they just hurt. And it's my fault. All my fault."

Gus said, "You think God operates that way, Captain? Hell, that sure ain't what you've been telling me all these years. And as for those sins of yours, I'm guessing you mean the war, and haven't you always told me that you and me and the others we could be forgiven? You told me you believed it as surely as you believed the sun would rise every morning. And I've got to tell you, Captain, you seemed so certain that you got me believing it too." Gus sat forward and looked at his hands which were wax-pale in the candlelight. "I can't see any way that the God you've talked yourself blue to me and everyone else about would be responsible for what happened to Ariel. I can't believe God would hurt that beautiful child in order to call you to account. No, sir, I don't believe that for one moment."

This seemed odd to me coming from Gus because mostly what I'd always heard from him was a questioning of everything my father spoke for.

"Seems to me you're just kind of reeling here, Captain. Like from a punch in the face. When you come around you'll see that you've been right all along. I know I give you a hard time about your religion but damned if I'm not grateful at heart that you believe it. Somebody's got to. For all the rest of us, Captain, somebody's got to."

Gus stopped talking and I became aware of an odd and disconcerting sound that was growing louder in the sanctuary. I didn't understand at first what it was or its source, and then I realized that it was my father crying. Huge sobs erupted from him and boomed off the walls. He bent and wept into his hands and Gus leaned to him and held my father dearly.

And as quietly as I could I crept outside into the night and the wind.

24

n light of Ariel's death, the district superintendent had offered to see to the services in all the churches under my father's charge that Sunday. My father agreed to this for the early service in Cadbury and the late service in Fosburg, but he insisted on leading the worship at Third Avenue Methodist in New Bremen himself.

The wind that had raged the night before had blown away the humidity and cleaned the sky and the day was sunny and beautiful. I'm sure services at Cadbury and Fosburg were poorly attended because I saw so many members of those congregations filling the pews of Third Avenue to hear my father preach. Mrs. Klement was there with Peter and I was surprised to see her husband Travis dressed in a rumpled suit and looking ill at ease beside her. Like the others they were curious, I'm sure, what this suffering man could possibly say that was good about God. My mother and Jake had both refused to come and my father would never have forced them. But my grandfather and Liz, who were Lutheran, came with me, and Gus was there and we all sat together in the first pew up front. After forty years I still remember that service well. The processional hymn was *A Mighty Fortress* which was one of my favorites and although my mother wasn't present to lead or to lend her clear soprano, the choir sounded lovely. Lorraine Griswold on the organ didn't miss a note. The scripture lessons were taken from

Ecclesiastes and Luke. Bud Sorenson, who was the lay reader and who often stumbled over the text, on that morning read perfectly. And I imagined that they were all so flawless because they wanted to do their best for my mother and my father and in memory of Ariel.

When it came time for my father to deliver his sermon I was concerned because I hadn't seen him prepare at all. He stepped up to the pulpit and for a moment simply looked out over the pews, every one of which was full. And then he began.

"It isn't Easter," he said, "but this week has caused me to think a lot about the Easter story. Not the glorious resurrection that we celebrate on Easter Sunday but the darkness that came before. I know of no darker moment in the Bible than the moment Jesus in his agony on the cross cries out, 'Father, why have you forsaken me?' Darker even than his death not long after because in death Jesus at last gave himself over fully to the divine will of God. But in that moment of his bitter railing he must have felt betrayed and completely abandoned by his father, a father he'd always believed loved him deeply and absolutely. How terrible that must have been and how alone he must have felt. In dying all was revealed to him, but alive Jesus like us saw with mortal eyes, felt the pain of mortal flesh, and knew the confusion of imperfect mortal understanding.

"I see with mortal eyes. My mortal heart this morning is breaking. And I do not understand.

"I confess that I have cried out to God, 'Why have you forsaken me?'"

Here my father paused and I thought he could not continue. But after a long moment he seemed to gather himself and went on.

"When we feel abandoned, alone, and lost, what's left to us? What do I have, what do you have, what do any of us have left except the overpowering temptation to rail against God and to blame him for the dark night into which he's led us, to blame him for our misery, to blame him and cry out against him for not caring? What's left to us when that which we love most has been taken?

"I will tell you what's left, three profound blessings. In his first letter to the Corinthians, Saint Paul tells us exactly what they are: faith, hope, and love. These gifts, which are the foundation of eternity, God has given to us and he's given us complete control over them. Even in the darkest night it's still within our power to hold to faith. We can still embrace hope. And although we may ourselves feel unloved we can still stand steadfast in our love for others and for God. All this is in our control. God gave us these gifts and he does not take them back. It is we who choose to discard them.

"In your dark night, I urge you to hold to your faith, to embrace hope, and to bear your love before you like a burning candle, for I promise that it will light your way.

"And whether you believe in miracles or not, I can guarantee that you will experience one. It may not be the miracle you've prayed for. God probably won't undo what's been done. The miracle is this: that you will rise in the morning and be able to see again the startling beauty of the day.

"Jesus suffered the dark night and death and on the third day he rose again through the grace of his loving father. For each of us, the sun sets and the sun also rises and through the grace of our Lord we can endure our own dark night and rise to the dawning of a new day and rejoice.

"I invite you, my brothers and sisters, to rejoice with me in the divine grace of the Lord and in the beauty of this morning, which he has given us."

My father's eyes swept over the congregants who filled the pews silent as dandelions with upturned faces. He smiled and said, "Amen."

And after a moment Gus beside me called out, "Amen." Which was a most un-Methodist thing to do. And then I heard another voice echo, "Amen," and I turned and saw that it was Travis Klement who had spoken and I watched as his wife laid her hand lovingly on his arm.

I left the church that morning feeling, as I do to this day, that I had experienced a miracle, the one promised by my father who had spoken a truth profound and simple. I walked across the street to our house where my mother sat with Emil Brandt in the living room with the curtains drawn against the morning light. I went upstairs to my bedroom where Jake lay on his mattress, still in his pajamas.

I sat down on my bed and said, "There's something I haven't told you. Something important."

"Yeah?" he replied with no interest at all.

"You're my best friend, Jake. You're my best friend in the whole world. You always have been and you always will be."

I could hear outside the calls of the congregation one to another bidding good-bye and the sounds of doors slamming and of wheels crushing gravel as cars left the church parking lot. Jake had been staring up at the ceiling with his hands clasped behind his head. He didn't move. Finally the sounds from across the street died out completely and it was just Jake and me and silence.

"I'm afraid you'll die, too," he finally said.

"I won't ever die, I promise."

His eyes slid from the ceiling to my face. "Everybody dies," he said.

"I won't. I'll be the first person who never died. And you'll be the second."

I thought that at least he would smile but he didn't. He looked serious and thoughtful and he said, "I won't mind dying. I just don't want you to die."

"Cross my heart, Jake, I'm not going to die. I'm not going to leave you ever."

He sat up slowly and swung his legs off the bed. "You better not," he said. Then he said, "Everything feels wrong, Frank."

"Everything?"

"The daytime. The nighttime. Eating. Just lying here thinking. Nothing feels right. I keep waiting for her to come up the stairs and poke her head into our room and, you know, goof around with us."

"I know what you mean," I said.

"What do we do, Frank?"

"I think we just keep going on. We keep doing what we always do and someday it'll feel right again."

"Will it? Really?"

"Yeah, I think so."

He nodded. Then he said, "What do you want to do today?"

"I've got an idea," I said, "but you might not like it."

My grandfather and Liz had gone home after church. To rest awhile, Liz had told us. She'd promised they would be back later to fix supper. They'd been with us constantly since Ariel first disappeared and I realize now looking back that they must have been sucked dry by our need and must have been hurting too but they never said a word of complaint.

Jake and I found them sitting in the shade of their long front porch. They were surprised to see us and looked concerned until I explained why we were there.

"It's the Sabbath," my grandfather said. "A day of rest."

"Honest, it'll be more restful than sitting home all day," I told him.

Jake and I set to the yard work that in a normal week would have been done the day before and while I worked I looked often toward the shaded porch. Ariel's disappearance and death had given me a different picture of my grandfather and Liz. Liz I'd always liked but I liked her more now. My grandfather, I realized, I'd badly misjudged. I'd always seen him in light of my own understanding which was like a match flame in a huge dark. My grandfather had his faults. He was demanding. He was proud. He could be narrow-minded. He expected a big deal to be made over the things he gave as gifts. But he loved his family, that was clear.

When we'd finished and had put away the yard things we went to the porch where Liz had a big pitcher set out with some glasses. She offered us lemonade.

My grandfather looked at his lawn which was buttery green in the afternoon sun and smelled of freshly cut grass. He said, "I don't know that I've ever told you boys how much I appreciate the job you do. I get comments all the time on how good this property of mine looks."

It was true that he never complimented us. He usually said something like, I pay you boys well. Be sure you do a good job now. And although we busted our butts in the work we did under his watchful eye and according to his constant direction he never once that I could recall had remarked favorably on our efforts.

"Here," he said. "I think a bonus is due."

We were usually paid two dollars apiece for the yard work but that day my grandfather gave us each a ten-dollar bill. I remember a heated discussion my parents once had in which my father said that my grandfather was a man who believed that money could buy you anything in life including love. Although I hadn't really thought about it, I'd pretty much agreed with his assessment. That Sunday afternoon

I saw something else. Whether my eyes had been opened by Ariel's death or whether it was my grandfather's understanding and behavior that had altered I couldn't say, but in the shade of his porch with a glass of cold lemonade in my hand, I looked at him with greater appreciation and affection than I ever had before.

Liz finally suggested that it was time we all get back. She needed to begin thinking about supper that night. My grandfather said, "You boys ready?"

"I'd like to walk home," I told him.

"Are you sure? What about you, Jake?"

"If Frank's walking, I'll walk too," he said.

"All right then." My grandfather stood up from his rocker.

Walking home was different from the day before. Easier somehow. It felt more normal with Jake beside me and the streets didn't seem as strange. But everything was different, there was no mistaking that.

Jake stopped suddenly and stood kind of slumped in the road as if all the air had suddenly gone out of him.

I said, "What's wrong?"

His voice was choked. "I can't stop thinking about how much I want her back."

"It'll get better."

"When, Frank?"

I knew nothing about death. We'd never even had a pet that died. But I thought about Bobby Cole's parents who'd lost everything when they lost Bobby. And I thought about an evening only a week before when I'd walked past their house on my way home from goofing around with Danny O'Keefe. Mr. Cole had been in the yard and he'd been looking up at the evening sky and when he realized that I was passing on the sidewalk he smiled and said, "Beautiful evening, eh, Frank?" I thought if a man who'd lost everything could still see the beauty in a sunset then sooner or later things would look up for Jake and me and our family.

I put my arm around my brother and said, "I don't know. But it will."

When we got home Dad was gone. Gus was in the church parking lot sitting on his Indian Chief talking through the open window of Doyle's cruiser. Jake and I drifted over.

"Hey, guys, "Doyle said.

I knew him in so many ways now that I felt a creepy kind of kinship with him.

"I was just telling Gus here that they found Morris Engdahl and the Kleinschmidt girl."

"Where were they?" I asked.

"Cozied up in a motel in Sioux Falls. The girl's only seventeen so the sheriff over there's holding Engdahl on violation of the Mann Act, but they'll be bringing him back here for questioning."

I didn't know what the Mann Act was and I didn't care. All I wanted was to hear what Morris Engdahl knew about Ariel's death. I believed absolutely that he was low enough to have done it and I was sure everyone else did too.

But the next day the medical examiner from Mankato came to New Bremen and conducted a thorough autopsy and what he found changed the thinking of us all.

25

On Mondays, Jake went to Mankato for a weekly session of speech therapy designed to help him overcome his stutter.

I didn't know why my brother stuttered; I just knew he always had. The therapists who worked with him were nice folks, patient and encouraging. Jake told me he liked them. So far as I could tell in all the years they'd worked with him they hadn't made much progress. He still stuttered when he was nervous or angry and just the thought of having to say something in a public way flustered him no end. Teachers seldom called on him in class because waiting out his halting answers was torture for everyone, Jake included. He always sat in the back of a classroom. Usually his therapy was scheduled for early afternoon and my mother would pick him up at lunch and he wouldn't go back to school that day. He told me it was the one good thing that came of being a stutterer.

If you weren't around Jake all the time you would have had trouble gauging him. I know that he gave some people the creeps because of the way he held to silence and watched things. Maybe because he was content to observe he often took the measure of a situation and of people much more accurately than others might have. At night in our room I'd be going on and on about a circumstance we'd both been a part of and Jake would listen to me from his bed and when I was finished he'd ask me a question or make a simple statement that had the effect of pointing out something I'd missed in the dynamics of the situation but Jake had not.

Normally my mother took Jake to his speech therapy but the Monday after Ariel died she didn't. That morning, she'd left us. She had simply stood up at the breakfast table after I asked for some orange juice and had announced she couldn't stand another minute in that goddamn house and she was going to Emil Brandt's. She'd stormed out and the screen door had slammed behind her and she'd stomped across the yard heading toward the railroad crossing on Tyler Street while my father stood at the kitchen window watching her go.

"What's she mad at?" I'd asked.

Without turning from the window my father had said, "Right now, Frank, I'd guess everything." He'd left the kitchen and walked upstairs.

Jake, who'd been trying to make a sentence with his Alpha-Bits cereal, stirred the letters back into incoherence and said, "She's mad at Dad."

"What did he do?"

"Nothing. But he's God."

"God? Dad? That's crazy."

"I mean for her he's God." Jake said this as if it should have been obvious then went back to making his sentence.

I didn't have the slightest idea what he was talking about, but I've thought about it since and I believe I understand. My mother couldn't rail directly at God and so she railed instead at my father. Once again Jake had seen and understood something I hadn't.

My father returned to the kitchen and Jake asked listlessly, "Do I have to go to Mankato today?"

This seemed to catch my father by surprise. He thought it over then said, "Yes. I'll take you."

So I was home alone that afternoon when the sheriff showed up looking for Dad. He knocked at the front screen door. A Twins game was on the radio and I was slumped on the living room sofa dividing my time between the game and one of Jake's comic books. The sheriff was dressed in his khaki uniform. He took off his hat which was something folks did respectfully when my parents came to the door but no one had ever done it for me. It made me nervous.

"Is your father home, Frank? I tried the church," he said, "but no one answered."

"No, sir. He's in Mankato with my brother."

He nodded and looked past me into the dark at my back. I wondered if he thought I wasn't telling the truth or if it was just something he'd become used to doing as part of his job.

"Will you do me a favor, son? Will you have him call me when he gets back? It's important."

"My mother's at Emil Brandt's house," I told him. "If you want to talk to her."

"I think I'd rather discuss this with your father. You won't forget?"

"No, sir. I'll remember."

He turned and put his hat on and took a couple of steps and paused and turned back. "You mind coming out here a minute, Frank? A couple of things I'd like to ask you."

I joined him on the porch wondering what answers I had that he could possibly want.

"Let's sit down," he suggested.

We sat together on the top step and looked out at the yard and the church on the other side of the street and beyond that the grain elevators mute beside the tracks. Everything was quiet in the Flats. The sheriff was not a tall man and sitting we were not that different in height. He spun his hat in his hands, fingering the sweatband inside.

"Your sister, she was pretty sweet on the Brandt boy, is that right?"

The Brandt boy? I thought. Karl Brandt had always seemed to me mature and sophisticated. Yet here was the sheriff calling him boy just as others called me.

I thought about Ariel and Karl and how well they seemed to get on. I thought about all they did together. I thought about the nights Ariel sneaked from the house in the dark hours and slipped back just before dawn. But I also thought about the question I'd posed to Karl Brandt the day Jake and I had ridden in his fast little car: Are you going to marry my sister? And I thought about how he'd backed away.

I finally said, "They had a complicated relationship."

Which was something I'd heard once in a movie.

"Complicated how?"

"She liked him a lot but I think he didn't like her as much."

"Why do you say that?"

"He wouldn't marry her."

The sheriff stopped turning his hat in his hands and his face swung slowly toward me. "She wanted him to?"

"She was supposed to go to Juilliard in a couple of months, which was what she always wanted to do, but lately she was different. I got the feeling she wanted to stay here with Karl."

"But the Brandt boy's going off to St. Olaf."

"Yes, sir. I guess he is."

With his mouth closed he made a sound that stayed mostly in his throat and then he went back to spinning the hat in his hands.

"What do you think of him, Frank?"

Again I thought about the car ride and what had struck me as his refusal to marry Ariel but instead of replying I simply shrugged.

"You notice anything different about your sister lately?"

"Yeah. She was sad for no reason. And mad sometimes too."

"Did she say why?"

"No."

"Do you think it might have been because of Karl?"

"Maybe. She really loved him."

I said that last part not because I knew it to be true but because it felt true. Or felt to me as if it should have been true.

"She spent a lot of time with Karl?"

"A lot."

"Did you ever see them argue?"

I made a good show of thinking hard although I knew the answer immediately. "No," I said.

Which didn't seem to be the answer he wanted.

"Once," I said quickly, "Ariel came back from a date pretty mad."

"At Karl?"

"I guess. I mean, he was the guy she was on the date with."

"Recently?"

"A couple of weeks ago."

"Did she talk to you, Frank? Maybe tell you things she wouldn't tell your folks?"

"We were very close," I said trying to sound mature.

"What did she tell you?"

I realized suddenly that I'd made a trap for myself, suggesting a situation that wasn't exactly true, and the sheriff was expecting something from me I didn't know how to give, confidences Ariel might have shared.

"She went out at night sometimes," I said in a panic. "After everybody was asleep. And she didn't come back until almost morning."

"Out? With Karl Brandt?"

"I think so."

"She sneaked out?"

"Yes."

"You knew? Did you tell your parents?"

This was getting worse by the moment.

"I didn't want to rat on her," I said, realizing even as the words tumbled out that it was probably not a great way to phrase what I meant because it sounded very James Cagney and I was feeling very *Public Enemy*.

The sheriff looked at me a long time and although I couldn't read his expression clearly I was afraid that what was there was complete disapproval.

"I mean," I stumbled on, "she was grown up and all."

"Grown up? In what ways?"

"I don't know. Big. An adult. Me, I'm just a kid."

I said this hoping like crazy that being just a kid would get me off the hook. Whatever the hook was. I didn't know for sure. What I understood clearly was that I was in way over my head.

"Grown up," the sheriff repeated sadly. "That she was, Frank." He rose slowly from the step and settled his hat on his head. "Don't forget to tell your father to call me, you hear?"

"I won't," I said.

"All right, then."

He descended the stairs and went to his car which was parked in the gravel drive in front of our garage and he backed out and disappeared up Tyler Street and just after that a train came rumbling through and I sat on the steps while the porch boards shook and the engine whistle screamed and I realized I was shaking too and it had nothing to do with the passage of the train.

*   *   *

I stayed on the porch watching for the Packard and in the late afternoon I spotted it bumping over the tracks. As soon as my father
had parked, Jake leaped out the passenger side and sprinted toward
the house and ran past me and inside. I heard the hammer of his
feet on the stairs then I heard the bathroom door on the second floor
slam shut. Jake had a notoriously small bladder. My father came more
slowly.

"The sheriff was here," I told him.

His eyes had been on the old porch steps as he mounted but now
he looked up. "What did he want?"

"He didn't say exactly. He just asked me some questions and then
he said you should call him when you got back."

"What kinds of questions?"

"About Ariel and Karl."

"Karl?"

"Yeah. He was pretty interested in Karl."

"Thank you, Frank," he said and went inside.

I went in too and flopped on the living room sofa and picked up
the comic book I'd been reading when the sheriff came. I was near
enough the phone stand at the bottom of the stairs that I could hear
my father's end of the conversation.

"It's Nathan Drum. My son told me you stopped by."

I heard the toilet flush on the second floor and water ran through
the pipe in the wall.

"I see." My father said this heavily and I could tell it wasn't good.
"I could meet you in my church office in a few minutes, if that's con-
venient."

Upstairs the bathroom door opened and Jake clomped into the
hallway.

"Fine. I'll be waiting for you."

My father put the receiver down.

I asked, "What did he want?"

The room was dark. Even though my mother hadn't been home
all day I'd left the drapes pulled shut. My father stood outlined in the

rectangle of sunlight in the front doorway. His back was to me and I couldn't see his face.

"The autopsy's finished, Frank. He wants to talk to me about it."

"Is it bad?"

"I don't know. Your mother, have you seen her?"

"No, sir."

"I'll be across the street if she calls."

He left the house and I followed to the screen door and watched him walk toward the church. Halfway there he stopped and stood dead still in the middle of the street. He seemed lost and I was afraid that if a car came by he would be hit because he wouldn't even know it was coming. I pushed open the door thinking I should call to him but he pulled himself together and continued on.

Jake galloped down the stairs and sidled up beside me.

"We got milk shakes," he said. "Dad and me. At the Dairy Queen in Mankato."

I knew he was baiting me but I had other things on my mind. I didn't even bother to reply.

He asked, "Where's Dad?"

I nodded toward the church and said, "He's waiting for the sheriff to come back."

I stepped out onto the porch.

Jake came too, glued to me, and said, "The sheriff was here? What did he want?"

"Mostly to see Dad. But he asked me some questions about Karl and Ariel."

"What kind of questions?"

"It doesn't matter."

I spoke to Jake curtly in a way meant to cut off his probing because something else had captured my attention. In the aftermath of Ariel's death I often found myself noticing some unusual convergence of natural circumstance that I took as a sign. Not necessarily from God but clearly from forces beyond my own constricted understanding. The night before, I'd observed two shooting stars whose paths crossed in the sky to the east and I knew it meant something extraordinary but what I couldn't say. And after my father and Jake had left for Mankato

as I listened to the Twins game on the radio I'd heard, during a few
moments of transmission static, a voice speak from a different broadcast source and I thought I made out two words, though not clearly:
The answer. The answer to what? I wondered at the time.

Now as I stood on the porch I saw that the sun was behind the
church steeple and the steeple shadow had fallen across the street and
was pointing directly at me like a long proscriptive finger.

"Frank, are you okay?"

The sheriff's car came down Tyler and swung onto Third and
pulled into the church lot. The sheriff got out and walked to the front
door of the sanctuary and went inside.

Jake tugged on my arm. "Frank!"

I pulled loose from his grip and started quickly down the porch
steps.

"Where are you going?"

I said, "Nowhere."

In an instant he was at my side. I didn't want to argue so I let him
come. I raced to the church's side door that opened onto the basement
stairs. Gus's motorcycle had been gone all day and as I descended into
the cool under the church I knew he wouldn't be there to stop me. I
went to the disconnected furnace duct that ran up to my father's office
and pulled out the rags meant to block the flow of sound. Jake watched
and his eyes told me he considered it an enormous transgression.

"Frank," he whispered.

I shot him a look that shut him up.

There was a knock on my father's office door and the boards above
us squeaked as he crossed to greet his visitor.

"Thank you for coming," he said.

"Could we sit down, Mr. Drum?"

"Of course."

They walked to my father's desk and chairs scraped.

My father asked, "What did the medical examiner find?"

The sheriff said, "He confirmed van der Waal's initial assessment.
Your daughter sustained a head trauma from an elongated instrument,
maybe something like a tire iron, but the actual cause of death was
drowning. There was water in her lungs, silty like you'd find in the

Minnesota River. But there's something else. Mr. Drum, your daughter wasn't the only one killed."

"I don't understand."

"I wish to God I could keep this from becoming public but this is a small town and sooner or later everyone's going to know, so I wanted you to know first. Ariel was pregnant when she died."

There was no sound from above, nothing down the duct at all, but beside me Jake sucked in an astonished breath and I grabbed him and clapped my hand over his mouth to ensure his silence.

"Did you know, Mr. Drum?"

"I had no idea," Dad said and I could hear his astonishment.

"The medical examiner estimated that Ariel was five or six weeks along in her pregnancy."

"A baby," my father said. "Dear God, what a tragedy."

"I'm truly sorry, Mr. Drum. And I'm sorry but there are some questions I have to ask you."

A painful silence followed then my father said, "All right."

"How long had your daughter been seeing Karl Brandt?"

"They'd been dating about a year."

"Did you believe they might get married?"

"Married? No. They both had other plans."

"This afternoon your son told me that Ariel had changed her mind about going away."

"She was just nervous about leaving home, I think."

"Do you still think that? In light of what the medical examiner found?"

"I don't know."

"Your son also told me that Ariel sometimes sneaked out at night and didn't come back until almost morning."

"I can't believe that's true."

"It's what he told me. If it was true, any idea where she might have gone?"

"No."

"Is it possible she was sneaking out to be with the Brandt boy?"

"I suppose it's possible. Why are you so interested in Karl?"

"Well, it's like this, Mr. Drum. All along I've pretty much figured that Warren Redstone or Morris Engdahl was responsible for what happened to your daughter. Now I've looked at Redstone's past and although the man isn't any stranger to jails he has nothing violent on his record. And those items Officer Doyle found in Redstone's little camp on the river, they were none of them worth anything and exactly the kinds of items you might find dropped somewhere along the railroad tracks or a riverbank or in an alley. So I don't have a real strong feeling at this point about him being responsible for Ariel's death. And first thing this morning, I went out to Sioux Falls to have a talk with Morris Engdahl and Judy Kleinschmidt. They're sticking to their story about being in Mueller's barn together the night your daughter went missing. Aside from the minor altercation with your son, I don't really have any reason to suspect Engdahl, except he's the kind of kid who always seems to be shaking hands with trouble. The Mann Act charge'll let me hold him and pump him good, so maybe we'll get something out of him yet."

My father said, "But you think because Ariel's pregnant and she and Karl have been dating that it's more likely Karl had something to do with her death?"

"Look, Mr. Drum, this is the first homicide investigation I've ever conducted. Things like this don't happen in Sioux County. Right now, I'm just asking questions and trying to find someplace to go with my thinking."

"I can't imagine Karl would ever harm Ariel."

"Did you know they had a huge argument the day before she went missing?"

"No."

"I talked to some of Ariel's friends who witnessed it. Anger on both sides, apparently. They couldn't tell me what it was about. Can you?"

"I haven't the slightest idea."

"Maybe about a baby, a child that would complicate both their lives enormously?"

"I don't know, Sheriff."

"Your son told me that Ariel was a lot more fond of Karl than Karl was of her."

"I don't know how he would know that."

"Would your wife?"

My father didn't answer right away. I glanced at Jake and even in the dark I could see that his face was flushed and he gripped the furnace duct as if it was a horse that might gallop away.

"I'll talk to her," my father finally said.

"I came to you first, Mr. Drum. Now I have to talk to Karl Brandt. And then I'd like to talk to your wife, after you've told her what I've told you, of course. Will she be here later?"

"I'll make certain she is."

"Thank you."

A chair scraped and a moment later another and the floorboards gave noisily under the weight of the men as they left and above us there was no sound and in the basement there was only a kind of stunned silence until Jake stuttered astonished and angry, "K-K-K-Karl."

26

My father went from the church to our house and when he could not find us there returned to the front porch. A wind had risen out of the southwest sweeping in thick clouds the color of soot. He saw us coming from the church parking lot under that oppressive sky and he eyed us with concern.

"We were looking for Gus," I lied with amazing ease and Jake made no attempt to contradict me.

"I'm going to Emil Brandt's house," my father said.

"Can we come?"

"You both stay here." His tone told us he would brook no argument. "Wait for Liz. She should be arriving soon to fix you something to eat. Your grandfather will probably come with her."

"Will you be home for dinner," I asked, "and will Mom?"

"I don't know," he replied brusquely. "We'll see."

He hurried to the Packard and backed out of the gravel driveway and drove fast up Tyler Street. As soon as he was gone, I bounded off the porch and headed for the river. Without asking where we were going Jake came running behind.

Beneath that sky which had turned cast-iron black the Minnesota River ran dark as old blood. I raced along the water's edge breaking through bramble and ignoring the suck of mud and whenever possible keeping to the sand flats on which I could make good time. I heard the desperate wheeze of Jake's breathing behind me and somewhere in my thinking I realized he was struggling to keep up but I had something more important on my mind and Jake for his part made no complaint.

We reached the narrow trail that led through cottonwoods, across the tracks, and up the slope to the old farmhouse home of Emil and Lise Brandt and we followed it. At the gate in the picket fence that surrounded the Brandt property we stopped. Jake doubled over struggling to breathe and I was afraid he might puke. When he caught his breath I thought he would in his usual way chide me for my disobedience. Instead he said, "What now?"

In so much of what had occurred I'd been informed only because of artfulness, because of heating grates and furnace ducts and my own willingness and ability to be a shadow against a wall or a fly hovering beyond a screen. I wanted to know everything the adults knew and everything they were thinking and I believed it an absolute wrong to be kept in the dark like a child. I was not a child nor was Jake any longer.

I looked past the vegetable garden Lise Brandt had planted and with our help had expanded. Across the long open yard stood the farmhouse. I had it in my mind that we would rush the house and skulk along the perimeter until we were positioned under an open living room window and could easily hear the voices inside. If we were quick and careful I believed it could be done.

I unlatched the gate and was about to lead the way inside when the back door of the farmhouse shot open and Lise Brandt stormed out. She was dressed in dungarees and a T-shirt and her hands flew in the air before her angrily signing words for which she had no voice. She hurried across the yard toward the garden shed so caught up in her rage that she didn't see us and she vanished inside.

Jake whispered again, "What do we do?"

I eyed the house and thought that if we ran for it immediately we might reach it before Lise came out of the shed.

I said, "Let's go," and I bolted.

Which turned out not to be the best plan I'd ever devised.

We were only a few fast strides beyond the garden when a banshee scream came at our backs. The sound was so awful I would gladly have kept running but Jake stopped dead in his tracks and turned. Caught and cowering I turned, too, ready to face the wraith that was Lise Brandt. In her right hand she gripped a gardening tool, something with crooked tines, and she threatened us in such a way that it appeared she had claws. I was certain she was about to tear us apart.

In the instant she saw Jake she changed. She rushed to him and began gesticulating and speaking quickly with what sounded to me like half-formed words. She shook the claw tool at the house and I couldn't tell if she was about to attack something there or if she was going to break into tears.

In the end it was tears. The first and only time I ever saw Lise Brandt cry. And it was the first and only time I saw something else. Lise Brandt who'd gone ballistic whenever I'd seen her touched put herself into my brother's arms and let him hold her while she wept.

He said to me, "She's upset because ever since Ariel died Emil has ignored her. He's gone all the time to our house and now Mom's been here all day and to Lise it feels like she's lost her brother and her home."

I'd picked up none of this during her tirade but somehow Jake had caught it all.

Lise finally pulled herself from his arms as if suddenly realizing what she'd allowed and Jake spoke to her: "You were going to work in the garden. Can we help?"

She handed him the claw tool and although she didn't smile she seemed happier.

I stood under the brooding sky and looked toward the house and knew that whatever was occurring inside my chances of overhearing were shot now. I followed Lise to the garden shed where she chose a hoe from the wall and gave it to Jake who passed it to me. For herself she took a trowel and we all trooped together into the garden.

We hadn't been long at work when I heard the front door of the farmhouse open. A moment later both my parents appeared at the side of the house and came to the garden.

"I thought I told you to stay home," my father said. He wasn't happy but neither did he sound angry.

I couldn't think of a lie quickly enough so I told the truth. "We wanted to know what's going on."

Lise Brandt remained on her knees furiously turning dirt with her trowel and clearly ignoring my parents.

"Let's go home," my father said. "We'll talk there."

Jake went to Lise but she wouldn't acknowledge him. He laid the claw tool in the dirt near her and I set down my hoe and we followed my parents to the Packard parked outside the front gate. Emil Brandt stood on the porch of the house and although he was sightless he turned his head as we passed as if following our every move. The look and color of his face seemed to mirror the threatening sky and I knew that he'd been informed of everything. I hated him for that. What my father had refused to tell Jake and me Emil Brandt knew and, although I couldn't say at all why, it felt to me like betrayal.

Not a word passed between us on the ride home. When we arrived I saw my grandfather's Buick parked in front of our house. He came out to the front porch with Liz and they both looked concerned.

"We were worried when no one was home," he said.

"Let's go inside," my father told them. "There's something we all need to talk about."

"I hate the Brandts," I said as I lay in bed that night.

The clouds had let loose another summer storm. We'd closed the windows against the rain and the bedroom felt hot and suffocating. Jake hadn't said much of anything all evening. My grandfather had blustered a good deal when he heard about Ariel's condition and said if he could just get his hands on Karl Brandt he'd wring that boy's neck. He used a few expletives which he was prone to do when angered and my father cautioned him that Jake and I were present and he said, "Hell, they're not kids anymore, Nathan, and they damn well ought to hear how men talk." And then he repeated his threat against Karl Brandt using even harsher language. Liz laid a hand on his arm but my grandfather shook it off and stood and wore the floorboards with his pacing.

Liz asked quietly, "Has anyone talked to Karl yet?"

"The sheriff," my father said.

"What did he say?"

"I don't know."

"Before we convict him, maybe we should hear his side," she offered gently.

My mother said, "The Brandts have always taken what they wanted. And thrown away what they didn't. Why should Karl be any different?"

My father said, "I intend to talk to Karl and his parents."

"We intend," my mother said.

"By God, I want to be in on that," my grandfather cried.

"No," my father replied. "This will be between the Brandts and Ruth and me."

"The sheriff is in there somewhere," I said.

They all looked at me as if I'd just come in from Siberia and had spoken Russian and after that though it nearly killed me I didn't say another word.

After we'd got ourselves ready for bed my father had come up and we'd talked.

"Maybe he forced himself on her," I said, using a term I'd pulled from God knows where.

"I'm pretty sure that didn't happen, Frank. People in love sometimes make bad decisions, that's all."

"So that's why Karl killed her? He just made a bad decision?"

"We don't know that Karl had anything to do with her death."

"We don't? That baby would have complicated Karl's life enormously," I said, nearly repeating words the sheriff had used that afternoon in my father's office.

"Frank, you know Karl. Do you think he's capable of doing what was done to Ariel?"

"You mean knocking her up?"

"Don't ever say that again. And you know what I mean."

"Jesus, I don't know."

My father could have cut into me for taking the Lord's name in vain but he sat on my bed calmly and calmly tried to reason me out of my bitter rage.

"Killing someone, Frank, that's not something most people could do. It's so unbelievably hard."

"You killed people."

I thought he would tell me that it was war and a different situation but he didn't. He said, "And if I could I would undo that." He said this with such sad conviction that it kept me from going further though it was a line of questioning I deeply wanted at some point to pursue, those mysterious killings which Gus had once drunkenly alluded to and had spoken of again in the dark of the church sanctuary only a few days earlier.

"You've always liked Karl," he reminded me. "We all have. He's always been a decent young man."

"Apparently not always," I said. Which was an exact phrase I'd heard my mother use in response to almost the same statement my father had made during the discussion downstairs.

"I'm going to ask this of you. Of you both," he said looking toward silent Jake. "Don't make any judgments until after your mother and I have had a chance to talk to Karl and his parents. Don't say anything to anyone even if you're pressed. It would be a further tragedy to have vicious rumors spread. Do you understand me?"

Jake answered immediately, "Yes, sir."

"Frank?"

"I understand."

"And you'll do what I ask?"

It took me a moment to make that promise but finally I said, "Yes, sir."

He stood up but before he left he said, "Guys, we're all moving in the dark here. Honestly, I don't know any more than you do what's right. The one thing I do know is that we have to trust in God. There is a way through this, and God will lead us. I believe that absolutely. I'm hoping you do, too."

After my father left I said toward the ceiling, "I hate the Brandts."

Jake didn't reply and I lay alone listening to the rain against the windowpane and wondering if it would really be so hard to kill someone because right at that moment I thought maybe I could.

27

n a small town nothing is private. Word spreads with the incomprehensibility of magic and the speed of plague. It wasn't long before most of New Bremen knew about Ariel's condition and the sheriff's suspicions regarding Karl Brandt.

Karl's friends were interviewed and the males among them revealed that Karl had said things lately that made them believe he'd been sleeping with Ariel.

Ariel's friends confirmed that she'd been upset but whatever had bothered her she'd kept fiercely to herself. They all suspected it had something to do with Karl and a couple of them indicated they'd suspected the possibility of a pregnancy.

Karl Brandt's parents, Axel and Julia, were keeping quiet and keeping their son out of public sight in their mansion on the Heights. My father tried his best to arrange the meeting that he believed was absolutely necessary to everyone's understanding of the situation but he never got past Simon Geiger who worked for Brandt and who'd been tapped to screen all calls coming into their home. He tried the direct approach and with my mother drove to the Brandt mansion but was refused entrance. Though he believed absolutely in God's good guidance my father was clearly upset at being stonewalled.

The sheriff was more forthcoming. He shared with my parents

what he learned in his interviews of Karl Brandt which, because a lawyer was always present, wasn't much. The young man would neither confirm nor deny his part in Ariel's pregnancy and he was adamant in asserting that neither he nor Ariel had had any intention of getting married. He held to his earlier story that the night she disappeared he'd drunk too much and had lost track of her at the party on the river. The sheriff shared with my parents his own concern that Karl sounded as if he was repeating a script he'd memorized.

Emil Brandt seemed to have dropped from our lives. He'd been my mother's constant companion from the moment Ariel vanished, but once my sister's pregnancy had been revealed and the Brandt name had been dragged into the thick of things and the family had sequestered themselves, my mother's affections shifted away from anything Brandt. Which left her adrift in a way. She seemed angry all the time. Angry at my father. Angry at the Brandts. Angry at me and Jake if we happened to stray into her path. And as always those days angry at God. As best we could we stayed out of her way.

Wednesday afternoon my father went to van der Waal's to complete the arrangements for Ariel's burial which was scheduled for Saturday. Jake and I were left home with our mother who sat in a rocker on the front porch smoking cigarettes in plain view of anyone who happened by and looking with a hard eye at the church across the street. Her hair was unbrushed and she wore slippers and her housecoat. Before he left my father had tried to talk her into dressing but had finally given up.

When Gus pulled into the church lot and parked his motorcycle I was in the garage with my bicycle flipped upside down working on removing the tube of a flat tire. Gus walked across the street so focused on my mother that he didn't see me. There were cobwebs across the garage window and the panes were in need of washing but even so I had a pretty good view of the front porch and could hear what transpired there.

At the bottom step Gus stopped. "Nathan around, Ruth?"

"Gone," she said and blew a flourish of smoke.

"Know when he'll be back?"

"I have no idea. He's getting everything ready to bury Ariel. Do you have news from your friend Doyle? Is that why you're looking for Nathan?"

"I'd rather talk directly to Nathan."

"If you know something, I'd rather you talked to me."

Gus looked up at the woman rocking slowly in the shadow of the porch. "All right," he finally said. He took the steps and faced her. "According to Doyle," he said, "the sheriff had been hoping to find the instrument used to crack Ariel's skull before she was thrown into the river. He believed it might be a tire iron and that Karl might still have it somewhere in his possession. But the county attorney has refused to petition a judge. Says there's not enough evidence. The sheriff thinks it's more a lack of backbone on the part of the county attorney."

Smoke vined from my mother's nostrils as she spoke: "Arthur Mendelsohn has always been a toad. He was a toad as a child and he's a toad as a man. He would never stand up to Axel Brandt."

She put her cigarette to her lips and her eyes held on Gus's face. She asked, "What do you think of the tire iron?"

Gus seemed to weigh his response or perhaps simply the advisability of any response. He said, "It's handy and would be effective, I imagine."

"Have you ever wielded a tire iron as a weapon?"

"No," he said, "but I'd guess that it does a lot of damage."

"You've killed people, Gus. In the war."

He didn't answer but watched her closely.

"Is it a hard thing?"

"I killed people at a distance. They were shapes to me, never faces. I imagine it would be a different thing killing someone whose face you could see."

"It would take a cold heart, don't you think?"

"Yes, ma'am, I imagine it would."

"People can fool you can't they, Gus."

"I guess they can."

"Is there anything else you wanted to tell Nathan?"

"No, that's pretty much everything."

"I'll let him know."

My father's friend left the porch and went to the church where he disappeared through the side door that led to his basement room. My mother finished her cigarette and lit another.

Within the hour my father returned from van der Waal's. It was almost lunchtime and he went directly to the kitchen to prepare the meal. My mother followed him and I drifted in after them. My father was relaying the final plans for the funeral which my mother had refused to have any part in. I saw her—maybe we all saw her— retreating, her world daily becoming a smaller and smaller box. She sat with her elbows propped on the table and a cigarette in her hand and she listened as my father pulled items from the refrigerator and told her the details. He'd acknowledged my entrance but my mother paid me no heed.

When she had apparently listened enough she said abruptly, "The sheriff tried to get a warrant to search the Brandt property for whatever it was that Karl used to shatter Ariel's skull. The county attorney refused to help him."

My father turned from the refrigerator with a half-gallon bottle of milk in his hand. "How do you know this?"

"Gus came by while you were gone."

"Doyle?"

"Yes."

My father set the milk on the table. "Ruth, we don't know at all Karl's part in Ariel's death."

She put a curtain of smoke in the air between them. "Oh, but I do," she said.

"Look, I'm going to give the sheriff a call."

"You do that."

When he'd left the room my mother finally looked where I stood by the screen door. She raised an eyebrow and said, "Do you know your Old Testament, Frankie?"

I watched her but didn't answer.

She said, "Let the battle cry be heard in the land, a shout of great destruction."

She drew on her cigarette and breathed out smoke.

28

Mother disappeared after dinner and only a short while before dark. She said she was going for a walk. My grandfather, who along with Liz had taken to eating with us regularly, had asked where she was headed. They'd all been sitting on the front porch, my parents and Liz and my grandfather, trying to get some benefit from a cooling breeze that had blown in with the evening. I'd been lying in the yard grass watching the light dissolve from the sky above the valley. My mother had said, "Around the block." And got up and just like that she was gone before anyone could object or offer companionship. Afterward my grandparents and my father talked about her. They were worried. Hell, we all were.

When she didn't come back by hard dark my father left in the Packard and my grandfather left in his big Buick and they went looking. Liz stayed with us. She kept near the telephone in case someone called with information. Jake had been upstairs all evening working on one of his model airplanes and after the men drove off he came down and when I told him what was going on he said that he'd seen Mother walking along the railroad tracks headed toward the trestle outside town.

"Why didn't you say something?"

He shrugged and looked chagrined and answered, "She was just walking."

"Along the tracks? Have you ever seen her walk along the tracks? Jesus."

I hurried to the kitchen and told Liz and then I said I would go and find Mother.

"No," Liz replied. "I don't want you on those railroad tracks at night."

"I'll take a flashlight and I'll be careful."

"I'll g-g-g-go with him," Jake stuttered and I figured he must be pretty scared.

Liz clearly wasn't happy with the idea but I pointed out that if somebody didn't go soon who knew what might happen and she gave in.

We both brought flashlights though once we were out of the Flats they were almost unnecessary because the moon had risen nearly full before us and it was easy to see our way along the railbed.

"She's ok-k-kay," Jake kept repeating.

And I repeated to him, "She's fine. She's fine."

In this way we reassured ourselves because Ariel's death had shattered any sense of normality, any firm sense that what any future moment held was predictable. If God could allow Ariel to die—allow little Bobby Cole to be so gruesomely slaughtered as well—then Mother who was not at all on good terms with the Almighty was, I feared, stepping directly into harm's way.

Moonlight turned the polished surface of each rail silver and we followed the tracks through the dark all the way to the trestle where we found our mother sitting above the flow of the Minnesota River. As soon as we saw her, I turned to Jake and said, "Go back and tell Liz where we are. I'll keep Mom here and make sure she's okay."

Jake looked back at the long dark tunnel of the night between us and town. He said, "Alone?"

"Yeah, stupid. One of us has to go and I need to stay here."

"Why c-c-c-can't I stay?"

"What if Mom decides to jump or something? You want to go in after her? Go on. Hurry."

He thought about arguing some more but finally accepted his duty and headed back following the jerky finger of his flashlight beam.

My greatest fear was that a train might at any minute come roaring toward us and, with Mother in the middle of the trestle in God knew what mental state, I wouldn't be able to get her to safety in time. The good thing was that it was night and the headlight of an engine ought to be visible a long while before it reached the river. I crept out onto the railroad bridge. Mother didn't look my way and I wasn't certain if she even realized I was there. But when I was a few steps from reaching her she said to me, "This is the place isn't it, Frankie?"

I stood beside her and looked down where she looked. The river below us was all moonlight. I said, "Yes."

"What did you see?"

"Her dress. Her hair. That's all."

She looked up at me and I saw thin iridescent trails down her cheeks and I realized she'd been crying and still was.

"I used to swim in this river," she said. "When I was a girl. There's a deep clear pool a couple of miles downstream where Cottonwood Creek comes in. Have you ever been there?"

"Sure," I said.

"Sit down. Here." She patted the crossties next to where she sat and I did as she asked.

"I never thought of the river as dangerous, Frankie. But you found someone else dead here."

"Yeah, the itinerant."

"Itinerant." She shook her head faintly. "Someone's entire life reduced to a single word. And little Bobby Cole, didn't he . . . ?"

"Yeah. Him too."

"It's pretty here," she said. "You wouldn't suspect all that death, would you? Do you and Jake come here often?"

"We used to. Not anymore. I think we should go home, Mom."

"Are you worried about me, Frankie? I know everyone else is."

"You kind of scare me sometimes these days."

"I scare myself."

"Come home, Mom."

"See, it's like this. I can't talk to your father. I'm too angry with him. I'm angry with everybody."

"With God?"

"Frankie, there is no God. I could jump right now into that river and there would be no divine hand reaching out to save me. It would simply be the end."

"Not for me or Jake or Dad."

"My point exactly. There is no God to care about us. We've got only ourselves and each other."

She reached her arm around me and pulled me gently against her and I remembered how when I was small and afraid she'd done the same thing.

"But your father, Frankie, he cares more about God than he does about us. And to me that's like saying he cares more about the air and I hate him for that."

I wanted to tell her about the night I'd seen him cry in Gus's arms at the altar. And I wanted to tell her about his sermon the next day and how from that air she faulted him for caring about he'd somehow taken remarkable strength. Instead I just leaned into her and felt her weeping and looked up at the moon and listened to the frogs along the river's edge and then I heard voices coming from the dark in the direction of town and I saw flashlight beams approaching along the railroad bed.

"Damn," my mother said quietly. "Saint Nathan to the rescue." She looked at me, looked me straight in the eye. "Will you do something for me, Frankie, something that you can't tell your father about?"

The lights were not far down the tracks and in only a couple of minutes they would reach us. I had to decide and decide quickly. She seemed so alone, my mother. And because God and my father wouldn't listen I figured I had to.

I said, "Yes."

In the dead of night I rose. When I was getting ready for bed I'd folded my clothes on a chair and because I was not known for my neatness Jake had watched me with suspicion. But it had been a strange evening and everything was strange those days and so Jake didn't question me.

I grabbed my clothes and went into the hallway where the door to my mother's bedroom was closed. I wondered if she was awake listening for the sound of my leaving. I crept down the stairs careful to avoid the steps I knew would cry my presence to my father who had taken to sleeping on the sofa in the living room. In the kitchen I saw by moonlight that the hands of the wall clock read two-thirty-five. I slipped out the screen door into the yard where I put on my pants and shirt and socks and sneakers. I folded my pajamas and carried them to the garage and put them on a shelf beside an oilcan. I rolled my bicycle out, climbed on, and followed the road that was milk white in the moonlight into town.

I'd lived other places before New Bremen, other towns where my father had been the pastor, and although I got to know them quickly and discovered easily what was special and fun about them none had been as close to my heart as New Bremen. Ariel's death had changed that. The town became alien to me and at night especially threatening and I biked each deserted street with a sense that menace was all around me. The unlit house windows were dark eyes watching. Awful things lurked in the shadows cast by the moon. The whole two miles to the Heights I pumped hard on the pedals as if chased by demons.

The Brandt estate was a football field of grass cut even as carpeting and set here and there with lush flower garden enclaves all of it tended by a groundskeeper, a man named Petrov whose son Ivan was in my class at school. A tall wrought-iron fence surrounded the entire property and the only way in was through a gate opening onto a long drive that led to the house. Ornately crafted into the iron of the gate was a great wrought-iron letter *B*. Two enormous stone pillars flanked the entrance and as I drew up before the gate I saw in the bright moonlight that a word had been spray-painted in black on one of the pillars: *Murdrer*.

I stood before the gate and stared at that angry misspelling. A can of spray paint lay on the ground not far away. I looked down the street which ran empty through the ghostly light. The houses on the far side were large and sat upon substantial properties though none even began to approach the extent of the Brandt estate. They all stood completely dark.

I continued a hundred yards farther to a place where a big maple grew outside the fence but with some branches that arched over the wrought iron. I laid my bike against the trunk, shinnied up the tree, scooted out along the thickest branch, and dropped into the Brandts' yard. Across a broad lake of moonlight I raced toward the house that was all white stone and white columns and had been built in the days when New Bremen was young. I veered toward the garage, a converted carriage house. Parked on the drive in front was Karl's little red sports car.

I did as my mother had asked then I sprinted back to the fence. Without the tree to help me I had some difficulty scaling the wrought iron but I finally made it over and leaped onto my bike and pumped hard toward home.

I hadn't gone far and was just turning a sharp curve in the road that led downhill toward the main part of town when headlights from an oncoming car blinded me. I swerved quickly and almost fell off my bike. I stopped and the car stopped too. I heard a door open and close. Because of the headlight glare, I couldn't see who it was. Then Doyle's big shadow fell over me and I figured I was dead.

"Got a call someone was messing around the Brandt place," he said. "Why am I not surprised it's you? Off the bike, Frank, and let's go."

I followed Doyle to the back of his cruiser. He opened the trunk and said, "Put your bike in there." When I'd done what he asked, he pointed toward the passenger side and said, "Get in."

We continued up the road to the gate of the Brandt mansion where Doyle's headlights illuminated the graffiti. He looked over at me but said nothing. He got out and picked up the can of spray paint and got back in. He turned his cruiser around and we descended slowly from the Heights. For a long time Doyle said nothing, just drove with his wrist draped over the top of his steering wheel. The radio of his cruiser squawked now and then but he didn't bother to pick up his mic.

I sat silent beside him, feeling doomed. I saw my father coming down to the jail in the middle of the night in just the way he'd come for Gus and I could already see the look on his face.

At the junction with Main Street, instead of turning toward the town square and the jail, Doyle turned toward the Flats.

He said, "A lot of folks around here, they think the Brandts are kind of big for their britches. You understand what I'm saying?"

"Yes, sir."

"What happened to your sister, it's got people upset. The Brandt boy, I'm betting he goes scot-free. I'm sorry to say that, Frank, but that's the way the world works. The rich, they walk on stilts and the rest of us, we just crawl around under them in the dirt. So what do you do? Well, you spray-paint the truth where the world can see it, I guess that's one thing. Rub their noses a little in the stink of what they've done and who they are, huh?" He smiled and laughed quietly.

I thought I hated the Brandts but the way Doyle talked made me feel uncomfortable, like we were both part of some larger darker conspiracy, and I wasn't sure I wanted that. Still it was better than being taken to jail.

He pulled to a stop in front of our house and we got out and he opened the trunk so I could get my bike. He held up the can of spray paint I'd seen lying near the Brandts' gate. "I'll keep this, if you don't mind," he said. "Dump it somewhere nobody'll find it. Frank, this is between you and me, understand? You say a word to anyone, I'll swear you're a liar, we clear?"

"Yes, sir."

"All right then. Get some sleep, kid."

He watched me lean my bicycle against the garage wall and then go quietly in the side door to the kitchen. Before I went upstairs to bed I looked out the front window and he was gone.

29

First thing next morning the sheriff arrived. We were eating breakfast, all of us except my mother who was still in bed. My father answered the front door and the sheriff stepped inside. I got up from the kitchen table and stood in the doorway listening to the two men talk and I could barely breathe.

"We had some vandalism last night out at the Brandt home, Nathan. Somebody spray-painted those folks' front gate. Wrote *Murderer* there. Except the vandal wasn't too bright. Left out an *e* and spelled it *Murdrer*. But it's pretty clear what the intent was."

"That's a shame," my father said.

"I don't suppose you or your family know anything about it."

"No. Why would we?"

"Didn't figure as much but I've got to ask. The truth is it could be just about anybody in town. Sentiment against the Brandts is pretty sour these days. By the way, heard you almost lost Ruth last night."

"Nothing like that. She just took a walk and didn't tell any of us where she was going. It got a little late and we got a little worried."

"Ah," the sheriff said. "Must've heard it wrong." Then he looked past my father into our house the same way he'd looked past me a couple of days earlier. His eyes found me in the kitchen doorway and held on me in a way that made me believe he was certain who the vandal was.

"Is that all, Sheriff?"

"Yeah, I guess so. Just thought you ought to know."

He left and got into his car and drove away and when I turned back to the kitchen table Jake was sitting there looking at me in the same way the sheriff had. My father returned to the table and Jake didn't say anything and we finished our breakfast.

Later in our room Jake said, "Murdrer? You couldn't even spell it right?"

"What are you talking about?"

"You know."

"No, I don't."

"I wondered why you went to bed in your pajamas but got up wearing your underwear and T-shirt. You went to the Brandts' last night, didn't you?"

"You're crazy."

"I'm not." He sat there on his bed looking up at me but he didn't look angry or worried. "Why didn't you take me?"

"I didn't want you to get into trouble. Look, Jake, I was there but I didn't paint that word."

"What did you do?"

"Mom asked me to put an envelope on the windshield of Karl's car."

"What was in it?"

"I don't know. She made me promise not to open it."

"Who spray-painted the gate?"

"I don't know. It was that way when I got there."

I was about to tell Jake the whole story when I heard the feisty growl of a little automobile engine and when I looked out the window Karl Brandt drove up in his sports car. Jake and I both went downstairs where our mother was finally up and eating some toast and drinking coffee. My father had gone to his office in the church but he must have seen Karl arrive because he came quickly home.

Karl knocked on the front screen door and I opened it. As he walked in, Dad bounded up the porch steps behind him. Karl looked like death. He stood in the house with his shoulders slumped and his eyes downcast and there came from him, as if it held an actual scent, the air of despair. My mother stepped in from the kitchen with her coffee in her hand. She didn't seem surprised at all. Karl's dark eyes lit briefly on each of us then settled at last on my mother. He held up the envelope which I recognized. Not a word passed between them yet my mother came forward and put her coffee cup on the dining room table, took the envelope, and walked to the living room. Karl followed her. The rest of us watched as if it was a silent play being performed. Mother sat down at the piano. She opened the envelope, took out a couple of pages of sheet music, settled them on the music rack above the keyboard, and began to play and to sing.

The song was *Unforgettable,* the great Nat King Cole standard. She played flawlessly and sang in a way that was like a pillow inviting you to rest all the weariness of your heart upon it. Karl had sung this same song with Ariel at the Senior Frolics in the spring, a duet that had brought down the house. We'd all been there and after I had heard them sing together I'd figured I knew pretty well what love was all about.

Karl Brandt stood with his hand on the piano and I thought if he hadn't had that great instrument to lean against he might have collapsed. He'd always seemed to me to be old and mature and sophisticated but at that moment he looked like a child and like he was going to cry.

When my mother finished he whispered, "I didn't kill Ariel. I could never hurt Ariel."

"I never thought for a moment that you did, Karl," my father replied.

Karl turned and said, "Everyone else in town does. I can't even leave the house anymore. Everyone stares at me like I'm a monster."

From where she sat on the piano bench my mother looked up at Karl and said, "You got my daughter pregnant."

"It wasn't me," Karl said. "I swear it wasn't me."

"You're telling me my daughter slept around?"

"No. But I never slept with her."

"That's not what you told your friends."

"That was just talk, Mrs. Drum."

"Hateful, hurtful talk."

"I know. I know. I wish I'd never said those things. But all the guys say them."

"Then all the guys should be ashamed of themselves."

"I didn't kill her. I swear to God, I didn't touch her."

We heard the pound of steps on the front porch and the hammer of a fist on our door and there were Mr. and Mrs. Brandt looking at us with their faces dark through the mesh of the screen.

My father let them in and Mrs. Brandt rushed to her son and put herself between him and my mother and said to Karl, "You shouldn't be here."

"I had to tell them," he said.

"You had to do nothing of the sort. You owe no one an explanation."

"Oh, but he does, Julia."

Mrs. Brandt turned on my mother. "He had nothing to do with your daughter's death."

"What about her pregnancy?"

"Or that."

"He's been telling two different stories, Julia."

I couldn't believe how calm my mother seemed, how solid, like cold iron.

Mrs. Brandt said to her son, "Karl, you go home and wait for us there. We'll take care of this."

"But they need to understand," he pleaded.

"I told you, we'll take care of this."

"Go on home, Son," Axel Brandt said. He sounded tired and some of Karl's despair was in his voice.

Karl slowly crossed the room, cowering, and I saw him in the same way the sheriff and Doyle must have seen him when they called him the Brandt boy. He reached the front door and paused a moment and I thought he was going to turn back and say something more. Instead he simply pushed out into the morning light. A minute later I heard the sound of his car pulling away.

"Now," Julia Brandt said returning her attention to my mother. "Is there something you want to say to me, Ruth?"

"Just one question, Julia: What are you afraid of?"

"What makes you think I'm afraid?"

"Because you've been hiding. Nathan and I have been trying to talk to you and Axel and Karl, but you've refused to see us. Why is that?"

"Our lawyer," Axel Brandt said. "He advised us against speaking with anyone."

"Given the circumstances," my father said, "I think the least you could have done was to have agreed to see us."

"I wanted to, but . . ." Mr. Brandt didn't finish. Instead he cast an accusing glare at his wife.

"I saw no reason," Julia Brandt said. "Karl didn't hurt your daughter. Nor did he impregnate her. Nor, despite speculation to the contrary, did he ever intend to marry her."

"And how do you know all this, Julia?" My mother stood up from the piano bench. "You're privy to Karl's every action and every thought?"

"I know my son."

"I thought I knew my daughter."

"We all know about your daughter, don't we?"

"I beg your pardon?"

"She's had her eye on Karl for a long time. Why do you think she got herself pregnant?"

"Julia," Mr. Brandt said horrified.

"It needs to be said, Axel. Ariel got herself pregnant in order to force Karl into a marriage he didn't want. None of us wanted. The truth, Ruth, is that we would never have allowed such a union."

"Julia, will you just shut up," Mr. Brandt said.

My mother said quietly, "And why would you have objected, Julia?"

"What kind of family would Karl have married into? Look at the risk," Mrs. Brandt replied. "Just look at your children, Ruth. A girl with a harelip. A son with a stutter. Another son wild as an Indian. What kind of children would Ariel have produced?"

"Nathan, Ruth, I'm sorry," Axel Brandt said. He strode across the room and grabbed his wife's arm. "Julia, I'm taking you home now."

"Just a minute, Axel," my mother said with unnerving calm. "Julia, that horse you're on is pretty high. But I remember when you were the daughter of a drunkard who fixed other people's automobiles. And everyone in this town knew you had your eye on Axel, and we've all done the calculations regarding your marriage and the birth of your son so don't you say one more word to me about Ariel's condition, you of all people."

"I'm not going to stand here and listen to this, Axel," Julia Brandt said and spun away from my mother.

"Whatever it is you're hiding, Julia, I'll find out," my mother said to the woman's back.

Axel Brandt mumbled more apologies and followed his wife out the front door.

A great quiet was left in their wake, the kind I imagined that might have fallen on a battlefield after the guns had been silenced. We all stood looking at the screen door.

"Well," my mother finally said brightly, "I think we should be grateful to whomever it was that flushed out the Brandts."

My father turned to her. "Flushed out? Ruth, they're not quails we're hoping to shoot."

"No, but they are adults and they should be accepting responsibility."

"Responsibility for what? We don't know anything for certain."

"Don't you feel it, Nathan? There's something they're holding back, something they know and aren't telling."

"The only thing I feel is great dismay at how the Brandts are being treated by the people of this town."

"That's because you didn't grow up here. The Brandts have always sidestepped responsibility for their trespasses and everyone in this town knows it. But not this time."

My father looked truly distressed. "How can I help you let go of this anger, Ruth?"

"I suppose you could pray for me, Nathan. Isn't that what you do best?"

"Ruth, God isn't—"

"If you mention God to me one more time, I'll leave you, I swear I will."

Now my father looked startled as if she'd struck him with her fist and he held out empty hands, offering her nothing. "I don't know how to do that, Ruth. For me, God is at the heart of everything."

Mother walked past him to the telephone, lifted the receiver, and dialed. "Dad," she said, "it's Ruth. I wonder if I could stay with you and Liz for a while. No, just until . . . well for a while. No, Dad, everything's fine. And, yes, I could use a ride, the sooner the better."

She hung up and the room was a fist of silence.

30

Mother left with a suitcase full of her things. After she'd made the phone call, my father didn't try to talk her out of her decision. He offered to help carry the suitcase but she refused and hauled it to my grandfather's car herself. The two men shook hands and then stood awkwardly and watched while my mother settled herself in the big Buick.

Jake and I hung back in the porch shade and after my mother had gone my father walked to us and looked at us bewildered as if he had no idea what to say. Finally he shrugged. "I guess she needs some time, boys," he said. "It's been hard for her."

Hell it's been hard for us all, I thought but didn't say.

"I'll be in my office," he said. He left us and walked slowly toward the church in a drifting way that made me think of a man wandering lost.

Jake kicked idly at the post that supported the porch roof and asked, "What do you want to do now?"

"Let's find Gus."

Because it was a hot day and still early I figured the pharmacy and we found Gus's Indian Chief parked in front. We went inside. No Gus. Mr. Halderson was talking with a customer but when he saw Jake and me he excused himself and came right over. Like we were special or something.

"Well, boys," he said. "What can I do for you this morning?"

"We're looking for Gus, sir," I said.

"He was in here earlier but he left a while ago. Went next door for a haircut, I believe. Say, I heard there was some vandalism up at the Brandt place last night."

"We heard that too," I said.

He gave me the same kind of conspiratorial smile Doyle had offered me the night before and it was clear he didn't at all condemn the guilty party and it was just as clear whom he considered the guilty party to be. I wondered if Doyle had been spreading the word.

I thanked him for directing us to Gus and went next door. Sure enough, he was sitting in the chair with a white sheet draped over him and his head bent while Mr. Baake ran an electric razor over the back of his neck. The barber looked up and said, "Come on in, boys."

Mr. Baake cut our hair too and my father's. Once a month or so we'd all troop down to his barbershop on a Saturday morning and get the deed done. I liked the barbershop, the way it smelled of hair oil and bay rum and had a million comic books and magazines of the kind my father would never let us read. I liked how men gathered there and talked and joked and seemed to know each other in the same way Jake and I knew our friends when we met on the ball field for a game of workup and afterward sat on the grass and learned what was what in New Bremen and to a smaller extent the world.

"Hey, Frankie, Jake," Gus said with a grin. That was one thing I loved about Gus. He was never not happy to see us. "What are you two up to?"

"There's something we wanted to talk to you about," I said.

"Okay, go ahead."

I looked past Gus's face to the face of Mr. Baake behind him and Gus saw and interpreted correctly the flick of my eyes and said, "Tell you what. Why don't you guys sit there for a few minutes and do some reading and when I'm finished here we'll talk, okay?"

Jake and I sat down. Jake picked up one of the *Hot Stuff* comic books which was about a little devil whose temper was always getting him into trouble. Me, I picked up a magazine called *Action for Men* that had on the front cover an illustration of a guy in a safari outfit holding a powerful looking rifle and with a voluptuous blonde

at his side who wore a very short khaki skirt and a blouse ripped away
enough to show a lot of bare skin and a little bit of her bra and they
both were facing a lion that looked pretty damn hungry. The woman
was clearly scared. The guy looked cool of nerve, exactly how I imagined myself reacting in that situation. I opened to an article that was
supposed to be true about a man who'd been attacked by killer spiders
in the Amazon. But I didn't read much because within a couple of
minutes Gus was finished and striding out the door with Jake and me
at his heels. On the street he turned to us.

"So what did you want to tell me?"

"Mom left," I said.

"Left? What do you mean?"

"She's gone, went to stay with our grandparents."

Gus ran a hand over his newly clipped hair. "How's your dad?"

"He went to his office, so I don't know."

"All right," Gus said, thinking. "All right." He looked toward the
Flats. "You guys want a ride back?"

And of course we did.

Gus threw a leg over his motorcycle. I hooked up behind him on
the seat and Jake settled into the sidecar. It took only minutes to reach
the church lot where Gus parked the Indian Chief. He nodded toward
our house and said, "You guys go on and have some lunch. I'll be over
in a bit." He headed into the church and we crossed the street to home.

We threw together a couple of peanut butter and jelly sandwiches
and ate them with potato chips and cherry Kool-Aid in the kitchen.
Then we headed to the living room to watch television. I thought
that with our mother gone the place wouldn't feel drowned in despair but breathing the dark air of that room full of the stale smell
of cigarette smoke was like breathing death. Mother in her grieving
had forbidden us to open the drapes. My father and Emil Brandt
both had tried to talk reason to her but she was almost vicious in
her resistance. In truth we often kept the drapes closed in summer
during the worst of the heat but my mother's desire for the dark
had nothing to do with that. Jake flopped on the sofa and turned
on the television. I went to the south window and yanked back one
of the drapes and then the other and July brilliance caromed off the

floor and smacked the wall. Jake jumped up and looked stricken, as
if I'd broken one of the Commandments, then he realized the freedom that had suddenly become ours and he ran to the east window
and threw back the drapes there. It wasn't just sunlight that flooded
in. The good scent of summer came with it. I was sure I smelled the
wild daisies in the pasture behind our house and the fresh wet of the
laundry Edna Sweeney had hung on her clothesline and the grapes
in the arbor of the Hansons' house two doors down and the almost
sweet aroma of the grain in the elevators beside the tracks and even,
I swore, the luscious mud smell of the river two blocks away. Jake
stood in the sunlight that poured in. He glowed as if electrified and
he wore a smile that stretched his cheeks until they nearly snapped.

Gus came in the front door and put his hands on his hips and
looked at us keenly. "What are you two up to now?" he asked.

"Nothing," I said, thinking he was going to chew our rear ends for
what we'd done with the drapes.

"Not anymore." He held up the keys to my family's Packard. "We're
going for a horseback ride."

We drove north out of the valley and onto rolling farmland. We followed back roads that were a mystery to me and that threaded between fields of corn and soybean and cut alongside farmyards and
skipped through towns that were there and gone in less than a breath
and finally we dipped into a valley much smaller than the one carved
by the Minnesota River and filled with emerald alfalfa fields outlined
by clean white fences. We turned off the main road onto a long dirt
lane that led to a house with a big barn and several outbuildings all
canopied by the leaves of a dozen great elms. A woman stood in the
shade near the house watching us come and when Gus pulled up she
stepped forward to greet us.

"Gentlemen," Gus said after we'd piled out, "I'd like you to meet
Ginger French. Ginger, my friends Frankie and Jake."

We shook her hand and I thought Ginger French was the pretti-
est woman I'd ever seen, tall and willowy, with long brown hair that
fell straight down over her shoulders. She wore a light blue shirt that

I thought of as Western because it had pearl snaps and she wore black leather riding boots.

She kissed Gus on the cheek and said to us, "You boys care for some lemonade before we hit the trail?"

"No, ma'am," I replied. "Let's ride."

She laughed and Gus did too and she took his arm and led the way to the barn where she had horses saddled and waiting.

Ginger—she insisted we call her by her first name—I learned that afternoon had not grown up in Minnesota but was raised in Kentucky and had come west with her husband, a man who'd worked for a company called Cargill. They'd lived in the Twin Cities but she'd been lonesome for the horse country so her husband had bought the land in the little valley and they'd started a kind of ranch there where they spent weekends and much of the summer. Her husband had died two years earlier of a heart attack and she'd moved permanently to the ranch and ran it by herself. Gus, she said, had been a big help during the first haying that year, doing most of the alfalfa baling by himself. Fine muscles, she'd said and she'd given him a long smile.

I knew some things about Gus. I knew that what living he made was done by working odd jobs all over the county. He did maintenance on the churches in my father's charge, dug graves for the cemetery in New Bremen and helped keep the grounds, got calls sometimes from Monk's Garage when they needed motorcycle work done, cleared jimsonweed from cornfields, strung wire for fences, put up rip rap along creeks prone to flood erosion, worked occasional construction jobs. And now I knew he did haying as well. Hell I'd've done haying for Ginger too and never asked a dime.

I rode a mount called Smokie and Jake got a horse called Pokey. Gus rode a big tawny beast named Tornado and Ginger rode, of course, Lady. We followed a trail along the creek that threaded the bottom of the little valley. We passed a small tractor that had no wheels but was mounted on blocks. A belt ran from the back axle to an irrigation pump that drew water from the creek for the alfalfa fields.

"Gus's creation," Ginger told us and reached out and touched his arm gently.

Gus and she rode up front side by side, talking quietly. Jake and I brought up the rear. We'd been on horses before, a couple of summers when we both attended a church camp, and we figured that made us experienced riders and we wanted to gallop, but Ginger said that it was better to take things easy this time around and let the horses get to know us and for us to get to know them. I didn't really care that much anyway. I loved being out on that beautiful day with butterflies like snow flurries over the alfalfa and the hills humped green against the blue sky and the air cool with the mist from the sprinklers that watered the fields. When we came back Ginger served us lemonade and sugar cookies on her porch and told us about the Kentucky Derby which she went to every year and it sounded to me like the most exciting thing imaginable. And too quickly it was time to go.

We said our good-byes and Jake called shotgun and got in the front seat and I slid in the back and Gus and Ginger French spent a moment talking quietly several paces away from the car and then he kissed her on the lips and she held his arm as if she wouldn't let him go and then the connection broke and she lifted her emptied hand and waved to us as Gus drove up the dirt lane and headed back to New Bremen.

On the way home Gus stopped at a liquor store and bought beer. It was suppertime when we reached the house. He came in with us and said, "I'm going to fix dinner." He didn't ask what we might want, just opened the refrigerator and took a look and launched into things. He put Jake and me to work peeling potatoes. He pulled a carton of eggs from the fridge and a block of cheddar cheese and set them on the kitchen counter and took a can of Spam from the cupboard. He put a skillet on the stove and poured in some oil. He grabbed the potatoes as they were peeled and diced them and coated them with a little flour from the canister near the sink. He started the oil heating and when it was hot let Jake and me toss in the potatoes and gave us a spatula and told us not to let them burn. He grated a mound of cheese and set it aside on a plate. He put a frying pan on another burner and started the flame underneath and diced the Spam and threw it into the pan with a little butter. He beat eggs into a bowl with salt and pepper and poured the mixture over the frying Spam and rolled them all together as they cooked and at the end he sprinkled the cheese over the eggs and Spam and put a lid on the pan. The potatoes were done by then and he used the spatula to remove them to a paper towel that soaked up the excess oil. He told me to set the table and told Jake to go across the street and let my father know that dinner was ready. He put everything into serving dishes and then on the table and instructed me to pour milk for myself and Jake and he cracked the tops on two of the bottles of beer and my father when he walked into the kitchen stood there stunned.

Gus held out an opened beer toward him. "I know it's against your religion, Captain, but how about it, just this once?"

We ate and my father and Gus drank their beer and we all talked, even Jake, and laughed and Christ for a while we were happy.

31

Karl Brandt came while Jake and I were doing the dishes. Like a beggar he appeared at the screen door off the kitchen. He stood there with his eyes downcast and when he asked for my father his voice wasn't much above a whisper as if what he wanted was something he believed he had no right to ask for and no hope of getting.

Gus had left after dinner, taken off on his motorcycle, and although he didn't say where my own thinking was that he'd gone back to see Ginger French. My father had gone to his church office to tend to some details of Ariel's funeral.

I stood with the wet dishcloth still in my hand and told Karl where my father was and offered to go get him and asked if he wanted to come in and wait.

Karl shook his head. "Thanks, Frank. I'll find him myself."

When Karl had gone Jake and I looked at each other and it was clear we were both reading the same book. I put down the dishcloth and dried my hands on the legs of my pants and started for the door.

"Wait," Jake said. I thought he was going to argue with me but he said, "We should give him a minute."

We waited until we saw Karl enter the church then we broke from the house and ran across the street with the long yellow light of the

low sun in our faces and hurried down the side stairs to the dark of
the basement where I quickly pulled the rag stuffing from the furnace
duct and we leaned close and barely breathed.

"... I swear it," Karl was saying. "I messed up I know. I shouldn't
have been drinking and I should have been watching out for Ariel, but
I swear I would never hurt her, Mr. Drum. Ariel was my best friend.
Sometimes I thought my only friend."

"I've seen the group you run with, Karl. It's not insignificant."

"Nobody understood me like Ariel. Nobody."

"Did you father her child?"

"No."

"Yet, as Ruth pointed out this morning, you apparently told your
friends that you were having sexual relations with Ariel."

"I never said that, not outright. I said things that they took to mean
that."

"They misinterpreted?"

"Not exactly. Look, when you're with guys, you've got to be a certain way, you know?"

"And that way is to appear to be sleeping with your girlfriend?"

"Well, yeah."

"Even if it's not true?"

Karl was quiet a long moment, then he said so low we almost
missed it, "Maybe especially if it's not true."

"What do you mean?"

We heard the floorboards above us give as someone stood and
began to pace. Nothing came down the duct for a while. Me, I'd've
been pressing for an answer but my father's patience was remarkable.
A bug with about a million legs crawled out from under the furnace.
Normally I would have stomped it but the silence in that church at the
moment was profound and I didn't want to risk giving us away. I saw
Jake looking at the bug too but he made no move to kill it.

"It wasn't me who got Ariel pregnant," Karl said at last.

The pacing above us had stopped far to my left and I figured Karl
was at the window which looked toward the setting sun. In my mind's
eye I could see his face lit with that dying yellow light.

"Ariel and I were friends but not that way," he said.

"I don't understand, Karl."

"Mr. Drum, I . . ."

He faltered and his voice broke and what came to us next was the sound of deep heartbreaking sobs.

The floorboards above us gave again as my father crossed the room to where Karl Brandt stood.

"It's all right, Karl. It's all right, son."

"No . . . it . . . isn't," Karl said between gasps. "It's sick. It's awful. It's depraved."

"What is it, Karl?"

"Don't you understand?" Karl's voice was suddenly vicious, a wet rage of tears. "I didn't like Ariel that way. I've never liked girls that way. I don't think of them at all that way. See? Now do you see?"

"Ah," my father said. And it was clear that he did.

"I'm a faggot. I'm a freak. I'm a sick freak. I'm a—"

"Karl, Karl, it's all right."

"No, it's not all right. All my life I've watched other boys to make sure I was acting just like them. I'd say to myself, 'This is how a boy walks. This is how a boy talks. This is how a boy doesn't notice other boys.' When I was a kid, I didn't understand what was going on with me. And when it finally dawned on me, I couldn't stomach who I was. Who I am."

"You're a child of God."

"A sick God."

"No, a God who loves you."

"If he loved me he'd have made me just like other boys."

"I don't think you're a freak. I don't think you're sick."

"No, you just think I'm a murderer."

"I don't. I never did."

"Right."

"What I saw in you always was a young man who befriended my daughter and who entered my house respectfully. I know you made mistakes, but not once in all this horrible mess have I ever thought you might have killed Ariel. That's the absolute truth."

My father spoke in a voice that held no heat of argument but only a gentle invitation to believe. It was the way he spoke about God in his sermons.

"Karl, does anyone know about this?"

"I've never told anyone, not even Ariel."

"But she knew?"

"I think she figured it out, but we never talked about it."

"Did you know she was pregnant?"

"The argument we had that everyone keeps bringing up, it was about the baby."

"What about the baby?"

"I told her—Mr. Drum, I'm sorry about this, but I thought it was best—I told her I knew of a doctor in Rochester who could take care of the situation."

"An abortion?"

"Yes, sir, an abortion. But she absolutely refused. She was going to have the baby and raise it here in New Bremen."

"Did she talk about the father?"

"She never would tell me that."

"Do you have a speculation?"

"No, sir, I don't."

"She was sneaking out at night to see someone, but you have no idea who that was?"

"I don't, honestly. Ariel, when she wanted to, could be very secretive. That's one of the things that I liked about her. She kept secrets, her own and those told to her. I guess you'd call it integrity. Mr. Drum, you won't tell anyone what I've told you?"

"No, Karl."

"I don't know what I'd do if people knew. The only reason I told you was because you have integrity, like Ariel, and I didn't want you to go on thinking I had anything to do with what happened to her, because I never would. I miss her, Mr. Drum. I miss her terribly."

"We all do."

The door at the top of the basement steps opened and I thought Gus had come back and because I was afraid he'd make noise and give us away I quickly stuffed the wadding back into the furnace duct. Jake and I turned and found to our surprise that it wasn't Gus but Doyle. He wasn't wearing his uniform. When he saw where we stood he didn't have to be a genius to know what we were up to.

"I'm looking for Gus," he said.

"He's not here," I replied.

Doyle came toward us slowly. "That's Karl Brandt's Triumph in the church lot. He's talking with your dad?"

I said, "Yes."

"Have they finished?"

"Pretty much."

"You boys get an earful?"

Doyle kept coming and Jake took a step back.

"Anything I should know?" Doyle looked at me first but what we'd just heard was something I knew my father wouldn't want us to share. He moved between us, separating us, and he turned fully toward Jake and towered over him.

"So tell me, Jakie, did he confess to killing your sister?"

Jake squeezed his face together and whether it was an effort to hold words in or to get them out I couldn't say.

Doyle leaned down so that his face and Jake's were separated by no more than the length of a Popsicle stick. "Well? Did he confess?"

Jake's lips trembled and his fists clenched and he finally spat out, "He's not a m-m-m-murderer. He's just a f-f-faggot, wh-wh-whatever that is."

Doyle's eyes bloomed wide with surprise and he straightened up. "Faggot?" he said. "Jakie, you're going to tell me everything."

I lay in bed that night more confused than ever. Too many things had happened in the day—the altercation between Julia Brandt and my mother, Mother's desertion of us, Karl Brandt's astounding confession, and our buckling under the questioning of Doyle who'd hounded Jake and me until he knew the whole of what we'd heard—and I felt twisted and wrung out. I was almost able to make some sense of these things but something else had happened that day which was far worse and for which I had no explanation or understanding and that made me feel absolutely lousy. It was simply this: For a little while I'd forgotten about Ariel and I'd been happy. Jesus, Ariel was dead only a week and not even in the ground yet and I'd forgotten her. It hadn't been a long lapse in grieving, only the time with Ginger French and fixing dinner with Gus and eating and talking around the table and laughing. Her death had come back to me the moment Karl Brandt's tragic face appeared at the screen door. Still I felt like a traitor, the worst kind of brother Ariel could have had.

Jake said, "Frank?"

"Yeah?"

"I've been thinking."

"About what?"

"Karl. About him being a faggot and all."

That was the word Doyle had kept coming back to when he hounded us, using it like the word was a nail and his voice a hammer.

"Don't say that word," I told him. "If you've got to say anything, say homosexual."

Which was the term my mother employed occasionally in her discussions of artists. She never said the word in a derogatory manner and I knew she didn't care if someone was inclined that way. Among my friends, however, *fag* was the word you typically used and you used it like a sharp stick.

Jake was quiet and I said, "Sorry, go on."

Jake said, "He's afraid people will make fun of him, and that's why he never told anyone."

"So?"

"I don't like to talk to people because I'm afraid I'll stutter and they'll make fun of me. I feel like a freak sometimes."

I rolled over and looked at his bed. The bulb over the bathroom sink was on and some of the light splashed off the wall in the hallway and fell into our room. Mostly all I could see was the gray outline of my brother under his sheet. There wasn't much to him and I thought about all the times he'd taken crap from other kids when I was around and I realized it was probably only a small percentage of all the crap he'd taken over all the years for something that was not his fault and that he could not help. And I felt even more like a rotten brother and a rotten person in general, the kind who only let people down.

"You're not a freak," I said almost angrily.

"Do you think Karl's a freak?"

I thought about that and decided there was probably something different about everybody and Karl's way of being different was no worse than anybody else's.

"No," I said.

"Do you think he was telling the truth about him and Ariel?"

"Yes."

We were quiet a long time. I didn't know what he was thinking but I was thinking that I wanted desperately to be someone better than I was. Finally I heard him yawn and saw him turn toward the wall to sleep and the last thing he said to me that night was, "So do I."

32

Friday was the day of the visitation before Ariel's funeral. My father wanted us to look decent and he gave Jake and me money for haircuts and after breakfast we walked to the barbershop while he drove to my grandfather's house to speak with my mother. Although I had no idea what he was going to say to her I figured it had to be about Karl Brandt. Maybe he was going to try to convince her to come home too. I wasn't sure how I felt about that. The house was a different place without her, and not necessarily in a bad way.

The morning was sunny and the day promised to be hot. We walked into the barbershop and found it already busy. There was a customer in the barber's chair. Two others waiting. I didn't recognize any of the men. Mr. Baake barely glanced our way. He pointed with his scissors toward a couple of chairs near the window and said congenially, "Have a seat, boys. May be a while."

Jake picked up a comic book and sat down. I rummaged through the magazines until I found the issue of *Action for Men* that I'd started the day before. We sat down to read and the discussion that had been in progress among the men when we came in recommenced.

"I don't believe it for one minute," one of the waiting men was saying. "Why, I saw that boy lead the Warriors to two regional championships. Coach Mortenson said he'd never seen a more natural athlete."

"I'm telling you," Mr. Baake said. "The boy's a fairy. Didn't you ever think it was strange that he sings and acts pretty good?"

The man in the barber's chair said, "John Wayne acts pretty good, too, but I don't see anybody calling him a faggot."

I looked up from the comic book. Jake looked up too.

"If that boy's a flit then I'm a zebra," the waiting man said. "And, Bill, seems to me a dangerous thing spreading a rumor like that. Can do a lot of damage."

"Look, I got it from Halderson who claims he got it from a cop," Mr. Baake said. "Cops know things, and they don't lie."

The man in the chair said, "Ouch."

"Sorry, Dave," Mr. Baake said.

The man named Dave said, "How about you finish this discussion when my haircut's done? I don't want to end up missing an ear."

I put down the magazine and stood up. Jake followed my lead.

"We'll come back later," I said.

"Sure, boys. Any time." The barber waved his scissors in good-bye.

Outside we stood in the shade of the awning that overhung the barbershop window.

Jake said, "What are we going to do, Frank?"

I looked across the square to the police station, wondering if Doyle was inside, wondering who else Doyle had told. "I don't know," I said.

"Maybe we should talk to Gus?"

"Yeah," I said. "Maybe Gus."

Jake said, "I didn't see his motorcycle at the church."

Which didn't matter. I knew where he was that day.

It was a long walk to the cemetery and we barely said a word the whole way. I was thinking how one bad thing seemed to lead miserably to another and how somehow I felt responsible for much of it. I hated Doyle who was not only a bully but a blabbermouth and I wished I was a lot bigger and could call him out. I figured we were going to have to tell my father everything and I wasn't looking forward to that experience at all.

We found Gus's Indian Chief parked near the little building where all the equipment was kept. The cemetery was large and I didn't know exactly where Ariel's grave was to be and we wandered awhile. The

whole valley basked under a cloudless sky. The distant fields were vibrant green. The call of birds was everywhere. I was in a place I'd been
many times before—on Memorial Day or attending a burial service
for some member of the congregation and most recently for the buri-
als of Bobby Cole and the itinerant—and I'd always thought of it as
peaceful, beautiful even. But this time was different. I saw it now for
what it really was, a city of the dead, and even though a wrought-
iron fence was all that separated me at the moment from the rest of
New Bremen I felt as if I'd stumbled a million miles from anything
familiar or comforting. We passed Bobby Cole's grave which was still
mounded and upon which sat bouquets of wilting flowers. I came to
the grave of the itinerant and remembered the day I'd helped lower
him into the ground and how I'd thought then that it was a lovely spot,
but now I decided there could be no such thing as lovely in a place
where headstones grew.

"There he is," Jake said.

It was on a slope on the far end of the cemetery beneath a linden
tree. I could see a wheelbarrow and a pile of fresh dirt and Gus in a
hole that was already knee deep.

Gus had once told us that he came from a long line of Missouri
gravediggers. "Famous in that part of Missouri," he said, only he pronounced it *Missoura*. "Folks would call on my grandpap or my dad to
come dig the grave of a loved one. It's not just digging, you know, boys.
It's carving a box in the earth that's meant to receive and hold forever
something very precious to someone. When it's done right, folks look
at it different from just a hole in the ground, and the time'll come
when you understand this for yourselves."

Gus was a good storyteller but you never knew, especially when he
was drinking, what to believe.

He wore a T-shirt soiled from the work and was so intent on his
labor that he didn't see us coming.

"Hey, Gus," I said.

He looked up, the shovel gripped in his gloved hands and the blade
cradling earth. He was startled and clearly not pleased. "What are you
doing here?"

"Could we talk to you for a minute?"

"Now?"

"Yeah, it's important."

He added the dirt to the pile beside the hole and stuck the shovel there. He tugged off his leather gloves, stuffed them into the back pocket of his jeans, and stepped up to where we stood. "Okay," he said.

But I didn't say anything right away. I stared at the dirt Gus had already dug and I saw movement there, the crawl of earthworms. And then I stared into the hole where Ariel would be laid the next day and it didn't look at all like a carved box and I felt like crying. Jake stared dumbly where I stared and I figured maybe he was thinking pretty much the same thing and I was sorry I'd brought him.

"Come on over here," Gus said. He put a hand on Jake's shoulder and turned him toward the linden tree and did the same with me. We sat on the grass in the shade and I told Gus everything. By the end he looked pretty unhappy.

I asked, "What should we do?"

"You're going to have to tell your father," he said.

I nodded and said, "I figured."

"It's not all your fault, guys. I should never have shown you that damn furnace duct." Gus got up from the grass. "You two find your father, tell him everything."

"He'll be pretty mad," Jake said.

"I guess he will. But it's really Doyle he should be angry with."

I said, "What about Doyle?"

Gus looked toward town. "I'll deal with him," he said.

Liz met us at the door and told us our father was no longer there and our mother was resting. She asked if we'd like something to eat, cookies and milk maybe. We said no thank you and left the shade of her porch and headed toward the Flats.

Liz called to us as we walked away and we turned back.

"This will pass, boys," she said. "I promise."

But I'd just come from the city of the dead where everything that was lost was lost forever and although I replied, "Yes, ma'am," I didn't believe her at all.

We walked to the Flats in perfect silence. The Packard was parked in the garage but my father was not at the house. We walked across the street to the church and found him in his office. He didn't appear to be working on anything, just sat with his back to us staring out his window at the railroad tracks and the grain elevators. I knocked on the frame of the door and he swung around. Right off he noticed our hair.

"Was Mr. Baake too busy to take you today?"

"No, sir," I said. "That's not why we didn't get our hair cut."

"No?" He waited.

"We know about Karl."

His face didn't change. "What do you know about Karl?"

"That he's a homosexual."

My father worked at not showing his surprise but I could see it. "Why do you think you know this?"

"We heard him tell you."

I explained to my father about the furnace duct. And then I told him about Doyle.

"Oh, dear God," he said. "That poor boy." He stood up and put a hand to his forehead. I heard a train coming and it rumbled by and all that time my father was deep in thought. When the freight cars had passed he leveled his eyes on us. "I'm not at all happy that you've been eavesdropping," he said, "and we'll deal with that. And I'll have some words for Gus, too, but right now I need to talk to Karl."

He left the church and we followed him to the garage. He dug into his pocket for the car keys. "You boys fix yourselves some lunch and get cleaned up and dressed for the visitation this afternoon."

Jake said, "What about Mom?"

"She'll be there. You worry about yourselves right now."

He got in and backed the Packard out and headed up Tyler Street.

We had bologna sandwiches for lunch and then went to our room to put on our good clothes for the visitation. If my mother had been there she'd have insisted we take baths but I figured we'd just wash our faces and Brylcreem our hair and put on clean shirts and ties and that would be okay.

I was in the middle of tying Jake's tie for him when the telephone rang. I went into the hallway and answered it. It was Officer Cleve

Blake whom we'd met the night we picked up Gus at the jail after his fight with Morris Engdahl. He asked for my father.

"He's not here," I said.

"Your mother?"

"She's not here either. What's wrong?"

"Well, son, we've got your friend Gus down at the jail. We're holding him for assault. He got into a fight with one of our officers."

I said, "Doyle?"

"That's right. He asked me to call your dad and let him know."

"Can we get him out?"

"I'm afraid not, at least not right away. He'll be our guest until municipal court convenes on Monday. You'll tell your father?"

"Yes, sir, I will."

I hung up and Jake said, "What's wrong?"

"Gus beat up Doyle."

"Good," Jake said.

"Except now he's in jail."

"He's been in jail before."

"He didn't finish digging Ariel's grave."

"Somebody will, won't they?"

"Maybe, but I don't want just somebody digging Ariel's grave. I want Gus."

"What do we do?"

I thought a moment then said, "We spring him."

33

The Indian Chief was parked in front of the drugstore. Because I knew Gus was in jail I figured maybe he'd tracked down and attacked Doyle at Halderson's. Jake and I kept on going until we reached the police department on the other side of the town square. I started inside but Jake held back.

"What are we g-g-going to s-s-say?"

"Don't worry, I'll do the talking."

"Maybe we sh-sh-shouldn't be here."

"Fine, you wait outside. I'll take care of this."

"No, I'm c-c-coming."

I wasn't nervous at all. Mostly I was angry and desperate. But it was different for Jake. He came because I came and walking into the jail was clearly something he didn't want to do but he was doing it and I thought again how there was so much to him that people who heard only his stutter didn't understand.

There were two men inside. One I'd talked to on the phone, Officer Blake. The other was Doyle. Doyle wasn't in uniform. He wore dungarees and a Hawaiian shirt red with yellow flowers. There was a purple bruise around his right eye leaking down his cheek, and his lip on that side looked puffy. He was drinking from a bottle of Coca-Cola. He made no comment, just watched us.

Officer Blake said, "You boys come to talk to Gus?"

When we entered he'd been pinning some papers to the bulletin board on the wall behind the main desk. He still held a couple of sheets in his hand and I saw that they were honest-to-God wanted posters.

"Not exactly, sir," I said approaching the desk. "There's something important Gus needs to do."

"It'll have to wait until Monday, son."

"It can't wait. He has to do it now."

Officer Blake laid the remaining posters on the desk. "You're Frank, right? What's this important thing, Frank?"

"Gus was digging our sister's grave. He didn't finish it."

"That's important," Officer Blake allowed. "Tell you what, boys. I'll call Lloyd Arvin. He's in charge of the cemetery. I'm sure he'll get someone over there to finish the job."

"I don't want someone else, sir. I want Gus."

The chair in which Doyle was sitting squeaked and I glanced his way and saw him sipping idly from his Coke. I figured he was probably enjoying the scene.

"Look, boys, I can't help you out here," Officer Blake said. "I'm sorry."

"But, sir, this is really, really important."

"So's the law, son. I told you, Lloyd Arvin'll get someone else, and whoever that is will do a fine job, I'm sure."

"No, please," I said. "It has to be Gus."

Doyle put his Coke down. "Why Gus?"

I wished that Doyle weren't there and wished that I was older and bigger and could have finished the job Gus had started on him. I didn't even want to acknowledge him let alone actually talk to him. But I was desperate.

I said, "Because he comes from a long line of gravediggers, and he won't just dig a hole."

"But, son, that's what a grave is," Officer Blake said. "Just a hole."

"No, sir, it's not. When it's done well, it's a box carved into the earth that will hold something precious. I don't want just anyone carving Ariel's box."

"I sympathize, Frank, I really do. But I can't just let a prisoner go."

Doyle picked up his Coke bottle and said, "Why not, Cleve?"

Officer Blake fisted his hands and leaned his knuckles on the posters on his desk and bent toward Doyle. "Because I've already done the paperwork. And I don't have that authority. How do I explain it to the chief?"

Doyle said, "What's to explain? You let him go, he finishes the girl's grave, he comes back."

"What makes you so sure he'll come back?"

"Ask him."

"Look, Doyle—"

"Just bring him out here and ask him, Cleve."

"Bring him out?"

"Are you afraid he'll overpower you or something?"

"You're one to talk," Officer Blake shot back.

Doyle put fingers to his bruise. "Sucker punched me," he said. "Bring him out, Cleve."

"Jesus," Officer Blake said. He eyed Doyle and then me and then Jake and finally shook his head and gave in. He took a ring of keys from the desk and unlocked the metal door in the back wall and went into the jail.

Doyle didn't say anything to us while the other cop was gone, just sat and idly drank his Coke as if a bruised face and a friend in jail and a couple of naïve kids on a hopeless mission were normal events for him.

Me, I wondered if I should spit in his eye for causing all this trouble, or if I should offer him grudging thanks for helping us now.

Gus who was still wearing his soiled T-shirt and who himself was sporting a black eye came out ahead of Officer Blake.

"Hey, guys," he said to us.

Doyle said, "They came to spring you." He could have laughed but he didn't. He gave the words serious weight.

"I explained the situation to him," Officer Blake said.

Doyle said, "What about it, Gus? Cleve lets you go so you can finish digging the Drum girl's grave, will you come back?"

Gus said, "I'll come back."

Officer Blake didn't look convinced. He opened his mouth to say something more but Doyle cut him off.

"Gus says he'll be back, he'll be back. Let him go, Cleve."

"The chief—"

"Screw the chief. It's the right thing to do, and you know it." Doyle looked at Gus. "You need a hand?"

"No, I got it."

"All right." Doyle dug into the pocket of his dungarees and brought out something he tossed to Gus. "The key to your motorcycle," he said.

"Thanks."

Doyle swung his eyes to Jake and me and I couldn't read what was on his mind. Did he expect a thank you? Did he believe we were square now? He said, "Your old man know you're here?"

"No, sir."

Doyle lifted a big arm and checked his watch. "If I'm not mistaken, the visitation for your sister begins pretty soon. If I were you boys, I'd get my ass home."

To Officer Blake I said, "Thank you, sir."

"Go on," the policeman said. "Gus, you're not back in two hours, you'll regret it."

Gus followed Jake and me outside. "I'd give you a lift on my motorcycle," he said, "but I need to get to the cemetery."

"We can walk," I told him.

"I'll give Ariel a grand grave, I swear," he promised. He loped across the square to his Indian Chief, swung a leg over, and was quickly gone.

Jake and I were halfway home just turning onto Tyler Street toward the Flats when the Packard pulled to a stop alongside us. My father leaned out the driver's window. "Get in," he said. The iron in his voice was a dead giveaway that he wasn't happy. I figured it was because of our mysterious absence from home but knew it could also have been because of whatever had gone on at the Brandts' home.

For once Jake didn't call shotgun and I sat up front with my father.

"I've been driving all over town looking for you two," he said shifting into gear and taking off.

I explained what had happened. He listened without interrupting. At the end he looked at me with what seemed like amazement and said, "Well, I'll be."

And as for any anger he might have felt toward his sons that was that.

I asked, "Did you talk to Karl?"

"I couldn't get past the front gate, Frank."

"Do you think they know?"

"I'm sure someone has told them. I just wish I could talk to that boy."

"Maybe when things quiet down?"

"Maybe, Frank," he said but didn't sound hopeful at all.

At home we finished getting ready for the visitation while my father called my grandfather's house to tell him we'd been found. Then we piled back into the Packard and headed to van der Waal's.

We arrived at four o'clock and Mother was already there with my grandfather and Liz. She was different from when she'd stormed from the house because my father had once too often said the name of God in her presence. The hardness was gone and maybe, I hoped, the anger. She looked frailer, fragile somehow, and it made me think of those hollowed eggs that sometimes people elaborately painted. She'd always been a powerful force in our family, a kind of empowering fury, and it was hard seeing her this way.

She smiled gently and straightened my tie. "You look very nice, Frank."

"Thanks."

"You guys doing okay?"

"Yeah," I said. "Sure."

"I'll be back," she said. "I just need . . . oh time, I guess." She looked away, across the room where the closed coffin sat flanked by two great displays of flowers. "Well, here we go."

She took my hand unexpectedly as she walked toward the casket and so I walked with her thinking that it should have been my father's hand she was holding. And I understood that something had been lost between them, something that had kept my mother anchored to us and now she was slipping away and I understood too that we hadn't just lost Ariel, we were losing each other. We were losing everything.

I had been to visitations before and have been to many since and I've come to understand that there's a good deal of value in the ritual accompanying death. It's hard to say good-bye and almost impossible to accomplish this alone and ritual is the railing we hold to, all of us together, that keeps us upright and connected until the worst is past.

They came in great numbers, the people of Sioux County, to pay their respects. They came because they knew Ariel or they knew my father and mother or they knew us as a family. Jake and I stood mostly in a corner and watched as our parents received the public condolences person after person and were offered only the best of words about their daughter. My father as always was a pillar of respectfulness. My mother continued to be a hollow egg and it was painful to watch her and feel as if I was waiting for her to break. Liz stood with Jake and me and I appreciated her presence. After we'd been there for what seemed a very long time and yet there was still a very long time to go I said to Liz, "I need some fresh air."

And Jake said quickly, "Me, too."

"I think it would be all right," Liz said.

"Would you tell Mom and Dad?"

"Of course. Don't go far."

We slipped from the room and out the front door and into the peach-colored evening sunlight that bathed New Bremen. The funeral home was a beautiful old structure that had once belonged to a man named Farrigut who'd very early on built a big cannery in the Minnesota River valley and had got rich. We drifted far away from the porch where those who came and went might notice us and feel obliged to say something. I didn't feel like talking to anyone.

Jake reached down into the thick grass at the edge of van der Waal's property and pulled up a four-leaf clover. He had an uncanny knack for spotting them. He idly plucked the leaves and said, "Think Mom'll come home tonight?"

I was watching a couple of older people totter up the walk and slowly mount the funeral home steps and I was thinking it probably wouldn't be long before one or the other or both would be lying in coffins inside and I said, "Who knows?"

Jake threw the denuded clover stem back into the grass. "Everything's different."

"I know."

"I'm afraid sometimes."

"Of what?"

"That Mom won't come back. I mean she might come home but she won't come back."

I knew exactly what he meant.

"Come on," I said. "Let's take a walk."

We left van der Waal's and drifted down the street and took a left at the next corner and after another block came to Gleason Park where a dozen kids were playing baseball. Jake and I stood at the edge of left field and watched the game for a while. I knew a few of the players, kids younger than me, Jake's age mostly. He probably knew them too and maybe they were kids who gave him a hard time for stuttering because he wasn't paying much attention to the game. One of the kids, Marty Schoenfeldt, hit a double and slid into second and kicked up dust and Jake said, "I saw Mr. Redstone."

"Redstone? Jesus! Where?"

The summer had done much to change us and Jake didn't even flinch at the name I'd taken in vain.

"I dreamed him," he said.

"Like a nightmare, you mean?"

"It wasn't really a nightmare. Ariel was in it, too."

I never dreamed about Ariel but she haunted my waking hours. Although we kept the door to her bedroom closed I sneaked in sometimes and just stood there. The smell that lingered most powerfully was the scent of Chanel No. 5, a perfume which she could never have afforded herself but was one of the gifts my grandfather and Liz gave her on her sixteenth birthday and which she dabbed on for special occasions. She'd worn it the night she disappeared. When I closed my eyes in her room and drew in the scent of her it was as if she'd never left us. Usually I ended up crying.

Warren Redstone was another matter. I often chased him in my nightmares, stumbling across the railroad trestle trying to tackle him before he escaped.

I said, "What were they doing in the dream?"

"Ariel was playing the piano. Mr. Redstone was dancing."

"Who with?"

There was some sort of altercation between Marty Schoenfeldt and the kid who was playing second base. We watched for a few seconds, then Jake said, "Alone. They were in this big place like a ballroom. Ariel seemed happy but he didn't. He kept looking behind him like maybe he was afraid somebody was sneaking up on him."

Since that moment in the rain when I'd chosen to let the man who'd probably killed my sister get away I'd wanted desperately to tell someone what I'd done. It was a secret whose weight I carried every minute of every hour of every day and I longed to be free from it. Sometimes I thought that if I just confessed, the burden would be gone, and for a second I thought I would tell my brother because maybe if anyone could understand it would be Jake. But I didn't. I kept the sin to myself and said bitterly, "I wish you'd dream him burning in hell."

Marty Schoenfeldt shoved the second baseman and the players from both teams came running to gather around them. I watched what looked like a fight developing, the two kids taking stances.

"I talk to Ariel," Jake said.

I looked away from the coming fight. "What do you mean?"

He shrugged. "It's like praying only it's not exactly. I just talk to her sometimes like she's in the room and listening, like she used to, you know? I don't know if she can hear me, but I feel better, like she's not really gone."

I wanted to say, She's gone, Jake, she's really gone, because that's how I felt but I held my tongue and let Jake hold to his own imagining.

The kids pulled Marty Schoenfeldt and the second baseman apart and it looked like the game would resume. For some reason I felt an enormous sense of relief.

"Come on," I said to Jake. "We better get back. They'll be missing us."

In the middle of the long dark of the night that followed, I woke to the brittle ring of the telephone. My father came from his bedroom and I got up too and stood in the doorway and watched him as he shuffled to the telephone in the upstairs hallway and answered. As he listened, I saw his face change and throw off all sleepiness and I heard him whisper, "Oh, dear God." He shook his head in disbelief and then he said, "Thank you, Sheriff."

He put the receiver in the telephone cradle and stood dumbstruck staring into the dark at the bottom of the stairs.

"What is it, Dad?"

His eyes swung slowly toward me and when he didn't speak immediately I knew it was bad.

"Karl Brandt," he finally said. "He's dead."

34

On Saturday afternoon we buried Ariel. The sky was nearly cloudless yet something heavy hung in the air over New Bremen and the valley of the Minnesota River. It was a hot day, another in a long line, and windless and I breathed the stale heat and felt the weight and could barely move.

By then I knew some of the details of Karl Brandt's death. He'd been out in his beloved Triumph, driving back roads, the way he'd driven Jake and me on a day that seemed very long ago. He'd been going way too fast, had missed a turn, and had run into a big cottonwood tree. The impact had thrown him through the windshield and he'd died instantly. He'd been drinking from a bottle of his father's scotch and there was no sign that he'd tried to make the turn in the road where the cottonwood stood. Whether the tragedy occurred because of the drink or the dark design of his own confused thinking no one could say.

Ariel's funeral service was scheduled for two o'clock and was to be held in the Third Avenue Methodist Church across the street from our house. My father had requested that his district superintendent, Conrad Stephens, preside at both the full service at the church and the brief graveside ceremony after. He'd chosen music and made arrangements for Lorraine Griswold to be the organist and had asked

Amelia Klement if she would lend her fine alto in leading the songs. He'd spoken with Florence Henne about arrangements for a meal after the burial for those who would be attending. He'd been through this dozens of times as a minister and knew exactly what he was doing although I'm certain that this time was quite different for him.

The visitation seemed to have drained my mother of what strength remained to her and she had not come home afterward. On Saturday morning my father drove to my grandparents' house and talked with her, probably about Karl Brandt among other things, and when he came back he looked tired and empty but he assured us that we would see our mother at the service. Which was something I wasn't convinced was necessarily a good idea. Funerals weren't just about the dead. They were about the dead leaving this world to reside with God, someone Mother wasn't seeing eye to eye with at the moment, if she ever had, and I couldn't shake the concern that in the middle of the service she would spring from her pew and find some way to spite him.

People began to gather half an hour before the service began. They drove into the parking lot and got out of their cars and entered the church and stood inside the sanctuary and visited. I was pretty sure what they were talking about—Ariel, Karl, the whole mess. I figured it would be a story people in New Bremen would tell for a hundred years, in the same way they told about the Great Sioux Uprising, and they would use words like *skag* and *faggot* and *bastard child* and they wouldn't remember at all the truth of who these people were. I watched them from the porch of our house where I sat with Jake. It was just him and me at home. My father had gone in the Packard to get my mother. He wanted us to enter the church together as a family.

Jake had been quiet that day, even quieter than usual, and I wondered if it was because of what had happened to Karl, something I was still trying to make sense of. I was praying that it had been an accident due to the scotch he'd been drinking because if I thought he'd really killed himself then I knew I'd had a hand in it. And Jake too, though I hoped like crazy my brother didn't see it that way. I should have been the one to stand up to Doyle and refuse to tell him what we'd overheard but I'd knuckled under and Jake had talked and now Karl Brandt was dead. I argued with myself: Karl didn't have to do what he did. Some people lived with dark secrets all their lives, secrets that threatened to crush them. Something had happened to my father in the war, something terrible, but he'd found the strength to continue on. And me, I was living with the knowledge that I'd let the man who'd probably killed my sister go free, a secret that at moments was almost unbearable, but I'd never think of killing myself. It seemed to me that if a place or situation bothered you, became intolerable, you could find a way to deal with it. Talk to someone maybe or maybe just go some- where where no one knew you and start a new life. Killing yourself seemed like the worst possible choice.

Out of nowhere Jake said, "There are some things you can't run from, Frank."

He was staring into the sun which from our perspective seemed to be hanging directly over the steeple of the church. I thought if he didn't look away soon he'd blind himself.

"What do you mean?"

"Who you are. You can't run from that. You can leave everything behind except who you are."

"What are you talking about?"

"I'll always stutter. People will always make fun of me. Sometimes I think I should just kill myself."

"Don't say that."

He finally turned from the sun and swung his eyes toward me and his pupils were like dots made with a pencil point. "What do you think it's like?"

"What do I think what's like?"

"Dying. Being dead."

What I thought was that they were two different things. Dead was one thing. But dying, that was another. I said, "I don't want to think about it."

"That's all I've been thinking about all day. I can't stop."

"You better."

"It scares me. I wonder if Karl was scared." Jake held still a moment then looked back into the sun and said, "I wonder if Ariel was scared."

Which was something I'd managed up to that point not to think about. It was the difference between being dead and dying. Being dead was a thing and not a horrible thing because it was finished and if you believed in God, and I did, then you were probably in a better place. But dying was a terribly human process and could, I knew, be full of pain and suffering and great fear and because I didn't want to think about it I felt like grabbing Jake and shaking all those awful thoughts out of his head.

The Packard came down Tyler Street and thumped over the tracks and right behind it was my grandfather's Buick. The two cars pulled into the church lot in an area outlined with yellow tape to reserve the spots for them. My father helped my mother from the car and even at a distance I could tell that if a solid wind blew it would tumble her.

"Come on," I said with a sigh and stood up.

We entered the church together as my father wished. My mother took his arm and walked ahead and then Jake and I and then my grand-parents. Deacon Griswold handed us programs and people broke off their conversations and made way for us. We walked to the first pew up front and filed in and sat down. Ariel's casket had been laid before the altar rail, flanked with flowers that looked much like those that had accompanied the visitation. Although I'd had no trouble looking at the casket the day before, on that Saturday I did my best to keep my eyes averted. I stared instead at the stained-glass window behind the altar and imagined shooting the panes out with a slingshot. Lor-raine Griswold came in from the side door and sat down at the organ. Pastor Stephens entered from the same door and took his seat behind the pulpit. Amelia Klement came up the aisle from where she'd been sitting with her husband and her son and sat alone in the choir section next to the organ. A hush fell over the church and Lorraine began to play, something soft and sad and classical, and I could have looked at the program to see what my father had chosen but I was already dis-tancing myself from the whole experience. All day I'd been thinking that if something became intolerable you could simply remove your-self from it and that's what I did. I thought about the things that had happened that summer, played them over in my head—sweet Bobby Cole and the dead itinerant and the day I pushed Morris Engdahl into the quarry and Warren Redstone slipping away across the trestle in the rain and riding horses with Ginger French and Karl Brandt plowing his little Triumph into a cottonwood tree—and the result was that I remember almost nothing about the funeral service except that it went on forever. People came to the pulpit and said things—later I learned that they'd shared wonderful memories of Ariel—but I wasn't present and didn't hear them. Everyone sang and I suppose I must have sung too because the music, what penetrated, was familiar. I don't remember a word of what Pastor Stephens said but I had the sense that it was appropriate though dry.

And then it was time to go to the cemetery and I walked out with my family into the swelter and got into the hot Packard and sweated while we waited for Ariel's casket to be loaded into van der Waal's hearse and then we followed.

I'd hoped for a kind of miracle that day, hoped for something like the joy that had filled me on the Sunday before when my father had stood and delivered his brief, miraculous sermon. And if not joy then peace at least. But as we entered the gate of the cemetery I felt only grief knifing deep into my spirit. And when I saw the grave I was devastated. Somehow I'd imagined it would be as Gus said, a beautiful box carved from the earth. It was indeed a lesson in geometry, a perfect rectangle with ninety-degree angles and straight sides and rigidly perpendicular walls and a level floor, but it was still only a hole in the ground.

Pastor Stephens conducted the graveside service which was blessedly brief and then we prepared to leave. And oh that was the hardest thing of all. To abandon Ariel. I knew in my head that her spirit had long ago been released but to think of her as I'd known her all my life—funny and kind and smart and understanding and pretty—to think of my sister being lowered into the ground and covered with dirt and left alone forever, that was too much. I began to cry. I didn't want anyone to see me this way so I kept my face bent toward the ground. I got into the Packard with Jake and heard my mother crying up front and saw my father reach out to take her hand and he was crying too.

I looked at Jake and his eyes were dry and I realized that he hadn't cried at all that day and I wondered at this, but I didn't have to wonder long.

35

We returned to the church, to the fellowship hall which had been set up with round tables and chairs. Food had been prepared in the kitchen—ham and fried chicken and au gratin potatoes and green bean casserole and a couple of salads and some rolls and cookies and dessert bars. There was cold lemonade and Kool-Aid and coffee. By the time we arrived we had all, except my mother, composed ourselves. Although she no longer wept, grief lay like a weight on every feature of her face and she walked like someone too long in a desert without water. My father stood on one side of her and my grandfather on the other and I realized they were afraid that she might fall. They sat her quickly at a table and Jake and Liz and I sat with her.

Some people had taken places at tables and others stood talking and no one had yet entered the serving line because the blessing hadn't been said. That was a responsibility I knew would fall to my father who, after he'd seated my mother, had become involved in a quiet conversation with Deacon Griswold. Although folks spoke in voices moderated by the solemnity of the occasion there was still a lot of noise.

Amelia Klement separated from her husband and came our way and Peter followed a few steps behind. Mrs. Klement sat next to my mother and spoke to her quietly and Peter stood near enough to me that I figured he wanted to talk so I got up from my chair and went to him.

"I'm sorry about your sister," he said.

"Yeah, thanks."

"You know, my dad's teaching me about motors and stuff. He's showing me how to take them apart and put them back together and how to figure out what's wrong if they don't work. It's fun if you ever want to come over and goof around with me."

I remembered the day I'd stood in the doorway of the Klements' barn and had been amazed by all the disassembled machinery inside and had seen the bruises on Peter's face and on his mother's, and I recalled how I'd felt sorry and was afraid for them as a family. I realized that although I hadn't acknowledged it I'd thought that my own family was better, special somehow, and that we were indestructible. That day seemed to be on the far side of forever ago and now I saw on Peter's face the same look I'd probably given him back then and I understood that he was afraid for me and for my family and I knew he was right to be.

"Sure," I said, but I figured I probably wouldn't.

Mrs. Klement stood up and held my mother's hand a moment then returned to her husband and Peter went along.

My father came back to the table but didn't sit.

"Could I have your attention?" Deacon Griswold called. "I'd like to ask Pastor Drum to offer a blessing for this meal."

The room became quiet.

My father composed himself. He always spent a moment in silence before he prayed. His blessings tended to be comprehensive and include not just the immediate food on the table but reminders of all we had to be thankful for and very often a reminder of those who were not as fortunate as we.

In that silence while my father's head filled with the words he deemed proper, my mother spoke. She said, "For God's sake, Nathan, can't you, just this once, offer an ordinary grace?"

There had been silence in the room, a respectful silence awaiting prayer. But that silence changed and what we waited for now was something filled with uncertainty and maybe even menace and

I opened my eyes and saw that everyone was staring. Staring at the Drums. At the minister's family. Looking at us as if we were a disaster taking place before their very eyes.

My father cleared his throat and said into the silence, "Is there anyone else who would care to offer the blessing?"

No one spoke and the silence stretched on painfully.

Then at my side a small clear voice replied, "I'll say grace."

I stood dumbfounded because, Jesus, the person who'd spoken was my stuttering brother Jake. He didn't wait for my father's permission. He rose from his chair and bowed his head.

I looked at all those people present none of whom could bring themselves to close their eyes and miss the train wreck that was about to take place and I prayed as desperately as I ever had, *Oh, dear God, take me away from this torture.*

Jake said, "Heavenly F-F-F-." And he stopped.

O God, I prayed, *just kill me now.*

My mother reached up and put her hand gently on his shoulder and Jake cleared his throat and tried again.

"Heavenly Father, for the blessings of this food and these friends and our families, we thank you. In Jesus's name, amen."

That was it. That was all of it. A grace so ordinary there was no reason at all to remember it. Yet I have never across the forty years since it was spoken forgotten a single word.

"Thank you, Jake," my mother said and I saw that her whole face had changed.

And my father looked mystified and almost happy and said, "Thank you, Son."

And all the people as if released from some hypnotic trance began to move again though slowly and got into line and filled their plates.

And me, I looked at my brother with near reverence and thought to myself, *Thank you, God.*

My mother came home that night. She left the drapes open to a cooling breeze that had blown in with evening and when she went to bed my father went with her.

I lay awake late into the dark hours wondering.

I hadn't asked Jake about the blessing. In a way I was afraid to open the door on the mystery of it because I knew that what we'd all heard was a miracle, the miracle I'd been hoping for ever since Ariel died. It had come from the mouth of a boy who never in his entire life had said three words in public without stumbling in the most horrible ways imaginable. With Mother home I liked the idea that we'd been saved as a family by the miracle of that ordinary grace. I didn't know why God would take Ariel or Karl Brandt or Bobby Cole or even the nameless itinerant or if it was God's doing or God's will at all but I knew that the flawless grace delivered from my stuttering brother's lips had been a gift of the divine and I took it as a sign that somehow the Drums would survive.

The grieving in fact went on for a long time, as grieving does. For months after Ariel's burial I would stumble upon my mother in a moment when she believed herself to be alone and find her weeping. I'm not sure that the beauty of her vivacious smile ever fully returned but what remained was all the more touching to me because I understood completely the reason for what was missing.

36

The next day, Sunday, Nathan Drum preached in all three of the churches in his charge and he preached well. My mother led the choir and Jake and I sat in the back pew as we always had. Gus sat with us because Doyle had talked to the chief of police and somehow squared things and no charges were going to be filed.

It felt as if life might again assume a normal course but for two things: Nothing would ever be the same without Ariel, and the authorities still hadn't apprehended Warren Redstone, the man I was sure had killed my sister. I was beginning to think they never would and I was trying to understand how I felt about that. I was afraid I would carry forever my guilt at letting Redstone get away and I knew I would have to find a way to live with it. But my anger over Ariel's death seemed to have passed. Though I still felt her loss deeply, sadness was no longer a part of every moment for me and I thought I understood why: Her death hadn't left me completely alone. There were still so many people whom I loved and cared about deeply: Jake and my mother and father and my grandfather and Liz and Gus. And so I'd begun to think about the question of forgiveness which had become a real consideration in my life, not just part of Sunday rhetoric. If they ever caught Warren Redstone, how would I respond? There was the question of law, certainly, but there was a question of deeper concern and it went straight to the heart of what I'd been taught by my father all my life.

After the final service on Sunday afternoon Liz and my grandfather came for dinner and Gus joined us. We still had food left from everything that had been given by the community during the days of our uncertainty and the days of our early grief. We ate and then Gus went off on his motorcycle and my grandparents went home and my mother and father sat in the porch swing and talked while Jake and I tossed a baseball in the front yard. Although they spoke quietly I caught the gist of their conversation. It was about the Brandts.

Emil alone among that family had come to Ariel's funeral. He'd been brought by one of his colleagues at the college in town and he sat in the back of the church and at the grave site he stood well away from the others gathered there.

My mother told my father she'd seen him but couldn't bring herself that day to talk to him. She felt bad about it. And she felt terrible about Karl and her heart went out to Julia and Axel and she wanted to tell them but was afraid they would refuse to see her.

As they drifted back and forth in the swing she asked, "Do you think if I spoke to Emil, he could arrange it? I need to apologize to him anyway."

"I owe him an apology as well," my father said. "I haven't been much of a friend lately."

"Could we go today, Nathan? Oh, I'd love to get this weight off my chest."

Jake must have been listening too because he said from the lawn, "I want to see Lise."

I kept quiet but there was no way I'd let myself be left behind.

"All right," my father said rising from the swing. "I'll call."

Half an hour later we piled out of the Packard at the front gate of the restored farmhouse. Emil stood on the porch holding to one of the posts, tracking our procession with his sightless eyes in that way that made me think he could actually see us coming up the flagstone walk.

"Emil," my mother said taking him warmly in her arms.

Brandt held her, then stepped back and extended his hand which my father grasped with both of his own.

"I've been afraid this would never happen again," Brandt said. "It's been almost unbearable. Come, sit. I've asked Lise to fix lemonade and a plate of cookies. They should be here any minute."

There were four wicker chairs around the wicker table. The adults occupied three and I leaned against the porch rail. Jake said, "I'm going to look at the garden," and he took off and disappeared around the side of the house.

"Emil," my mother said, "I'm so sorry for what's happened between us and what's happened with Karl. It's horrible. It's all so tragic."

"The tragedy continues," Brandt said. "Julia has lost her mind. I mean really lost it. Axel says she's threatening to kill herself. She's heavily sedated most of the time."

My father said, "Axel must be in hell. Is there any way I could talk with him?"

"And I with Julia?" my mother asked.

Brandt shook his head. "I don't think that would be a good idea. It's complicated." He reached out with both hands and although he could not see he immediately found my mother's hand and took it. "How are you, Ruth? Really."

It was such a simple question on the surface but nothing these days was simple and the delicacy with which he held my mother's hand made me recall my own hollowed-egg image of her.

But she was no longer fragile that way and she said, "It hurts terribly, Emil. Maybe it always will. But I've survived and I believe I'll be all right."

The screen door opened abruptly and Lise stepped onto the porch holding a plate of sugar cookies and giving us an evil eye. She was dressed in dungarees and a dark blue blouse and red canvas slip-ons. She put the cookies on the wicker table and quickly went back inside.

"Lise doesn't seem happy to see us," my father remarked.

Brandt said, "She's been in seventh heaven for a while. Had me all to herself. For Lise to be happy, all that's necessary is this little sanctuary and someone in it who needs her. In a way, it's enviable. When you arrived she was about to work in the garden, which she dearly loves. Now she'll just sulk."

Jake reappeared and mounted the steps just as Lise came out with a pitcher of lemonade and ice cubes. When she saw my brother her attitude changed. She hastily put the pitcher on the table, went back inside, and returned almost immediately with a tray of glasses which she set next to the pitcher. She made signs to Jake that I didn't understand but to which Jake nodded and said, "Sure."

"I'm going to help Lise," he said, and they both left the porch and headed toward the shed where she kept her yard and gardening tools.

When they'd gone, my father asked, "Will you finish your memoir, Emil?"

Brandt was quiet a long while. "Without Ariel I don't think I can go on," he finally said.

"You could get someone else to transcribe," my father suggested.

Brandt shook his head. "I don't want someone else doing for me what Ariel did. I don't think anyone could."

I'd been so deep in my own experience and emotions that I hadn't considered the effect of Ariel's loss on those outside my family but I saw now that Emil Brandt who'd mentored my sister and encouraged her talent and championed her work and who, after Ariel's disappearance, had given my mother so unselfishly of his time, this man had suffered great loss as well. His face was turned in profile and I realized that if you didn't know about the scars on the other side you would think him in every way normal, maybe even handsome for an older man.

And then an extraordinary possibility occurred to me, a possibility paralyzing in its magnitude.

Brandt and my parents went on talking but I no longer heard them. I stood up and in a kind of daze drifted down the porch steps. My father said something and I mumbled in return that I would be right back. I walked through the yard, passed the garden where Jake and Lise were at work, and went to the fence gate that opened onto the path leading down the back slope to the cottonwoods and the railroad tracks and the river. I closed my eyes mimicking blindness and fumbled with the gate latch. I pushed the gate open and started down. I went slowly, my eyelids clamped shut, feeling my way carefully. It wasn't difficult at all to sense the difference between the thick undergrowth that edged the path and the worn thread of the path itself. I cleared the cottonwoods and came to the raised bed of the railroad tracks where I was sorely tempted to open my eyes but did not. I mounted the roadbed and felt the crushed rock and stumbled over the first rail but caught myself and kept going. On the other side I descended and felt through the soles of my tennis shoes the place where hard ground gave way to the sand along the river. And finally I stepped into water up to my calf and opened my eyes and looked down into the murky flow. I drew my leg back and glanced upriver and saw that I was standing only a few hundred yards from the stretch of sand at Sibley Park where bonfires were sometimes lit and where Ariel had last been seen. I stared back at the path I'd blindly walked, at the thread that was visible if only you knew where to look, and I understood with icy clarity how Ariel had come to be in the river.

37

Jake came looking for me, sent by my parents who'd begun to be concerned by my long absence. He found me sitting in the sand.

"What are you doing down here?"

"Thinking," I said.

"Will you come back up?"

"Tell everyone I'll walk home. I'll walk along the river."

"Are you okay?"

"Just tell them, Jake."

"All right. Don't bite my head off."

He started away and then came back. "What is it, Frank?"

"Go up and tell them, and if you want to talk, come back down."

He returned in a few minutes, huffing so I knew he'd run the whole way. He sat down beside me.

It was late afternoon and we sat in shadows cast by the tall cottonwoods near the tracks. The river swept before us fifty yards wide and beyond that was the other bank and the lowland of the floodplain where a cornfield formed a green wall and beyond that a mile or so distant rose the hills that had once channeled the great surge of the River Warren.

"He killed her," I said.

"Who?"

"Mr. Brandt. He killed Ariel."

"What?"

"All this time I've been blaming Warren Redstone and not looking at what was right in front of me."

"What are you talking about?"

"Mr. Brandt killed her. He killed her and brought her down here and threw her into the river."

"Are you crazy? He's blind."

"I closed my eyes, Jake, and pretended I was blind. I came down here without a problem. If I could do it, he could do it, too."

"But why would he hurt Ariel?"

"Because she was pregnant and the baby was his."

"No. He's too old. And his face is all scarred up. I mean, if I didn't know him so well, I'd get the willies just looking at him."

"That's the point. You know him well, and it doesn't bother you. I think it didn't bother Ariel either. She was in love with him."

"That, well, that's just stupid."

"Think about it. She talked forever about wanting to go to Juilliard, and then suddenly she didn't. She wanted to stay here. Why? Because Mr. Brandt is here."

"Maybe it was because of Karl."

"Karl was leaving for college," I said. "He told us so. When I asked him if he loved Ariel and was going to marry her he said no. Now I understand it was because he didn't love her that way. Who else was Ariel seeing? If it was another boy, wouldn't we know? The only other guy she's been close to is Mr. Brandt. Think about it, Jake. She was over here all the time."

"But wouldn't Lise know?"

I remembered the afternoon when I'd stood in the doorway of her bedroom watching her iron naked and she hadn't been aware of me at all and I said to Jake, "She's deaf. And I think Ariel sometimes sneaked over at night when Lise was asleep."

"But why would he kill her, Frank? Was he mad at her or something? It doesn't make sense."

I picked up a rock and threw it at the river and said, "Adults do a lot of things that don't make sense."

"Why haven't Mom and Dad thought about it? I mean, if you're so sure, why aren't they?"

"I don't know. Maybe they like him too much to even let that thought in."

Jake drew his knees up to his chest and wrapped his arms around them and stared at the river. "So what do we do?"

"We tell Gus," I said.

We had a hard time finding him. It was Sunday afternoon and almost everything was closed. We checked Rosie's parking lot and didn't see the Indian Chief there. We wandered around town awhile and didn't talk much because what we were thinking drove out all desire for conversation between us. Once the idea of what Mr. Brandt had done to Ariel came to me I couldn't stop playing the scene over and over in my head. I kept seeing him heave her onto his shoulder like a rolled-up rug and stumble his way down the path and discard her in the river. I grew angrier and angrier and my insides knotted and I thought about just going up to Emil Brandt and throwing my accusation in his face. And I imagined the police—Doyle—grabbing him roughly and slapping on handcuffs and shoving him into the cruiser and taking him away.

"I hope he didn't do it," Jake said out of nowhere.

We were walking down Tyler Street toward home. It was nearing suppertime and I didn't want our parents worrying about us so we were walking quickly but I was also propelled by sheer anger.

I said, "He did it and I hope he goes to hell for it."

Jake didn't say anything so I pressed him. "Don't you?"

"Not really."

I stopped and turned to him, seething. "He killed Ariel, Jake. He killed our sister, and if the police don't kill him, I will."

Jake turned from my anger and kept walking.

"Well?" I said to his back.

"I don't want any more killing, Frank. I'm tired of feeling mad. And I'm tired of feeling sad. And I'm happy that Mom's back home and I just want things to be okay again."

"They won't be okay, not until Mr. Brandt's in jail and on his way to the electric chair."

"All right," Jake said and kept walking.

I hung back because I didn't want to be with him anymore. I wanted to be alone with all the wretchedness of my mood. So we continued in that way with Jake leading and me grumbling behind until we reached home.

Mother had food on the table, leftover ham for sandwiches and macaroni-pea salad and watermelon slices and potato chips and while we ate I heard the sound of Gus's motorcycle and I got up and saw him park in the church lot.

"I'm finished eating," I said.

"But you've barely touched your food," Mother said.

Jake glanced toward the window. "I'm finished too."

My father eyed us both. "You two have been awfully quiet. What are you up to?"

"Nothing," I said.

Mother smiled on us and said, "Go outside and have a good time. And if you happen to see Gus, tell him that if he's hungry he's welcome to come over and help himself to whatever we have."

We went to the church basement and heard the shower running in the little bathroom and when the water stopped I called out, "Gus?"

"Just a minute," he hollered back.

He came out a couple of minutes later with his hair wet and a white towel wrapped around his waist. He grinned and said, "What's up, guys?"

"We were looking for you," I said.

"Took a motorcycle ride. Something about the wind in my face that gives me a sense of freedom. Guess I'm still trying to get rid of the feel of that damn jail cell penning me in." He looked at us both carefully. "This is serious, isn't it?"

While he stood there naked except for the towel I told him what I thought. He listened and at the end said, "Jesus." He idly rubbed his bare chest and said again, "Jesus." Then he said, "Have you told your father?"

"No."

"I think you should."

"Does that mean you think I might be right?"

"I hope not, Frank, but it's worth considering."

I asked, "Could you be with us when we tell him?"

"Sure. Just let me get dressed."

We waited upstairs in the sanctuary. Jake sat in the front pew with his hands folded in his lap in the same way he sat when he listened to my father preach. I paced in front of the altar rail with my guts all twisted. The sun was low in the sky and the stained-glass window in the western wall at the back of the chancel was alive with the fire of a dozen colors.

"Frank?"

"What?"

"What if we didn't tell Dad?"

"Why would we do that?"

"Does it really matter who killed Ariel?"

"Of course it matters. It matters a lot. What's wrong with you?"

"I'm just thinking."

"What?"

"Miracles happen, Frank. But they're not the kinds of miracles I thought they'd be. Not like, you know, Lazarus. Mom's happy again, or almost, and that's kind of a miracle. And yesterday I didn't stutter, and you want to know something? I think I never will."

"Terrific, I'm happy for you."

Which was true, although the happiness was greatly overshadowed by the terrible enmity I felt toward Emil Brandt.

"I just think maybe we should let things go, maybe put everything in God's hands is what I'm saying, and hope for some kind of regular miracle."

I stopped pacing and looked at Jake's face. There was something so guileless about it and—I don't know another word except beautiful. I sat down beside my brother.

"What was it like?" I asked him. "Your miracle?"

He thought a moment. "It wasn't something that came over me, like I saw a light or heard a voice or anything. I just . . ."

"What?"

"I just wasn't afraid anymore. I mean, maybe nobody else would even think of it like a miracle, but for me it felt that way. And that's what I'm saying, Frank. If we put everything in God's hands, maybe we don't any of us have to be afraid anymore."

"I thought you didn't believe in God."

"I thought so, too. I guess I was wrong."

Gus walked into the sanctuary. "Okay," he said. "I think it's best if we have this discussion here, keep your mother out of it for the moment. Who wants to fetch your dad?"

I knew Jake wouldn't go so I turned and left the church. The sun was just beginning to set and above the hills the clouds were already ablaze with an angry orange glow. I walked into the house and the first thing I heard was my mother playing the piano, the Moonlight Sonata. She hadn't played since Ariel disappeared and I realized how empty the house had been without music. And there was my father on the sofa reading the newspaper as he often did on Sunday evenings when the business of the day was finally finished for him. I almost stopped and turned back because as much as I wanted Ariel's killer known I wanted more for life to be normal again. But once the question of Emil Brandt's guilt had come to me it was a consideration too awful to hold on to alone and so I went to where my father sat and said, "Gus wants to see you."

"What about?"

"It's important. He's at the church."

"Where's Jake?"

"He's there, too."

My father gave me a puzzled look and folded his paper and set it down. "Ruth," he said, "I'm going to speak with Gus. I'll be gone a bit. Frank and Jake are with me."

She continued playing and without looking up from her keyboard said, "Stay out of trouble."

As we walked to the church my father put his arm around my shoulder. "It's going to be a beautiful sunset, Frank."

I didn't answer because I didn't give a crap about the sunset and in another minute we were standing with Gus and Jake.

Gus said, "Do you want to tell him, Frank, or do you want me to?"

I told my father everything.

When I finished Gus said, "He makes sense, Captain."

My father leaned against the altar rail, deep in thought.

"I need to talk to Emil," he finally said.

"I want to be there," I blurted.

"Frank, I don't think—"

"I want to be there. I have a right to be there."

My father shook his head slowly. "This won't be the kind of discussion that a thirteen-year-old needs to be a part of."

"Captain, beg your pardon, but I think Frank has a point. He's been involved in this mess all along. It was him who pointed you toward Brandt. Seems to me he has a right to be there, if that's what he wants. I know I'm an outsider, but I thought you might want another point of view."

My father considered then he looked at my brother. "What about you, Jake? You feel a burning need to be there?"

"I don't care," Jake said.

"Then I'd rather you didn't come. You either, Gus. I don't want Emil to feel ganged up on."

I was amazed. My father didn't sound angry at all. He seemed far too calm.

I said, "He did it, Dad."

"Frank, it never pays to convict someone in advance of knowing all the facts."

"But he did it. I know he did it."

"No. What you're thinking makes a certain sense, but it doesn't take into account the kind of man Emil Brandt is. I have never sensed from him the depth of violence what you're talking about would require. So I'm believing that we know only part of the story right now. If Emil is truthful with us, we may know it all and understand."

Through the chancel's stained-glass window the setting sun shot fire and the altar and the cross blazed and the chancel rail and the pews and the floor all around my father burned and I couldn't understand how amid all that flame he could stand so calm. His reasonableness was something that in the past I'd admired greatly but I found it maddening now. Me, I just wanted to get Emil Brandt strung up.

"If you go with me, Frank, you have to be quiet and let me do the talking. Do you promise?"

"Yes, sir."

"I mean it."

"I promise."

"All right. Gus, why don't you and Jake go keep Ruth company. She's in a mood to play, and I know how she appreciates an audience."

Gus said, "If she asks where you've gone?"

"Tell her anything you like," he said, "except the truth."

38

The drive to the home of Emil Brandt was no more than five minutes but it felt like forever getting there. Because of my father's doubts, seeds of doubt had been planted in my own thinking and I thought maybe Jake was right. Maybe I should have said nothing and left the resolution of the whole mess in God's hands. But what was done was done and when we parked in front of the old farmhouse I got out and steeled myself for the ordeal ahead.

As we approached the porch I could hear Emil Brandt playing his grand piano inside. I knew the piece. It was something Ariel had composed and in the wash of its beauty I swore I could feel Ariel's presence. We stood on the porch until the piece was finished then my father—reluctantly, I could tell—raised his hand and knocked on the screen door.

He called, "Emil?"

"Nathan?"

Through the screen I saw Brandt rise from the great piano and come to greet us. He pushed open the door and said, "Who's with you?"

"Frank," my father said.

He smiled with pleasant surprise. "What brings you both back so soon?"

"We need to talk."

The smile fell away and Brandt looked troubled. "This sounds serious."

"It is, Emil."

Brandt stepped outside and we took the wicker chairs where not long before he'd sat in good friendship with my parents. With the sun down, we sat in the moody blue of dusk.

"Well?" he said.

"Did you father my daughter's child, Emil?"

My father asked it so directly that it startled even me and I could see that Brandt was clearly taken aback.

"What kind of question is that, Nathan?"

"An honest one. And I would appreciate an honest answer."

Brandt turned his face away and held himself motionless for a long time. "She was in love with me, Nathan. Blind and battered as I am, she loved me."

"Did you love her, Emil?"

"Not in that way, not really. I'd come to rely on her greatly, and I loved her presence in this house, and she reminded me so much of . . ."

"So much of whom?"

"Of her mother, Nathan."

"And that's why you made love to an eighteen-year-old girl? She reminded you of her mother?"

Was it anger I heard in my father's voice? Profound indignation? Betrayal?

"I know how terrible it sounds, but it wasn't like that, Nathan. It happened once. Just once, I swear, and I was so ashamed. But Ariel, for her it was so much more. Of course. Something like that to one so young, it means everything, I know. She talked marriage. Marriage to me, can you envision that, Nathan? A man more than twice her age, blind as a bat and with the face of a monster. What kind of marriage would that be for her once she opened her eyes and realized the poor bargain she'd struck? And what about Lise? Lise could never have accepted someone else in our retreat here, especially someone who might, in my sister's understanding, steal all my affection. Nathan, I told Ariel no. Honest to God, I did everything in my power to dissuade her from throwing her life away on a wreck like me. But she . . . oh, the young, they're always so certain of what they want."

Brandt stopped talking and the silence was a great, heavy stone that settled on us all. He was blind but he nonetheless looked down as if his eyes were weighted with shame.

"I tried to kill myself once before," he finally said. His voice was like something that had come from a distance on the wind. "Did you know that? In the hospital in London after I was wounded. I fell into such a darkness. I couldn't imagine a life for myself this way." He put his fingertips to his monster of a face and then went on. "Do you want to know why I tried to kill myself this time? A more noble reason, or at least that's what I told myself. I wanted Ariel to be free of me, and I simply couldn't see any other way."

"Except killing her," I said.

"Frank," my father cautioned.

"Killing her?" Brandt raised his head and a terrible understanding blossomed in his sightless eyes. "That's what you think? That I killed Ariel? That's why you're here?"

The screen door opened and Lise Brandt stepped outside and looked at us with concern and irritation as if we were trespassing. She said, "Emil?" Except that because of her deafness and the resulting oddness of her speech it came out something like *Emiou?*

Brandt signed to his sister.

"I wan them to go away," she said in a drone.

Brandt turned so that she could read his lips. "We have business to finish, Lise. Go back inside." She didn't immediately obey him and he said, "It's all right. Go on. I'll be in soon."

Lise drew herself back slowly like mist being sucked into the house and I thought that if I were her I'd hide myself and listen but of course that would do her no good. I watched through the screen as she vanished into the kitchen and I heard the faint sound of cookware rattling.

"It's true then," my father said. "The baby was yours."

"She didn't tell me about the baby, Nathan. She never said a word. And when I found out that she'd died pregnant, I hoped against hope that Karl might be the father."

"You hoped that Ariel might be sleeping around?"

"That's not what I meant. It just seemed impossible. Ariel and I had been together only once."

"She came here often after dark," my father said. "Frank saw her leave the house several times."

"Yes," Brandt admitted. "But she came late at night and all she did was stand out there in the yard and watch my window."

"You're blind, Emil. How could you know this?"

"Lise saw her. She wanted to chase her off, but I asked her not to interfere. I talked to Ariel and she promised to stop her nocturnal visits."

"Did she?"

"I suppose so but I don't really know. It was right after that that I tried to kill myself. And then so much happened."

"Did she come the night she disappeared?"

"I'm sure she didn't. If she had, Lise would have said something to me. Look," he pleaded, "I didn't kill Ariel. I couldn't have killed Ariel. In my wounded way, I loved her. Not as she would have liked, but in the only way I was able. You have to believe that, Nathan."

My father closed his eyes and in the gathering dark sat in silence and I believed he was praying. "I do," he finally said.

Brandt looked as if he was in physical pain. "You'll have to tell Ruth, I suppose."

"No. That's something you'll have to do, Emil."

"All right. I'll talk with her tomorrow. Will that do, Nathan?"

"Yes."

"Nathan?"

"What is it?"

"We're finished as friends, aren't we?"

"I'll pray for the strength to forgive you, Emil. But I have no wish to see you again." My father rose. "Frank?"

I stood too.

"God be with you, Emil," my father said in parting. He didn't say it in the way he sometimes did to a congregation as a blessing at the end of a service. This sounded more like a criminal sentence. I followed him to the Packard and we got in. I looked back before we drove away and Emil Brandt and the dark of the coming night were merging and if he stayed there long I figured you wouldn't be able to tell one from the other.

At home my father parked in the garage and turned off the engine and we sat together in the stillness.

"Well, Frank?"

"I'm glad I know the truth. But I kind of wish I didn't. It doesn't make anything better."

"There was a playwright, Son, a Greek by the name of Aeschylus. He wrote that he who learns must suffer. And even in our sleep pain, which cannot forget, falls drop by drop upon the heart, until, in our own despair, against our will, comes wisdom through the awful grace of God."

"Awful?" I said.

"I don't think it's meant in a bad way. I think it means beyond our understanding."

"I guess there are graces I like better," I said.

My father slipped the car keys into his pocket. He put his hand on the door handle but didn't get out. He turned back to me. "There's something I haven't told you yet, Frank. A congregation in Saint Paul would like me to be their pastor. I'm going to accept."

"We're moving?"

"Yes."

"When?"

"In a month or so. Before school begins."

"I guess that would be all right," I said. "Does Mom know?"

"Yes, but not your brother. We should go inside and tell him."

"Dad?"

"Yes?"

"I don't hate Mr. Brandt. In a way, I feel sorry for him."

"That's a good beginning. It would be nice to leave this place with a heart that's not full of enmity."

I saw a firefly blink in the dark of the garage and I realized it was getting late but I didn't move.

"Is there something else, Frank?"

There was and it was Warren Redstone. Although I knew the sheriff intended to question Morris Engdahl and Judy Kleinschmidt further about the night Ariel was killed, I didn't believe anymore that they had something to do with her death. Redstone had murdered my sister. I accepted that now. I'd fought against believing it, a battle whose real purpose was simply to keep me from being overwhelmed by guilt because I didn't do anything to stop Danny's great-uncle when he made his escape across the river. I was finished with blame, finished with feeling lousy, and so I told my father everything. The whole horrible story spilled from me in a torrent I couldn't stop, a complete unburdening. I'd been afraid that he would be angry, that he would condemn me. In my worst imaginings, he ceased to love me. Instead he held me and pressed his cheek to the top of my head and said, "It's okay, Son. It's okay."

"No, it's not," I insisted between sobs. "What if they never catch him?"

"Then I suppose God'll have a lot to say to him when they meet face-to-face, don't you think?"

I drew away a little and looked into his eyes. They were brown and sad and gentle.

"You're not mad at me?"

"I'm ready to be done with anger, Frank. I'm ready to be done with it forever. How about you?"

"Yeah, I guess I am."

"Then let's go inside. I'm kind of tired."

I opened my door and walked with my father toward the house where Jake and Gus were waiting and where my mother at her piano filled the night with music.

39

The days came hot one after another but there was decent rain and by mid-August the farmers in my father's congregations were commenting guardedly to one another that the crops in the valley all looked pretty good. What they really meant but would not allow themselves to say openly was that they were anticipating the best harvest in years.

My mother began to organize for our move. The most difficult part, I suspect, was clearing Ariel's room. She did this alone and over a long period and I often heard her crying as she boxed. Most of what had been Ariel's we didn't take with us to Saint Paul. My father donated her things to an agency that distributed clothing and other items of necessity to the migrant families who came in large numbers to work the harvests.

We weren't the only ones who left New Bremen for good that summer. Danny O'Keefe's family moved too. His mother got a job teaching in Granite Falls and they put their house up for sale and by the second week in August, Danny and his family were gone.

In those final days New Bremen for me had a different feel. Whether this was because of our move or because of all that had happened that summer I couldn't say. It seemed as if the town and everything in it was already a part of my past. At night sometimes I tried to reach out and grab hold of what exactly I felt toward the place but everything was hopelessly tangled. I'd lived there five years, the longest I would live anywhere until I married and had my own family and settled down. I'd been a child there and had crossed the threshold, perhaps early, into young manhood. In the daylight I walked a lot, usually alone, visiting the places that would become monuments in my memory. The trestle that had been the scene of so much tragedy that summer. The quarry where I'd taken such childish pleasure in challenging and besting Morris Engdahl. Halderson's Drugstore with its frosted mugs of root beer. I walked along the river, passed the place where Warren Redstone had built his little lean-to. The sides were already collapsed and I knew that in the flooding which came every spring all sign of the man's presence would be washed away. I lingered at the place below the home of Emil Brandt and his sister where the trail threaded up the rise through the cottonwoods, the trail I'd been so certain was the way my sister had been carried to the river. And a little farther on I stood below Sibley Park where the cold black ash of many bonfires lay on the sand like leprous sores and where Ariel had last been seen alive on this earth. If understanding was what I sought, I was disappointed.

After Ariel's funeral my mother took Jake to only one more session of speech therapy. He told me afterward that they questioned him mercilessly about the inexplicable disappearance of his impediment. When he insisted that it was the result of a miracle they looked at him as if he said he'd kissed a frog and been granted three wishes. Then my mother calmly told them it was the absolute truth, a miracle by the grace of God, and they had no reply.

Gus spent more and more time away and although he was reluctant to talk I knew because my father told me that he was helping Ginger French at her ranch. He'd put the brakes on his drinking and didn't hang out anymore with Doyle.

As the day of our departure drew nearer we had a lot of visitors, folks stopping in to say their good-byes. Many were a part of my father's congregations but others were a surprise. Edna Sweeney came with cookies. I had no idea if she and Avis were finally doing okay in the sack but she was such a good woman at heart that I hoped so.

I knew I would miss the view of her underthings drying on the line, swinging a little in the summer breeze as if beckoning. The Klements dropped by one evening and while our parents talked on the porch Peter and Jake and I spent an hour sitting in the pasture behind our house kicking around the Twins and *The Twilight Zone* and speculating on what living in Saint Paul would be like. Peter was not hopeful. He thought a place like Cadbury—or even a town like New Bremen—was infinitely preferable. There were streets in Saint Paul, he warned, where people couldn't walk safely at night. And everybody locked their doors. Before he left he repeated his invitation to come anytime for a visit and he'd teach us about motors and things. The Coles visited, too, briefly. They'd been old when they had Bobby and his death had made them even older. They were not much more than fifty then but in my memory they are always ancient. They held hands as they walked away and I thought that although they'd lost Bobby they were lucky. They still had each other.

A week before we left town Morris Engdahl was killed in an accident at the cannery where he worked. He was out on bail, awaiting his hearing on the Mann Act charges that had been filed against him. He'd gone to work drunk and the foreman had told him to go home and Engdahl had taken a couple of swings at his boss. He'd missed and, off-balance, had tumbled from the platform where the altercation took place and had broken his neck in the fall to the cannery floor below. In a kind of irony, Engdahl's father, who was not a churchgoing man, requested that my dad preside at the burial service. I asked if I could be there and my father allowed it. It was one of the saddest funerals I've ever attended. Engdahl had no mourners at all, not Judy Kleinschmidt or even his father, who we later found out was dead drunk in a town bar.

Two days out from the move to Saint Paul the house already had the feel of abandonment. Mother had directed Jake and me to pack up our things in the boxes she provided and we emptied our dresser and our closet. Jake had carefully packed his model airplanes and his comic books. I had nothing special that I cared about in the same way and threw in my own collected junk haphazardly. Walking through the house we negotiated a path between stacks of boxes: linens and towels and tablecloths; my father's books; table lamps and vases and framed pictures; kitchen utensils and pots and pans. We still had curtains on the windows but not much else to cozy the place.

In those last days Jake had begun to divide his time between our house and the home of Lise Brandt. My parents had severed their relationship with Emil. When Brandt told her the truth about his relationship with Ariel my mother had been outraged but she hadn't held long to that useless emotion. "What's done is done," I heard her tell my father, and I believe she meant it. I don't know that she ever forgave Emil Brandt. Maybe like Jake she was simply tired of being angry. As far as I know she never saw Brandt socially again. I suppose that in its way this, too, was a loss she suffered.

But with Jake it was different. He told me he felt sorry for Lise. As far as he could tell, the only people in the world who cared about her at all were him and Emil, and although Lise seemed fine with the company of her brother her face lit up with undeniable delight whenever she saw Jake. He visited often using the garden as an excuse to offer his companionship. He told me that he sometimes saw Emil Brandt sitting on the porch or heard the music of his playing drift from the house but he never talked to the man. It wasn't because he felt any anger. He claimed that he sensed something coming from Brandt that was like strong waves pushing him away. I figured Jake was onto something. The Brandt family had always seemed a kind of island, separate and distant and a little forbidding, and there had never been, as far as I could see, the kind of energy, whether love or the yearning for simple human connection, that held them together or drew the larger world to them. As a family they seemed to have no center and I figured they would fall apart. Because my own family was healing and because wholeness seemed possible again, I kept the Brandts in my prayers.

On the day before we were to leave New Bremen my brother asked if I would help him and Lise with a project. She wanted to build a little wall around one of her flower beds using the rocks she'd pulled and piled when creating all her garden spots. Jake said it would be easier with three of us, especially because some of the rocks were big. I wasn't excited about returning to the Brandt home but I agreed to give a hand.

We arrived after lunch and found Lise at work loading a wheelbarrow with the smaller stones from the huge pile beside the shed. The flower bed itself was in the middle of the yard, positioned in a sunny area between deep pools of shade that lay beneath a couple of tall hackberry trees. It was circular and at its center was a birdbath. Jake had explained that what Lise had in mind was to use the smaller stones to build the wall maybe a foot high and to put the large rocks inside, placing them carefully among the flowers so that the effect in the end would be a touch of wildness within the circular geometry of the wall.

She wore a loose short-sleeved yellow blouse and dungarees and tennis shoes and had soiled gardening gloves on her hands. It was hot and the blouse clung to her sides and back. We came from the river, through the gate in the back fence. She was intent on her work and didn't know we were there until Jake circled so that she could see him. She clapped her hands together like a child pleased at a new toy and she signed something to Jake who signed something back and then he said, "Frank came too." He pointed toward me and she turned and although she didn't beam as brightly as she had with Jake she nonetheless looked pleased to see me. In her drone she said, "Thang you, Frang."

We got to work. Mostly it was a question of transport, hauling the rocks from the pile to the garden thirty yards distant. Jake and I did this part while Lise constructed the wall. We filled the wheelbarrow half full because any more was impossible for us to handle and crossed the yard through the hackberry shade and dumped the stones in jumbles spaced along the edge of the garden. Lise carefully fitted the stones together with a bit of mortar that she'd mixed in a bucket.

We worked late into the afternoon. Toward the end I heard the swell of a piece I recognized as Rachmaninoff coming through the windows of the house and saw Emil Brandt step onto the front porch and sit down in his rocker and I figured he was playing a record on his stereo or maybe a tape on his reel-to-reel. Not long afterward the wall was complete. Jake and I were sweating like a couple of pack mules. Lise put down her mortar trowel and pulled off her garden gloves and said, "Wan pop?"

"Yes," Jake and I answered together.

She smiled and made gestures to Jake who understood clearly. When she turned to go, he said, "She wants us to get the crowbar out of the shed. We'll need it to pry the big rocks loose that she wants to put in with the flowers."

"I'll get it," I offered.

The door of the shed was open and I stepped inside. Sunlight streamed in at my back. The shed smelled of damp soil and faintly of a mechanical odor like cutting oil. Lise kept the little place neatly organized. Clay pots and potting soil stood stacked beside each other against the far side. The tools of her yard work—rake, hoe, edger, clippers, shears, shovel, spade, pick, trowels—all hung neatly from hooks or nails set into a row of two-by-fours that ran horizontally along the inside of the wall midway between floor and roof. To the right was a narrow workbench with a vise and above the bench a Peg-Board that was hung with hand tools—hammer, screwdrivers, hacksaw, wrenches, chisels—and beneath the bench was a small cabinet with half a dozen drawers. The cabinet was honey-colored and decorated with hand-painted flowers. Leaning in one corner of the shed was a long pry bar and cradled across a couple of nails next to it lay the smaller crowbar. The crowbar I remembered well. That day in early summer when without thinking I'd touched her and she'd gone berserk, I'd've been dead if I hadn't been so quick to dodge her wild swing. I reached for the crowbar and as I pulled it off the wall I cut my finger on the head of one of the nails. The cut wasn't bad but it was bleeding and my hands were dirty. I took the crowbar out to Jake and showed him my wound.

"Lise keeps a box of Band-Aids in one of the drawers in the shed," he said. "I don't know which one."

I returned to the honey-colored cabinet and began opening drawers. Mostly they held nails and screws and washers. But when I opened the middle drawer something else caught my eye. Amid a collection of bolts and nuts lay a delicate gold watch and a mother-of-pearl barrette.

Jake was stretched out on the grass. As I walked to him he glanced at my face and then he sat up. "What's wrong?"

I held out my hands that were soiled with dirt and blood.

Jake looked at what I held in my palms, the little treasures that had gone missing with Ariel, and his eyes crawled up and met my gaze and I saw something in them that made me go cold.

"You knew," I said.

"No." Then he said, "Not for sure."

He looked away toward the house where Emil Brandt rocked on the porch like a metronome keeping time with Rachmaninoff. I moved closer to him and leaned down. "Tell me."

"I didn't know," he said.

"You said you didn't know for sure."

"I thought . . ." He stopped and I was afraid he was going to commence to stuttering but he just spent a few seconds collecting himself and then he went on. "That day you told me Mr. Brandt killed Ariel I began to think about it, and I thought probably it wasn't him."

"Why not him?"

"Jesus, Frank, he's blind. But Lise, she's strong and can see, and she never liked Ariel. But I figured if she did it, it had to be an accident. Like when she almost hit you with this crowbar," he said and picked up the iron tool. "You remember?"

"Yeah, I remember. But maybe it wasn't an accident."

Jake looked down. "I thought about that too," he said.

"Why didn't you say something?"

"She doesn't have anything, Frank. Just this place and her brother. And maybe she thought Ariel was going to take that away from her. And what if people knew and she went to prison or something?"

"She should go to prison," I said.

"See? I knew if I said anything you'd get mad."

"Jake, this isn't like she just did something a little bad. She killed Ariel."

"Putting her in prison won't bring Ariel back."

"She has to pay for what she did."

"Why?"

"What do you mean why?"

"Look around you. She almost never leaves this yard except to go down to the river sometimes. And she never has visitors except me. Isn't that what a prison is?"

"She might hurt someone else. Did you ever think of that?"

Jake put the crowbar down in the grass and didn't answer.

I stood above him pissed as hell and at the same time marveling. He'd once again seen something that the rest of us had missed, an awful truth that he'd held to alone. Even in my anger I understood what a terrible burden that must have been.

"Did you say anything to Lise?"

He shook his head. Then he said, "Seventy times seven, Frank."

"What?"

He lifted his face in the sunlight. "Seventy times seven. It's how we're supposed to forgive."

"This isn't about forgiveness, Jake."

"What's it about then?"

"It's the law."

I heard the back door of the deck slide open and looked up and saw Lise come out carrying a tray that held three Coke bottles and a small plate of cookies.

Jake didn't take his eyes off me. "The law? That's really what you're thinking about?"

Lise descended the steps and started across the yard toward us.

"Frank," Jake said pleading.

I could see the smile on Lise's face. I could see how lightly she walked.

"Please," Jake said.

"Warren Redstone," I replied.

Jake looked at me, confused. "What?"

"The sheriff's still looking for him. What if they catch up with him and he tries to run and gets himself shot? Could you live with that?"

Jake considered this and his shoulders dropped and he shook his head in defeat.

I'd lived for weeks with the belief that I'd let Ariel's killer escape and although my father had helped me understand how to carry that burden it still weighed on me. Standing in that shaded old farmyard, I finally felt it evaporate. Warren Redstone was not a killer. He'd never done a thing to harm my family. And what I was about to do would free him too.

I put my hands out. Lise Brandt when she reached us glanced at what I held and I saw by her look that she recognized these things.

She quickly composed herself and said with a smile, "Wha tha?"

I said, "You know what they are."

She kept smiling and shook her head.

"You killed Ariel," I said.

She frowned dramatically. "No," she replied and it came out like a small moan.

Jake looked up at me. "What are you going to do, Frank?"

I kept my eyes on Lise Brandt and my face toward her so that she could read my lips. "I have to tell someone. I'm going to start with Mr. Brandt."

I left Jake sitting on the grass and walked past Lise where she stood with the tray still in her hands. I'd taken only a few steps when I heard the clatter of the tray and bottles as they hit the ground and a banshee cry at my back and Jake screaming, "Lise, no!"

I turned and saw her stoop and grasp the crowbar and charge at me, the whole time wailing like a wounded beast. She swung the bar at my head. I dodged and hit the ground and rolled and tried to get to my feet as she came again with the hard iron in her hand but I felt my ankle twist painfully and I crumpled to the grass. I lifted my arm in a feeble attempt to deflect the blow I knew was coming.

Then Jake was on her, grabbing her arm and holding fast. She screamed bloody murder and tried to shake him loose and slapped at him with her free hand.

From the porch, Emil Brandt yelled, "What's going on?"

She turned and turned again and finally flung Jake from her and he fell to the ground. She stood over him with the crowbar raised high, breathing deeply and loud. I tried to rise but my twisted ankle prevented me from moving quickly enough. Jake just lay there looking up at her helplessly. He didn't even lift a hand to defend himself.

And then the final miracle of that summer was delivered. Something—only God knows what—stayed the hand of Lise Brandt.

I heard breath rushing from her in and out and in. I watched paralyzed as the crowbar held still, poised high in the air. I nearly wept as she slowly lowered it and let it fall to the ground at her feet. She collapsed onto her knees facing Jake and she clasped her hands as if in prayer and droned, "Sorry. I'm sorry."

Jake gathered himself and knelt beside her. He reached out but did not touch her. "It's all right," he said.

Emil Brandt hollered, "Is everything okay out there?"

Jake looked at me and I saw no child left in him at all. He said, "I'll stay with her, Frank."

I stood and held fast to the things that had once been Ariel's and limping because of my injured ankle I began to make my way through the deep shadows of that August afternoon toward the porch and Emil Brandt.

Epilogue

There's a math problem everyone is familiar with. It involves two trains. One leaves from one location, New York, for example, and the other from another location, say San Francisco. The trains are traveling toward each other at different speeds. The idea is to calculate how far each train will have traveled by the time they meet. I was never any good at math and didn't waste time trying to solve this problem but I did spend a lot of time thinking about it. Not about how many miles the trains would have covered but about the travelers on them. Who were these people and why were they leaving New York and San Francisco and what were they seeking at the other end of the line? Most especially I wondered if they had any idea what awaited them when the two trains met. Because I thought of them as traveling on the same set of tracks, I imagined their meeting as a catastrophic collision. So it always struck me not as a math problem but rather a philosophic consideration of life, death, and unhappy circumstance.

In my own life, the two trains of this problem are the summer of 1961 and the present. And they collide every year on Memorial Day in the cemetery in New Bremen.

This year my father is waiting for me in the shade, sitting patiently on the porch of his condominium in Saint Paul, staring at the world from under the brim of a clean white ball cap. A tall man, slender all his life, he's grown thin and fragile over the last few years, with a heart that worries us both. When I pull into the drive, he rises from the bench and hobbles to my car. He walks like a man built of toothpicks, afraid that the connections will not hold. He opens the door and eases this body, this awkward construction of brittle bone and loose flesh, into the passenger side.

"Good afternoon, sir," he says with chipper energy, and he gives me a smile, telling me with that flash of stained enamel that he's happy to see both me and another day.

As we head south out of the Twin Cities toward New Bremen, we talk about things that in the grand scheme matter not at all. Baseball: The Twins are playing well this year, but it's still a long season ahead. The French Open: Who's out, who's still in, and why aren't there any Americans who can play on clay? And of course the weather. In Minnesota weather tops all other topics of conversation. My father, once a voracious reader, seldom picks up a book anymore. His hands tremble, he complains, and he has trouble concentrating. He's well over eighty. Things fall apart.

At Mankato, we turn west and follow the broad valley of the Minnesota River. It's been a good spring, plenty of rain but not too much, and the crops have all been planted and the fields are green. My father comments on their appearance with approval, as if he has a personal stake in the harvest still far ahead. I know him and I know that it's more than idle talk. He hopes good things for these farmers whose lives are so helplessly bound to the whim of nature. Too much rain, too little rain, a devastating hailstorm, a plague of locusts, blight, they've all swept through this valley like the horsemen of the Apocalypse and the only recourse for those who stand and watch the sky is prayers or curses.

A few miles outside New Bremen we grow quiet, as we always do, and our thoughts begin to slide into a consideration of the past.

It seems to me that when you look back at a life, yours or another's, what you see is a path that weaves into and out of deep shadow. So much is lost. What we use to construct the past is what has remained in the open, a hodgepodge of fleeting glimpses. Our histories, like my father's current body, are structures built of toothpicks. So what I recall of that last summer in New Bremen is a construct both of what stands in the light and what I imagine in the dark where I cannot see.

Entering town we drive a new road across a recently built bridge spanning the river. Only a hundred yards east stands the trestle that is one of the solid fixtures of both past and present. The grain elevators along the tracks are gone but I can see down Tyler Street all the way to the Flats. The church, remodeled and enlarged over the years, is still there and in late afternoon the shadow of the steeple still falls across the house where the Drums once lived.

Halderson's Drugstore is now a video store and tanning salon. The shop where Mr. Baake once held forth with barber scissors and gossip is now called The Shear Delight and caters mostly to women. The police department still borders on the square, housed inside the same stone walls that were laid when the town was first platted. The interior, I've been told, has been modernized but I have no desire to see it. For me it will always exist as it did that long ago summer night I first saw it when Jake and I went with our father to bring Gus home.

My grandfather and Liz passed from this world nearly twenty years ago and the family that bought their house has never taken particularly good care of the property, a circumstance that would have had my grandfather spewing forth a few choice expletives.

The Brandt mansion is still the Brandt mansion and is still occupied by someone who bears the family name. Axel and Julia Brandt adopted a child, a little boy from Korea, and raised him and loved him and willed to him the brewery. His name is Sam and on the few occasions I've met him I've found him pleasant but patronizing in the way of many people of wealth.

When we arrive at the cemetery Jake is waiting at the gate. He's driven from Winona where he's pastor of a Methodist church. He's grown into a tall, graceful man and is just beginning to bald. He greets us both with a powerful hug.

With a nod toward his station wagon he says, "I've got the flowers."

He drives ahead of us on the lane among the gravestones which are decorated with flower bouquets and various items of tribute and memory. We come every year on this day to pay our respects. In earlier times our families often accompanied us but our children are grown and our wives have made this trip too many times and today have made other plans so it's just the three of us. It's our intention after we've finished in the cemetery to head to a German restaurant in town and drink some Brandt beer and have a good German dinner.

Every year we visit a lot of graves. A number of them were dug in the summer of 1961. We lay flowers at the headstone of Bobby Cole, whose death seemed the beginning of everything terrible that summer. Despite the early suspicions of Officer Doyle, I have always believed that Bobby's death was nothing but a tragic accident in all probability due to his tendency to lose himself in daydreams, something I'd often witnessed when he was alive. We also lay flowers at the headstone with no name where the itinerant is buried and at the headstone of Karl Brandt. We always lay a small bouquet and spend a moment at the graveside of Morris Engdahl. It's clear every year that we're the only ones who bother but my father insists. We lay flowers on the graves of Emil and Lise Brandt who are buried side by side. Emil Brandt died first, a relatively young man at age fifty-one. Lise Brandt lived to be nearly seventy and after the summer of 1961 spent the rest of her life in the Minnesota Security Hospital in Saint Peter. She claimed not to remember actually killing Ariel. She'd found my sister on the lawn at the farmhouse that night and had gone outside to shoo her away. Ariel had reached out, touched her—who knew why?—and the next thing she remembered was standing with the bloodied crowbar in her hand and Ariel on the grass at her feet. She'd panicked, carried Ariel to the river, and delivered her to the current, hoping it would take the whole problem away. In truth she was not unhappy at the hospital in Saint Peter. She worked a garden and had a room to herself and, until his death, her brother visited regularly. Jake never deserted her and was with her at the end praying her into a peaceful final rest.

We spend time at my grandfather's grave. He's flanked by my grandmother on one side and Liz on the other and we lay flowers for them all.

We visit the graves of Ginger French and Gus who were married a year after we moved away. They were a happy couple, given to adventure. Ginger loved to ride with Gus on his Indian Chief. They both eventually took up flying and bought their own little Piper Cub and would take off for the Black Hills or Yellowstone or Door County at a moment's notice. A dozen years into their marriage, on a flight to Valentine, Nebraska, they ran into severe weather and crashed in a cornfield and were killed. At their funeral my father delivered a moving eulogy.

There's another grave I would visit if it were here, the grave of
Warren Redstone. When I was in college at the University of Minnesota I ran into Danny O'Keefe. We recognized each other immediately and I was happy to find that he held no grudge because of the
events that summer which drove his family from New Bremen. He
told me his great-uncle had returned and was living near Granite Falls
and he gave me an address and a telephone number. I went to see the
man I'd wrongly condemned in my sister's death. I found him fishing
on a stretch of the Minnesota River, a spot where meadow ran along
the bank and poplar trees gave shade.

He nodded for me to sit beside him and he said, "You're a couple
of heads taller, boy. Damn near a man now."

I said, "Yes, sir, I guess I am."

He watched where his fishing line disappeared in the cider-colored
sweep of water. He wore a black hat with a wide, round brim and a
colorful band. He'd let his hair grow long and it lay in two gray braids,
one over each shoulder.

"I figure I owe you my life," he said.

Which surprised me because mostly I'd come to apologize for having put him in jeopardy.

"Always been grateful you kept your mouth shut while I crossed
that trestle," he said. "Those policemen, they'd've shot first and asked
later."

I didn't necessarily agree with him but it seemed pointless to say so.
I asked, "Where'd you go?"

"Family on the Rosebud rez. Thing about family is they got to take
you in."

We didn't say much more. With the exception of that summer in
which our lives had converged in a few dramatic moments, we had
almost nothing in common. But when I left, Warren Redstone offered
something I've never forgotten. As I walked away he called to me and
when I turned back he said, "They're never far from us, you know."

"Who?" I asked.

"The dead. No more'n a breath. You let that last one go and you're
with them again."

It was an odd thing to say in parting and I thought it probably had

more to do with where Redstone was in the declining arc of his own
life than anything to do with me.

Our final cemetery stop always is the small section beneath a linden tree where Ariel and my mother lie buried. Mother died at sixty,
a victim of breast cancer. My father cared for her lovingly to the end
and, when she was gone, never remarried. When his time comes, he
will join her in the shade of the linden tree.

I'm a teacher of history in a high school in Saint Paul and what
I know from my studies and from my life is that there is no such
thing as a true event. We know dates and times and locations and par-
ticipants but accounts of what happened depend upon the perspective
from which the event is viewed. Take the American Civil War. The
residents of the beleaguered Confederacy recounted a very different
history from the one touted by the victorious Union. It's the same
with the history of a family. Whenever we talk about New Bremen
I'm aware that Jake and my father recall things I don't and what we
remember together we often remember differently. I'm sure that each
of us has memories that for reasons our own we don't share. Some
things we prefer remain lost in the shadows of our past. My father, for
example, has never said a word about the incident in the war in which
both he and Gus played some terrible part and although I have often
wondered I have never asked. And of that summer in New Bremen in
which so much death occurred we hardly speak at all.

We stand the three of us where an important part of our lives lies
buried. We can see the river brown with silt and on the far side the
patchwork of fields and beyond them the wooded hills that long ago
channeled the glacial flood of the River Warren. The sun is low in the
sky and the light is pollen yellow and the afternoon is blessedly still.

"It's been a good day," my father says with satisfaction. "It's been
a good life."

In the way he did as a child whenever my father finished a sermon,
Jake whispers, "Amen."

Me, I throw an arm around each of them and suggest, "Let's go
have a beer."

We turn, three men bound by love, by history, by circumstance, and
most certainly by the awful grace of God, and together walk a narrow

lane where headstones press close all around, reminding me gently of Warren Redstone's parting wisdom, which I understand now. The dead are never far from us. They're in our hearts and on our minds and in the end all that separates us from them is a single breath, one final puff of air.

This reading group guide for *Ordinary Grace*
includes an introduction, discussion questions,
and ideas for enhancing your book club.
The suggested questions are intended to help
your reading group find new and interesting angles
and topics for your discussion. We hope that
these ideas will enrich your conversation and
increase your enjoyment of the book.

Introduction

I n 1961 New Bremen, Minnesota, all is quiet and serene. The Minnesota River flows through the countryside, the town barber knows everyone's name, and folks dutifully attend church every Sunday. But that serenity is thrown into turmoil as a series of tragic deaths lead thirteen-year-old Frank Drum and his family on a hunt for terrible truths. But at what cost comes wisdom?

In this powerful novel from the author of the Cork O'Connor mysteries, a boy must leave his childhood behind and confront the dark nature of the adult world and its myriad moral questions: What secrets will destroy us? How do we deal with grief? And what solace is there in the ordinary grace of the world?

Topics & Questions for Discussion

1. Discuss the final revelation of Ariel's whereabouts. Had you guessed correctly?

2. Much of Frank and Jake's knowledge comes from overhearing and snooping. Which instance of eavesdropping provided them with the heaviest, most important information? Is there a particular overheard conversation that led most directly to the loss of their childhood innocence?

3. Along those same lines, in what ways have the two boys been transformed by story's end?

4. Who is ultimately responsible for the death of Karl Brandt?

5. A number of characters carry secrets that eventually come to light. Was there a certain catharsis once they were able to unload the truth? Did it do them any good? Consider especially Frank's father, whose deeds in the war remained a mystery. Is there some merit to carrying the burden of a secret alone?

6. Though the title of the novel refers to a particular "ordinary grace," what other small graces did you find in the book?

7. Why does Ruth leave her family? Do you think she was truly mad at Nathan? At God? Discuss the ways in which she and the other characters deal with their grief over Ariel.

8. Do you agree with Frank's insight in the epilogue that, "there is no such thing as a true event"? What makes a story real? How do we deal with varying perspectives and reflections of history?

9. Do you think Frank had a responsibility to tell Emil about Lise? Was there merit to Jake's argument that her fenced-in estate was prison enough?

10. Do you forgive Emil for his moment of indiscretion? Is he in some way to blame for everything that happened in New Bremen?

11. Frank and Jake often make a case to come along to the sheriff's office, crime scenes, and pivotal confrontations during the upheaval in New Bremen. Should they have been allowed to bear witness to these things? Should children be shielded from the occasional darkness of adult life?

12. What do you make of Gus? Is he in some ways the backbone (though not a true relative) of the Drum family?

13. Do you agree with the sentiment of the older Warren Redstone? Is it true that the departed are never far from us?

Enhance Your Book Club

1. Tragedy and controversy will occasionally befall a small town like New Bremen. Has something similar ever happened in your town? Discuss the details of that incident, and how/if it changed things for you.

2. Much of our perspective in *Ordinary Grace* comes through Frank and Jake's by-foot travels throughout town, through the hidden passages and remote clearings. Make a similar journey through your own neighborhood. What places are ripe for a secret? Where can you go for peace and meditation?

3. List and discuss the ordinary graces and miracles you've experienced. How do small moments help us deal with larger-than-life trouble?

4. Read any one of the novels in William Kent Krueger's Cork O'Connor mystery series and discuss how the suspense of the Minnesota that O'Connor inhabits compares to the more pastoral mystery of the Drum family.

Turn the page to read an exclusive excerpt
from William Kent Krueger's

THIS TENDER LAND

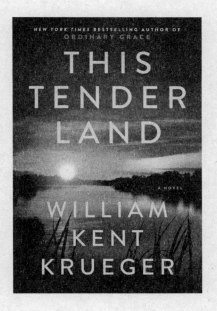

Coming September 2019 from Atria Books

PROLOGUE

I n the beginning, after he labored over the heavens and the earth, the light and the dark, the land and sea and all living things that dwell therein, after he created man and woman and before he rested, I believe God gave us one final gift. Lest we forget the divine source of all that beauty, he gave us stories.

I am a storyteller. I live in a house in the shade of a sycamore tree on the banks of the Gilead River. My great-grandchildren, when they visit me here, call me old.

"Old is a cliché," I tell them, with mock disappointment. "A terrible trivializing. An insult. I was born along with the sun and earth and moon and planets and all the stars. Every atom of my being was there at the very beginning."

"You're a liar." They scowl, but playfully.

"Not a liar. A storyteller," I remind them.

"Then tell us a story," they plead.

I need no goading. Stories are the sweet fruit of my existence and I share them gladly.

The events I'm about to share with you began on the banks of the Gilead. Even if you grew up in the heartland, you may not remember these things. What happened in the summer of 1932 is most important to those who experienced it, and there are not many of us left.

The Gilead is a lovely river, lined with cottonwoods already ancient when I was a boy.

Things were different then. Not simpler or better, just different. We didn't travel the way we do now, and for most folks in Fremont County, Minnesota, the world was limited to the piece of it they could see before the horizon cut off the land. They wouldn't have understood any more than I did that if you kill a man, you are changed forever. If that man comes back to life, you are transformed. I have witnessed this and other miracles with my own eyes. So, among the many pieces of wisdom life has offered me over all these years is this: Open yourself to every possibility, for there is nothing your heart can imagine that is not so.

The tale I'm going to tell is of a summer long ago. Of killing and kidnapping and children pursued by demons of a thousand names. There will be courage in this story and cowardice. There will be love and betrayal. And, of course, there will be hope. In the end, isn't that what every good story is about?

CHAPTER ONE

lbert named the rat. He called it Faria.

It was an old creature, a mottle of gray and white fur. Almost always, it kept to the edges of the tiny cell, scurrying along the wall to a corner where I'd put a few crumbs of the hard biscuit that had been my meal. At night, I generally couldn't see it but could still hear the soft rustle as it moved from the wide crack between the corner blocks, across the straw on the floor, grabbed the crumbs, and returned the way it had come. Whenever the moon was just right and bright beams streamed through the high, narrow slit that was the only window, illuminating the stones of the eastern wall, I was sometimes able to glimpse in the reflected light the slender oval of Faria's body, its fur a dim silver blur, its thin tail roping behind like an afterthought of the animal's creation.

The first time I got thrown into what the Brickmans called the quiet room, they tossed my older brother, Albert, in with me. The night was moonless, the tiny cell as black as pitch, our bed a thin matting of straw laid on the dirt floor, the door a great rectangle of rusted iron with a slot at the bottom for the delivery of a food plate that never held more than that one hard biscuit. I was scared to death. Later, Benny Blackwell, a Sioux from Rosebud, told us that when the Lincoln Indian Training School had been a military outpost called Fort Sibley, the quiet room had been used for solitary confinement. In those days, it had held warriors. By the time Albert and I got there, it held only children.

I didn't know anything about rats then, except for the story about the Pied Piper of Hamelin, who'd rid the town of the vermin. I thought they were filthy creatures and would eat anything and maybe would even eat us. Albert, who was four years older and a whole lot wiser, told me that people are most afraid of things they don't understand, and if something frightened you, you should get closer to it. That didn't mean it wouldn't still be an awful thing, but the awful you knew was easier to handle than the awful you imagined. So Albert had named the rat, because a name made it not just any rat. When I asked why Faria, he said it was from a book, *The Count of Monte Cristo.* Albert loved to read. Me, I liked to make up my own stories. Whenever I was thrown into the quiet room, I fed Faria crumbs and imagined tales about him. I looked up rats in the worn *Encyclopaedia Britannica* on the school library shelf and discovered that they were smart and social. Across the years and the many nights I spent in the isolation of the quiet room, I came to think of the little creature as a friend. Faria. Rat extraordinaire. Companion to misfits. A fellow captive in the dark prison of the Brickmans.

That first night in the quiet room, Albert and I were being punished for contradicting Mrs. Thelma Brickman, the school's superintendent. Albert was twelve and I was eight. We were both new to Lincoln School. After the evening meal, which had been a watery, tasteless stew containing only a few bits of carrot, potato, something green and slimy, and a little ham gristle, Mrs. Brickman had sat at the front of the great dining hall and told all the children a story. Most dinner meals were followed by one of Mrs. Brickman's stories. They usually contained some moral lesson she believed was important. Afterward, she would ask if there were any questions. This was a conceit, I came to understand, to make it seem as if there were an actual opportunity for dialogue with her, for the kind of conversation that might exist between a reasonable adult and a reasonable child. That evening, she'd related the story of the race between the tortoise and the hare. When she asked if there were any questions, I'd raised my hand. She'd smiled and had called on me.

"Yes, Odie?"

She knew my name. I'd been thrilled at that. Amid the sea of children, so many that I didn't believe I would ever be able to learn all their names, she'd remembered mine. I'd wondered if maybe this was because we were so new or if it was because we were the whitest faces in a vast room full of Indian children.

"Mrs. Brickman, you said the point of the story was that being lazy is a terrible thing."

"That's true, Odie."

"I thought the point of the story was that slow and steady wins the race."

"I see no difference." Her voice was stern, but not harsh, not yet.

"My father read that story to me, Mrs. Brickman. It's one of Aesop's fables. And he said—"

"*He* said?" Now there was something different in the way she spoke. As if she were struggling to cough up a fish bone caught in her throat. "*He* said?" She'd been sitting on a stool that raised her up so everyone in the dining hall could see her. She slid from the stool and walked between the long tables, girls on one side, boys on the other, toward where I sat with Albert. In the absolute silence of that great room, I could hear the *squeak, squeak* of her rubber heels on the old floorboards as she came. The boy next to me, whose name I didn't yet know, edged away, as if trying to distance himself from a place where he knew lightning was about to strike. I glanced at Albert, and he shook his head, a sign that I should just clam up.

Mrs. Brickman stood over me. "*He* said?"

"Y-y-yes, ma'am," I replied, stuttering but no less respectful.

"And where is *he*?"

"Y-y-you know, Mrs. Brickman."

"Dead, that's where. *He* is no longer present to read you stories. The stories you hear now are the ones I tell you. And they mean just what I say they mean. Do you understand me?"

"I . . . I . . ."

"Yes or no?"

She leaned toward me. She was slender, her face a delicate oval the color of a pearl. Her eyes were as green and sharp as new thorns on a rosebush. She wore her black hair long, and kept it brushed as soft as cat fur. She smelled of talcum and faintly of whiskey, an aromatic mix I would come to know well over the years.

"Yes," I said in the smallest voice I'd ever heard come from my own lips.

"He meant no disrespect, ma'am," Albert said.

"Was I talking to you?" The green thorns of her eyes stabbed at my brother.

"No, ma'am."

She straightened herself and scanned the room. "Any other questions?"

I'd thought—hoped, prayed—this was the end of it. But that night, Mr. Brickman came to the dormitory room and called me out, and Albert, too. The man was tall and lean, and also handsome, many of the women at the school said, but all I saw was the fact that his eyes were nothing but black pupils, and he reminded me of a snake with legs.

"You boys'll be sleeping somewhere else tonight," he said. "Come along."

That first night in the quiet room, I barely slept a wink. It was April, and there was still a chill in the wind sweeping out of the empty Dakotas. Our father was less than a week dead. Our mother had passed away two years before that. We had no kin in Minnesota, no friends, no one who knew us or cared about us. We were the only white boys in a school for Indians. How could it get any worse? Then I'd heard the rat and had spent the rest of those long, dark hours until daylight pressed against Albert and the iron door, my knees drawn up to my chin, my eyes pouring out tears that only Albert could see and that no one but him would have cared about anyway.